Praise for *The Sist*

'The novel we've all been wa... fresh and funny – a brilliant read.'
Holly Miller, author of *The Sight of You*

'You know it's good when you are snorting with laughter one minute and ugly crying the next!'
Amanda Prowse, author of *Very Very Lucky*

'Funny, warm, poignant – totally brilliant . . . Another triumph.'
Becky Hunter, author of *One Moment*

'Witty, touching, uncannily perceptive and so funny . . . An absolute must read.'
Jenny Bayliss, author of *The Twelve Dates of Christmas*

'Funny, heartwarming and oh-so-relatable . . . a fabulously comforting and uplifting read!'
Fiona Lucas, author of *The Memory Collector*

'Funny, touching and uplifting . . . the perfect tonic to a stressful day.'
Clare Swatman, author of *Before We Grow Old*

'A refreshing take on the switcheroo storyline . . . filled with all of the warmth, love and laughs of family life.'
Julie Ma, author of *Love Letters*

'What a treat! Charlotte has once again carried off a brilliant idea with pace, humour and enviable detail – what's not to love?'
Norie Clarke, author of *The Library of Lost Love*

'Equal parts hilarious and heartwarming, this twin-switch tale brilliantly captures the complexity of modern womanhood.'
Kathleen Whyman, author of *Would You Ask My Husband That?*

'Charlotte's best book yet . . . It isn't just for sisters, it's for everyone.'
Sheila McClure, author of *The Break-Up Agency*

'A true laugh-out-loud story showing life through a different lens and filled with charm and wit.'
Jessica Ryn, author of *The Extraordinary Hope of Dawn Brightside*

'An absolutely stunning read that will make you laugh out loud.'
Helga Jensen, author of *Twice in a Lifetime*

'A funny and moving reminder that other people's lives are not always as they seem.'
Melanie Rose, author of *Could It Be Magic?*

More praise for Charlotte Butterfield

'Wonderfully original'
Katie Fforde, *Sunday Times* bestselling author *of Island in the Sun*

'A delight'
Sophie Cousens, *New York Times* bestselling author of *This Time Next Year*

'Gloriously life-affirming'
Heidi Swain, *Sunday Times* bestselling author of *The Book-Lovers Retreat*

'The funniest writer I've ever come across'
Debbie Johnson, Million-copy bestselling author of *The Moment I Met You*

'A heartwarming triumph'
Holly Miller, author of Richard & Judy Book Club pick *The Sight of You*

'Moving, page-turning and snort-laugh funny'
Becky Hunter, author of *One Moment*

'Hilarious, life-affirming and such a clever concept'
Jessica Ryn, author of *The Extraordinary Hope of Dawn Brightside*

'A pocket of joy'
Emma Cooper, author of *The Songs of Us*

'Zippy and confident'
Niamh Hargan, author of *The Break-Up Clause*

'What a fun place Nell's world is!'
Helga Jensen, author of *A Scandinavian Summer*

'Fun and witty'
Julie Ma, author of *Love Letters*

'Warm, funny and absorbing'
Emily Critchley, author of *One Puzzling Afternoon*

'The perfect page-turner'
Norie Clarke, author of *The Library of Lost Love*

'Deeply joyous'
Jenny Bayliss, author of *The Twelve Dates of Christmas*

A former magazine editor, Charlotte Butterfield was born in Bristol and studied English at Royal Holloway. She moved to Dubai by herself on a one-way ticket with one suitcase in 2005 and left twelve years later with a husband, three children and a 40ft shipping container. She now lives in the Cotswolds, where she is a freelance writer and novelist.

By the same author:

Me, You and Tiramisu
Crazy Little Thing Called Love
A Beautiful Day for a Wedding
One More Yesterday
The Family Fix
The Second Chance

The SISTER SWITCH
Charlotte Butterfield

avon.

Published by AVON
A division of HarperCollins*Publishers* Ltd
1 London Bridge Street
London SE1 9GF

www.harpercollins.co.uk

HarperCollins*Publishers*
Macken House, 39/40 Mayor Street Upper
Dublin 1, D01 C9W8, Ireland

A Paperback Original 2025

1

First published in Great Britain by HarperCollins*Publishers* 2025

Copyright © Charlotte Butterfield 2025
Emojis © Shutterstock.com

Charlotte Butterfield asserts the moral right to be identified as the author of this work.

A catalogue copy of this book is available from the British Library.

ISBN: 978-0-00-864297-6

This novel is entirely a work of fiction. The names, characters and incidents portrayed in it are the work of the author's imagination. Any resemblance to actual persons, living or dead, events or localities is entirely coincidental.

Set in Birka by HarperCollins*Publishers* India

Printed and bound in the UK using 100% Renewable Electricity at CPI Group (UK) Ltd

All rights reserved. No part of this text may be reproduced, transmitted, downloaded, decompiled, reverse engineered, or stored in or introduced into any information storage and retrieval system, in any form or by any means, whether electronic or mechanical, without the express written permission of the publishers.

Without limiting the author's and publisher's exclusive rights, any unauthorised use of this publication to train generative artificial intelligence (AI) technologies is expressly prohibited. HarperCollins also exercise their rights under Article 4(3) of the Digital Single Market Directive 2019/790 and expressly reserve this publication from the text and data mining exception.

This book contains FSC™ certified paper and other controlled sources to ensure responsible forest management.

For more information visit: www.harpercollins.co.uk/green

To my sisters, my best friends

CHAPTER ONE

Alice & Edie

Sisters were meant to share everything. But the only thing Alice and Edie shared were their faces.

Finding identical twin sisters with such opposing views – one a qualified relationship therapist, and one with an Instagram following most reality stars tried to manifest every sunrise – was television gold. And as for Alice and Edie, well, they couldn't believe their good fortune; they were now being paid to do what they'd spent the last forty-five years doing for free: bicker.

'Welcome back to *Britain in the Morning*.' Lauren the co-host smiled brightly into Camera Three. 'And we're joined on the sofa by our resident agony aunts, sisters Alice and Edie.'

At the mention of their names, both sisters smiled brightly down the camera lens while tilting their heads ever so slightly to the left the way the producer had told them to, just to hammer home the whole shared-womb creation story of the two women.

'They're here to help you with some of your festive problems,' Lauren continued, 'and golly, our inboxes have been heaving under the weight of the nation's worries. The first conundrum of the day comes from Janet in Yorkshire, whose three children are all in their late teens and early twenties and have all asked if they can bring their new partners to Christmas. She and her husband were looking forward to a Christmas just the five of them, and are now worried about the change in dynamics – what advice would you give to her? Alice?'

Sitting beside her sister on the sofa, Alice pushed her bottom lip out far enough to convey a sense of heartfelt empathy. 'Oh this is a tricky one. Perhaps you could have a quiet word with each child in turn and tell them how excited you were about getting together, just you, and perhaps offer to host a bigger party with partners for Boxing Day? That way everyone is happy. Maybe it might be better coming from your husband if you don't feel you could say it?'

Edie shook her head vehemently, her large earrings jangling as she did so. 'No, no, no, I have to interrupt—'

Upstairs in the studio control room the producers simultaneously leaned forward in their seats, while in homes across Britain, the eyes of millions of viewers widened in anticipation of the fireworks just about to be let off, which was, after all, why most of them had tuned in.

'First off,' Edie said, 'Janet is a strong confident woman and is perfectly capable of handling this herself, no need to bring her husband in to save the day, and more importantly,' Edie added, staring directly down the camera lens as if talking directly to Janet herself, 'I just want to say how lucky you are Janet that you've created a home that your kids want to bring their new partners to! At Christmas! So chuck on double the amount of sprouts, get yourself a bigger turkey, and when you think you've bought enough booze, buy some more, and just bloody well enjoy it!'

'We'd just like to apologise to the viewers for the language there, sorry about that,' the co-host Gareth simpered, while shooting Edie a warning look which she didn't seem to pick up on. To be fair, it was a mistake she made almost weekly.

'Ah, now here's an interesting one from Molly in Llandudno,' Lauren said, looking at the card in front of her. 'She writes that she feels an enormous amount of pressure to create the perfect Christmas for her family, but as a full-time supermarket manager, the minute the Closed for Christmas sign goes on the shop door she feels like sinking into an armchair and not getting up again. Now, I don't think Molly's alone in feeling this way, is she?'

'No she's . . . not!' Edie exclaimed, looking pleased with herself that she'd managed to omit a profanity in between the three words. 'There is a huge and grossly unfair expectation of women up and down the land to make Christmas—' she put air quotes around her next word '—perfect. And it's outdated and just plain wrong. Retail workers have had a hell of a month . . .' She shot a look at Gareth to check that 'hell' was an allowable adjective. He blinked back suggesting it was on the cusp. 'And if Molly wants to sink into an armchair, put a straw in a bottle of Baileys and give herself the downtime she deserves, well then it's up to the rest of her family to step up, muck in and share the load.'

'Alice, do you agree?' Gareth asked with more than a little smugness to his voice, suggesting that he knew full well that his question was akin to lighting a stick of dynamite and throwing it onto the studio floor. But then again, that's why the sisters were hired.

Alice smoothed down her pleated skirt, adjusted the cuff of her satin blouse and replied politely, 'I'm afraid I don't, Gareth no, I think that creating a wonderful Christmas for your family is a privilege, and as a change is as good as a rest, I think Molly should not give in to the tiredness and push on through. The joy she'll feel when she's glammed up in something sparkly, her family are enjoying the food she prepared, the presents she bought and wrapped, the music she's chosen, the ambiance she's created, she'll be very thankful that she put the effort in.'

'She's been putting the effort in all f. . . ricking year!' Edie exclaimed, rounding on her sister. 'Surely she deserves a rest now?' Edie swivelled to face the camera head on again and looked intently into the lens. 'Molly, listen my love, use your staff discount on some lovely ready meals, put your feet up and enjoy Christmas however you want to spend it, wearing what you want to wear and doing what you want to do. And thank you for all the hard work you and everyone in retail has been doing, especially this last month.' Edie sat back on the sofa in triumph at a point scored.

Alice side-eyed her sister, clearly knowing that she could hardly combat that moment of gratitude with a postscript to her argument.

'Hear hear,' Gareth said. 'The next question is from Laura, from Kettering. She says, "I am extremely houseproud, and am already having palpitations about the mess that happens over Christmas. We've just had a new stair runner put in, and I am losing sleep over it surviving the festive period, have you got any tips as to how I can keep my house clean without putting my guests on edge?"'

'I'll take this one, shall I?' Alice said over-amiably to Edie. 'I'm guessing you think a stair runner is someone who exercises vertically.'

Lauren and Gareth laughed, while Edie opened her mouth to give a haughty reply, but then closed it sheepishly, proving her sister right.

Alice clapped her perfectly manicured hands together. 'The best investment I have made is a basket of house slippers just inside the front door, where all guests exchange their shoes for fur-lined moccasins as soon as they walk in; it immediately makes everyone more relaxed as they are extraordinarily comfy, and it saves your carpet as well! Incidentally, I also double up on the number of coasters at Christmas time, so each occasional table has at least four.'

'Oh great tips there,' Lauren said, nodding along. 'Edie, anything to add?'

Edie smiled sweetly. 'No, not really, Alice has nailed it there.'

The look on confusion on the co-hosts' faces was nothing compared to the bewilderment on Alice's. Edie had never agreed with her, on any topic.

'Apart from saying,' Edie added, 'that the Canaries are really lovely this time of year, and the thing that would keep your new stair runner really looking pristine is an empty house.'

'Well, we've got to break for the news now,' Lauren said quickly, 'but remember to keep your questions coming in for the new year, when the sisters will be back to answer more of your dilemmas. Stay tuned for our pick of the best sequinned jumpsuits for all your party needs. Molly in Llandudno, this one's for you.'

The four of them kept their smiles in place until the camera's red light went off, when all four faces dropped simultaneously.

'Spain?' Alice said angrily, rounding on her sister.

Gareth spat, 'In the two months since you started with us, we have had five bloodys, four buggers—'

'Three French hens, two turtle doves. . .'

'I'm serious Edie. It's not hard to keep your potty mouth in check for a six-minute weekly segment.'

'Potty mouth? Bloody's hardly a swear word. You're lucky I didn't say—'

Alice bundled her sister off the studio floor, calling behind her, 'Right well, we'd better be off, see you in the new year

5

Gareth, Lauren, have a really lovely Christmas in the Lake District.'

'I'm going to go and buy ten pairs of slippers this afternoon, Alice,' Lauren said.

'Oh lovely, get the ones with the non-slip surface, much safer,' Alice added with a wave. 'Cheerio.'

Once Alice had distributed a Christmas card to each member of the crew backstage, along with a hamper for the security team at the gate and a bottle of wine for James the floor manager, the sisters walked across the parking lot to their cars. 'I signed the cards from you too,' Alice said, her voice suggesting she was hopeful for a thank you, but knowing she wouldn't get one.

Edie's brow furrowed. 'Why did you do that?'

'Because I knew you wouldn't do any.'

Edie shrugged. 'I made a donation to charity instead of cards this year.'

'But they didn't know that.'

'No one expects cards anymore.'

'They might not expect them, but they're pleased when they get them.' Alice unlocked her car and leaned into the passenger seat for a handful of red envelopes, which she presented to Edie. 'For you, and the kids.'

'Thank you. I'll drop yours off in a day or two.'

'Once you've bought them.'

'Once I've bought them,' Edie repeated, her eyes twinkling.

'You could always just bring them when you come for Christmas lunch – you are still coming for Christmas lunch?'

Edie's phone alarm buzzed in her bag. She had to race home if she was going to make her lunchtime client. 'Yes of course,' she said a little distractedly – she should make it in time. 'Same as last year? Around eleven-thirty?'

'Yes, first canapés will be at eleven-forty-five.'

'Lovely. Oh and Iris is a vegan now. Did I mention that?'

Edie was probably the only person in the world that had ever witnessed Alice's transformation from human into beast firsthand. It was a rare, but dramatic phenomenon that only happened once every few years, and encompassed a full-body stiffening, a sharp intake of oxygen, followed by a long exhalation of flames. 'She's ten years old,' Alice said from between her teeth.

'Yes,' Edie replied. 'And?'

'Ten-year-olds don't just decide to be vegan.'

'Iris has.' There was more than a hint of pride to Edie's voice at the emergence of her young daughter's social conscience.

Alice put her hands on her hips, 'Well tell her she can't be.'

'I'm not telling her that. Her beliefs are perfectly valid.'

Alice's voice moved up an octave. 'No they're not! She's *ten*.'

'If it's that much of a problem, she'll just have the roast potatoes and vegetables.'

'I'm cooking the potatoes in goose fat!'

'Can't you use vegetable oil?'

Alice put her hand on her chest as though to soothe the onset of a coronary, 'Do you even know what you're asking?'

'I don't know why you're overreacting. She'd be happy with pasta.'

'Pasta? *Pasta?*' Never in the history of the English or Italian language had the word *pasta* been said with such an intense disdain, except perhaps at a keto convention.

'Look,' Edie replied, holding her hands up in a conciliatory way, 'I can bring a packed lunch for her.'

'Packed lunch? *Packed lunch?*'

'Why are you repeating everything twice?'

Alice flapped her hand in the air. 'We might as well just call it all off.'

'Well, that seems an entirely logical and proportionate response to learning about your niece's dietary requirement.'

'It's not a dietary requirement! It's a ridiculous fad that you are absolutely idiotic for entertaining.' Alice turned her back on her sister and held onto the roof of her car with both hands, breathing in through her nose for three and out for three. In for three, out for three.

'You seem a little wound up. Would you like an armchair, a bottle of Baileys and a straw?'

When Alice eventually spoke, every syllable was sounded out. 'Do you have any idea how many hours I have put in to making this Christmas perfect? No, you don't. Because you've never hosted one. You're only too happy to leave your hovel of a house for a few hours' respite, eat my food, drink my drink—'

'Wear your slippers,' Edie said cheerfully, knowing full well the impact of every one of her words on her sister. 'Speaking of which, have you noticed that set number three have been missing since last Christmas? I stole them. You're right, they are extraordinarily comfy. You won't approve, but I also wear them outside to take the bins out.'

'I can't even . . .' Alice choked out, her knuckles turning white with the strength of her grip on the car's roof rack.

'Eleven-thirty Christmas Day you said? See you then, we'll try not to be late. Don't worry, I'll bring my own moccasins.'

CHAPTER TWO

Edie

Edie stood at the bottom of the stairs looking up at her daughter, who had slept through present-opening and the Christmas croissants, which were still just ordinary croissants but made festive by inserting a seasonal prefix. 'Rosie, please get dressed.'

'But you said on TV a few days ago that you should wear what you want to wear at Christmas.'

Edie held onto the banister for moral support. It was baffling how teenagers could choose which parts of their mother's advice they listened to like they were at a pick'n'mix. 'If you go to Auntie Alice's wearing pyjamas that say *On the naughty list and I regret nothing* she will spontaneously combust into a little pile of ash all over her expensive rug, none of us will know the timings for the turkey and we'll end up eating fast food.'

'Yum. That's a win.'

'She's not wrong,' Seb, Edie's partner, said, giving his daughter a fist bump as he passed her on the stairs.

'Reports say that fast food companies are responsible for the slaughter of more than seven million cows a year,' Iris piped up from the kitchen table, where she'd been building the Taj Mahal out of paper straws since term had broken up the week before.

'And I reckon this family might be personally responsible for a million of them – obviously not you Iris, well not in the last three weeks, anyway,' Edie said. 'Right, Rosie, back upstairs, wear anything other than nightwear.'

Seb opened a chocolate coin, threw it up into the air, caught it in his mouth and raised his arms in victory. 'Twenty quid says she'll come down next in a bikini.'

Edie slammed the dishwasher shut, the handle of a ladle stopping it from closing completely. She bumped her bum against the door until it relented. 'Shit, course she will. Did you wash her jeans?'

'Which ones?'

'The flared ones?'

'Yeah I think so,' Seb said, 'I put them on her bed a couple of days ago.'

'Which means she'll have been sleeping with them in her bed since then.' Edie checked her watch; they were edging into the danger zone of being late, which only ever bothered her when she was meeting Alice. 'Right, are we ready to go as soon as Rosie's ready?'

Seb motioned towards the Christmas tree. 'You haven't unwrapped your present yet.'

'I did, you put the theatre tickets in my card.'

'No, there's another present behind the tree.'

'I didn't see one? We agreed a budget remember, and the tickets must have taken you over that already.' Edie went back into the living room; standing behind it was a foot-tall present, wrapped in Christmas paper with a ribbon rosette pinned to the top of it. 'You didn't need to get me anything else!'

Seb rocked back on his heels in excitement. 'Open it. Be careful though, it's fragile.'

Edie ripped the paper off gently, and the layer of bubble wrap beneath it, to uncover a beautiful ceramic vase, glazed in a mottled gold with a bold thunder bolt of pink running down its side.

'Do you like it? I'm trying something new.'

Edie turned it over in her hands, the gold subtly changed its hue as the light caught it, revealing a depth of colour that made her gasp. 'You made this? It's incredible. And so different from your others.'

'It's the first of the batch, and I wanted you to have it, to say thank you for believing in me and for letting me go for it.'

'I didn't *let you go for it,* you had a dream, and if this is what you're capable of, then it was absolutely the right decision to jack in teaching for it. You are one talented beast, and I love it.' She kissed him full on the mouth, squishing their lips together.

'Even though I've only put two hundred quid into the joint account this month?'

'Bash out a few more of these and we'll be holidaying in the Maldives before too long.' Edie moved her mum's mantle clock to one side to make room for the vase to have pride of place above the fire, and stood back for a moment, admiring it.

'I think I'd settle for just being able to buy you the engagement ring I've been promising you for the last sixteen years.'

Edie cupped Seb's face in her hands. 'We are blissfully happy as we are, I don't need an overpriced rock on my finger to know that you're my person.'

'No, but—'

Iris wandered into the living room, holding her shoes. 'Do you think Auntie Alice will have used meat juices in the gravy?'

'Almost certainly. Grab a green stock cube out of the cupboard, you can make yours in a mug when we get there.'

Iris perched on the edge of the sofa to lace up her trainers. 'Did you know that the United Kingdom will eat ten million turkeys today? The USA eat forty-six million on Thanksgiving. Forty-six *million*!'

'Okay Iris, quick chat.' Edie moved a pile of clean laundry off the sofa and patted the seat next to her. Edie had meant to do a full clean of the house before Christmas so she wouldn't need to spend the only day of the year where one could legitimately not do anything staring at glaring reminders of how rubbish she was, but the run-up to Christmas and the first few weeks in January were the prime time for relationship crises and she'd been flat out cramming in clients day and night. If she could inflate her counselling fees for the holiday season like hotels did, she'd be a lot less stressed about meeting the mortgage this month. 'Sweetheart,' Edie started, gently, 'your life choices are your own to make, as are mine, and your sister's and Dad's, and anyone else's that walks this planet.'

Iris shook her head. 'Not the turkeys'.'

'No,' Edie said softly, 'not the turkeys'. People. Talking about people.'

'Bob didn't choose to be homeless.'

'Who's *Bob*?'

'The man outside the Tesco Express,' Iris replied, her tone suggesting to Edie that there should be a *duh* at the end of the sentence, but thankfully Iris wasn't Rosie.

'When were you talking to Bob?'

'When I gave him the blanket from the back of the sofa to keep him warm.'

To be fair, Edie hadn't noticed it was missing amid the chaos that was her living room, so Bob would get a lot more practical use out of it, but she felt bad that Alice's expensive present had just been re-gifted without her knowing about it. She had given it to her for their birthday last May, handing it over with a reverence Edie didn't think a blanket deserved, even if it was Peruvian alpaca, which meant nothing to her, but Edie was clued up enough on social cues to know that her response demanded an impressed 'ooooo'.

'I'm not really talking about Bob,' Edie told Iris, 'I'm talking generally. We all make decisions about how we live our lives, and that's great, but you need to tone down the animal-killing facts, particularly today.'

'Why?'

'Because when someone is eating an animal, they don't like to be reminded that they're eating an animal. They just want to enjoy their meal without thinking too hard about where it came from.'

Iris scrunched up her face. 'That's stupid.'

'Maybe. But my point is, you choose to live one way, which is great, but don't expect other people to think or behave the same.'

'Your mum's right.'

Edie shot Seb a look across the room that said, *of course I'm right, I don't need you validating my rightness by affirming it.* He rolled his eyes as if to say, *hey, give me a break, I've got your back here.* She glared back at him over Iris's head and he merely gave a lazy smile in response, which completely thawed her, and had her glancing at her watch to see if they had time to nip back upstairs to 'wrap presents, don't come in' before heading out. December had been an excellent month for grabbing alone time in the middle of the day, it really had. It did mean that she had to stay up until gone two am last night in order to actually wrap the presents, but it had been totally worth it.

'This better?' Fourteen-year-old Rosie stood in the doorway, hands on hips, teaming a Christmas jumper with a sarong and flip flops.

'My purse is in my handbag,' Edie said to Seb with a sigh, 'help yourself.'

Alice

'So from my home to yours, on this wonderful Christmas morning, have an absolutely fabulous day, enjoy the fruits of all your hard work and make sure you enjoy it! Lots of love for now, and merry Christmas!' Alice kept her smile in place while she counted to five in her head before turning the video off on her phone; it would make trimming it so much easier. She'd scheduled a fifteen-minute window to edit it and get it posted between taking the turkey out and resting it, and putting the carrots and peas on. She checked her watch. It was eleven-forty-eight, eighteen minutes since Edie was meant to arrive, three minutes since the miniature Yorkshire puddings with slivers of rare beef and a tiny dollop of homemade horseradish were due to be distributed round the front drawing room to sighs and exclamations of wonder. But they weren't being passed around with the reverence they deserved, they were sitting on the kitchen island, drying out, congealing. If Alice cling-filmed them that would squash the horseradish, if she left them uncovered then the last hour would have been completely wasted and the next canapé would make no sense at all as it was part of a culinary journey.

Alice's eldest son Teddy wandered in, pulling at his tight shirt collar. 'Can I have one of those?'

'No you cannot,' Alice replied, slapping her son's hand away.

'I'm starving.'

'You had pancakes and bacon two hours ago. Have an apple.'

'Oh those look delicious, darling.' Alice's dad, Kenneth, came into the kitchen, eyes trained on the canapés. He stretched out his hand to take a Yorkshire pudding, and the blend of Alice's good manners and deferential belief in familial hierarchy stopped her dishing out the same sharp smack, so she just stood by withering as the symmetrical pattern of the canapés on the plate was now ruined. 'It's delicious,' he said, popping it into his mouth whole. 'Are they meant to be cold?'

'Danny! Danny!' Alice's voice as she called her husband was shrill and bordering on hysteria. 'Can you call Seb and see where they are?

'No need, they're walking up the drive now.'

'Right, take these plates through, Teddy, call your brother and sister downstairs. Alexa – play the playlist Best Christmas Carols. Who's been outside in their slippers? There's mud on the bottom of this one, these are inside shoes, *inside*. No, don't put it there Teddy, the cat will eat it, put it on a high surface. Did you tell Rufus and Emily to come down?' Alice speedwalked through the hall calling out instructions as she went, before opening the front door wide and plastering on her most hospitable smile. 'Hello! Welcome! Happy Christmas, no, don't worry about it Seb, we're very relaxed today, things happen when they happen. Didn't you drive? You got an Uber? On Christmas Day? Are they still running? What's this? A green Oxo cube? Thank you, Iris. Oh, Rosie, what a lovely sarong.'

'Hi sis.' Edie gave Alice a kiss on her cheek and handed over a yule log still in its supermarket packaging, complete with a thirty percent off sticker as it was due to expire that day. 'Dessert,' Edie explained, but she must have known that there was a Christmas pudding getting steadily more drunk in a cupboard since October and two trifles fully prepped and ready to go in the utility room drinks fridge, one even topped with vegan custard and cream.

Edie wandered into the kitchen after Alice to ostensibly 'help' but as every work surface was devoid of chopping boards or industry of any kind, it was unclear to both of them what assistance she might be. 'I thought I could chop something,' Edie offered.

'It's all done,' Alice said, wiping her hands on her new apron. She was pleased that all her hints to her family had paid off, telling each of them whenever they'd passed the little cooking shop on the high street that she'd love the apron with bees on it in the window, and then that morning she'd unwrapped one from each of them, so that was brilliant. She'd also bought one for herself as an early Christmas present, as last year her entire family took her at her word that she 'didn't want anything', resulting in a morning of her looking longingly at everyone else as they all opened the mountain of gifts she'd spent months lovingly picking out for each of them. Danny picked up on her disappointment and the next day gave her a card with a £500 Amazon voucher in it.

'Nice apron,' Edie remarked. 'Is it new?'

'Yes,' Alice replied, a little cagily, knowing full well what her sister's brain would make of her next sentence. 'Danny bought it for me.'

Edie was by the hob, lifting up saucepan lids to see what was inside each one. 'If Seb bought me an apron I'd leave him.'

'He didn't *just* buy me this.'

'Let me guess . . . don't tell me . . . he also bought you a kitchen mixer?'

'No,' Alice replied indignantly, while quickly assessing whether a blender constituted a kitchen mixer. Admittedly, she was a little taken aback on opening it, because she'd never mentioned liking smoothies, or blending anything of any kind. If anything, Danny himself would have been the perfect recipient of that present as he'd just started subscribing to one of those expensive green powder companies and up until that morning she'd been mixing his morning green pond water with a whisk. She supposed that he just wanted to make her life easier, and to be fair to him, it wasn't a cheap brand. 'I'll have you know that he also got me this.' Alice held her wrist out to show Edie a giant yellow gold, diamond-encrusted watch, the size of which would have had championship footballers weep with envy.

'Wow. That is very . . . wow.' Edie said, her eyes wide like saucers. 'How are you going to lift your arm up to reach things?'

Danny sidled into the kitchen and slid one arm around his wife's slim waist. 'Did Alice show you what I bought her?'

'She did.' Edie nodded. 'Very impressive, and so very . . . her.'

Danny smiled and whistled happily to himself as he left the room, oblivious to the sarcastic undercurrent in Edie's tone. Alice, however, was attuned to every nuance in her sister's voice and knew exactly what she was insinuating. 'What did Seb get you then?'

'Tickets for us to go to a one-woman theatre show I've been wanting to see, as well as something rude that you wouldn't approve of, and an amazing vase that he made himself.'

Alice grimaced. Not one of those three presents appealed to her. Watching a woman moan about inequality, childbirth and the menopause for two hours, no thanks, nor would she want something for the bedroom designed for a woman half their age and double their flexibility, and handmade gifts were very thoughtful, she'd given her spiced Christmas chutney to all the neighbours, but not from your husband, and judging from the photos Edie had shown her of his pottery, Seb should really have just kept it as a hobby. 'What's with Rosie's beachwear?' Alice added, changing the subject, 'Isn't she freezing?'

'Probably. I'm calling her bluff, but she thinks she's calling mine.'

Alice's middle child, Rufus, chose that moment to enter the kitchen, dressed impeccably in the beige chinos, blue shirt and navy bow tie his mother had laid out for him on his bed, looking like he'd just emerged from page seventy-two of the Next catalogue, which was exactly the look she was after.

'Hi Auntie Edie,' Rufus said, returning the fist bump Edie offered him. 'You're wearing jeans. Mummy told Daddy he can't wear jeans because it's Christmas.'

'Good job I'm not married to Mummy then, isn't it?' Edie winked at her nephew.

Alice was thankful she was facing the fridge and not her sister then so her flared nostrils would go unnoticed. She was very clear about the dress code on her invite, she wrote 'Festive partywear'. Edie's jeans, Rosie's sarong, Iris's frog onesie and Seb's shorts – shorts! – were a deliberate attempt to wind her up. Well, it wasn't going to work.

'Uncle Seb wants to know if Iris's onesie is flammable because she's poking the fire in the log burner.'

Alice swivelled round, aghast at the query, looking in horror first at her son for asking the unthinkable, and then at her sister, who was taking far too long to reply.

Edie considered the question for a beat too long before saying, 'Yes, I think it is, so tell her not to poke it too hard.' Obviously catching her sister's open-mouthed horror, she said innocently, 'What? Honestly, this horseradish is really delicious.' She licked her finger. 'Is horseradish a herb?'

'Root vegetable,' Alice muttered, trying not to scream as she watched her sister merrily double dip her licked finger back into the ramekin of creamed horseradish.

'What's that you were looking at on the fridge?'

'My timings for the day.'

Edie hopped off her bar stool and went around the island to stand next to her sister in front of two pages of A4 taped together and stuck up with magnets. 'Wow. There are like thirty different timings on here.'

'Thirty-three,' Alice corrected with pride.

'When's the next one?'

Alice looked at her watch. She didn't trust the timer on the oven, the minutes always seemed too short on it. 'In three minutes I have to turn the potatoes.'

'Three minutes seems the perfect amount of time to open the bottle of prosecco I bought and pour us all a pre-dinner drink.'

Alice waved the suggestion away, 'Not me. I need to keep a clear head, but you go ahead. None for Danny though, he's on a health kick, and I read the instructions of Dad's tablets and he can't have any either. He was very upset when I took his Buck's fizz away from him this morning.'

'Well we got an Uber so me and Seb could both get bladdered. I'll open it while you crack on. Those potatoes aren't going to turn themselves.'

Edie

Edie walked into the living room holding the two champagne flutes, and bent down, dispatching one to a grateful Seb.

'None for me?' her dad said sadly.

'Alice said no. You can share mine though if you want.'

'Don't I get one?' Danny asked from the other sofa, seemingly put out at being overlooked.

'Alice said you wouldn't want one.'

'I'm off the booze normally, but it is Christmas. Alice!' Danny called. 'Be a love and bring me a glass.'

'She's just sorting out the potatoes,' Edie said.

'Oh. Can you get me one then?'

Edie had just sat down, sandwiched between her dad and Seb, and although getting up wouldn't have been impossible, there wasn't any compelling reason for her to go instead of him. 'Why? Is something wrong with your legs?'

Alice rushed in, one hand still in an oven glove, the other holding a spatula. 'Did you call?'

Danny stretched his arm out along the back of the sofa. 'Oh hello there love, can you bring me a glass of prosecco?'

Alice blew a tendril of hair out of her face. 'I didn't think you'd want one.'

'I wasn't going to, but I quite fancy one now.'

'Oh okay. Bear with me a second, I just need to put the parsnips in.'

'You know, you could always get one yourself, Danny,' Edie said to him once Alice had scurried back to the kitchen to add one more thing to her To Do List.

'She doesn't mind, she likes taking care of us.'

The annoying thing was, he was right. Seb wouldn't dream of dispatching her to fetch something for him, but if Edie knew her sister – and she was so confident she did she would put money on the fact – then any minute now Alice would glide back into the living room, not only carrying Danny's bubbly, but also an hors d'oeuvres of some kind to 'keep him going'.

Just then a plate was shoved underneath her nose.

'Salmon blini?'

Edie smiled to herself. This was too easy.

While Alice beavered away in the kitchen, Kenneth was poring over the television schedules in the *Radio Times*, the blocks of Jenga the kids were playing with had reached a crucial height and Seb was feeling down the side of the couch, because he'd recently found nine pounds down the side of their sofa. He'd be out of luck here though, Edie thought, as Alice was one of those people who even removed the sofa cushions to vacuum it.

'I'm just going to see if Alice needs any help,' Edie said, getting up, and giving Danny a bemused glance as she walked past him. She didn't mind the guy. He wasn't her cup of tea at all, all coloured chinos and a voice that was far too loud for indoors, but Alice seemed happy enough. Edie found him utterly unfanciable, back when Alice and he started dating, and now, but she supposed that was nothing but a good quality in a brother-in-law. Every one of Danny's limbs was double the thickness they needed to be in normal life outside of a rugby pitch, and despite not playing professionally for over a decade, having swapped his gum shield for a suit, he still walked with the swagger of someone who once had a stadium of people shout his name. That sort of thing had to change a person, you couldn't be signing shirts one minute and then happily take the bins out the next. Ten years of not giving an autograph should have been enough time for normality to be restored, but in this house he still walked into a room expecting it to erupt into applause.

'Oh good, you're here. Does anyone want a refill?' Alice handed Edie the half-filled bottle. 'And ask Danny if he wants any more blinis, there's still forty-five minutes to lunch.'

'Have you got a small bell I can give him as well so that we know when he needs anything else?'

Alice kicked the fridge door shut with her foot and used scissors to snip the smoked salmon packet open. 'No, he'll probably just shout.'

'I was joking.'

'Oh, yes, haha. Very funny.'

A couple of minutes later, Edie begrudgingly carried Danny's drink in with the replenished plate of blinis, trying not to feel like a servant girl waiting on a Roman gladiator, and deliberately sloshed a little prosecco over his chinos as she handed it over. 'Canapé?' She smiled, proffering the plate.

He took one and popped the whole thing in his mouth. 'Yum'.

Her nephews, Rufus and Teddy, took one and in unison parroted, 'Thank you Auntie Edie,' while her little niece said the same, then added, 'I love Mummy's blinis.'

Edie held out the plate to Iris, who shook her head, but viewed the offering with narrowed eyes, 'Do you know if the smoked salmon is wild or farmed?' she asked.

'Does it matter if you're vegan?'

'It matters to the salmon.'

Edie reached for her wine glass, but it was empty. She looked at her dad, the obvious culprit, only to find he'd dozed off, then from the corner of the room came a little hiccup from her fourteen-year-old daughter, shivering stubbornly in her sarong.

Alice

'Trifle or Christmas pudding? Trifle or pudding?' Alice knew her voice had taken on a tinge of hysteria, but that was what nine hours standing up in a kitchen forgetting to hydrate would do to you. She looked round the table at each of her family members in turn while brandishing a large silver serving spoon in the air. 'I've got homemade custard, or homemade brandy sauce, or homemade brandy butter, something for everyone, what would you all like?'

'Where's the chocolate log we brought?' Edie said, getting up from the dining table to fetch the packaged dessert, which Alice had discarded onto the countertop conveniently close to the bin. 'I think I'll have a bit of this.' Edie started tearing the plastic wrapper off with her teeth.

'Ooo, you bought a chocolate log? I'll have a slice of that too,' Kenneth said.

Alice's eyes snapped from her sister to her father, 'But Dad, I made the trifle using Mum's recipe, you always loved Mum's trifle.'

'Yeah, but I'm in the mood for a bit of chocolate, love.'

'But I used four different types of fresh berries.' Alice omitted to add that two ingredients on her mum's neat handwritten recipe card, which had survived five decades, took pretty much a whole day of googling and an expensive delivery cost to receive.

Kenneth pulled a face and patted his tummy. 'Berries and my stomach aren't great friends these days to be honest.'

Emily leaned forward in her chair and put her hands on her chin. 'What does that mean, Grandpa?'

Teddy laughed, 'He means it gives him the squits.' Cue laughs from all the grandchildren and Seb.

'Have some Christmas pudding then,' Alice said quickly, picking up a bowl ready to spoon some pudding into. 'I've been feeding it a blend of amaretto and a special Spanish sherry, and I've even used quince, which is really hard to find these days, but someone told me about a farm shop out in Kent that sells it, so I took a day trip out there.'

Kenneth shook his head. 'Sounds a bit rich for me; no, a little slice of yule log will do the job.'

Alice turned to Seb, waving the spoon dangerously close to his face. 'Seb? Pudding or trifle?'

'I'm going to have yule log too, I think, Alice.'

Alice turned to her husband, and when she said his name it came out of her mouth as though she was being strangled. 'Danny? Pudding or trifle?'

'I'm off desserts, you know that.'

'It's Christmas.'

She recognised that if there was a way to say those two words in an entirely opposite way to Noddy Holder's jubilation, then that would be it. But the fact remained, it *was* sodding Christmas. And Danny could eat *some* sugar. And Iris, who was eyeing up the very non-vegan chocolate log with very non-vegan yearning could have eaten roast potatoes cooked in goose fat rather than Alice having to make all forty of them with vegetable oil which meant they hardly crisped up at all, and took much longer, which meant there wasn't room for the cauliflower cheese in the oven, so that only got added to the table in time for seconds and insult added to injury, Iris only took one potato anyway. *One*.

Alice swivelled her glare to the younger members of the family sitting at the table. 'Kids? Trifle, pudding?'

'Didn't you say both were very boozy?' Seb asked, for the first time in his life choosing to be an appropriate adult.

Alice's nostrils flared. 'They can have the jelly and fruit part. Or Iris's vegan one.' Her tone suddenly became brighter with her brainwave. 'That one doesn't have any alcohol at all in it. Shall I just divide Iris's trifle up five ways for you all?'

'Can I have the chocolate log please, Auntie Edie?' Rufus asked.

'Me too,' Teddy added.

'I don't really like trifle,' Iris admitted. 'I guess a little bit of the log wouldn't hurt. It *is* Christmas.'

Rosie and Emily plumped for it too, prompting Edie to amiably exclaim, 'I should have bought two of these! Can you believe it was only one pound fifty? What a bargain.'

Alice spooned out a big dollop of each of her homemade desserts into a bowl for herself with the enthusiasm of a prison guard manning the canteen's porridge pot, while everyone else busied themselves with moans of ecstasy over the log.

'You okay, love?' her dad asked Alice once his plate was clean. 'You've gone a bit quiet.'

Alice gave Kenneth a small grateful smile. 'I'm fine.'

'It's all really lovely, today, isn't it everyone? Let's have a toast to Alice.' Kenneth picked up his glass. 'To Alice, thank you for a super spread.'

Everyone picked up whatever liquid-holding receptacle was nearest them and toasted her, which was lovely. Or it would have been lovely had she not noticed her sister and Seb exchange a wry smile and what was that, an eye roll? Alice picked up her own wine glass, which hadn't been touched at all, and said, 'Let's not forget Edie. Without whom everyone would have had to suffer my desserts.'

'What's that supposed to mean?'

Alice folded her napkin into a neat little square and laid it softly down next to her bowl. 'Nothing at all. Just lucky you were here to save the day, that's all.' She gave her sister the tightest of smiles.

Edie sighed and leaned back in her chair. 'Spit it out.'

'What?'

'Well clearly you have something to say.'

Alice ran her hand over the napkin square, not meeting Edie's eye. 'I just feel like you ruined it a little.'

'*I* ruined it?'

'Yes. You. Actually. You bowl in here with your bag clinking with alcohol, your shop-bought, bargain-bin chocolate log, and just take over the whole thing. And it's not really fair. I have spent nine hours in the kitchen so far today.'

'No one asked you to.'

'Well, who else was going to? You? We'd have all been eating a jacket potato if it was left to you.'

'I like jacket potatoes.'

'Not now Seb,' both sisters said in unison.

'You do this every time,' Edie continued, filling her wine glass up again from the near-empty bottle on the table in front of her. 'You set your expectations way too high, you set unrealistic goals for yourself, you expect everyone at the end of every mouthful to declare how amazing you are, how selfless and brilliant, and then when we don't, you sulk about it.'

'I do not! I enjoy doing all this!'

'Looks like it.'

All five children, and the three men at the table were watching this like spectators at a tennis match, on the sidelines of the action, knowing they weren't allowed to speak until a suitable break in the action.

'Well, no,' Alice admitted, 'I'm not enjoying this moment right now, but I like the prepping and cooking and hosting. I just wanted today to be okay. It's the third Christmas without Mum, and I just wanted it to be special.'

'And it is, but it would have been just as special without sodding quince.'

'Quince adds a perfect tang without the sharpness of lemon.'

'No one cares, Alice. Christmas pudding is Christmas pudding. There's a reason you only eat it once a year. It's gross. We didn't eat Mum's, we're not eating yours, it's nothing personal.'

'Okay girls, give it a rest now, we're having a lovely day,' Kenneth said, once again trying to quell the storm between his daughters, a task he'd been attempting for forty-five years. 'Seb, Edie tells me you answered the Wordle in one the other day. That's brilliant.'

'The thing is Edie,' Alice said, not yet willing to let it go, 'don't you think that I would have loved to sit on the sofa drinking prosecco all day and lying on the floor playing Jenga with my kids and nieces? Of course I would have done, but this dinner wasn't going to cook itself.'

'The key is to start with a word with four vowels,' Kenneth said. 'I like "audio" myself. What's your first word, Seb?'

Seb looked at Edie before answering just to check he was allowed to speak. 'Adieu,' he said quietly.

Kenneth nodded. 'Oh that is good. Four vowels, see?'

Edie leaned forward in her chair and folded her arms in front of her on the table. 'Alice, I have asked you continually whether you needed help today, and every time you said no, or that you had things under control, or I'd just be in the way. Any one of those times you could have said, "do you know what Edie, I'm a bit snowed under here, drain the carrots," and I would have drained the fucking carrots.'

In unison all three of Alice's children's eyes widened at the f-bomb being used at their dinner table, especially in the context of vegetables. Edie's own children didn't seem to notice.

Alice sniffed. 'Well I think that's the final nail in the Christmas coffin, we might as well take the tree down now.'

Emily gasped.

'Oh, for Christ's sake Alice, stop being so dramatic, pour yourself a glass of wine, go and sit down and we'll clear up.' Edie scraped her chair back and stood up, leaning over to collect everyone's dessert bowls. 'Come on kids, look lively, Teddy, I just heard the dishwasher beep, so you and Rufus start unloading that, and we'll bring all the dirty things over.'

Alice looked at Danny to get his support, and under her glare he attempted to bluster some sort of unintelligible 'now now ladies,' type of response, which both sisters completely ignored. Edie stacked the dishes on top of each other with a far louder clatter than Alice's nerves could take. 'Stop, just stop!' she shrieked, 'I'll do it, none of you know where anything goes, one of you will break something, there's a special way of loading it, just leave it, please.' She could feel tears teetering on the brink of falling, and really wanted an empty kitchen when they did.

'But it'll be faster—' Edie countered.

'—I mean it. Leave it. Please!' Alice begged.

A couple of seconds of silence blanketed the room and everyone stood stock still as though the music had just stopped in a game, each child still holding whatever dirty or clean plate they had been tasked with moving. Their eyes jumped from their mother to their auntie, waiting for another signal as to what their next move should be.

'Fine, if you're sure,' Edie said, putting the plate she was carrying back on the table. 'In that case, I think we'll leave you to it and head home. Thank you for dinner Alice, it was lovely. Kids, enjoy the rest of your day. Dad,' Edie said, bending down to graze her dad's cheek with her lips. 'Always a pleasure, never a chore. Danny, bye. Rosie, put on your flip flops.'

As soon as the front door had closed behind them, all three children followed their dad and grandad into the living room and flicked the television on, while Alice retreated to the kitchen and sank onto a bar stool at the kitchen island, which was piled high with dirty plates and dishes. She wasn't being a martyr when she said she'd prefer to do it, she would. She'd only have to rearrange the dirty dishwasher and reshuffle the crockery cupboard if she'd have let everyone loose in here. She picked up her phone; amid the madness of the day she hadn't checked her Instagram post once. She allowed herself a satisfied smile when she saw that her pre-meal video had amassed nearly fifty thousand views. Not bad when you considered that all her followers would have been very busy cooking their own family Christmas dinners. She scrolled through the comments:

Your family are so lucky! said one.
Adopt me please! exclaimed another.
I wish I was having Christmas at your house!
Everything about this is perfect!

Alice breathed in slowly, closed her eyes and tilted her head back, feeling a sense of calm and accomplishment once again trickle through her body.

CHAPTER THREE

January

Edie

Edie was trying to remember the moves for 'Oops Upside Your Head' as she'd been the one to request it. It surely must be more complicated than just two hand-pats to the left, two to the right, two forward, then back – that couldn't sustain a whole dancefloor for a whole song, surely? Turns out the eighties were simpler times because a quick google confirmed that yes, they were doing it right. Anyway, everyone was dancing with at least one bottle of wine sloshing around inside each of them, and everything mattered less when that was the case. When the song was over, the women helped each other up, laughing. Edie didn't notice that after three minutes of sitting on her kitchen floor each of them were wearing some element from that week's dinners – a grating of cheese on Amanda's bottom, a hardened pea on Helen's, a stray piece of fusilli pasta on Sam's, while most of Scooby the Alsatian's winter coat had ended up glued to Sarah's.

'Should we talk about the book at all?' Helen asked, holding onto the back of a chair to catch her breath. Before this song, they'd gone through Steps' '5, 6, 7, 8' and Whigfield's 'Saturday Night', which made the whole group grateful for their robust pantyliners.

'I didn't really like it if I'm being honest,' Sam added, with a grimace and a shake of her head to help the others interpret her words through the slurring.

'Me neither. It was shit,' Amanda said, pouring herself another glass of red wine. 'Edie?'

'Four hours of my life I will not get back. Not my cup of tea.'

Alice

'Another cup of tea?' Alice held a teapot aloft to the women assembled in her living room three tube stops across London. 'What I thought was done really well was the narrative arc of the antagonist. Now I know we were meant to dislike him, but after the denouement, I really felt an enormous amount of sympathy for him.'

The five other women murmured their agreement. One tentatively took a homemade biscuit from a plate Alice was proffering. 'I shouldn't, but okay, let's be naughty,' she said, with a little giggle.

'What did you think about the use of pathetic fallacy throughout? I liked it at first as a mood-setter, but felt it quite intrusive, and dare I say it, a little heavy-handed as the novel went on,' Alice's friend Ruth said.

Alice scanned her notes in front of her. 'I must admit, I felt the same about the use of dramatic irony; at the start I liked being aware of the different subplots and character motivations, but I did feel a little dissatisfaction at not experiencing the thrill of the various twists and reveals alongside the protagonists.'

'Mmmm I see your point, but I really enjoyed being *in the know* as it were,' Louisa said, 'and it wasn't really about the big reveals, more the intricacies of each character's reactions to them.'

'Absolutely.' Alice nodded in agreement. 'My sister Edie's book club is doing the same book tonight at her book club, so it'll be interesting if they've come to similar conclusions. We're talking about it on the show on Friday.'

'I thought you were only the agony aunts?'

'We are, normally. But during the holidays the normal presenters have a couple of weeks off, so they get different guest presenters in for other segments too, so we're also doing the monthly book club. But you've all given me so much to go on, thank you so much.'

Edie

'Please tell me you read it,' Alice whispered to her sister as they sat side by side on the sofa getting their foreheads powdered. It was a fair question.

'We're live in twenty,' James called from the side of the studio.

'Of course I read it,' Edie replied. 'It was rubbish.'

Alice's eyes widened. 'Please don't say that on air.'

'Why not?' Edie shrugged. 'The viewers deserve to know our honest opinion.'

'Did you read the script?'

'No, it's going on the autocue, I can read it then.'

'Three, two . . .' James held his finger up and the light on camera three went on.

'Hello, and welcome back,' Alice started with a wide smile. 'We're delighted to be with you this week hosting the *Britain in the Morning* Book Club, and we hope that, like us, you were glued to this month's pick over the festive season. I do have to say, this novel was a step out of my comfort zone, but it did not disappoint, wouldn't you agree, Edie?'

Edie made a face. 'Not really, I found it a bit paint by numbers if I'm being honest. The whole, you should be feeling angry at this point, so it's going to take place in a storm, and then, this chapter is about hopefulness, so let's put some blue sky in it.'

'But I found that just added to the emotion of the writing, which I don't think you can deny was an incredible feat of storytelling, wasn't it?'

Alice seemed to be telling Edie with her eyes to agree with her, almost as though Alice's own child had written it, which Edie conceded, might have made it better.

'See, I'd have to disagree again, I didn't really feel anything.'

Alice seemed oddly uncomfortable, her eyes were wildly boring into Edie trying to transmit a message Edie couldn't decipher. 'I know you discussed it at your own book club this week though, what did your friends think about it?'

'Sam wasn't keen either, and Amanda thought it was utter shi. . . urely not destined for greatness.'

Alice swivelled to look straight down the lens of the camera. 'Well, I think you need new friends Edie, ones with better taste, because this has bestseller written all over it, and here to tell us more about his inspiration for writing it, is author Clive Williams.'

Edie's blood ran cold as a very angry Clive Williams stalked on to the set, shaking Alice's hand and leaving Edie's hanging in mid-air like a beaten piñata. Her face flushed with embarrassment as she gingerly took her seat beside her sister. For the next six and a half minutes, Edie added nothing but non-committal murmurs of interest, and a well-timed appreciative laugh at a very unfunny anecdote involving a llama.

'Why didn't you tell me he was coming on?' Edie hissed as soon as the cameras were off.

Alice shuffled her notes into an orderly pile and smiled at someone in the distance. 'Maybe if you read the notes?'

'Why was he here? They never normally have the authors on?'

'They always have the authors on! Have you ever actually watched this segment before?'

Edie had never admitted to anyone on the team, or even her sister, that she'd never even watched the *programme* before getting hired to be on it. When Alice had excitedly called her last summer after getting an email from the producer of the show inviting her for a screen test, her words tumbling out in one go with the magnitude of the invitation, Edie made all the right noises of congratulations, while having no clue what she was going on about. From an early age, if something was popular Edie swerved it. The must-have toy, the boy everyone else gravitated to, no thanks, they were welcome to them. Daytime television firmly fell into this category too. Alice, meanwhile, was as proudly mainstream as it was possible to be, jumping on the yummy mummy Instagram bandwagon as soon as it had built up enough momentum for her not to be considered a trailblazer. After all, Alice never did anything experimental. Soon she started amassing hundreds of thousands of followers, all keen to see the picture-perfect life she'd carefully curated. She filmed it all: tutorials on cleaning your oven without chemicals, arranging flowers in three easy steps, creating family meals from scratch in under thirty minutes with all five food groups in, all of them seamlessly edited in a way that made her followers feel she was in their room with them helping them all be better versions of themselves. If Edie was a producer on the UK's top morning show, she'd hire her sister in a heartbeat as well. She couldn't, however, fathom why the hell they offered her the job too.

Edie's inclusion in the show had happened entirely by accident. Alice's car was booked in for a service the day of her screentest, and while Danny was able to drop her off at the studio, Alice called on Edie to pick her up: a favour Edie knew Alice had regretted asking her for ever since. The executives had liked Alice so much they'd whisked her down to the studio floor after the audition in their offices, to see her in situ on the famous pink sofa and record some sample segments with her. Edie, fed up with waiting in her car, had just wandered in through the door that said *Strictly No Entry*, and strode straight onto the set, shouting out for Alice to 'hurry the hell up' because she had a tantric massage class to get to and she absolutely couldn't be late lest she 'miss out on the most sensual part of the session.' A perfectly reasonable thing to do, Edie had maintained since then. Those 'no entry' signs were usually just there to keep overeager fans off the lot, anyway. As a mortified Alice chastised Edie for trespassing and snapped at her to get off the set, the producers watched on in amazement. The twins were so used to the double takes and stares, they didn't even register them anymore. They didn't think they even looked that alike any longer: Alice's highlights were religiously done every five weeks by an Italian man in Covent Garden, while Edie's were done by her friend Helen once before Christmas, and again before school broke up for the summer holidays. Alice's clothes were tailored, a subdued medley of beige, and expensive, while Edie didn't own anything that hadn't already been worn by someone else. Alice's nails were shaped and her cuticles trimmed by a lovely lady who had also been waxing her bikini line every four weeks for years, while Edie only cut her nails when they started making a clicking sound on her keyboard, and her bikini line had joined up with her leg hair years ago, so it was pointless trying to work out where one began and ended. Yet as Edie huffed onto the studio floor, looking pointedly at her watch, the crew fell silent and their gaze yo-yoed between the twins as they bickered. That very same afternoon, the executives offered them both jobs as the show's resident agony aunts – with a ten-minute segment on-air every week.

If Alice was put out that Edie, who wouldn't know how to even sign up to social media, let alone get a coveted blue tick and sponsorship by three major lifestyle brands, had landed a presenting job purely on her genetic similarity to Alice, then she didn't show it. Not then anyway. 'You want both of us?' she'd exclaimed. 'Oh how thrilling, it would be wonderful to work together!' Three months in, after this latest debacle, it was a slightly different story. It was as though being given a hall pass to air their different views live on television had opened the floodgates for that to spill over into their real lives too. They'd had forty-odd years of keeping a lid on how baffling each found the other, doing exactly what their mother had always told them to do and just 'get along girls,' but now she was gone and here they were, being paid to be as opposing as possible. It was actually incredibly liberating.

Alice

'You made us both look like fools then Edie, and it's not fair. You need to start taking this more seriously, because if you don't, we're both going to get fired, and—' Alice stopped her tirade as they passed one of the show's runners in the corridor, who gave them a reverential head nod.

Alice smiled at the younger woman. 'Hi Priya, is your mum any better? Oh good.' She then retained her silence with her sister until the girl had rounded the corner. 'Look, it's a new year, it's a new chance to make a fresh start. After you left on Christmas Day I promised Dad that we'd try to be more, I don't know, more understanding of each other's personalities. More patient.'

'What aspects of my personality do you need to be patient about exactly?'

Alice searched for the right words, 'You're a little... chaotic.'

'You think that I'm chaotic?' Edie put her hands on her lips as she waited for a reply.

It astounded Alice that this was news to her sister. 'Don't you?'

'No. I'm just not very rigid in my behaviour like you.'

Alice, affronted, replied, 'You think I'm rigid?'

'Don't you?'

'No! I am not rigid at all! I am just organised.' Rigid. *Rigid?*

'You're a complete control freak.'

Alice's eyebrows knotted together as she shook her head. 'I am not.'

'You are! You plan everything to a minuscule level leaving no room in your life for spontaneity, and if it's this claustrophobic watching it from the sidelines I dread to think what it's like being in your actual family.'

'At least my family are all relatively normal.'

Edie laughed. 'There is nothing normal about a thirteen-year-old boy wearing beige chinos and a bow tie, believe me.'

'It was Christmas! I don't make him wear that around the house on a random Tuesday. And if we're talking normal Christmas attire, one of your kids came dressed for an all-inclusive holiday in the Balearics and the other one came dressed for bed! And don't even get me started on Seb.'

'What was wrong with Seb?'

Was she for real? 'He was wearing shorts! Doesn't he have trousers?'

'He's a grown man, I'm not going to tell him what to wear.'

'I did seven different side dishes, roast turkey *and* beef, not to mention the nut roast Iris didn't even touch, and he couldn't even be bothered to cover his knees.'

'How on earth are the two related? You don't eat with your legs?'

Alice didn't know if it was anger or disbelief with how unreasonable her sister was being that made her stand there, mouth opening, then closing, her fists clenching at her side. It was a question of respect; going to the trouble of picking something out of your wardrobe that showed that you understood the gravitas of the day and the effort she'd put in was just basic human decency. 'And you have no idea how much time worrying about Dad takes up in my day as well. I don't see you taking him to his appointments or picking up his prescriptions. When he wanted to move nearer to one of us, I wasn't aware of you offering to show him round your neighbourhood?'

'We live three tube stops away from each other, your neighbourhood is basically my neighbourhood.'

'And another thing,' Alice continued.

'Oh good, there's more, because I was sorry that this conversation had ended,' Edie replied sarcastically.

'Teddy told me that Rosie was drinking on Christmas Day.'

'Teddy told you that?'

'Yes, he was concerned about her.'

'Oh, that's lovely, that level of cousin concern. But I knew about that already. And it was one glass of prosecco, which isn't really the first step on the ladder to heroin addiction.'

Alice pulled the strap of her handbag further up onto her shoulder. 'I just thought you should know, that's all, it might be a sign that you need to actually start parenting.'

'Absolutely. Yes, thank you for that. And in the spirit of

helping each other 'parent', I'm pretty sure I saw Teddy vaping out of his bedroom window while the King's Speech was on.'

Impossible. Teddy wouldn't know a vape if it came up to him and introduced itself as such. This was typical Edie, finding herself cornered like a wild ferret and then swiping out in defence at anyone trying to help. 'That is extremely unlikely,' Alice said, her chin lifted, 'it was probably the smoke from his scented candle, he does love a scented candle.'

Edie pursed her lips together, looking as though she was trying not to laugh; god she was maddening, trying to lower everyone down to her level. 'Right,' Edie said finally, 'I don't think it's helpful for us to say any more, do you? Quite clearly you think you and your family are perfect and me and mine are a chaotic mess. That is fine. We will agree to disagree. I am going home now, to my hovel and my reprobate kids before the local young offenders' institute come knocking. See you next week.'

'Edie—' Alice called after her sister, but Edie didn't turn around again. Alice sighed and looked at her watch – it was midday. She had to collect the cat's medication from the vets, pick up Danny's suits from the dry cleaners and lodge an official complaint about one of his ties going missing, transfer the money for Rufus's residential school trip, organise the Ocado delivery for her mother-in-law who had just had a hip replacement, and get to the supermarket and do the big shop before the kids got home from school. She really didn't have time for her sister's moods.

CHAPTER FOUR

February

Alice

If Alice and Edie were merely friends, not bonded by 99.9% of their DNA, their relationship would have fallen by the wayside long ago. They'd occasionally give a well-meaning heart to each other's Instagram posts, but face-to-face contact would have ceased fairly early into their paths crossing. They both knew that if a friend recounted a story identical to theirs, their advice would be to accept that shared genetics mean good bone marrow matches, not necessarily harmonious lifelong unity. Since their fight after the book-club fiasco, an uneasy truce had been agreed, and was working reasonably well, as long as they stayed out of each other's way. Audiences had no idea that as soon as the red light on the camera stopped blinking, the twins' smiles and easy banter completely evaporated and they would peel off and exit through different sides of the studio floor. The winter was unseasonably warm, and as the frost was disappearing from people's back gardens, it was still settled and showing no sign of thawing on the sisters.

'Happy Valentine's Day!' Lauren shrilled into the camera. 'It is the day of love, and we have a jam-packed show for you today. We are joined by Alice and Edie on the sofa who are going to tackle all of your relationship dilemmas.'

'Happy to be here.' Alice smiled.

'Hello,' said Edie, beside her.

'Is Valentine's a big thing in your houses?' Lauren asked. 'Well, I know the answer to that, I saw your fantastic decorations on Instagram Alice, they must have taken hours!'

Alice shook her head modestly. There was no need to admit that it had taken the best part of three days to master the giant origami hearts that she'd hung in each bay window, or the wreath for the front door made from over a thousand silk rose petals that she'd painstakingly glued together before finding an almost exact replica on Amazon for under a tenner. 'I just love the romance of it all.'

'And is your husband equally as romantic?'

Alice smiled, adjusting her sitting position slightly, a little embarrassed about discussing her own love life on TV. 'He is. He gave me the most beautiful designer handbag this morning. He has the most exquisite taste.'

'If you were a footballer's WAG maybe,' Edie murmured alongside her, just quiet enough for Alice to hear but not for the microphone to pick up on. Alice shot her a look.

'And your partner, Edie? Any big romantic gestures this morning in your house?'

'None that I can talk about on air,' Edie replied with a wink.

Alice's insides started withering and dying. Why did she have to do that? How difficult would it be to say, *I got a lovely card thanks*. It was as though Edie went through life taking a big red pen to normal, acceptable conversation, constantly seeking to shock or challenge.

'Lucky you,' Lauren laughed. 'Well, our first caller this morning is Becky, from Padstow, that's a lovely part of the world. What's your conundrum, Becky?'

The viewer's voice rang out excitedly, 'Hello! Firstly can I say to Edie and Alice, that I'm a big fan . . .'

It always rankled Alice when people did that, reversing their names. A came before E. You would never say Dec and Ant, would you? It just sounded wrong.

'Hi Becky,' Edie answered. 'Lovely to hear from you, how can we help?'

'I'm going to a singles speed-dating event tonight, and I want your advice on the questions I should ask to know quickly if the person is right for me. I have four minutes with twelve different men.'

'That sounds like an amazing night!' Edie said excitedly. 'Reminds me of an evening I spent in Ibiza when I was twenty, but again, probably can't talk about that on air.'

Alice hurriedly cut in. 'I would go straight for the main three topics that you need to be aligned on in every successful relationship: politics, religion and financial stability. Oh, and I would absolutely ascertain very early on if they want children if that's what you want. There's nothing worse than getting on with someone, only to discover years later that their vision of their future is different to yours.' Alice was vaguely aware of her sister swivelling around to stare at her with an ever-dropping jaw, but she honestly didn't know what was so bad about what she had said.

'What are you talking about, woman?' Edie exclaimed. 'Politics? Religion? Money? It's a wonder you managed to find a partner at all if that was your opening gambit. Who gives a toss what box you both put a tick in at the last election or if one of you has an ISA? No, just no. You find out so much more about someone by asking things like what animal they think represents them the best, or if they could swap places with anyone else for a day who it would be, or when the last time they cried was and what was it about? Having a long-term partner is a long hard slog, and believe me, you're going to want to choose someone based on so much more than the fact both your parents decided to christen you and you both have a private pension.'

Alice had been shaking her head the whole way through Edie's monologue, so much so, she was now feeling a little seasick. 'I have to disagree I'm afraid, I've been married for eighteen years and I can honestly say that I have no idea at all what animal my husband thinks he would be, or why on earth that would matter?'

'Because if he said sea cucumber that would be a giant red flag.'

'She's not wrong,' Gareth said.

'Yes she is!' Alice retorted. 'Sorry, didn't mean to raise my voice, but that's nonsense. You'll have your whole lives to have silly chats about these type of things if you want, but you need to find out right at the start that he has a good job, savings, a pension, and isn't going to drag you into debt.'

'I'd rather be in debt with a flamingo than live in a mansion with a tapeworm.'

Alice looked at her sister, aghast. 'That makes no sense, you're being ridiculous.'

'*You're* being ridiculous. But there's no surprise there.'

Lauren smiled straight into camera three. 'And we'll be back after the break with another caller, stay tuned.'

*

March

Edie

'It's Dad's seventieth in June,' Alice said to Edie as they sat side by side in the hair and make-up chairs backstage, a black cape around both their necks.

'I know.'

'We should do something to mark it somehow.'

Edie wasn't really listening. She and Seb had had words that morning, and she hadn't had a chance to call him and make things right. It was the anniversary of them meeting, and he'd got her a beautiful card and the girls had made a gorgeous breakfast, which she had to wolf down to shoehorn in a client Zoom counselling session before leaving for the studio. He'd even reminded her a few days before and asked her to swap her appointments around so she could enjoy it, but it had flown clear out of her mind, and she hadn't even got him a card. She couldn't afford a grand gesture to apologise, but she knew she needed to do something to patch up his hurt feelings, not to mention the girls'.

'Sure,' she replied, 'whatever you think.'

'We'll need to send the save the dates out soon.'

'It's three months away.'

'Exactly.'

The sisters stared ahead at their own reflections, conscious that the stylists had been told very early on in their employment to make them look as similar as possible to maximise their currency on live television. Edie's prep time always took twice as long as Alice's, who arrived in the studio looking broadcast-ready, while it took a good hour to tease Edie's hair into submission with the help of an ozone-melting amount of lacquer, but it was Edie's monobrow that was the chief area of concern that morning.

'Shall we hire a private room in a restaurant?' Alice continued, reaching for her slim diary in her handbag to check the shortlist of venues Edie bet she'd already rung who had availability. Yep, there it was, a neat handwritten list of venue names with ticks next to at least five of them.

Edie caught the eye of Petra, the hair stylist, who smiled warmly back at her in the mirror. Clearly six months of having both sisters in her chair every week had been more than enough time to suss out their dynamics.

'Hello and welcome back to *Britain in the Morning*, school has started again after half term, we're on the home straight to the Easter holidays, and parents up and down the land are starting to think about how they can keep their little ones entertained for a much longer break. We're joined by our resident agony aunts to help us with some ideas – Alice and Edie, hello ladies.'

Edie's nose crinkled, as it always did, at this greeting. Firstly, it really rankled her that Alice's name always came before hers; she knew alphabetically it did, but varying it occasionally wouldn't hurt, they weren't bloody Ant and Dec, were they? And secondly 'hello ladies' was so cringe, as Rosie would say.

'Hi Gareth, Lauren, lovely to be back,' Alice answered chirpily.

'You're both mothers, and am I right in thinking that half term has been a hectic family time for you both?'

'Oh absolutely,' Alice agreed, smiling, 'I feel I need a break after the break!'

Gareth, Lauren and Alice all laughed.

'Edie, what did your family get up to this week?' Lauren asked good-naturedly.

The truth was, half term came and went without Edie even noticing. Seb had been away all week sourcing new materials in Scotland, and she'd been squirrelled away in her home office having back-to-back client Zooms, and writing a column for a magazine she'd been asked to contribute to on laissez-faire parenting and was using her own children as guinea pigs for the hands-off approach. The food she'd stocked the fridge with at the start of the week had gradually disappeared as the days wore on, so she was confident Rosie and Iris had fed and watered themselves; she saw that the washing machine had been used throughout the week, so they had also changed their clothes occasionally; and they'd been back at school for three days, and there hadn't been any angry emails from teachers saying their homework hadn't been done, so they'd obviously cracked on with that too. The column she wrote was incredibly complimentary about the technique. 'I have absolutely no idea!' Edie answered honestly.

The two presenters alongside Edie both laughed again, thinking her 'joke' hilarious, but Alice sat stonily alongside her. Edie could tell that Alice thought that she did this on purpose, pretending to be laid back and too busy to spend loads of time with the girls, thinking it made her appear cool, but the truth was, she couldn't afford not to work right now. After the twins' mother had died, and Kenneth didn't feel able to live at the family home alone anymore, Edie – in her grief – had bought her parents' home from her dad and had moved her family in. It was a beautiful house, and living in her childhood home again made her feel closer to her mum somehow. Edie loved that her own children now slept in her and Alice's childhood bedroom, and she could almost feel her mum watching over her when she worked on the sofa late at night. But it was slowly vacuuming up every penny she and Seb had, even at the heavily reduced price they'd got it for. So, while she'd have loved to take the day off to spend it with Rosie and Iris, cancelling clients just wasn't an option. Plus, the kids were old enough to look after themselves – and she *was* there if they needed her. It wasn't like she'd buggered off on holiday for a week, she was still at home for god's sake.

'I think it's actually quite sad,' Alice countered, 'when parents deliberately swerve spending time with their children when they're young. I know it's different if parents really need to work and can't take the time off, but you're a freelancer, so you can. I had hundreds of tasks to do, but I still managed to take my children ice skating, to the London Transport Museum and the Imperial War Museum, we had dinner together every night, we had an afternoon journalling and we all worked on a 1500-piece jigsaw together every evening. I got up at five am to do my own work before waking them up at eight. It's just a question of priorities.'

'Well, it sounds like we know who would win the best parenting award,' Gareth laughed.

Edie stared at him for a beat before turning her stare back to her sister. This style of one-upmanship between the two of them wasn't new – they'd been compared all of their lives and had practically come out of the womb as competitors; what was new was the uneasy truce wobbling live on TV. And she had a choice to make. She could smile and say, 'That does sound like a lot of fun,' and then move on to the phone-in, or she could slap the smugness out of her sister's face with a counter argument. *What to do. What to do.*

Edie took a deep breath and went for it. 'I think good parenting is rather subjective, Gareth, if I'm honest. If you have the type of kids who will happily go to a museum and learn about the history of the underground system, then fair play, knock yourself out, but if you have children, like I do, who would prefer to wrap themselves in a duvet and reacquaint themselves with the inside of their eyeballs for a week to get over the stress of school and the myriad challenges of adolescence, then they should be allowed to do that.'

'But perhaps they're only being lazy because you've never

opened their eyes to the rich culture around them?' Alice said, peppering her words with deliberate lightness, making sure to finish on a smile.

'You say lazy, I say normal.'

'There's nothing normal about not leaving your room for a week,' Alice added a little chuckle at the end of her sentence along with a little 'am I right?' eye roll at the camera to gain support from the invisible thousands at home.

Edie, meanwhile, had completely forgotten about their audience for this conversation; the cameras had ceased to exist, Lauren and Gareth were no longer in her eyeline. It was just her and Alice. And the gloves were coming off.

'There's nothing normal about a fifteen-year-old boy sitting with his mum in the evening doing a jigsaw after spending the day unwillingly learning about the history of the RAF. Let your kids just relax and just be teenagers. You don't need to fill every second with educational value or formative experiences. Rest and recuperation are just as important.'

'Bored children are boring children,' Alice said in an annoying singsong voice.

'Are you calling my children boring?'

'If the cap fits.'

Edie's eyes flashed with anger as she sat up as straight as her spine would allow. 'My children are not boring.'

'Lazy then.' Alice's voice was still calm and measured, which had the opposite effect on her sister, whose voice was so loud when she replied the producers had to lower the volume of her microphone.

'Or lazy! They are catching up on vital rest to replenish their reserves for when school starts again!'

'Well, what would they tell their teachers when they went back to school when they asked them what they did over the holidays? I slept.'

'Their teachers probably spent the week sleeping too, god knows they bloody deserve it!' A flicker of Edie's spit landed on Alice's cheek, which she rubbed away with a grimace.

'Parents have a responsibility to show their children that the world is an exciting place full of diversions and activities that can enrich their lives.'

'And I think parents have a responsibility to take their cues from their kids, and not force-feed them a litany of must-do activities because they'd feel lesser or "bad" parents if they don't. So, Gareth,' Edie threw her gaze across the set to the other sofa, 'I'd argue that the best parenting award goes to the parent who knows her kids best, not the one who completely ignores what her kids *actually* want in favour of ticking off a ridiculous to-do list created for the sole purpose of feeling pompous and self-righteous and showing off about it on Instagram.'

'Pompous? Self-righteous?'

'Careful Alice, you're doing that repeating thing again.'

Lauren coughed, and smiled sweetly straight into camera two. 'Well sadly, we don't have time to go to any of the viewers' questions today, but Alice, Edie, you've certainly given us a lot to mull over. We'll be back after the regional news and weather with a wonderful recipe for a weeknight dinner using offal that the whole family will love.'

The studio floor was silent. The pink sofa was silent. Everyone was waiting for the inevitable eruption from the executive producer. Edie sighed. Bollocks.

Alice

Alice ran over the last few minutes in her head. Had she sounded pompous and self-righteous? Might the viewers side with Edie? She shouldn't have called Rosie and Iris lazy and boring. Lazy yes, but they were definitely not boring.

A voice came through their earpieces. 'Alice, Edie, upstairs now.'

In the ten minutes since they went off air, there had been over three hundred complaints. Shaun, the executive producer, who both sisters had only met once before, told them to come in but didn't offer them a seat. They stood like naughty schoolchildren in front of his desk while he held a sheaf of notes at arms-length, which he read from: 'How are we supposed to be teaching our children tolerance and politeness when your own employees are brawling on air?' He put that paper to the back of the pile and read the next one: 'Your programme is supposed to spread joy, not all-out war. We can watch the news for that.' There were more, but both sisters tuned them out in their mutual shame.

Finally, he put the pages down and looked up at them. 'I can't deny that bringing you two on board has made viewing figures spike, but today they spiked for all the wrong reasons. I don't want to terminate one of your contracts, but I am going to have to if you can't find a way to sit alongside each other without flinging insults at each other.'

'I don't think we did that?' Edie retorted defensively. 'I mean, yes, it perhaps got a little heated, but I don't think we resorted to hair pulling and name calling?'

'You said Alice was pompous and self-righteous.'

'Ah. Yes.'

Alice tried not to look pompous and self-righteous as she felt her twin squirming beside her.

Shaun must have clocked her expression and added, 'I'm not sure what you're looking so smug about, Alice, you called her children lazy and boring.'

Alice opened then shut her mouth, realising that there was nothing she could say that would prove that to be untrue.

'I mean it,' he said. 'One of you will have to go unless you can understand the other one's perspective a bit more. You don't have to agree all the time, in fact, we don't want you to, but we do want you to at least look as though you don't hate each other. Is that too hard to do? I mean you're identical twins for goodness' sake, surely there's something about the other one you actually like?'

They left his office too stunned to speak. Alice was still reeling from Edie's hand grenades, and she knew that Edie was far too stubborn to forget the insults that she threw her nieces' way any time soon. They walked to the car park, still in silence, got into their adjacent cars without a word and slammed their car doors in a perfect synchronisation. Alice reached into her bag for her phone, and exhaled shakily at a text from her friend Ruth that said: *How are the two of you even related? On behalf of all good mothers, well done for calling her out.*

The one that hit the hardest was from her dad: *I am relieved your mother never saw that. Find a way to appreciate each other rather than constantly find fault.*

Alice looked out of her window across to Edie's car and saw her, mobile in hand, obviously reading the same message, feeling the same punch to the stomach she had a few seconds ago. Alice watched as her sister leaned her head back against her headrest and closed her eyes in shame.

Alice's car slowly reversed out of her space and out of the car park.

CHAPTER FIVE

April

Edie

'You're not going to believe this.' Edie stomped into the kitchen holding her phone and thrust it under Seb's nose at the sink where he was washing up.

Seb peered at the screen. 'What am I looking at?'

'Dad's refusing to come to Easter lunch.'

'What do you mean?'

'He just sent me and Alice a message saying that he's not going to come to any event or anything where we're both at until we start getting on. That's ridiculous! Isn't that ridiculous?'

Seb was concentrating really hard on getting the final bit of burned-on lasagne off the bottom of the Pyrex dish.

'Seb? Isn't that ridiculous?'

'This pasta really isn't coming off.'

'Say it then. That is ridiculous.'

Seb shrugged. 'He may have a point.'

'He does not have a point! We're sisters, sisters argue, everyone's making such a big deal about it.'

'To be honest I've been trying to think of an excuse why I can't go either,' Seb said, wiping his hands on the tea towel and turning to face Edie. 'It's just not fun Eeds; everyone's waiting for one of you to start something and then we're all just caught in the crossfire. I think the time's come for you two to realise that you don't like each other and just call it a day.'

'I can't *call it a day* with my twin! It's not like choosing not to use the takeaway that always gives you food poisoning but you keep going back because it's the nearest. She is my sister. And yes, we may not agree on most things, but she does have qualities that I like.' Edie picked up a tea towel and started drying the plates.

Seb smiled encouragingly. 'Name them.'

Edie paused for a moment to think, then triumphantly replied, 'Her house is very clean.'

'You said it looks like a furniture showroom before the store opens to the public.'

'Well yes,' Edie conceded, 'it does.'

'You said that at your sister's postmortem they'd cut her open and she'd bleed bleach.'

'You see, I was wrong there, she doesn't use bleach, it would be a white vinegar and bicarb mix.'

'So, just to get this right,' Seb said, 'the quality you admire most, is the one you mock most often.'

'You say mock, I say tease with affection.'

'I must have always been in the loo when the affection bit happens.'

Edie flicked him with her tea towel. 'It's not just me, it's her too, I feel that I'm perfectly reasonable most of the time.'

Seb nodded, his eyes twinkling. 'Perfectly reasonable.'

'Now who's mocking?'

Seb pulled Edie in closer to him and kissed the top of her head. 'Only affectionately.'

Alice

'You're not going to believe this!' Alice said, walking into the living room where Danny was watching the rugby.

'What?'

'Dad's sent me and Edie a message saying that he's not going to come to Easter lunch, or anything where we're both at until we start getting on.'

'Oh well,' Danny said, motioning for Alice to move a little to the right so he could still see the whole screen.

'What do you mean?' Alice said, sidestepping out of his eyeline.

'To be fair your sister and her family are a bit nuts.'

Alice thought that was slightly unfair, Edie was unconventional certainly, but not what he said. And tradition was tradition. 'But we've always had Easter lunch together.'

Danny threw a peeled pistachio in the air and caught it in his mouth. 'Time for a change then.' He held out the bag for Alice to take one.

She shook her head distractedly. 'But I've ordered a massive leg of lamb, and prepaid for it.'

'Can't you freeze what we don't eat? That's what I bought you the big freezer for.'

May

Alice

The television studio had been transformed into a shrine to the sisters, which ordinarily would have been embarrassing, but when you spooned in the fact that they hadn't talked to each other since Alice had cancelled Easter (not the whole Christian celebration, just their family lunch), it was teeth-numbingly mortifying. Having to stand shoulder to shoulder making appreciative aahs and oos as everyone sang them happy birthday and asked them what *they* were doing to celebrate was taking every ounce of acting skill Alice possessed to smile through. For the first time in their lives, they had woken up without any fanfare from the other at all, no message, no voice-note, no card in the post, no barbershop quartet – Edie had organised that to embarrass Alice at the temping firm she was working at on their twenty-first. This year, they hadn't even wished each other happy birthday yet, as Edie had arrived at the studio with seconds to spare, meaning that Petra had had to run behind her brushing her hair all the way down the corridor to the studio. In typical Edie-style she muttered one apology and thought that was sufficient for all the waiting around and anxious clock-watching everyone else had been doing.

A cord was strung across the studio with blown-up photos of the twins at various ages clipped onto it and Gareth and Lauren were cooing over each one in turn, the camera zooming in on each. Kenneth must have provided them all to the producers who thought up this segment – who doesn't love cute pictures of twins? The first two photos were sweet enough: two chubby identical infants sat on a sheepskin rug looking up at the Kermit the frog hand puppet their dad had dutifully brandished just out of sight, although even at that tender age Edie's expression definitely displayed a little hint of pity for her father's lack of dignity. By their third year of this humiliating birthday portrait tradition, Edie's smile had an edge of defiance about it, a clear intent to soil her new big girl pants while smiling at the camera, while Alice sat primly alongside her with her hands neatly folded in her lap. Alice remembered that there had been a massive argument the fourth year as Edie had point-blank refused to take off her Minnie Mouse ears that she'd got at Disneyland Paris; the fifth year Edie had refused to wear a smile, and by the sixth they were lucky she was wearing anything. On their seventh portrait they were each allowed to bring their favourite possession into the photograph: Alice brought the cute teddy bear she'd been given that morning, which had a green ribbon around its neck and tweed paws, while Edie had dragged in the dog's bed. The eighth one had been lost in the house move from their Ealing maisonette to the Victorian terrace in Clapham Edie now lived in. And the ninth only had the back of their heads in, as that was the year they both had faces full of chicken pox, resulting in the first physical difference between the sisters: a tiny little scar above Alice's right eyebrow. Thankfully most photographic evidence of the sisters as teens were lost to landfill, apart from two: one taken on their fifteenth birthday, which in hindsight should have heralded the divide to come. Edie's goth phase was in full swing, black lipstick, a heavy metal band T-shirt, kohl-rimmed eyes and a scowl that would turn milk sour, while Alice sat on the other side of their parents' sofa wearing a namesake hairband and a dress their mum picked out. The last one in the twins' portrait series was from their surprise eighteenth birthday party; their parents had to organise a surprise because a planned one would have probably resulted in two no-shows from the guests of honour. Oh who was she kidding, Alice thought, of course she'd have gone.

And almost three decades after that last photograph was taken, a camera was once again pointing at the twins, and once again, they were both thinking that the shot would be so much better if the other one wasn't in it.

'Alice,' Lauren asked cheerfully, 'what did Edie get you?'

The question caught her off guard. The simple and honest answer was nothing, but she could hardly admit that to the nation. Her mind raced with the possibilities. She thought about last year, when Edie had given her a first edition of a book their mum used to read them. She'd thought it was a really lovely gift until she opened it up only to find it inscribed to someone called Marion and a pencil price of £4.50 written in the top right corner along with an Oxfam stamp. 'A first edition of a book I loved as a child.'

'Oh lovely. Edie?' Lauren prompted, 'what did you receive from Alice?'

Edie had obviously followed the breadcrumbs Alice had dropped for her as she replied, 'A lovely Peruvian alpaca blanket.'

'Oh what a super present,' Lauren said, prompting Alice to beam with the present-choosing praise. 'I bet that's lovely to snuggle under on a cold night.'

Edie looked a little sheepish. 'My youngest actually gave it to a homeless man called Bob who sits outside Tesco – other supermarkets are available,' she added quickly, remembering what channel she was on.

Alice shook her head a little. Did she just hear that right? A homeless man now had her blanket? 'Sorry – can I just – you gave the blanket to a homeless man?'

'Well, Iris did, but he loves it, bless him, he's always got it round him.'

Edie didn't even look embarrassed about it, or at least a little apologetic. 'That was a hundred and fifty pounds!' Alice exclaimed.

'Wow, for a blanket?' Edie said, open-mouthed. 'That's crazy! If I knew that I would have sold it and given Bob the cash.'

'I can't believe you did that.'

'I can't believe you think spending a hundred and fifty quid on a blanket is perfectly reasonable!' Edie retorted, giving an eye roll to the camera, which only served to fan the flames slowly building inside Alice.

'You wouldn't know perfectly reasonable if it bit you.'

'Speaking of biting,' Edie said, marching down the line of photos until she was standing in front of the one of their fifth birthday with her scowling. 'The reason I'm not smiling here—' she pointed at the photo '—is because Alice bit me on the arm just before our mum took the photo.'

Lauren laughed nervously. 'Kids eh?'

Alice stormed over near to where Edie was standing, and jabbed her finger at the photo of seven-year-old them, 'You see this teddy bear, viewers? It was my new present, I adored it, and just after this photo was taken Edie tied it to ten helium balloons and I never saw it again.'

'That's nothing!' Edie shouted, while pointing down the line at the second to last picture. 'You see that one of us as teenagers? Well doesn't Alice look all prim and proper here? Well just out of sight is a sick bowl because she drank half a bottle of our mum's Malibu the night before and passed out in the dog bed.'

Alice ran to the end of the string. 'I can trump that! This was our eighteenth and an hour after this picture was taken, Edie was arrested!' She tugged on the picture much harder than she intended, her jubilation at getting the last word, at throwing the biggest hand grenade of all, making her lose all sense of decorum, and out of the corner of her eye she saw the false wall that the string was attached to give a little wobble. Time slowed down as Edie leapt in slow motion to push Lauren out of the way, who let out a long blood-curdling scream. Gareth gasped in horror, his hands flying to his head. Two cameramen ran on to try to stop the wall from crashing down, but were a couple of seconds too late, and as it loudly splintered into pieces across the set, the sisters' photos scattered like litter across the floor.

CHAPTER SIX

Edie

If they'd been standing on a precipice of severing their bond forever before, they were now jumping without a parachute, pockets laden with rocks, headfirst into a ravine. Final warning. That's what Shaun had bellowed at them. The irony wasn't lost on Edie that the only thing keeping them employed at the network was the fact they were identical twins, and yet that was their biggest problem. This time felt different though. In all their other moments of crisis, and god they'd had a few, their mum had been there to smooth it over and soothe them both. Now they had to try to do that alone. Or do what Seb said, and simply *call it a day*. As her mum's park bench came into view in the distance, just behind the third old oak, Edie saw someone seated on it. For a split second she thought it was Alice, drawn here for the same reason, but as she approached and the silhouette became heavier, bulkier, her heart sank in disappointment; if it had been Alice, at least that would show that occasionally they did have the same thought.

She really didn't want to make small talk with a stranger, and she knew that she had the type of face that welcomed it, and to be fair, she usually did. But not today. Today she just wanted to sit on her mum's bench and feel sad. Really, really sad.

Edie raised her gaze from the path as she heard a voice she knew so well.

'I thought if I waited long enough one of you would show up.'

She sank gratefully onto the bench and leaned in close to her father. He put his arm around her, pulling her closer. She didn't say anything, she didn't need to. They sat like that a while: father and daughter, their backs resting on the brass plaque they'd all chosen together.

'It's all gone to shit, Dad.'

The old man slowly nodded. 'That it has.'

Edie snuggled further into the crook of her dad's shoulder. 'Every time we see each other it's getting worse.'

'Some things have to break completely before you can fix them.'

'I think this time it's completely buggered.'

'So, then it's time to fix it.'

Edie raised her head to look at Kenneth. 'We have tried so many times to be nice to each other, but we can never keep it up.'

'That's because you're just pretending. You're doing what you think you should be doing, acting the part, not living it, believing it. God, your mum was great about helping you both see things from the other's point of view when you were kids.'

Edie smiled at the memories Kenneth was talking about. After one massive row over the state Edie kept her half of their bedroom compared to Alice's spotless side, their mum had made them swap beds for a week: Alice had to sleep in Edie's and Edie's in Alice's. It only took a day for Edie to realise that waking up facing a rubbish dump was not a great way to start your day. Another time, when Edie couldn't understand why Alice was so anxious about school, she made them swap clothes, backpacks, even packed lunches – Alice had Edie's jam sandwiches and Edie had Alice's horrid cucumber ones – and sent them off to school, knowing that Edie, by the end of the day, having walked the corridors alone as Alice, sitting quietly in the library alone, being jeered at by Edie's friends in PE after being the last to be picked for a team, she'd start to see the world through her sister's eyes and understand. They'd swapped at other times on their own accord, playing the twin card to their advantage: Alice's aptitude for languages meant sitting two GCSE French orals back-to-back was the only sensible thing to do, and when Alice couldn't find the right words to let down a boy, Edie couldn't remember his name – Neil maybe? – Edie stepped in and did it for her.

Kenneth patted Edie's leg. Were those *tears* in his eyes? 'Before your mum died, when she was sick, and I was sat with her at night, she made me promise that you two would find your way back to each other, and I fear I've let her down. She'd know what to say to you both, and I just don't. It was so much easier when you were kids. Do you remember when we were on holiday in Italy? We were camping by the lake, and you two had been fighting for the whole holiday over something or other, and she took off Alice's headband and plonked it on your head, and then bent down and rubbed her hands in the dirt and then rubbed the mud all over Alice's T-shirt to make it look like yours.' Kenneth laughed, which made Edie smile as well. 'God, Alice's face, and then she sent you both off in opposite directions – Alice to be with the boys that you had made friends with at the campsite who were making ant farms in the mud, and you to the little group of girls making friendship bracelets. You'd never made a bracelet in your life before that, but by the end of the holiday you loved making them so much we each had about five up our arms.'

'I'm not sure Alice ever made another ant farm though,' Edie smiled, remembering the length of her sister's shower that evening in the communal shower block, as she scrubbed the mud off her.

'I'm not sure she did either,' he chuckled. 'But my point is, it was a lot easier to heal rifts when you were little. Christ knows how you get over this one now.'

Alice

It wasn't a massive surprise to Alice when Edie had more or less summoned her to a meeting. Edie's stormy moods always passed overhead relatively quickly, it was her own that took longer to dissipate. She wasn't expecting, however, to be offered a cup of tea then immediately ushered up to what used to be their childhood bedroom, now Iris's, to have the chat. Alice had initially been pleased, albeit very surprised, when Edie had said three years ago that she and Seb were going to try to raise the funds to buy their parents' house after Kenneth said he couldn't stay there alone. Even at far below the market value, purchasing it still stretched Edie and Seb beyond what most people would have felt comfortable with. But the expense was only part of it, Alice wasn't sure that she'd have been strong enough to walk through the doorways of the past every time she needed to enter a different room. It was tough enough visiting the house, which was why she always suggested hosting things at hers – well, that was one of the reasons. The others were self-explanatory, she thought as she moved a Tupperware of vegetable peelings off Iris's bed in order to sit down.

Iris's bed was placed in the exact position Alice's used to

be, the headboard flush against the wall facing the window, the afternoon sunlight shining on a mural Seb had painted of a map of the world and the wild animals indigenous to each country; it was very good, but where did he find the time? Alice used to have a poster of the Friends cast blue-tacked to the exact same spot that caught the late afternoon sun in exactly the same way. She looked across the room, at the space that Edie's bed used to occupy, but which now had a desk with a big reptile vivarium on it, housing a solitary leopard gecko.

Edie must have seen Alice looking at it, prompting her to say, 'There were two in there. They were sisters. That one murdered the other one. Actually, that brings me nicely on to why I've asked you here today. . . we need to stop getting at each other, Alice. It's just making life difficult for both of us and for everyone else. Dad's really upset that we're on the verge of killing each other . . . So I think you should just apologise for being so judgemental and then we can just move on and stop snapping at each other all the time.'

Is Edie for real?

'Me? Apologise? You must be joking. You're the one who acts like your free-range parenting is superior to my actually being present with my family. You've insulted me, Danny and the kids hundreds of times now! Plus, you accused Teddy of vaping, for Christ's sake! Are you going to apologise for that?'

'You're being absolutely ridiculous, Alice. You were judging *my* family, judging *me!* Just as you always have, ever since we were kids!' Edie stood up and walked to the other side of the room, arms folded. 'I knew I shouldn't have even bothered asking you here. Dad's just going to have to deal with us not speaking.' She rolled her eyes and looked out of the window. 'I can't believe he thought it might be as easy as it was when we were kids.'

Alice raised one eyebrow, and said with a sneer that she made no attempt at veiling, 'Like when Mum used to make us swap places?'

'Yes. Dad reminded me of all the times that she made us switch places when we were kids. I thought it was ridiculous but he thought it would help us now.'

'Right, yes, you wear my hairband, I swear a lot and then we'll become best friends.'

Edie sighed in frustration. 'He's not wrong though, Alice. I don't understand you at all, I don't get your family dynamics, I can't name a single one of your friends, I have no idea what you do, or like, or why you spout such nonsense on the show every week. I don't know anything about your life, and I'm damn sure you have no idea about mine.'

'I know you don't own a vacuum cleaner.'

Edie slammed her hand down on the desk next to her. 'For fuck's sake Alice! This is what I mean! You're always trying to embarrass me. This is what you do every week on the show. I know you think I'm a lazy slattern who can't keep Mum's house in order, who lets her kids run wild, but there's so much more to me, to my family, than that, and you just don't see it.'

'You're right,' Alice replied, pulling her Valentine's gifted handbag closer to her chest rather than risk putting it onto the carpet. 'I don't. I don't see why you have to live the way you do, running, constantly running, between catastrophes, encouraging your children and all of our viewers to be as odd and contrary as you are, turning our parents' house – that Mum spent every minute polishing until it gleamed – into some sort of storage facility for a community jumble sale. Dad pruned the front hedge every other Saturday morning for our entire adolescence, I'd wager that Seb doesn't even own a pair of shears.'

'Why would it only be a man that can prune a hedge?'

'See, that's what I mean, you hang importance on to the wrong things. You advise people every week to take some kind of stand all the time rather than just getting on with their lives. I don't get how your brain works. But I don't think I'm alone in that, this isn't all on me. You go out of your way to make fun of me every single chance you get, which was bad enough when we were kids, but now you do it in front of the whole country *every week*! You think I'm stupid for caring so much about everything being perfect and—'

'It is stupid!'

'*You're* stupid!' Alice felt herself getting more and more frustrated. 'My life is difficult, too, Edie! You're not the only one with problems.'

'Oh leave off the sob story! How hard can it be to dress like a Stepford wife, take some selfies and totter around in your six-inch heels for a week?'

Alice's blood was starting to boil and she could feel her cheeks flushing red as she stood up and jabbed her finger towards her twin who it felt like she no longer knew at all. 'You would not be able to handle my life, Edie!'

Edie laughed. She actually laughed out loud. 'You'd absolutely fall to pieces if you had to live mine!'

'Doing what exactly? I would love to lock myself in a room, ignore your kids for a week and just let them scrounge for scraps in the fridge.'

Edie scoffed, the gloves clearly off now. 'Oh yeah? Be my guest. My family would suss you out straight away. You are far too uptight to fit in here. You'd have to have your head surgically removed from your own arse before you could even sit on the sofa!'

'You think it's so easy being me . . . well . . . fuck that!' Alice had to admit, it felt quite good to swear.

'Honestly, Alice, I bet you wouldn't even last a week in my life!'

That was the final straw. 'Fine,' Alice said, calmly, with an incredible show of confidence as an idea came to her. She paused, then stared right at her sister. 'I'll take that bet. And while we're at it, let's make it interesting.' She glanced at the solitary gecko in its cage on the desk. 'The first one to get found out has to step down from the show and let the other one keep their job. It was me they wanted first, so it has a nice symmetry to it that it'll be me that keeps the gig.'

Alice knew she was taking things too far but this was how it always was. Edie would poke and poke her until she snapped. But she wasn't backing down this time. Something about them arguing in their childhood bedroom had reignited a stubbornness, or competitiveness, within her. She stared at Edie with an eyebrow raised, questioning. Edie looked at her sister with a glint in her eye. Alice couldn't tell if she was furious or strangely impressed at Alice being the one to suggest something so out of the ordinary. Edie crossed her arms and smirked, and Alice saw a glimpse of her as a ten-year-old back in this very room.

'Now it's interesting. Game on, my friend.' Edie spat in her hand and offered her glistening palm out for Alice to shake.

Alice's eyes widened in abject horror. 'Just, no.'

Edie smiled. 'I give you less than a day.'

CHAPTER SEVEN

Edie

'You put a teabag in a mug for each of them before you go to bed ready for the morning?' This was the fifteenth question Edie had asked since they'd sat down opposite each other in a café a week later and handed over their manuals about their families. They both wanted to win the bet, but had agreed to help each other by creating guides so that they didn't get exposed by each other's families within the first ten minutes of the switch. Plus, once they'd had a chance to think about it for a week, Edie – and she suspected Alice, as well – realised this could be the chance they needed to be able to see eye to eye again. Edie had to concede that her manual had been hastily written, but Alice's, quite clearly, had taken slightly longer to compose.

'It just saves time in the morning, knowing that all I need to do is put the mug under the boiling water tap.'

'How on earth do you spend those seven seconds you've won back?'

Alice put down Edie's booklet. 'You promised you were not going to be judgemental.'

'That was before I saw the *War and Peace* epic that is the instruction manual. I'm still only on the pre-school routine, and I'm on page four.' Edie flicked through the full file for added emphasis.

'And you don't think it's odd that you have no idea how your kids get to school?'

'I didn't say I don't know. It clearly says that either one of us takes them, or they get the bus, or a lift with one of their friends.'

'But which one is it?'

'Depends on the day.'

'So write out the rota for me.'

'There isn't a rota, I just said, it depends on the day – Iris may want to take in a life-size model of Queen Nefertiti that she's just made out of loo roll holders, in which case, either me or Seb will give her a lift, or Rosie will yell out that one of her mates has pulled up outside and then they'll go with them. It's all quite spontaneous.'

Alice pulled her collar to one side to allow herself to breathe a little easier. She had honestly thought that Edie was going to have the hardest time slotting into *her* life, but now she had serious concerns about her ability to pull off Edie's way of living.

Alice scanned the page. 'You haven't written anything on here about what breakfast they all eat.'

'Why do you need to know that?' Edie asked. 'They just all grab whatever they want.'

'Packed lunches?'

'They make their own in the morning.'

'Make their own?' Alice said those three words like someone else would say *Caramelise their heads?*

'Yes.'

'What about Seb?'

'What about Seb?'

'Do you make his lunch?'

Edie made a big show of considering the question, she

even tilted her chin up and tapped it with her finger for added emphasis. 'Do I make the lunch of a forty-six-year-old man? No, of course I don't.' Edie looked at her sister's expression changing. 'What? Say it.'

'Nothing.'

'Say it.'

Alice shrugged, 'I just feel sorry for him, that's all.'

'You feel sorry for him?'

'He works really hard and—'

'*I* work really hard! Who's making my packed lunch? Please tell me I'm not going to have to make Danny's lunches.'

Alice leaned over the restaurant table, and pointed at a subheading halfway down page five. 'I've listed his favourite sandwich fillings there.'

'Roasted salmon? Chargrilled halloumi? Jog on.'

'I always put a little note in there as well. I've written twenty out here, they're in this little envelope, so there'll be enough for the whole month just in case we decide to swap for longer. Just slip one on top of the sandwich before you close the Tupperware lid.'

Edie made an exaggerated hand-flap near her mouth. 'It's difficult to taste my latte over the vomit in my mouth. But seriously, while we're on the subject of things that make us feel sick, how are we going to avoid any intimacy issues with each other's husbands? I mean, personally, I'm not planning to avoid it,' Edie said with a wink. 'A change is as good as a rest.' Seeing the look of horror on her sister's face, she quickly followed that up with, 'Joke. Joke!'

'I hadn't even thought of that,' Alice said, suddenly paling.

'I bet Danny snores. Does he snore?'

'He has a mouthguard to stop it.'

Edie wiggled her eyebrows. 'Sexy. That right there will sort out the intimacy issues.'

'I think we should swap back and be our normal selves

for the show though; it's one thing pulling the wool over our family's eyes, but we can't get away with it on live television?'

'But that's the point isn't it, that's part of the test. Which one of us is more convincing pretending to be the other? Look, either way one of us is going to lose our job – either through fighting or losing the bet.' Six months ago, Edie would have probably added the question, 'Would that be such a bad thing?' Being on national television had never been part of her plan; she'd never admit it, for risk of seeming mainstream or worse, fame-seeking, but she had begun to love their Friday slot in the studio. She loved being a therapist, but it was rather one-sided and not very uplifting. The whole concept of being paid to listen to someone else's woes was, well, rather depressing at times. It would be wonderful if there was a reverse-therapy role where people made appointments to talk about what fantastic childhoods they'd had, how healthy their relationship was with their parents, or how well their relationship was going. But Friday morning was different. For two hours, backstage and on the sofa, everyone seemed pleased to see her. She gossiped with the stylists, laughed with the runners, and apart from the viewers texting in with their conundrums, the mornings were happy and problem-free. Except now, she and Alice were the problem.

Alice clapped the table with both hands. 'Let's start the swap on a Monday, while the kids are at school, that way we can get to grips with each other's houses and routines before everyone comes home and the madness starts. Then we can see how we feel during the week about whether we want to swap back for the Friday show. But we can't bulldoze into each other's lives and immediately make changes, that's not the point of this. We need to literally be each other to really understand how we feel. You know those bracelets people wear that say What Would Jesus Do? Well, every minute you need to be thinking about what would *I* do, and I'll be channelling my inner Edie.'

'You do not have an inner Edie, that's the problem.'

'I can totally be spontaneous and carefree.'

'Sure.'

'I can! And I'm looking forward to proving it. But can I just ask you about meal planning? There's nothing on here for what to do for dinner each night?' Alice flipped over the one sheet Edie had provided her to check the other side, but it was blank.

'That's because we all just eat what we want to eat there and then. You can't plan on a Sunday what you'll fancy on a Thursday? And how can one person decide for everyone else? I might want lasagne and Seb might fancy a curry, Rosie might have made her own meal in food tech, while Iris had a big lunch and might want cereal. And a lot of it depends on what's marked down at the end of the day. You can get such bargains if you wait until just before closing.'

'But . . . but . . .' In order to help Edie out, Alice had actually provided a month-long meal plan on a separate colour coded spreadsheet along with pre-ordering supermarket delivery slots of all the ingredients she'd need. How could Edie have not put any thought at all into even the first night?

'How's the spontaneous and carefree looking now, sis?'

Baffling. Terrifying. Ludicrous. 'Absolutely fine.'

'Oh, before I forget, I've also got this for you.' Edie reached down into her bag and pulled out a bulging A4 folder, much to Alice's relief. She knew there was no way that Edie would actually hand over her life and family with just one page of notes to help her. 'This is everything you need to know about Scooby.'

'Scooby? Your dog?'

'Yes. He has loads of idiosyncrasies that you'll need to be aware of. And he's really particular about his routine.'

Alice sighed. It was going to take more than a week being her sister to understand her.

CHAPTER EIGHT

Alice

They decided on the third Monday of June to start the swap. It wasn't an arbitrary stick-a-pin-in-the-calendar sort of date, more the result of a considered and measured brainstorming how this arrangement could work best. Any later in the calendar and it would clash with Alice's middle son's jujitsu grading and cricket try-outs for the regional under-thirteens, her daughter's summer recital and LAMDA acting exam, her eldest son's Silver Duke of Edinburgh trek (and there was no way that Alice was going to leave the laundry from that epic weekend to her sister), and Danny had a really big few weeks at work and really needed her there to be supportive. When asked which dates worked best for her, Edie flicked through a largely blank pocket diary, shrugged and said, 'Whenever really.'

Alice knew that the hug she gave Teddy, Rufus and Emily was a little tighter than usual that morning, and that she'd taken more care with their sandwiches, making sure the Parma ham reached all four corners of their sourdough slices before she cut the crusts off, even slipping traditional fried crisps into their lunchboxes rather than the healthier oven baked versions as a silent apology for not being there when they got back from school. She knew none of them noticed any of these things, but *she* knew. She told Danny she loved him that morning, as she always did, reminding him to drive safely before handing him his Wellman multivitamin along with his freshly made green shake, that had somehow, seamlessly, become part of her morning routine since he bought her the blender at Christmas. It meant she had to get up ten minutes earlier to prepare all the various greens and the blender parts couldn't go in the dishwasher, so every morning she had to scrub it with a long-handled brush, but he seemed grateful.

'You too!' he'd shouted over his shoulder before running out of the door. And then she was left with only the sound of the tumble drier rumbling away from the utility room, on its second load of the day and it wasn't even half eight in the morning. She'd wanted to completely clear every last sock from the laundry baskets, throw away every last puckering pepper from the salad drawer, not that her peppers were ever actually puckered, and make sure every toilet roll holder next to the three toilets in the house had at least four spare rolls on them before meeting Edie midmorning at a café between their two houses to swap keys.

Edie

Edie surveyed the living room. When her mum and dad owned the house it was quite clearly a room fit for purpose: one sofa, two armchairs, a coffee table, a television, a nice rug and an ornate fire guard. Since Edie's family had moved in, its exact function was slightly more ambiguous. Despite appearances giving contrary evidence, she knew that under the pile of newspapers and school textbooks, and clothes that needed mending and a duvet one of the kids had come down wrapped in this morning and a plate with toast crumbs on it and a half a bottle of ketchup from last night's dinner on laps and an eleven-year-old, slightly smelly, German shepherd, was a lovely three-seater sofa, making this definitely the living room. Should she tidy up for Alice? That would be a bit disingenuous though; they were swapping their real lives, getting a glimpse of how their literal other half lived. She had a tiny bit of time between her Zoom clients this morning – her weekly check-in with her septuagenarians Margot and Roger, and a newlywed couple in their twenties navigating their first row – to do a quick sweep of the house banishing the detritus to their rightful places, but that would be cheating, wouldn't it? Pretending that her life was more ordered than it was. Anyway, it was too late, and too difficult, to make a dent in four people's debris now, so Edie made a tiny concession to the imminent arrival of one of Instagram's most followed housewives, by going round the toilet bowl with a loo brush. You couldn't say fairer than that.

She felt really bad that when Rosie and Iris left for school this morning, banging the front door behind them, she'd been in the shower with Seb and didn't realise the time, so she didn't even get to say goodbye to them. They'd have diagnosed her with a rare neurological disorder if she'd run down the road after them and wrapped them both in big bear hugs or made them toast in the shape of hearts as a farewell, so it was probably for the best they hadn't crossed paths, but she would have liked to have at least shouted an 'I love you' after them. Saying goodbye to Seb was hard though; she was sure he picked up on her edginess, as he asked her two, perhaps even three times, if everything was okay. 'I really love you Edie,' he told her, making sure his eyes said the same as his words.

'I really love you too,' she replied, breathing his scent in as she locked him in a hug.

'Fancy a re-run tonight?' he said cheekily, while fastening the chin strap of his bike helmet.

'Probably not tonight,' Edie said, 'I can feel a headache coming on.'

An hour later as they sat at a table in the café's window, two sets of keys were lying in the middle of the table. Alice's front door key was on a keyring attached to a Waitrose loyalty fob. Edie's key nestled happily next to a stainless-steel little rectangle engraved with the words *They can't burn us all*. Both women immediately made a silent vow to themselves never to flash their new house keys around in public.

'The chilli for tonight is already in the slow cooker on the side, it's ready at six. I've scheduled my Instagram posts for the next fourteen days, so that's two weeks taken care of, but you do need to keep on top of liking the comments, removing any offensive ones and replying to any that need replying to. And be *me* in them. Not you. The kids will be home at about four, the boys will shower before dinner, Emily will have a bath after, and make sure Emily uses the leave-in conditioner, or you'll never be able to get the tangles out. Danny will be back about six-thirty, unless he's at the gym, but there's a spin class on tonight and he doesn't like being surrounded by all the women when the class ends, as they all look at him funny, so he should be home on time. This is all in the folder, but tomorrow is swimming for Teddy, rugby for Rufus and Emily has to take in her wellies, so get those ready tonight and put the bags on the pegs in the hallway. I'm forgetting something, what am I forgetting?'

'To breathe?'

'Don't you have any last-minute reminders for me?'

'Scooby's lead is in the first drawer in the kitchen.'

'That's it?'

'I can't think of anything else. I've moved all my evening clients to the daytime to do them while I've got an empty house—'

'Oh,' said Alice, looking disappointed, 'I was hoping to take on a couple of your clients.'

'Um, I'm not sure that would be legal, or ethical?'

'Don't you just let them rant about the other one, then turn to the other one asking, "and how did that make you feel?" for an hour?'

'There's slightly more to it than that. Oh, and by the way, if Seb asks, you still have a headache, and you think it's going to last for a while.'

Alice looked confused, but didn't say anything. Edie could tell that nerves had started to kick in, and as she reached for her new keys on the café table, Edie saw a tremble in her sister's hand. She was no doubt fighting an almost overwhelming urge to cancel the whole plan and run back to her lovely ordered life, where all the herbs were in matching glass bottles with labels she'd made herself, and everyone's clothes were colour coded in their drawers and everything made sense.

As Edie also reached for her new keys, she felt her blood pumping faster than usual. She had no idea how she was going to remember the gargantuan list of tasks she was expected to complete; there were only twenty-four hours in the day and she was hoping to sleep for at least ten of them. At least Alice's lists were laminated and hidden in a variety of places all over the house in places the rest of the family never apparently went: the bottom of the laundry basket, on top of the tumble drier, in the pan drawer under the oven, in Alice's cleaning caddy – whatever that was. Edie didn't think that there was a single inch of her home where any one of her family wouldn't merrily have a rummage, as proven fairly early on in motherhood when an incredibly personal item from Edie's bedside drawer was incorporated into Rosie's game of Lego to give a car its buzzing engine sound.

'Look, let's see how tonight goes, and then let's talk tomorrow and see if we want to carry on. One day might be enough to understand each other,' Edie offered hopefully. 'Or Seb and the girls will have rumbled you by then.'

'Unlikely.'

'Right. Shall we go to the toilets to get changed?'

Alice looked confused. 'Changed into what?'

'Each other! Unless you've got Wonder Woman skills where you just turn around a few times on the spot, we're going to have to change into each other's clothes before going home.'

Alice looked like she hadn't considered this at all when she was choosing her clothes this morning – the look of horror on her face suggested that she'd done something unthinkable like pair black pants with a navy bra or something. As the sisters walked to the toilets to get changed together, Edie patted her own chest on top of her jumper to check that she'd remembered to put on a bra that morning. Nope. Oh well, at least that was one less thing to swap.

CHAPTER NINE

The swap: day 1

Edie

The only items missing from Alice's house, Edie thought as she wandered around it, were those signs you got in museums that said, 'please don't touch', or the posts in parks telling you to 'keep off the grass', or in this case, carpet. Everything was laboratory-standard clean and she had an overwhelming urge to bend down and lick the worktop, she wasn't exactly sure why. The fridge was completely devoid of the kids' artwork or certificates or postcards, it housed just a wipeable days-of-the-week chart where each dinner was carefully scribed in Alice's neat handwriting. Edie's gasp of awe on opening the fridge suggested that the door to a sacred vault had been released, and in a way it had: every shelf housed not a wobbling pyramid of half empty jars of pesto and past-expiry Greek yoghurt like Edie's, but pull-out glass boxes all categorised by food type: meat on the bottom shelf, cooked hams and cheeses on the second, what looked like a variety of dips in another, and jars of homemade chutneys and jams in another. This set-up vaguely chimed a bell with Edie, but it wasn't until she started humming *that's the way uh-huh I like it* that she realised that about a month ago her sister had dedicated a whole Instagram Reel to the organisation of her fridge, to that very song. If Alice wasn't related to her, Edie would have unfollowed her on every social media platform years ago.

Alice

Across town, knowing Edie the way she did, Alice had stopped at a supermarket on the way home to buy ingredients for that night's dinner. Well versed in teenage palates, she opted for a safe selection of Mexican-inspired items – avocados for homemade guacamole, peppers, onions, chicken for the meat eaters, and mindful of Iris's veggie fad, a plant-based alternative along with vegan cheese and sour cream. Opening the fridge to put it all away, Alice realised that she should have also picked up a roll of bright yellow crime scene tape and a hazardous waste warning triangle. How her sister hadn't succumbed to a fatal bout of Legionnaires', or at the very least a nasty spell of Salmonella was anyone's guess. She couldn't bear to place her newly bought spoils inside what was essentially a very cold garbage bin without bleaching it, but was also very mindful of not doing anything too out of character on the first day. She settled for a quick wipe of the shelves with a piece of kitchen roll. Clearing a space for the chopping board on the work surface was the next task. The cereal boxes from breakfast were still littering the worktop, along with two wine glasses with a teaspoon's worth of red wine pooling in the base of each. Slovenly as her sister was, Alice didn't have Edie down as a Rioja with Rice Krispies kind of woman, so these must have been from last night. Sunday night drinking before a busy week ahead, that was a bold move. She couldn't remember the last time she and Danny had shared a bottle of wine. Between his health kick and her trying to control her perimenopause through food group elimination, things like drinking together had stopped completely. They'd spent thousands of pounds a couple of years ago on an outside pergola and rattan sofa set, 'to enjoy sundowners together,' which they'd done the night the furniture got delivered, and then never again. What a waste.

An hour later, with dinner bubbling away on the stove, Alice opened her sister's crockery cupboard to lay the table, and immediately had a pang of homesickness for her own kitchen. One where plates matched and saucepans had lids, cups were uncracked and glasses weren't freebies collected from garages or fast-food restaurant tokens. She absolutely remembered Edie keeping lots of their mum's crockery, so where on earth was it? There wasn't a corresponding side-plate to a dinner-plate in sight, let alone a gravy boat. Had they broken everything? Sold it? Had Seb smashed it all intentionally to make mosaic plant pots? Surely Edie had a ball of shame inside her every mealtime watching her family eat off different-coloured plates with knives and forks from different sets? What about when they had people round? The one good thing, she supposed, was that she'd now got a mental list of Christmas and birthday presents for her sister so long it would last the rest of their lives. No more need for scented candles or plush Peruvian Alpaca blankets. Urgh, *the blanket*.

Edie

There was literally nothing for Edie to do. Dinner was slow cooking, every room looked ready and prepped for a magazine photo shoot, there wasn't even a pet to take care of because the section in the binder detailing the cat's routine had it roaming around outside all day and night, only coming back in for mealtimes. That must annoy Alice no end.

Edie looked at the clock: ten to four. The children would be home soon, where should she be when they came in the door? In the kitchen stirring something? Or would Alice welcome them at the front door? Pipe their arrival in like they do in castles? She should put on Alice's apron, yes, that would definitely work. Why was she so nervous? She tied the two strings in a bow behind her back. These were her nephews and niece for goodness' sake, she'd held each of them at a day old, changed their nappies, of course she could open the door and ask them about their day. 'Hi guys!' she practised in the empty hallway. 'Hey gang! What's up? How're you doing?' She puffed out her cheeks. They would suss it's her instantly. A key sounded in the lock and Edie had no more time for second guessing. *What would Alice do? What would Alice do?*

'Hi darlings,' she shrilled with a wide smile, 'shoes off, slippers on, coats and bags in the cupboard, spit spot.'

Nailed it.

Alice

Alice perched Edie's spare reading glasses on her head. They might share one hundred percent of their genes but Edie had overridden vanity sooner than Alice and was now able to enjoy reading things at a normal distance from her face again, whereas Alice was still firmly in the 'holding all packaging at arm's length' stage of her life. She wouldn't tell Edie this either, but wearing a baggy skirt with an elasticated waist was vastly superior in the comfort stakes than her own clothes. The trouble with having items tailored to your body was that they didn't allow for big plates of pasta, whereas a quick glance in

Edie's wardrobe earlier confirmed that eating carbs was not going to be an issue this week.

She knew that they'd agreed not to bowl into each other's lives and immediately make changes, but as she didn't really want to spend the next thirty days standing up, she had to clear some space to sit, so shooed a disgruntled Scooby off the sofa, put the ketchup in the fridge and the dirty plates in the dishwasher, stacked the books and magazines on the coffee table, and couldn't help herself running the hand-held vacuum over the seats too. Any more would have raised too many eyebrows, any less and she'd have been unable to sleep tonight.

She looked at the clock – half four, the girls would be home soon. Edie would probably be sitting on the sofa when the girls got in, laptop open, she'd probably call out a welcome, and they'd disappear upstairs until dinner, that's what her own kids did. Her heart was beating really fast as time marched towards the time they'd be back. Nonchalance, that's what she needed. Did she have time to give the TV table a quick polish? It would be a disaster for them to all arrive back while she still had a duster in her hand, but she also knew that she wouldn't be able to concentrate on any programme at all until it was wiped.

Her head was stuck in the under-sink cupboard in the kitchen trying to make sense of her sister's cleaning products when the front door slammed. Realising this wasn't a realistic look, Alice hurriedly backed out and scrambled to her feet, a tricky feat when wearing a maxi skirt.

'Rosie, hi, Iris, hello!' Alice shrilled enthusiastically.

Ten-year-old Iris eyed her suspiciously. 'Have you been drinking at lunch again?'

'What? No!'

'Mushrooms?' Fourteen-year-old Rosie piped up. 'Let me see your eyeballs.'

Alice backed away, flapping them away. 'I'm just pleased to see you, that's all.'

Rosie glanced over Alice's shoulder at the oven. 'Have you . . . cooked?'

'Are you and Dad getting a divorce?' Iris asked, wide-eyed.

Rosie took up the baton. 'Has someone died? Grandad didn't look great when we saw him last. Is it Scooby? Does he have cancer? He's not on the sofa, did you put him down?'

Some immediate damage control had to be done, or this was going to be the shortest swap in history. Even the twins in *The Parent Trap* lasted longer than this, and they had to master completely different accents.

'No one has died. No, we're not getting a divorce, Scooby is in the garden, very much alive. I just thought it would just be nice if we had dinner together.'

That seemed to ward them off. Iris perched up on a bar stool and immediately launched into a thousand-word-a-minute summary of her day, pausing occasionally to ask questions vaguely related to the context of her monologue: 'So do you think the Romans were justified in their barbarism?' and 'Sadie cut her own fringe, can I borrow the scissors after dinner?' and 'If I cheated on a maths test and got a hundred percent, is it okay if I still feel proud of myself for my achievement?' Alice could feel her face twitching as she tried to keep up. Meanwhile, Rosie had just finished the orange juice after drinking it directly from the bottle, then carefully swilled it out under the tap and put the bottle in the recycling box. Alice didn't think any of her kids could have told you where their recycling bin was actually kept, let alone be moved enough to put something in it. This very act gave Alice something of a conundrum: scold the swigging from the bottle or compliment the clean-up. She decided to stay true to her character and pretend not to notice either.

'Rosie, how was your day?' Alice asked, with just the right level of chirpiness in her voice. She'd learned her lesson on that score.

'Good. You're not going to believe this. Annabelle had her first kiss yesterday with a boy she met on the bus. They even used tongues.'

'Oh my lord!' Alice exclaimed without being able to stop herself. That was completely the wrong reaction though, as both girls were back to eyeing her beadily. 'I forgot to make salsa!' She hoped that covered up her gaffe, but as she collected the tomatoes from the fridge drawer she wondered which was more out of character, making salsa from scratch, being horrified at public displays of affection on public transport or being so shocked at having a teenager openly voice such an intimate detail to their mother. Forty minutes into her new life, and she was completely at sea.

Edie

'Mum?' Fifteen-year-old Teddy came into the kitchen. 'Coach says I need new shin pads for tomorrow's game.'

'What's wrong with your old ones?' Edie replied, really hoping after she said it that he did indeed have old ones.

'He said they're too small and don't cover enough of my leg.' Teddy waved a piece of paper inches away from Edie's face. 'He wrote down the ones I need. Can we go and get them now?'

'Now? But the shops shut in twenty minutes.'

Teddy shrugged. 'So we better leave now.'

'Why couldn't you have picked them up on your way home? You literally walk right by the sports shop.'

'But then I'd be spending *my* money on them.'

'But they are for *you*.'

Teddy narrowed his eyes at Edie. 'You've always got my things before. Why are you being so jarring?'

'I'm not being *jarring* Teddy, but I've got to put the rice on, and . . .' Edie tailed off, and channelled her inner Alice. 'Okay, I'll go, can you watch the rice and keep topping it up with water so it doesn't run dry, and then turn it off in fifteen minutes?'

'Turn it off?'

Edie grabbed her sister's designer handbag, which had an impractical number of buckles. 'Yes Teddy, turn it off.'

He looked horrified, like she'd just asked him to defeather some roadkill for dinner. 'How do I do that?'

Was he joking? Fifteen years old. Three years away from being the sole person responsible for his stomach being filled every day and he didn't know how to use the hob?

'And you're leaving us alone? With no adult?'

His reaction was baffling, it wasn't as though she'd booked an all-inclusive for herself in the Balearics, she was going half a mile away on an errand for him! 'You're fifteen,' she said.

'Which is legally not an adult.'

'Do you want new shin pads, or not?'

'Dad's not going to like this.'

At the mention of Danny, Edie had a brainwave. 'Why don't you call your dad and ask him to pick them up for you on his way back?'

'He'll just ask why you can't go. You always get our things, he works.'

Edie was about to launch headfirst into a vital life lesson about the misconception that 'work' solely related to the act of leaving the house for a place you needed to wear a lanyard for, when actually 'work' came in many forms, as did sharing the provision of essentials for the children two people created, but she managed to stop herself before her cover was immediately blown and she lost the bet an hour into the switch.

'Fine,' she said, looking at Alice's ridiculously ostentatious gold watch on her wrist and doing a very rough estimation on how late dinner was now going to be. 'Come on then. Rufus! Emily! We're going out again.'

They arrived back home forty-five minutes later, delayed significantly by Rufus remembering he needed a new mouthguard for rugby, and Teddy storming off in a sulk when she wouldn't buy him the new Man United strip which cost more than her own family's weekly groceries. Edie walked the entire length of the hallway and reached the door to the kitchen before she realised that she hadn't taken her shoes off and swapped them for her indoor moccasins. She scuttled back to the basket before anyone else noticed. Danny's work shoes were in the basket, and his own house slippers gone, so he must be back. It was one thing to trick children, but here was the big test. Danny and Alice had been married for eighteen years, surely he would rumble she wasn't his wife straightaway. She poked her head into the living room, but it was immaculately empty, same with the dining room. The smell of slightly burned food greeted her as she opened the door to the kitchen, but sitting on a bar stool seemingly unperturbed by it, was Danny.

'Hey,' she said, immediately second guessing her greeting. Had she ever heard Alice say 'hey'? Her sister wasn't a 'hey' sort of person, but it was out there now, swirling around the kitchen, so she had to roll with it.

'Something smells burned,' he said, not lifting his gaze from his laptop.

It looked like Danny wasn't a hey kind of person either. Or a hello, or hi, or, indeed, a fan of any cordial greeting to his wife at all.

Edie rushed to the slow cooker, where the dinner Alice had painstakingly prepared earlier was looking decidedly crispy. 'Oh bollocks,' she exclaimed, before her body immediately stiffened and her face grimaced. She wouldn't be able to tell you what exclamation Alice would have made on discovering an overcooked dish, because the circumstance had probably never happened.

She spun around to face her brother-in-law. 'You were just sat here,' she said, trying and failing to keep the accusation out of her voice, 'why didn't you turn it off?'

He looked at her with the same look of confusion his eldest son had an hour earlier. 'Turn it off?' he said.

'Yes, if you thought it was burning, you could have just turned it off.'

Danny looked as if he was at least considering the question, his head tilted slightly to the side, and there were a few seconds' pause before he shrugged and said, 'You don't like me touching things in your kitchen.'

Alice

It was clear that Seb was expecting his lips to land on hers, rather than get a mouthful of hair as Alice whipped her cheek swiftly to the side to avoid the mouth-to-mouth contact. 'Hello, there!' she said brightly.

'Hey,' he replied smiling, lifting the strap of his satchel over his head and putting it on one of the kitchen chairs she'd just cleared. 'Something smells amazing, have you cooked?'

'Mexican.'

'Oh wow, you didn't need to do that.' He sauntered over to the hob, where two pots of chilli, one beef, one vegan, were bubbling away and a wok of spicy chicken for fajitas was simmering. 'This smells incredible. What's the occasion?'

'No occasion, just thought we'd all have a nice dinner.'

Alice could tell he wanted to ask 'why' again, but cut him off before he could. 'Right, I think we're almost ready, do you want to get changed before we eat?'

'Changed? Into what?'

'Your home clothes.'

'Since when do we have home clothes?'

'I just thought you might want to be more comfy?' She realised as she said it that the work clothes Seb was wearing consisted of a pair of jeans and a sweatshirt, so she wasn't sure how much comfier he could be unless he went upstairs and came down in his pyjamas. She clocked him looking at her strangely. She'd blown it. She had to stop being so presumptuous about other people's routines and just let them take the lead or she was going to be busted before nightfall.

'Right, shall I open a bottle of red?' Seb asked, his tone and movement towards the wine rack suggesting this question was very much rhetorical.

Alice was about to say something about it being a Monday, when she remembered how precarious her position was, and also, the idea of having a nice glass of wine was very appealing. She'd have to drink it slowly though; it had been so long since she'd drunk alcohol, if she wasn't careful she'd be slurring her way through dinner.

'Right,' she said to Seb just after they'd clinked glasses, 'can you just call the girls, and I'll dish up.' Dish up, *dish up*, was that an Edie sort of saying? She was second-guessing everything now. It was also taking every ounce of self-control not to order immediate handwashing from the family as soon as each of them walked in the kitchen.

Seb almost dropped his glass in surprise. 'We're all eating together? What's happened?'

'What do you mean?'

He put his glass down on the worktop and picked up Alice's hand. 'Do you have to tell us all something? Oh god, are you ill?'

'No! I—'

'Is it Scooby?' Seb swivelled around in panic to check that the cushioned bed basket in the corner of the kitchen was still occupied by a breathing dog.

She had considered the fact that they might find the fact she'd gone to so much effort for the meal a bit odd. She hadn't actually meant to go to so much trouble over it, she had actually bought little pre-made supermarket pots of salsa and guacamole in the end, but when push came to shove she just couldn't bring herself to open them, and somehow, don't ask her how, found herself crushing up tomatoes and avocado, and before you could say *Jamie Oliver*, two bowls of homemade dips were clingfilmed, in the fridge, ready for their debut. So, she was fully anticipating a few raised eyebrows over this, but it hadn't occurred to Alice that the very notion of consuming food together as a family would be such a glaring red flag too.

Edie

This definitely wasn't the worst dinner Edie had ever eaten, but apparently, that wasn't the case for the other four people round the table.

'I don't like it,' Rufus whined, pushing a lump of hard meat round the plate with his fork.

'This definitely isn't your best effort,' Danny agreed.

'I'm not having any more,' Teddy said, decisively putting down his fork.

'I like it,' said Emily, smiling at Edie, although the full plate in front of her contradicted her words. Bless her.

Edie studied the males at the table, who had, in unison, pushed their fork and knife together on their plates and were staring expectantly at her, presumably for a hostess trolley to be wheeled out and a different main course unveiled from under a silver dome. Each of them had a hand in this dinner being ruined, but to look at their innocent faces, looking at her with a mixture of pity and anticipation of what she was going to whip up now for them, she realised that this had completely escaped their notice. She knew she should do what Alice would do, and start cooking something else from scratch while apologising profusely for her slip up, but she just couldn't bring herself to do that, so she started shovelling every mouthful of the chewy mince into her mouth, accompanying every third swallow or so with a murmur of appreciation of the food, which really wasn't that bad at all. When her own plate was sparkling clean, as was Emily's after watching her mother's actions, Edie got up from the table and took her and Emily's plates over to the dishwasher, leaving the other three sitting there, their chilli cold and congealing in front of them.

'Emily darling, you can go and play for half an hour, and I'll run your bath in a bit, okay love?' Edie said, noting out of the corner of her eye the look of utter bewilderment that was passing between father and sons. 'I've got a few bits of work to finish up myself,' Edie continued, to no one in particular, 'so feel free to make yourselves something else if you don't like this.' She couldn't help smiling to herself as she walked away with the satisfaction of her first victory.

Alice

Seb had just finished talking about something to do with work, and was staring at Alice intently. The curve of one of his eyebrows and his encouraging nod suggested that he'd ended on a question, but Alice had been directing all her listening skills to eavesdropping on Rosie and Iris's conversation about the afterlife. Iris was apparently dubious based on the scientific theory of particle dissolvement, but Rosie's friend Olive had the spirit of an Elizabethan servant girl living in her parents' bedroom, which Iris was considering as pretty compelling evidence.

'So, what do you think I should do about that?' Seb asked, his elbows resting on the table.

'Sorry?'

'I'd just really like your take on it,' Seb pressed on.

'You'd like *my* take on it?'

'Yes. You're much better at this kind of stuff than me.'

Alice honestly had no idea what kind of stuff Seb meant as her mind had hopscotched a few steps ahead to the different tasks that needed doing after dinner while he had started talking, then had been tuned into her nieces' bizarre existentialist debate after that, not having a clue that Seb was intending to pause his monologue to ask for her input. Whenever she'd asked Danny how his day was, she just received a shrug and an effusive 'good' if she was lucky, or more often than not a rather curter, 'fine', neither of which opened the door for much discussion.

'I think you know the answer already,' Alice said, remembering the advice Edie often gave on the show, 'go with your gut and you'll make the right choice.'

Seb smiled at her and reached across to stroke her hand.

Alice was thankfully saved from enduring any more of her brother-in-law's tactility by Rosie making vomiting noises and getting up to load her plate in the dishwasher. Iris followed her sister's lead, and even reached over to take the plates in front of Alice and Seb too. Alice couldn't remember the last time her own plate had been cleared by someone else, apart from in a restaurant. She watched incredulously as the two girls loaded all the pans from the sink into the top tray of the machine, quick-stepping around each other after scraping any leftover bits of food into the food waste bin, with all the practised flair of a choreographed dance. Seb hadn't seemed to notice, which suggested that this wasn't unusual in the slightest. It was absolutely killing her though that one of the girls had loaded a big pan on the bottom, which meant the dishes on the shelf above it wouldn't be rinsed very well, but she could always do what she did with the Christmas decorations at home, and just move it all about a bit once everyone was in bed. She'd also spotted Iris using the same cloth to wipe the floor where some guacamole had dripped, before then wiping down the surface. It took every ounce of self-restraint for Alice not to wrestle the cloth out of her niece's hand, and immediately set fire to it before dousing the kitchen in a thick layer of bleach.

Edie

What would Alice usually put in Emily's bath, Edie wondered, looking around the family bathroom for clues. Bubbles, salts, some sort of oil with an actual lavender sprig inside the bottle, what would she pick? Edie hadn't been involved in either of her own daughters' washing habits for a few years now, their bodies were their own business. She remembered seeing a section on baths in the folder Alice had prepared, she probably should have read it before turning on the taps. She picked up the most fun-looking bottle and generously slurped it under the running water, which almost immediately resulted in a foamy mountain that engulfed the taps and spilled over the sides. Perfect.

Emily's gasp of delight from the doorway made it quite clear that this wasn't usual bathtime practice. How could she be making so many mistakes in her first evening? While Emily was happily splashing about, Edie took out Alice's phone and started scrolling through her sister's social media feed. She could feel her face contorted into a withering grimace as account after account of middle-aged women showed off their homemade oven cleaners, and tips and tricks for prepping packed lunches, how to dress for your age, and embracing cortisol-reducing somatic yoga moves. No wonder Alice thought she was an anomaly if this was her benchmark of what a woman was.

Alice

'Oh Mum, you said you'd help me with my ethics homework tonight,' Rosie said, lugging her heavy school bag onto the table and pulling out her laptop.

Alice tried not to retch at the thought that this bag had undoubtedly been discarded on corridor floors all day, even regularly placed on the floor of a secondary school's toilet cubicle. The litany of germs happily multiplying all over it right now as though the table was an oversized wooden petri dish was horrifying – right there, where they ate for goodness' sake. She silently added giving the table a good sand down to her nighttime routine. She suddenly realised what Rosie had said: *ethics* homework. It was fair to say that her and Edie's ethics were pretty polarising. 'Why don't you ask your dad,' Alice said, nodding in Seb's direction where he appeared to be pulling Iris's dirty PE kit out of her games bag and loading it into the washing machine.

'I have to write a balanced essay about whether feminism has achieved all its goals.'

'That's easy,' Seb called from the corner of the kitchen where he was pouring out about half the amount of detergent actually needed to clean the clothes. 'On one side of the page write down what your mum would say about it, and on the other put what Auntie Alice would.'

That was a bit unnecessary, Alice thought. She was very

much in favour of equal pay, although it was a bit annoying that men rarely gave up their seat on the bus anymore.

'Okay Mum,' Rosie said, sliding onto the kitchen chair alongside Alice and opening up her laptop, 'we'll start with you.' Rosie hovered her hands above the keyboard. 'Thoughts about feminism. Go.'

'I, um, oh gosh, there is just so much I could say.'

Rosie nodded encouragingly. 'Go on then.'

'Well . . .' Alice searched her brain for any feminism-themed nugget she had unknowingly squirrelled away. 'I mean, getting the vote was a tremendous thing, wasn't it?'

'Yes, I've already got the suffragette movement, and the shockwaves of first wave feminism that acted as a catalyst to parliamentary change and legislation. What else? Come on Mum, you know loads about this.'

Alice tried not to look as flustered as she felt – was she blushing? 'Well, um, the wars changed things, didn't they?'

'What's the full name of that woman again, with the bicep and the spotty hanky on her head saying "we can do it"?'

Alice shook her head. 'No idea.'

Rosie pulled a face at her. 'You've literally got the poster up in your office!'

'Oh, um, I've forgotten.'

'You literally named me after her! It was Rosie something! Mum, are you *sure* you're not on mushrooms?'

Seb looked over at her and Alice immediately thought that he'd clocked that she wasn't his wife. But instead of calling her out on it, he told her that she looked tired, and would she like him to run her a bath. What was this parallel universe that her sister lived in? Where baths got run for her, people asked her opinions on things and everyone attempted to clear up after themselves, admittedly not very well, but at least they tried.

*

Twenty minutes later, Alice leaned her head back against the bath, letting the warm water soothe away the day. She tried not to think about the dehydrating effect her sister's supermarket own-brand bubbles were going to have on her skin, or the fact that seconds before the taps were turned on, the bath housed the family's collection of suitcases which were hastily moved to the hallway. It was nice to have a few moments to herself though. Emily would just have finished her own bath. She really hoped Edie had remembered to read the section on bedtime routines, and to warm Emily's pyjamas on the towel rail while Emily was washing; she hated putting on cold nightclothes before bed.

Alice forced herself to close her eyes, to breathe slowly in and out, and as she did, she could start to feel her concerns slowly ebb away when the sound of water gushing alongside her in the bathroom made her eyes spring open, and widen in abject horror as she realised that Seb was standing there, a foot from her head, flies undone, merrily having a wee into the toilet.

'Relaxed now?' he asked.

CHAPTER TEN

Alice

'What the hell are you doing?' she spluttered, simultaneously using her hands to cover the parts of her body that the bubbles weren't and also trying to shield her eyes.

'What do you mean?'

'I mean, I'm in here!'

'I know,' Seb replied, looking confused as he zipped up his flies. 'Is it warm enough? For some reason the hot wasn't running really hot.' And then, as if the scene wasn't horrific enough, instead of washing his hands in the sink, he merely dipped them into the bathwater, about an inch or so away from Alice's left thigh. Right. That sorted it, this swap was a ridiculous idea; it was one thing to pretend to be someone's mum, but wife? Quite clearly her sister and Seb had zero boundaries, and an astonishing degree of intimacy that was not only bizarre, it was totally unnatural. There was a reason that bathrooms had doors on them, and the ease with which he just sauntered in and relieved himself suggested that this was absolutely the norm. How could you live like that? In eighteen years she'd never once even broken wind in front of Danny, let alone done what Seb had just done. She'd even vetoed Danny's presence at the birth of his own children so that standards were maintained.

Seb crouched down next to the bath. 'Have I upset you?'

Alice tightened her folded arms across her chest and hoped beyond hope that the bubbles were covering the rest of her. She silently willed Seb to go away. Had he and Edie never heard of boundaries? 'No, honestly,' she gabbled, 'I just wasn't expecting company. I'll be down in a minute, if you could give Iris a ten-minute warning that it's almost bedtime, that would be great.'

'A what?'

'Just remind her that it's a school night, so she might want to think about going to bed soon . . .' Alice tailed off, remembering whose house she was in, whose rules she was following. 'Or not, it's totally up to her.'

Seb smiled, pulling himself up to standing. 'Okay, cool. But you go on up to bed, I've just got a couple more work things to do, then I'll be up.'

'But the girls—'

'Iris will take herself off to bed soon, and god knows when Rosie will, she's turning into a right old night owl.' Seb tapped Alice's bare arm with his finger, making her whole body tense up. 'Oh I know what I had to tell you—'

'Um, Seb, can we maybe have this chat after I've got out of the bath?'

'Oh yes, sure, do you want me to pass your towel?'

'No! No, I'm okay, thanks though, see you in a bit.'

Alice listened out for his retreating footsteps on each stair before risking getting out of the bath and wrapping herself in a fraying cardboard-hard towel at record speed.

Once she'd dried off upstairs in the main bedroom, faster than she ever had before as this family clearly mistook closed doors for welcome banners, Alice took her sister's phone out of her bag and unlocked the screen. They'd both changed the passwords on their phones to their mother's birthday to make it easier to remember; previously Alice had chosen the last six numbers from her national insurance number, whereas Edie had 061967, the date unmarried women were allowed to take the contraceptive pill in the UK, and Alice knew she'd never remember something as obscure as that.

Her phone number went straight to voicemail.

'It's me,' she said to the ether. 'You need to call me back. I think we'll call a halt to this first thing. You need to call me back.' She groaned, that repetition wasn't very eloquent. But as anyone else listening to that message would assume it was Edie, it was fine.

It felt so wrong to be getting ready to go to bed knowing that all the living room lights were blazing, and Rosie was still awake tapping away on her phone, some godawful show about marrying someone you'd never met before blaring on the television. Her thoughts then careered back to her own house, hoping that Edie had remembered to collect the family's phones and put them in the recharging station in the kitchen before turning all the lights off and locking up. But then if Edie had remembered, hers would currently be in there too, and so that was why she wouldn't pick up her call. Twelve hours. She just needed to get through the night, and then they could swap back and put an end to this ridiculous farce and call it a tie. She was so torn between wanting Edie to do everything to Alice's own standards and treating her family well, but then if she did, she'd win the bet, and Alice would lose the best job she'd ever had. It would be much better for them to just stop the switch now and find some other way to work out who would step aside.

She opened her sister's chest of drawers to try to find her

pyjamas, and rifled through all three drawers, clueless as to the demarcation or zoning of Edie's items. Pants were next to T-shirts, scarves, a cashmere jumper she'd once given Edie but never seen her wear, a belt, jogging bottoms, the mixed-up medley continued in every drawer. How was this in any way a practical way to live?

'Lost something?' Seb said from behind her as he came into the bedroom.

'My pyjamas,' she said, 'maybe they're in the wash.'

'I did all the laundry last night,' he said, 'the basket's empty. Anyway, since when do you wear pyjamas?'

Alice's heart plummeted.

Edie

There was a line of night potions on Alice's dressing table, which Edie didn't have a clue what to do with, and reading the back of them wasn't helping either. Retinol something, vitamin C, collagen, repair, anti-ageing, smoothing, correcting, plumping – this wasn't a moisturising routine, it was a workout for the face. No wonder it said in the folder that Alice usually started getting ready for bed around nine pm, it would take until midnight to work her way through all these tubes and bottles. She could sense that Danny was watching her from the bed, so she couldn't let her confusion show too much. She squeezed out a very generous amount from a bottle that looked to be nearly finished, suggesting its regular use, and started rubbing it upwards in circular motions that seemed quite Alice-like. There was another one that said the word 'eye' on it, so she dotted a bit of that around each eye too.

Almost immediately her face started burning. Not gently warm, or invigoratingly awakened. She didn't feel smoothed, corrected or plumped. She felt the same kind of pain she felt after falling into a bed of nettles when drunk on last year's camping holiday. 'I'm just going to the bathroom,' she exclaimed, running into the en suite and plunging her face into a basin-full of icy cold water. Her reflection in the bathroom vanity mirror prompted a loud gasp, her face was beetroot-red, her eyes sunk into her rapidly puffing-out face.

'Everything okay in there?' Danny called from the bedroom.

'Yes, absolutely. I'm just washing my face.' Edie opened the bathroom cabinet, and started rifling through its contents, looking for anything resembling a bottle of after-sun, or anything vaguely cheap and reassuring. There was an unopened sachet of a face mask, the type you wet and lay over your face for a few minutes with a couple of slices of cucumber on your eyes. Perfect. Edie snipped off the end of the sachet packet with Danny's nail clippers, gross, and carefully unfolded the white mask. Smoothing it all over her face, the relief was instant. She did however now resemble Casper the Ghost's perimenopausal twin, but the searing agony was diluted slightly, which was the main thing.

'Jesus Christ!' Danny exclaimed when Edie walked back into the bedroom.

'I thought I'd sleep with this on tonight. It's good for my pores,' Edie replied in way of explanation, getting into Alice's side of the bed.

Danny sat up in bed. 'You're going to keep that on all night?'

'Yes.'

'I'll have nightmares!'

'You won't,' she replied, 'you'll be sleeping. You'll have your eyes shut.'

'But what if I wake up and see you?'

'Well then you can just close your eyes again, can't you?'

Danny folded his arms over the duvet. 'Are you okay? You're being very prickly tonight.'

'Prickly?' Edie picked up the book next to Alice's bed, but then remembered she'd left her reading glasses at her house, and what's more, Alice didn't wear glasses, so she put the book down again.

'Yes. What was that about at dinner?'

'What part?' Edie replied innocently.

'The part where you serve up something pretty inedible and then expect me and the boys to make ourselves something else.'

'It was perfectly edible, me and Emily enjoyed it.'

'I'm sorry Alice,' Danny said gently, 'I can't have a conversation with you in that mask thing, go and take it off.'

'No, it feels nice. Anyway, we don't need to talk.'

'I'm not doing *that* with you while you're wearing that if that's what you're suggesting.'

Edie fought the urge to retch at the very idea of *that*, and made a mental note to go to the chemist tomorrow and buy lots more of these masks to see her through the whole switch. She reached over to the bedside table and turned her lamp off. 'Night Danny, try not to dream of ghosts and zombies.'

'Why would you say that?' he huffed, turning over and pulling most of the duvet with him. 'You're being really weird today.'

'You're being really weird today,' Edie mimicked back in a high-pitched whisper. It wasn't big, it wasn't grown up, and it definitely wasn't something Alice would do, but it felt really good.

CHAPTER ELEVEN

The swap: day 2

Alice

Alice had been so terrified of one of Seb's limbs accidentally being thrown over one of hers she had kept an anxious vigil clinging to the edge of the mattress all night. She heard Rosie eventually come to bed around eleven-thirty, far too late for a fourteen-year-old on a school night, and it was anyone's guess how long she was scrolling on her phone for in the dark after that. It wasn't just that keeping Alice awake, it was the knowledge that there were three coffee cups each with an inch of decaying brown sludge in the bottom of them on her sister's bedside table, a pile of paperwork next to the bed, including a passport which was poking out, so goodness knows how that would be found in a hurry next time a foreign trip came around, and there was a semi-dead plant in the corner desperately gasping all available oxygen out of the bedroom. Every one of these things in isolation would have been enough to disturb her slumber, but throw in her sister's naked life partner and it was no wonder she had insomnia.

She must have dropped off at some point in the early hours as she was woken up by Seb standing on her side of the bed nudging the old coffee mugs to one side to make room for a steaming new cup. He was thankfully fully dressed, ready for work.

'Hey sleepyhead, feeling any better?'

It took Alice a moment to remember the lies from the night before. 'Oh, yes, I think so.' She sat up in bed, conscious of her bra-less state under her thin white T-shirt, so kept the duvet firmly pulled up to her armpits. 'Thanks for the coffee, that's really thoughtful.'

The look of confusion that flashed across his face made her realise that this must be part of their normal morning routine. Was this how every day began for her sister?

'Busy day?' Seb asked, perching on the side of the bed.

The question threw her. Danny was not a morning person in any way, shape or form, so breakfast never came with a side order of conversation.

'Um, not really.' She took a sip of the coffee he'd made her, trying not to wince at its sweetness, and quickly tried to conjure up an answer her sister might give. 'I have a few bits to prepare for the show on Friday.'

'Really? I thought you preferred just to wing it.'

That explained a lot. 'I thought I might give the house a bit of a tidy round.'

'No need for that, it looks alright. Rosie ran the vacuum round a couple of days ago, remember.' He rested his hand on top of the duvet where her leg was. 'Haven't you got any clients today?'

'Um, no, it's slowed down a bit for the summer; everyone's getting ready to go away.' She adjusted her position so his hand slid off.

'Oh, that's rubbish,' he replied, his forehead crinkling a bit, 'but it always does, doesn't it?'

'Yes. Always does.' Good, that was obviously a good answer. 'You?' she said brightly, trying to be as Edie-like as possible. 'What have you got on?'

'Well, there's the big pitch I was telling you about to the gallery in Kent. I've got a couple of salad bowl commissions, and I've got to start designing the marketing posters for the exhibition in St Ives, nothing too taxing.'

'Great, great.' Alice still found Seb's decision to leave his safe career as an art teacher to set up his own pottery studio a very odd one. Surely you only left one job for another when you were sure of its success, and him being the man too made the whole idea completely nonsensical. Edie had got really cross at her when she'd voiced her thoughts on it at the time, even the term 'main breadwinner' was apparently 'irrelevant and outdated'. From what Alice could tell, based on her intimate knowledge of every pottery line John Lewis stocked, he did seem to be reasonably talented.

'Oh.' Seb patted Alice's knees again. 'I know what I meant to tell you: guess who came into the studio last week?'

'Who?'

Seb's eyes widened with excitement at his game – was he really forty-six? 'No, guess.'

'You know I'm bad at this.'

'Have a guess, we haven't seen them for two, maybe three years.'

Alice puffed out her cheeks and slowly exhaled, pulling the duvet even closer to her. 'Oh, this is hard, um, oh, do you mean that guy who went to that place, oh god, what's the name of it, but that guy? The one whose wife was called, oh god, what was her name now?' She tapped the side of her head, 'Come on brain, think.'

'Yes! That's the one, Lucas!'

'Oh god, yes, Lucas! How is he? And what was his wife's name again?'

'Sheba!'

'Sheba, yes, of course, gosh how could I forget that!'

Seb laughed. 'I have no idea, we even went on holiday with them!'

'Well, you know me with names! Anyway, shouldn't you be getting on?'

He looked at his watch. 'God, yes, okay, love you—' He moved in to kiss her lips but she moved her head just in time.

'Sorry, I still feel a bit ropey, don't want you to come down with anything with such a busy week on.'

He put his head on the side and surveyed her sympathetically. 'There's some paracetamol in the bathroom cabinet, do you want me to get you some before I go?'

'No, honestly, you push off. I'll be fine. Are the girls up?'

'Rosie has already gone to school, breakfast club are doing bacon sarnies today, so she went in early, and Iris got picked up by Scarlett's mum as they're going to swing by the protest on the Common about the new Tory councillor agreeing to the tree felling. She's made a sign that says "What a beech!"'

'They left without saying goodbye?' Alice felt so sad that the two girls had gone off to school without her waving them off, before remembering that you couldn't miss what you didn't normally have. She'd make it up to them. 'What do you fancy for dinner tonight?' Her question surprised her. In the early hours, she had been resolute about swapping back first thing, but now, she felt that would be giving up too easily. She'd be going back to her own life having learned nothing and Edie would win.

Seb shrugged. 'Why don't I swing by the shops and see what's just been reduced? We could have my world-famous random tapas.'

'No, no, I'm here today, so I'll prepare something, you don't want to be cooking after a long day at work.'

Seb smiled. 'You sound like your sister; are you morphing into a 1950s housewife too? Am I going to come back and you're going to hand me a tumbler of Scotch and a pipe?'

Alice forced a laugh to come out of her mouth. 'Only if you're really lucky.'

'Those slippers she makes us wear are really bloody comfortable though. I'd totally get on board with that. Can you nick me a pair next time you're over there?'

'I'll see what I can do. Now go!' She flapped her hands at him. 'Go.'

As soon as he left, Alice grabbed the phone, and ordered a pair of matching slippers for the whole family.

Edie

During the night someone had poured a bucket of plaster of Paris over Edie's face, or at least that's what it felt like. The mask had dried like cement, rendering her unable to move a single muscle. She'd meant to slip out of her sister's bed with its impossibly deep mattress and take it off once Danny was asleep, but every time she'd tried to move, he'd jerked awake. It had been so odd sleeping next to a man that wasn't Seb. Danny sounded different, he smelt different, he moved differently, and she didn't like it. Seb was really considerate when he turned over, delicately trying to samba his body in a way not to make the mattress bounce, whereas Danny just heaved his big rugby-playing body over, making her feel like she was sleeping on a trampoline. In the depths of the darkness Edie remembered a news segment a couple of years before about this family of wild boar that ran amok in a supermarket car park on the outskirts of Rome, and the grunts they made at coveting the contents of people's trolleys was the exact same sound that came out of Danny's mouth. All night. All things considered, it was a wonder her sister ever had any sleep at all, maybe that was why she was so tightly wound up all the time.

'I could murder a coffee when you're ready,' Danny murmured beside her.

And I could murder you. Was this really how her sister's day always started? Being woken up by an alarm at six am, and immediately having to wait on her husband.

'Come on Ally, get the kettle on,' he moaned into his pillow, not even opening his eyes. 'Chop chop.' *Chop chop?*

Edie had an idea. She shuffled her pillow right next to his, lay facing him, her statue-white face inches from his, and whispered out of the tiny opening between her concrete lips, 'Sugar and milk?'

His eyes opened and he recoiled in horror, shrieking, desperately scuffling his body away from her, getting his limbs tangled up in the duvet, screeching out words his real wife would definitely not have approved of.

If Edie's facial muscles would have allowed it, she would have laughed so hard. Instead, she had to reward herself with just the satisfaction of yet another point scored. 'Something I said?' she murmured, taking herself off to the bathroom to chip away at her face with whatever tools she could find in the cupboard.

Fifteen minutes later, while the kettle was boiling – she had conceded, and was actually making Danny a coffee, she did not want to lose this bet – she flipped through Alice's folder, reminding herself of the morning routine. In half an hour, at seven, she had to wake the kids up. By now, she should have done twenty minutes on the cross-trainer in the garage and ten minutes of gratitude mindfulness, but the mask removal had eaten into her exercise time, which she wasn't particularly sad about. Walking Scooby a couple of times a day kept her fit enough, and the only thing she was grateful for this morning was that this wasn't her life, and she definitely did not need ten minutes to ponder on that.

As per the manual, she got three bowls out of the cupboard and filled each one with a different cereal, even putting a spoon propped up in each. She diligently measured out the green powder for Danny's shake, and double checked the notes again to see the packed lunch requirements. She'd seen less complicated instructions on a flat pack wardrobe. She started to get into a rhythm: cut the bagel, spread the bagel, fill the bagel, wrap the bagel. She even made up a little rap to accompany it in her head as she did each one, feeling more pleasure than she thought she would at filling each compartment of each lunchbox with cut-up grapes, slivers of cheddar, carrot sticks and a dollop of hummus. She stopped short of actually saying 'Ta-da' out loud when she'd finished, but definitely said it in her head. There was also a very brief moment when she considered taking photos of the finished boxes for Instagram and then remembered who she was and felt a little nauseous that the thought had even crossed her mind. Less than twenty hours living as Alice and she was already feeling the need to document her small triumphs online.

'Where are the kids, don't they need to leave now?' Danny said, sauntering into the kitchen to pick up his smoothie, hair freshly waxed, expensive suit newly laundered.

'Oh my god! The kids!' Edie took the stairs two at a time, banging each of the three bedroom doors open with a frenzied flourish, shouting into each one. 'Guys, you have to wake up now, we're really late! No need to brush your teeth, I've got gum, quick, quick!'

Danny watched Edie rummage through a PE bag to check its contents. 'Doesn't being late mean an unauthorised absence or something? Won't it go on their record?'

Tears welled up in Emily's eyes when Danny said that, while Edie noticed that Rufus started biting his bottom lip so hard it started bleeding. 'It'll be fine kids, don't worry, Daddy's only joking.' She glared at her brother-in-law, 'You know, you could have woken them up too,' she hissed as she pulled on her trainers to drive them to school. 'You literally had to walk past their bedroom doors to come down the stairs.'

'I didn't want to interfere with your routine,' Danny said lamely, but Edie knew the real reason was that it simply hadn't occurred to him. He and the children had placed the smooth running of their lives in Alice's hands, and she, and only she, was responsible.

'Out, out of my way,' Edie said, flapping her hands at Danny. 'Teddy, remember your new shin pads! Rufus, your swim kit is on your peg, and Emily, grab that bag for life. It's got your wellies in.'

'Aren't you going to give me my vitamin and tell me to drive safely?' Danny asked, in a tone that very much suggested his bottom lip was sticking out.

Edie stopped still and stared at him. Was he serious? He had literally just spent the last hour primping and preening himself and now she had to offer *him* a nicety to take with him to work along with his sodding bagel. She gave him a saccharine smile. 'You're right. Drive safely darling, see you tonight. Have a lovely day at work.'

'Thanks,' he said, seemingly completely placated. Had he never heard sarcasm before? 'Bye.'

It was only after she'd dropped the kids off, that she realised that Danny would have to pass both the primary and secondary schools on his way to his office, yet hadn't offered to drive his own children there. She knew that she and Alice had promised not to make any changes in each other's lives, but some things had to be altered. The sooner the better.

Alice

Alice had come up with a plan while she was in the shower that she thought was foolproof. She couldn't spend another minute in this house the way it currently was, and had decided that before she left this house and retreated back to her clean and tidy sanctuary, she was going to leave her sister a little parting gift. The only problem was that Edie apparently didn't 'see mess'. 'I honestly don't notice it,' she used to say on an almost daily basis to Alice when they shared a bedroom as children and she would point out Edie's detritus edging its way over her half of the room like an incoming tide. The fact that there was dust gathering on top of the mess in Edie's house, suggested that maybe she was sharing her home with three other humans who had the same affliction. And Seb, Rosie and Iris would never believe that the woman they knew and loved would voluntarily spend her day off elbow deep in Marigolds, so Alice had decided to invent a cleaner, which was more believable, but would give the same end result.

She'd had to empty the vacuum cleaner three times and she hadn't even done upstairs yet. She found a screwed-up ball of wrapping paper under the sofa, the embossed Santa hats on it suggesting it had been happily nestled there for over six months since Christmas, three dog toys, one very dusty maths textbook with a school stamp on its flyleaf, and one solitary men's trainer. Alice also reckoned it housed Scooby's entire winter coat, probably from multiple years.

She listened to Radio 4 as she went from room to room, moving the smart speaker as she went, dusting her way through a programme about how science was used to solve crime, bleaching the bathrooms while pondering whether AI could ever replace GPs, changing the beds to a discussion on how fruity real ales had become cool, and tackling the ironing pile to *Woman's Hour*. She listened to the debate on reevaluating gender roles in the home with only half an ear as she wondered why the bottom of the iron was so sticky and wished she could use her own top-of-the-range one with three different steam strengths that Danny had bought her for her last birthday.

Once all Seb's shirts were done and hanging on hangers dotted all around the kitchen, she tried her own phone number again. This time, instead of going through to voicemail, it started ringing. She tapped her foot anxiously. *Pick up. Pick up.*

'Hey you,' Edie answered.

'Hello! Where are you? Are you at home?'

'No, I popped out to the shops to get some things. How's it all going?'

Alice paused. How was it all going? Well, she'd spent most of the last twenty-four hours either naked or with her sister's naked boyfriend, she'd made faux pas after faux pas in every interaction she'd had with her nieces, and somehow, what started off a little light clean, has turned into a massive home makeover worthy of a primetime television programme. She'd even found an old tin of paint in the garden shed and erased a decade worth of scuffmarks on the skirting boards. 'Yeah good. Just, you know, sitting back, observing, being you.'

'Yeah, me too.'

'Kids get off to school okay?' Alice asked.

'Yep, yep, all at school.'

'Danny all okay?'

'Of course, why wouldn't he be?'

'Well, you know, he's quite particular over how he likes things done.'

'Is he?' Edie asked innocently. 'I can't say I've noticed.'

She had definitely noticed. 'Be nice to him,' Alice begged. 'He has a really stressful job.'

'I am nice to him! I made him his morning coffee, a bagel and his smoothie.'

'Did you remember the note I prepared to put in his lunchbox?'

'Uh-huh.'

'That means no.'

Edie didn't contradict her, which meant that he'd be really sad. For such a gruff-looking man, little gestures like the notes meant a lot to him. It wasn't immediately apparent, having lived as her sister for about sixteen hours, what little acts of kindness or love Seb was on the receiving end of, aside from the obvious one which she could not and would not attempt. 'I was thinking of making Seb a sandwich to take to the studio in the mornings, do you think he'd like that?'

If lip curls had audio attached to them, Alice would have heard it as Edie replied, 'I think he'd think it was really weird. How's Scooby? Did he eat his breakfast? I'm trialling a new type of hypoallergenic biscuits and he's been really fussy about them.'

Despite sharing a womb with her for nearly nine months, and a life outside for forty-five years, Edie was utterly baffling to Alice. She hadn't enquired about her children's welfare, or her husband's, and now was harping on about her dog's diet. Madness. 'Iris cheated on a maths test and Rosie's friend Annabelle French-kissed a stranger on a bus.'

'I'm sorry, what?'

'I just thought you might want to know the headlines from your kids as well as your dog.'

'Are you mad at me?'

'No, I'm not mad at you. I'm just reminding you that the members of your family without fur also have stuff going on in their lives you should perhaps be more concerned about.'

There was a pause before Edie spoke. 'Did Iris get found out?'

'What?'

'Is she in trouble? Did the school message?'

'No, no I don't think so, she just told me that she got a hundred percent in the test, but she'd cheated on it.'

The relief in Edie's voice was palpable. 'Well, that's fine then. And did Rosie also get off with a strange boy?'

'Not that I know of, I think it was just her friend that did.'

'Well, that's fine too then.'

'I'd hardly call that fine Edie.' Honestly, what planet was her sister on? She'd be mortified with either one of these reports, let alone both on the same day.

'Alice, my name's Alice. You're Edie, remember.'

'That's actually why I'm calling, I'm not sure how much longer I can keep this up. Seb keeps trying to kiss me and—'

'Oh bless him. He's like a golden retriever puppy. Tell him you feel like you have a cold sore coming. I get one at some point every year and he's terrified of catching it, so won't go near you. There are little cold sore stickers in the bathroom cabinet – pop one of those on, and he'll keep a one-metre distance at all times.'

'He also went for a pee while I was in the bath.'

'That's disgusting, why would he pee in your bath? He's never done that before. I'm so sorry.'

'No! He went for a pee in the toilet, while *I* was in the bath.'

Edie laughed in relief. 'We only have one bathroom, and he obviously needed to go. Just count yourself lucky it was only a number one, he completely gassed me out the other day.'

Alice swapped the phone from one hand to the other, so that she could use her right hand to write down on her shopping list *door locks*. This job had better be worth it.

CHAPTER TWELVE

Alice

> Hey sweetheart, I'm in between meetings at the moment, thought I'd check in. I just saw a man on a unicycle! In central London! Anyhoo, love you, see you later xxxxx

This was Seb's third message of the day so far, and it wasn't even lunchtime yet. The first detailed the interesting facial hair his new Italian client had, the second was a meme he shared from Instagram, and then this one about the unicycle. It was a wonder he and Edie had anything left to talk about over dinner if he kept up a pretty constant monologue about the goings on in his day. Was it a monologue, Alice wondered, or did Edie reply with equally inane observations? She scrolled back through her sister's messages with Seb and saw that while the majority of messages did indeed come from Seb, Edie treated him to a titbit every third or fourth message, so he was probably going to be expecting one back. She looked around the spotless living room – no fancy moustaches or unicycles here. What could she possibly say that was entertaining? Her gaze flittered to the window, where a sparrow had landed on the windowsill. She quickly took a picture of it and wrote an accompanying caption.

A sparrow has just landed on the windowsill.

She'd pressed send before realising that was probably one of the most boring messages she'd ever sent, and she had sent a few.

The phone pinged with an immediate reply: *Aw that's so cute! Hang on, where are our curtains?*

Dammit. She didn't spot the bare bay window in the background. She was hoping to have the curtains dried and pressed and hung again before he noticed they were cleaned.

I was fed up with the mess, so hired a cleaning firm for the day, they've done an amazing job, so thorough! Alice smiled and added in her head, *even if I say so myself.*

How much did that cost??? I thought we were saving?

Can't put a price on cleanliness. Alice had almost pressed send on this message before she realised that those six words would spell the immediate end of this switch once and for all. What would Edie say? Alice closed her eyes, and imagined her sister typing her response and her thumbs involuntarily started flying across the keypad.

I hear you babes, and the saving has started again now, but oh my days, the house looks AMAZING!!!!!

The message was immediately hearted, signalling both the end of the conversation, and the fact that she'd managed to get away with it.

Edie

There was a reason none of Edie's waistbands had buttons, and she could swear Alice's expensive jeans were made from a non-stretch denim. Admittedly in recent years, she and Alice had become slightly less identical in the waist and hip area, not necessarily noticeable to those who only saw them fully clothed, but Edie was very aware that she didn't have as much restraint in the calorie department as her sister. A fact proven as she was merrily sitting in Alice's neighbourhood café tucking into a sugar-coated almond croissant with her latte when a 'naughty naughty' got whispered into her ear, making her jump.

The woman, fresh from the pages of the Joules catalogue, took the empty seat opposite Edie. 'Alice, you are such a devil, how the flip can you look the way you do after scoffing a thousand calories for lunch?'

'This isn't my lunch,' Edie said, 'this is a post-lunch pick-me-up.'

'Oh, you are such a hoot!'

Edie vaguely remembered there being a section in Alice's folder on her friends and neighbours – she should probably read that before venturing out of the house again. Meanwhile, the woman was looking at Edie intently. 'Something's different about you.'

Oh god. 'I don't know what you mean.'

'I can't put my finger on it.'

'How are the kids?' Edie took a leap of faith in this question, based on the fact that the woman was wearing the ubiquitous yellow raincoat with the Breton striped lining that was only allowed to be sold to middle-class mums.

'They're fine. Hughie got a yellow belt in Judo, and Lexie got chosen to do a clarinet solo for the Eisteddfod.'

'That is really splendid.'

'I know what it is! You've done your make-up differently.'

Edie had really tried that morning to replicate the barely-there-but-very-much-there look her sister had perfected, but Alice's cosmetics bag was really complicated, and she drew the line at drawing lines on her face, aka contouring.

'Just trying something new,' Edie replied, smiling.

'Now tell me, is it true that George and Bella have got a new au pair? What is this one, their third? Fourth this year?'

'I have no idea.' *Nor do I care,* Edie added in her head.

'Why do you think they keep going through them? Alison told me it's because they only let them eat off the kids' plastic Ikea plates and not the real China ones.'

'That's ridiculous.'

'Evelyn said it's because George keeps walking around in his underwear. Helena's au pair Jasmine said that she heard from another au pair that Bella refused to give her their Netflix password, and she can't get terrestrial on the TV in her room.'

'I really wouldn't know—'

'Oh you are losing your touch! I would have put money on you having all the goss. Not that I'm the gambling type, we'll leave that to Ursula, am I right?' The woman gave a theatrical wink to Edie, who recoiled in disgust. Women who gossiped about other women had no place in her day. Did her sister actually entertain people like that? Was this woman one of her actual friends?

Edie made noises about needing to get on, and the woman gave her a couple of dramatic air kisses, told her that she'd see her at book club tomorrow and departed, leaving trails of her cloying perfume in her wake.

She glanced at her sister's phone. It had been six hours since Danny had left the house and he hadn't messaged at all. Was that usual? Seb kept the invisible string between them taut and buzzing with communication all day; by this point in the afternoon he would definitely have messaged four or five times, with some little nugget about what he'd seen or done: his excitement at hearing someone use the word 'bamboozle' in a sentence, or passing a little boy with the face of a fully grown man. Often his messages came through at deeply inconvenient times, eliciting a sigh of annoyance from her at the interruption; she wondered what he'd been spamming Alice with this morning.

She scrolled through her sister's messages to find the last exchange with Danny. It was three weeks ago. He'd messaged Alice to ask her to cook steak for dinner. She had replied with just three words. *Rump or sirloin?*

There was a flurry of messages a week or so before that; apparently his mum's guttering had come away from the wall in a storm, and Alice was trying to find a handyman in Fife who could pop round and fix it, and was asking Danny if he knew anyone he'd grown up with that could help, or if he had the number of a neighbour. He left her message on read for four hours, then replied with a *no, sorry*.

Two weeks before that, he'd messaged to say that he was in Tesco, and could she send him a photo of the clubcard. She replied: *I'm on air in two mins, and my purse is in my dressing room, sorry!* He replied with *FFS, I wanted a meal deal*. She then felt the need to reply an hour later with, *I really am sorry, I'll order you a replacement card now*.

It was making Edie really sad scrolling through these messages. Her lovely sister reduced to nothing more than a personal assistant slash housekeeper. She knew that their dynamic was different to hers, but where was the warmth? The affection? She was nicer to the local binmen than Danny was to his wife. Maybe, hopefully, Alice had chosen to delete all the lovely messages before handing her phone over to Edie, not wanting her sister to see the gushing declarations of love and romance. She decided to test out this theory and tapped out a message to Danny.

Hi darling, how's your day going? Having a coffee, wishing you were here.

The message had two blue ticks almost as soon as it had sent, meaning he was obviously sitting with his phone in his hand and had read it immediately. Edie waited for his reply. And waited. It wasn't until three mums with pushchairs started hovering in a circle around her table like seagulls over spilled chips that she gave up on receiving a reply, shoved the phone in her bag and headed home.

Alice

'Fuck me, what's happened to our house?' Rosie said, staring around in open-mouthed wonder.

Part of Alice was horrified at her niece's flagrant use of an obscenity, the other part was thrilled at such a dramatic, and fitting, response to her hard day's work.

'This isn't our house. It can't be,' Iris said, doing a full three-sixty-degree turn to take it all in. 'Is that the colour our carpet was meant to be, or have you had new carpet put in?'

'I just got a cleaner round,' Alice explained, shrugging. While she would have loved the accolade for accomplishing such a makeover herself, she knew that it would be so out of character it would be impossible to pull off.

Rosie was so shocked, she still hadn't closed her jaws together. 'It looks like that show home we went round on the new estate when it was raining and McDonald's was too busy.'

'Did the cleaner go upstairs too?' Iris asked, one foot already on the bottom step

'She did the bathrooms, but not your bedrooms, apart from changing the sheets. If you want her to tidy your rooms and organise your wardrobe, I'm sure she wouldn't mind coming back tomorrow and doing that?'

Rosie swivelled round, from where she was holding the newly trimmed leaf of a previously half-dead plant in her hand. 'Hang on? This cleaner just out of the goodness of her heart will come back tomorrow and do more?'

'Well,' Alice tried to think quickly, 'I mean, I'll pay her of course.'

'With what money?' Rosie said, her hands on her hips.

'Sorry?'

'I heard Dad say to you at the weekend that we were only allowed to shop at Aldi from now on, and he had unplugged the tumble drier as it was too expensive. Where are we getting money for a cleaner?'

'I don't think you need to worry about that.'

'I know what's going on, you know.'

How could she know? 'What's going on?'

'You can pretend all you like, but it's pretty clear what's happening.'

'What is?' Alice croaked out.

Rosie held the trimmed leaf up to show Alice. 'You know where the only place I've ever seen leaves trimmed like this is?'

'No, where?'

Rosie paused for dramatic effect then announced theatrically, 'Auntie Alice's.'

'Yes!' chimed in Iris. 'I saw that too, at Christmas. She cuts all her leaves into leaf shapes. I googled "can plants feel pain" after I saw that, but the answers were a bit varied.'

Rosie spread her arms out wide and started a slow walk around the hallway. 'It's so obvious now I think about it. Look at all the shoes lined up in size order! The coats on the pegs are all colour coded, and I bet if I turn on the radio, it'll be that boring talking station it's tuned into.'

'I mean . . . I don't . . .'

Rosie shook her finger in Alice's face accusingly, 'Don't even try to pretend anymore. I can't believe that you'd lie to us like this. Does Dad know?'

Alice felt her face flush bright red. How could one good deed unravel everything? She managed to stammer that no, he didn't know, it was meant to be a secret, they didn't mean to upset anyone, or make them feel duped, it was just a silly idea and—

Rosie cut her off, 'Look, chill Mum, it's not that deep. If Auntie Alice wants to come round here and sort our shit out, then I say, let her crack on. And yeah, if you think she'll come back again tomorrow and do this to our rooms, then cool.'

'Yeah cool,' Iris added. 'But don't let her throw away my stick insects.'

Seb let out a very similar expletive to the girls when he wheeled his bike into the hallway.

Alice ran out from the kitchen to greet him. 'Before the girls have a chance to tell you, it wasn't a cleaner, it was Alice. Alice came round and did this for us.'

'Why would Alice do that? You're not even talking to each other at the moment.' He wandered between the rooms, eyes wide at seeing the house look like it never had before.

'I don't know, something about paying me back, I can't remember what for, I helped her out with something a while back, and she just turned up this morning with some cleaning products and a pinny and set about finding our house again.'

'It looks incredible!'

'I know! It took her all day pretty much. She worked so hard.'

'Let me guess, you sat on a bar stool looking gorgeous while she mopped under your feet?'

'Something like that.'

Seb pulled her in and joked, 'It's on days like this when I wonder if I chose the wrong sister.' Alice awkwardly detangled herself from Seb's grasp and laughed, stopping abruptly when he followed that up with, 'Only kidding, she'd drive me absolutely nuts.'

Alice followed him into the kitchen, and against all her better judgement asked as innocently as she could manage. 'In what way? Wouldn't you like having a clean house all the time?'

'Nah. Wouldn't be worth it.'

'Worth what?'

'The aggro every time I moved a cushion.'

'She's a great cook.'

'She is. But I'm not sure I'd like my life organised to the nth degree. Deciding on the first of the month what you'd like to eat three weeks on Tuesday, no thanks.'

'You'd rather decide half an hour before you want to eat it?'

'Pretty much.'

'Speaking of which,' Alice said, looking at the carrier bags at Seb's feet, 'what did you pick up at the shops?' It had been absolutely killing her that she couldn't menu plan ahead of time, and was now faced with the stress-inducing task of making a meal from random ingredients.

'Oh, you are going to love the selection I got.' He stuck his hand into one of the bags and brought out two tins of kidney beans, each with a big dent in them, a pack of risotto rice with a big yellow reduced sticker on it, a pot of fresh chicken stock, again with a yellow reduced sticker and a wrinkled aubergine. 'They gave me this for free!'

'Wow. That is . . . um, yes, so great. Yum.'

'I told you you'd like it. Right, let's get cooking.'

Edie

'Are we having something cold for dinner?' Danny asked as he dumped his gym bag in front of the washing machine.

Edie looked at it, and wondered if it was a magical gym kit that put itself in the machine, or whether he'd left it there by accident perhaps, or maybe, just maybe, it was a little gift for her in lieu of a hello, or any kind of greeting at all.

'I thought I saw on the menu planner that it was jambalaya tonight but I can't smell anything? I've been looking forward to that all day.'

For Christ's sake, Edie thought, Alice knew about the swap, why couldn't she have put something like cheese toasties on the menu for tonight, not a sodding dish that took hours of prep and much googling of the recipe.

'I thought I'd wait and see what kind of mood you were all in,' Edie replied.

'Mood for what?'

'Eating. What you all fancied eating tonight?'

'I don't know, that's what you decide. You're the chef.' He slumped on the sofa and put his huge moccasin-clad feet up on a footstool, spreading his forearms along the back of the cushions like a bald eagle during his downtime.

Edie asked Teddy, Rufus and Emily the same question, but all of them gave variations of the same response as their father, the boys using the exact same disparaging tone as Danny too, while at least Emily offered her shoulder shrug with a smile.

Cheese toasties it was then.

If she was back in her own house she would not be laying the table for sandwiches, hell, they even had Sunday roasts on their laps if her mum's antique dining table was too messy to clear it, but Edie already knew that the food she was serving up was unconventional, to offer it up on trays would make all their heads explode. It also said in the folder that Tuesday night was games night, so they'd need to be at the table for that anyway. Danny seemed to be sulking with her about something; she even brought him a glass of sparkling water and a ramekin of olives 'to keep him going', and he barely acknowledged her as he took them from her.

'Everything okay at work?' Edie asked.

He shrugged his shoulders in response.

'I messaged you earlier,' she said.

'I was busy.'

'Oh okay. Would have been nice to get one back when you were free.'

'I'm never free. I have meeting after meeting, call after call, you have no idea what it's like.'

She perched on the sofa arm next to him. 'So, tell me. Tell me about what you do and who you meet.'

'Alice, just leave it. You know I don't want to talk about work when I'm not at work; it stresses me out. You're acting a bit funny to be honest.'

'Funny?'

'Well, first you burned dinner last night, then you forgot to wake the kids up, you didn't write me a note in my lunchbox, and you know how much I like them; you haven't even taken my gym kit out of its bag and you always do that as soon as I come in, or it won't be dry for tomorrow. You're drinking wine in the kitchen, and now you're making sandwiches for dinner. Any one of those things in isolation would have me worried, but you've done all of them in the same twenty-four hours. Is anything seriously wrong?'

None of the things that he'd just listed were unusual, all of them happened on a daily basis in her own life, and yet he'd just itemised them like federal charges in a courtroom. How did she plead? Guilty, guilty, guilty. But if he was cataloguing all these misdemeanours, it was only a matter of time before he twigged and she was rumbled. But even if she was and this swap had to stop, twenty-four hours had been long enough for Edie to have serious empathy with how her sister lived. Alice was totally invisible in her own home, her function was solely to make her husband and kids' lives more comfortable, but who was doing that for her? At least over at her house, Alice should be having a taste of what proper family life should be.

Alice

'No!' Alice shrieked, almost falling off her garden chair with the combination of half a bottle of very strong Rioja and the punchline to Seb's story.

'So then I told him, get yourself dressed, put the bicycle pump back in the drawer, and we'll forget this ever happened.'

'You're lying! That never happened!'

'It did too. But on the plus side, I got a really big order from him.' Seb picked up his glass from the side of the barbecue where it had been balancing. 'Anyway, enough about me, how was your day?'

Alice's mind flitted back to the seven hours she'd spent with either a vacuum cleaner, mop or sponge in her hand. If she'd have known they'd be having drinks outside tonight, she'd have given the patio a clean too; as it was, she and Seb were seated on dusty garden chairs sandwiched between an out-of-control wild blackberry plant and a rusty trampoline, but it was lovely sitting outside in the sun just chatting. It was amazing how much fun you could have without a pergola. 'Oh, you know, fairly chilled. I did a couple of therapy sessions, when Alice wasn't using the vacuum, and I helped her sort out some of the cupboards.'

'She did inside the cupboards as well?'

'They were really gross, you wouldn't believe it.'

'How did the two of you get on?'

Alice nodded. 'Fine, yes, good.'

'Really?'

'Yes, really.' Why did he sound so shocked?

'Alice wasn't too . . . Alice?'

Alice bristled at the suggestion that she was *too* anything. 'No, not at all, she was great. Really helpful, and lovely, and really good company actually.'

'Wow.'

She didn't think that her description of herself deserved a 'wow', as though it was such an unusual and unexpected phenomenon. How badly did Edie normally speak of her that Seb would be actually awe-struck at the suggestion that she was nice?

'It reminded me actually of what a kind person she is,' Alice continued, searching Seb's face as she spoke, 'I mean, in many ways she's the perfect wife.'

Seb's face contorted into a grimace. 'Nah. I'd take you any day.'

'Really?' She tried and failed not to sound incredulous.

'Really. You bring out the best in me. She brings out the worst. You said it yourself, when you first met Danny you said he was pretty decent, I mean, totally wrapped up in his sport, but not as selfish as he is now.'

'And you think that's Alice's fault?'

'We've spoken about this before? It's not all down to her, of course not, but he was an alright bloke before she started peeling his grapes for him. Now he thinks he's a cross between Julius Caesar and Jesus.'

Alice was too stunned to speak. She opened and closed her mouth like a goldfish. Was this what they both thought? Danny wasn't that bad, he worked hard, that was all, and if he couldn't completely switch off in his own home then where could he? It wasn't as though she had a demanding job, she just kept everything running in the background, he was the one who had to put on a suit and be corporate all day. If anything, she felt a bit embarrassed about how much she was earning from her sponsored posts on Instagram and her telly slot; society really valued the wrong things sometimes. If the world worked the way it should, then people like Danny should be paid so much more than they were. And he didn't even know that her earnings had started outstripping his a couple of months ago. There was no need for him to know that, she would just keep squirrelling the money away and surprise him with a fancy holiday or a new car later in the year. Even as she had the thought, a clutch of nausea took hold deep in the pit of her stomach. He would never drive a car she had bought him, or enjoy the breakfast buffet of a holiday he hadn't paid for. She couldn't actually see a way that her money could be spent at all without turning his world upside down. She could give the money away perhaps? Maybe that would be the best thing? She could start donating it anonymously to a range of charities? Because as long as it sat there in a secret account, it was steadily burning a little hole deep into the roots of her marriage.

Seb nudged her knee with his. 'You've gone very quiet. Sorry, I know you hate it when I say anything bad about your sister. Only you're allowed to do that.'

'Do I do that often?' Alice asked innocently.

He smiled teasingly. 'Only on the hour, every hour.'

'Oh good. I was worried it was becoming a habit,' Alice managed to joke.

Edie

As much as the male members of the family initially turned their noses up at the cheese, ham and tomato toasties Edie served up, all of them asked for another round, so Danny could put that in his pipe and smoke it. She did Alice-them up though, by cutting them into triangles and placing them at jaunty angles around a serving platter, and sprinkled some fresh parsley over the top that she'd snipped from the herb tray on the windowsill. At least she hoped it was parsley. And she kept the bee apron on all of dinnertime. When they'd all finished, they all sat back in their dining chairs with their dirty plates in front of them, no one making a move to clear the table at all. Edie glanced at each of them in turn. 'So, games night?' she said, hoping that would prompt a flurry of housekeeping from each of them, but nothing. 'Emily, what game do you fancy playing tonight?'

Emily's surprise at being asked her opinion was palpable on her excited little face, and she could hardly get her words out, 'Um Scrabble? Bananagrams? Risk? Game of Life? A card game? Anything, whatever Teddy wants to do?'

'Teddy? What do you think?' Edie said.

Teddy gave a non-committal shrug that plainly said that he'd rather be upstairs with his Xbox.

'Rufus?'

'I don't mind. You usually pick.'

Edie turned to face Danny, who was now on his phone at the table. 'Danny?'

Danny looked back at her, equally as surprised at being asked for his input as his daughter. 'Games night's your thing with the kids, not mine. England's got a friendly against Spain at eight.'

'Can we watch it, Dad?' Teddy asked.

'Yeah, can I watch it too?' Rufus chimed in.

'As long as you don't talk through it. Come on, we'll get it set up, they'll be showing the pre-match commentary now.'

All three got up from the table, leaving their dirty plates behind them. No attempt to clear their part in the mess that was left behind. No thank you, or recognition of the meal being made by someone's hands and not by fairies. No thoughtful pushing of chairs in, or backwards glances of appreciation.

Edie looked over at her niece, whose eyes hadn't left Edie's face the whole time. 'That was lovely Mummy,' Emily said. 'What do you call that meal we just had?'

127

Edie narrowed her eyes at Emily. 'Toasted sandwiches?'

'Can we have that again tomorrow?'

Edie's face broke into a warm grin. 'Never change, Emily, you are perfect in every way.'

'Do you want to play a game with me?'

'I'd love to. You choose one while I put these in the dishwasher.'

'I'll help you, I'll be a mummy one day so I need to learn how to do it.' Then in Alice's singsong voice, Emily added, 'Can I wear one of your aprons? This kitchen isn't going to clean itself.'

Edie stood statue-still as Emily's words stabbed right through her and she had to do a few deep breaths before speaking or moving.

'Right boys,' she called, stalking through into the living room, 'you have fifteen minutes before the national anthems, which arguably is the best part of the entire match, so come into the kitchen, clear your plates away, sort the chairs out, load the dishwasher, and you can be back on the sofa in time to put your hand on your heart and sing along. Come on, Teddy, Rufus, now please.'

The boys didn't move, instead they just looked at their dad for his instruction on this bizarre turn of events.

Edie put her hands on her hips to show that she meant business. Danny deliberated, obviously wondering if this was a fight worth fighting. He sighed, then said, 'You heard your mother.'

'And Danny, your gym kit needs to go on a forty wash, you can put it in with Rufus's games kit and Teddy's swim stuff, which for some reason are dumped on the hall floor. And use two laundry tablets, they're filthy. Chop chop.'

CHAPTER THIRTEEN

The swap: day 3

Edie

After swerving Alice's lotions and potions, but very much enjoying her heated eye mask, Edie fell fast asleep on the second day, long before Danny eventually climbed in beside her. She stirred when he came up, because who wouldn't with a sixteen-stone hulk of muscle lumbering aboard a shared double mattress with memory foam topper, but she managed to drift back off fairly quickly, nimbly aided by some noise-cancelling earplugs she'd found in Alice's bedside drawer. She'd initially approached her sister's bedside drawer with trepidation, but was both relieved and disappointed in equal measure to find it just contained said earplugs and eye mask, a box of paracetamol, a pen and a notepad, the first few pages of which were just to-do lists. Did Alice have a single item in her home that brought her joy? Something that wasn't practical, or functional, or related to the smooth running of her house and body, but something, anything that was there purely for pleasure? Even the book she was halfway through was an autobiography of the wife of a successful billionaire called *Always One Step Behind*. If ever there was a depressing title or premise for a memoir, that was it.

The boys had avoided her all evening, but to their credit, they had cleared the table and sorted the dishes when she'd ordered them to. Seeing the look on Emily's face as she and Edie sat at the table dealing the cards between them while Danny crouched down on the floor in front of the washing machine peering at the dials, and her brothers watched a YouTube video on how to stack the plates into the dishwasher, was worth more than money. She wasn't sure she could repeat this particular life lesson every night of her stay, but maybe a small moral had been learned tonight.

Her alarm went off half an hour earlier than it had done the morning before. Until she got faster on the packed lunch production line, she was not making the same mistake twice. This time she remembered to pop one of Alice's handwritten notes in the top of Danny's. She unfolded it before popping it in, curious to see what sentiments her sister would want her husband to take to work with him. *You're braver than you believe and stronger than you think.* Oh pur-lease. Danny didn't need that type of crap being peddled to him along with his grilled halloumi, his life was already one long audition tape for a husband in *Mad Men*. Listening out for a creak of an upstairs floorboard, Edie quickly tore off a square from the bottom corner of a notepad, and trying her best to imitate her sister's uptight cursive handwriting, she wrote Danny a completely new mantra for his day. Pleased with it, she tucked it into his lunchbox, and popped the box into his messenger bag just in time to hear the pipes come to life upstairs with a toilet flushing.

Alice

Seb was still sleeping when Alice slid out of bed. She padded downstairs to make him some sandwiches to take to the studio. As she topped up the water in the coffee machine, she still couldn't shake what Seb had said last night, about her basically creating Frankenstein's monster. Was that true?

To say that she was unaware of her desire to please and her persistent quest for perfection would have been a complete lie, of course she knew that about herself. None of her other friends ran their home, their family, their lives with as much precision as she did, and yet nothing brought her greater joy than when she was complimented on it. 'Look at Alice,' their mother used to say. 'Can't you be more like Alice?' 'Alice doesn't feel the need to roll down a hill/cut a worm in half/play loud music/lick her plate/use bad words/stay out late.' 'Life would be so much easier, if you were both just like Alice.' It must have driven Edie crazy, constantly being held up for scrutiny next to her. And look at the marriages they'd ended up with: on paper, Danny should be the more attentive partner; he literally had everything done for him, you would have thought gratitude and love would be spilling out of him at every opportunity, and yet it was Seb who was far more proactive and busier in the home, who seemed so much happier and more caring. On second thoughts, maybe she wouldn't make Seb his lunch. He could make his own lunch, just like Danny could start making his.

She might just make Seb a coffee to have in bed though.

Her phone vibrated on the counter with a message. It was Edie, on Alice's number. She was up early.

> Is it your book club tonight? I bumped into an awful woman in a café yesterday, harping on about someone's new au pair, and she said 'see you tomorrow at book club' AAARRGGGHH What? Where? Who? And what book am I meant to have read?

> Yep. Book club tonight, sorry, totally forgot. That must have been Ruth, keep her on side, think Mean Girls X a million. It's at Louisa's house, she's lovely, newly divorced. You need to take a canapé dish – maybe do something easy like a cream cheese log with pistachio coating and take breadsticks. Book is on my bedside table, really interesting read. When's yours?

> You don't need to go to mine, I've already told my friends I can't make it.

> I want to! We said we would live each other's lives, when is it?

> Edie??? When is it?

> Fine. It's also tonight. It's at my friend Amanda's. Don't bring anything except wine. You're going to hear a lot of bad words and graphic details about their husbands. Don't do that judgy thing with your face. Please don't say anything to make them hate me.

> Sounds fun. What book is it?

> Book?

Edie

In the end, Edie only had time to upend a bottle of sweet chilli sauce on top of two scooped-out tubs of Philadelphia as her proffered dish of the day, but who didn't love Chilli Philly?

She had put aside an hour that afternoon to respond to all of Alice's Instagram DMs and comments on her latest reel, which Alice had scheduled to go live that morning showing her recent wardrobe organisation, and an hour was nowhere long enough to get through the barrage of audience interaction. Edie thought it was going to just be a case of hearting all the comments and typing a few *Thanks!* on some of the more heartfelt comments, but looking back on some of her sister's old posts, she realised that Alice was far more effusive with her time and replies. *You can totally do this!* she typed out in response to a woman asking for positive vibes on tackling her late mother's closet. *Keep going my lovely!* she wrote to another lady, who had posted a picture of a bed covered in a mountain of clothes, trapped in that terrible mid-sort-out phase, where you start to question the paths in your life that led you to that exact point. Before she knew it, the kids were home demanding snacks, and she'd needed to prepare dinner for them all to eat while she was out. She'd decided to make a macaroni cheese, partly in apology for turning their worlds upside down last night, and partly because it was the only meal she knew how to make without googling it, and Rufus was sitting at the breakfast bar the whole time, so she couldn't look anything up online.

'Are you okay Roof?' Edie had asked, using the abbreviation she'd heard Alice use in the past.

'Yes,' he replied, without conviction.

'What's up?'

'Can I tell you something without you telling Dad?'

'Of course.'

He looked at her with large deer-like eyes. 'Promise me you won't tell him?'

'I promise.' That was a very easy promise to keep. Depending on what this declaration was, Edie may well have to tell Alice, but as that's who Rufus thought he was telling anyway, then no trust was actually going to be broken.

'You know I have to choose my GCSEs next year?'

'Yes?'

'Well, I want to do food tech.'

'Okay? And?'

'And Dad's going to go mad. And you probably think that's really dumb too.' He hung his head, not wanting to meet her gaze.

'I don't think that's dumb at all. Why would you think I would?'

'Because you never let me or Teddy in here to help you with anything. Whenever you're making a cake or anything you always call Emily to do it with you.'

'Do I?' *Does she?*

'You know you do. You always shoo us out. You've taught Emily how to use the cooker, and the blender, and the waffle maker, but not me.'

'Well I . . .' How on earth could Edie legitimately justify something that she felt was so wrong? 'Well I . . .' *Say something*, she urged herself, *finish your sentence*. 'I had no idea you'd be interested in it,' she said brightly, 'and now I do, I'll get you involved all the time.'

'But only when Dad's not here.'

'Why would he mind?'

'He just would, wouldn't he? You know what he was like when I had to dance in the school play; he still calls me Twinkle Toes now.'

'Well he's not here now. Do you want to learn how to make macaroni cheese?'

'Yes!' Rufus jumped off his bar stool in glee, and ran to the drawer where his mother kept her aprons. Taking one out, he wrapped it round himself, grinning from ear to ear. Together they melted the butter, poured in the flour and milk, and gently stirred it, joking and laughing the whole time. Edie spoke into the end of a wooden spoon like a microphone. 'So, chef Rufus, can you tell me what you're doing now?'

'I am making a wonderfully rich cheese sauce, which will delicately coat each macaroni piece with its delicious creaminess.'

'Oh that does sound splendid. Do you think we should grate some more cheese for the top?'

'Absolutely. You may also want to serve this with a delightfully crisp green salad.'

'That is great advice to the viewers.'

They had just put the macaroni cheese under the grill, and were laughing about 'the one they prepared earlier' having gone missing when the front door slammed, and panic flashed across Rufus's face as his fingers desperately struggled to untie his apron, throwing it to the floor and kicking it under the breakfast bar just in time before Danny walked in, his face thunderous.

'Rufus, up to your room while I speak to your mother.'

'What's the meaning of this?' Danny brandished the note in his hand that Edie had scribbled hurriedly that morning. She had actually lamented doing it, concluding that she should have waited for her coffee to kick in before putting pen to paper, but there it was, in as close an impersonation of Alice's writing as she could muster: *Men should be grateful that women just want equality and not revenge.* It was funny for goodness' sake, not particularly offensive, although seeing the vein pulsing out of Danny's neck, perhaps her idea of humour wasn't necessarily universal. His brow furrowed as he read it again. 'What does it actually mean? Revenge for what? It doesn't make any sense.'

'The fact you don't know is incredibly troubling.' Just then the phone pinged, with a *Where are you?* from somebody called Louisa.

'Oh god, my book club!' Edie ran to the fridge, surveyed it for any inspiration at all; her eyes alighted on the Philadelphia and sweet chilli sauce, and bingo, her favourite late-night university snack saved the day.

'So you're just going to go out?'

Edie opened the cupboard under the sink. Where did Alice keep her carrier bags? 'You know I have a monthly book club.'

'But dinner's not even ready yet.'

Edie glanced up at the clock. 'It's only got another five minutes to go.'

'But won't it be too heavy for Emily to get out?'

Was he joking? He'd better be joking, or tomorrow's note would definitely be of the more offensive variety.

'It is definitely too heavy for Emily, so you can get it out. You can also put a bag of lettuce in a bowl to serve it with.' Edie opened and shut all the drawers in the dresser. Where would she have put all her bags?

Danny looked panicked. 'You know I can't cook.'

'Nothing of what I've asked you to do is cooking. The cooking part is done. Get the boys to lay the table, you get the hot dish out, everyone helps themselves, everyone's happy.'

Edie opened the final drawer, to find around twenty carrier bags, all folded into little triangle pouches. Genius.

Danny looked at her quizzically. 'I'm really confused, Alice. And not very happy about this.'

'No, no you're not, but that very much sounds like a you problem,' Edie muttered under her breath.

'What?'

'Nothing dear, have a lovely evening. Don't wait up.'

Alice hadn't mentioned anything about bringing a bottle to the book club, but Edie grabbed two from the wine rack anyway. She had a feeling she might be needing them.

Alice

Edie's friend Sam had just pulled her trousers down and was giving a live demonstration of how she rubbed her oestrogen HRT cream into her upper thighs every morning. Alice didn't think this was entirely necessary; after all, Sam had just said, 'I rub it into my thighs every morning,' and Alice didn't feel that there was enough ambiguity in this statement to warrant this show and tell, but the other women seemed to enjoy the display. Sam was wearing flowery knickers, which made Alice flush and look away, but not before silently reminding herself to book another session of lymphatic massage.

It was exhausting trying to look like she was enjoying herself. She was literally having to sit on her hands not to put all the wine glasses on the coasters they were standing next to. If a coaster was there, why on earth would you deliberately not use it? The coffee table looked like it was Indonesian mango wood as well, which would stain dreadfully. Also on the table were open containers of various supermarket tapas bits: olives, chorizo, mozzarella balls. They were even still in the plastic pots, with the film merely peeled back. Admittedly, they all looked very tasty, but why would you not at the very least pour them into little bowls and make your own breadsticks to go with them? It was almost like these women were proud of being so lazy. When Alice hosted her book club she'd spent the majority of the day baking and prepping. And no one had made the same groans of pleasure that Edie's friends were currently making over some pre-packaged sundried tomatoes. That said more about Edie's friends than Alice's cooking though; this group of women seemed to shriek with delight at the tiniest thing, whereas Alice's were a little more refined.

Edie

'I think what struck me the most is her unswerving loyalty to her husband, even in the face of five affairs, and three unproven fraud court cases. She is an absolute inspiration,' Ruth said, pouring herself more tea and brandishing the porcelain teapot in Edie's direction, who waved it away and held up her almost empty wine glass by way of an explanation.

'In what way is she an inspiration?' Edie asked politely.

'Well, her resilience and her classiness.'

'I think it would have been far classier to burn his clothes on the barbecue, change the locks and enlist a really amazing divorce lawyer. He sounds like a complete knob-end.'

Ruth looked absolutely shocked at Edie's turn of phrase, making Edie realise that Alice's friends were probably the ones who called into the show complaining about her.

'I must admit, I do agree slightly with Alice,' the host, Louisa, said. Edie liked Louisa, particularly after she took the bowl with Edie's cream cheese concoction in and exclaimed with sheer happiness, 'Chilli Philly! I haven't had this since I was at Durham!' Edie had however noticed that it was only she and Louisa who had been dipping Ruth's homemade breadsticks into it all night.

'I think the trade-off of being married to a really rich and successful man is his little foibles,' said a woman who Edie was pretty sure was Bella with the string of au pairs. Edie wondered if her husband's 'foibles' might be the reason for the rapid turnover of staff.

'I agree. You can forgive a lot when you know a fortnight in Fiji is just around the corner.'

The other women all laughed, but Edie didn't get the joke. They were talking about it being absolutely fine if men were arseholes, as long as they gave their wives an unlimited account at Selfridges. This was insane. Did these women have so little self-respect that they'd overlook basic human decency? No wonder Alice thought Danny's outdated behaviour was normal if these women's marriages were her benchmark. She noticed that Louisa wasn't laughing either, and it vaguely chimed with her that Alice had told her about her friend Louisa who had caught her husband in bed with a colleague of his when she got home after watching their child be the Pharaoh in the school's production of *Joseph and the Technicolour Dreamcoat*.

Edie coughed and adjusted her legs underneath her, saying, 'My sister's partner, Seb, doesn't really have two beans to rub together; he designs and makes his own pottery which he sells at a few independent shops, but he's literally the nicest man you could meet, who treats my sister with respect and love. If it was between being married to him and an arrogant millionaire who gave me vouchers for Christmas for a new designer handbag but treated me like dirt, I know which one I'd pick.'

Louisa caught Edie's eye and gave a small, sad smile.

After a few seconds of awkward silence, Ruth let out a guffaw. 'You're basically saying you'd rather be married to your brother-in-law than your own husband! Alice, really! Is there something you want to tell us?'

Five pairs of eyes bored into Edie's soul. She knew she shouldn't have said anything, but feminism wasn't a passive thing, it was active and political, and she felt she had a duty to shake these women until their eyeballs rattled and they realised quite what unhealthy cycles of patriarchal hegemony they were perpetuating.

But then, she looked at all of their faces. A mixture of confusion and concern etched on their smooth, plumped out skin, but without a shred of self-awareness or grasp of what point she was trying to make. She reached over, picked up a breadstick and bit the end off it. 'Lemon, pepper, and, no don't tell me . . . rosemary?' she said.

Ruth beamed. 'And baked with oil from Sicilian olives.'

'I knew it, you can absolutely taste the difference, can't you?' Edie smiled, hating herself never more than at that particular moment. 'It really is top notch.'

Alice

'Alice! Alice! Who the frick is Alice?'

Alice might have suspended all notion of propriety to belt out a nineties classic while standing on the Indonesian mango wood table – which, it turned out, did not stain at all when she spilt her wine on it – but she still couldn't bring herself to join in with the profanity that the song apparently demanded. Baby steps.

She had to admit it though, Edie's book club was a lot more fun than hers was. Possibly because it wasn't technically a book club. And aside from a complete lack of matrimonial privacy – she now knew far more about all their husbands than a woman should who wasn't married to the man in question – Edie's friends were really lovely. One of them, she couldn't remember her name, but she had the warmest hazel eyes she'd ever seen, pulled her aside in the kitchen as Alice took the dirty plates in.

'I just wanted to say Eeds, you know that Penny just mentioned going away for her fiftieth to a log cabin for a few days; we're really happy to cover your share my lovely, it wouldn't be the same without you, and please don't say no, we'd be really happy to, but we know that you'd be too proud to say yes, so I just wanted to tell you that it's done. We love you. We know things are tough, this is what best friends do.'

'But there's no way—'

'Hush. It's done. It's your turn to be looked after now, it might be mine next year, Amanda's after that. Give me a hug, you silly moose.'

Every part of Alice was cringing as this lovely, strange woman squashed her bosom against her. To talk so openly about not having money, to offer to pay for a trip because Edie obviously couldn't afford it, this was excruciatingly embarrassing, but somewhere, buried inside Alice's mortification, was the realisation of what true friendship was. It was this: pure and genuine non-judgement and support. Alice felt terrible that she and Edie didn't seem to have that sort of friendship anymore. The hug she'd just received stayed with her long after the woman let go of her and they went back to join the others.

'Edie! You choose the next one!'

Oh god, Alice's mind went blank; the only music she listened to had a part for the string section. *Think brain, think*. What did Edie used to belt out in their bedroom when they were teenagers? That was obviously the genre of the night . . . The one that made their floor shake and always had one parent or the other running upstairs yelling about the thin ceilings of old houses . . . '"Jump Around" by House of Pain!' she shouted triumphantly, her grin growing even wider when her suggestion was met with cheers and whoops.

As Alice jumped up and down, with three of her sister's best friends' arms around her, shouting the words of a song she remembered watching her fifteen-year-old twin lose her mind to, she couldn't remember ever being this happy.

CHAPTER FOURTEEN

The swap: day 4

Edie

They had to swap back as soon as possible. Today. Now. This very minute, no time to waste. Forget the bet. Edie was competitive by nature, but the idea of spending another hour in this sterile (admittedly it was getting less sterile by the day, Edie hadn't realised cat litter trays needed to be changed), toxic environment was making Edie's heart hurt. She wasn't a runner by any stretch of the imagination, but she would quite literally sprint the three miles home barefoot if it meant she could sleep in her own bed that night and cuddle Seb and her girls and promise never to take them for granted again. The trouble was, she'd just intimated as much to Alice on the phone, obviously not citing Alice's family as the reason for her incredible homesickness, but Alice was adamant that they needed to stay put, that the bet was still on; plus she felt not enough time had elapsed yet for them to get a full understanding of each other's lives, that another week, or two, perhaps even three, *three!* was warranted for a real sense and appreciation of the other's world. Edie was sorely tempted to do something so outrageous that there would be no doubt which sister she was just to be able to get her own life back, but she had to be sensible and remember how important winning this bet was. The money the programme paid was currently keeping them afloat; without it, they'd have to sell the house and Seb would have to give up on his dream. She couldn't let that happen; she couldn't be the one to lose.

Edie was absolutely sure that after an evening with Edie's friends, Alice would be up at the crack of dawn hammering on her own front door, desperate to decamp back to the land of homemade hummus – that was Ursula's offering last night – and impassioned debate about why on earth someone would go to the trouble of making their own scented candles when they could just pay seventy-five pounds for a half-decent one – that was Ruth's standout contribution to the evening. But no, it was very strange, Alice seemed absolutely gung-ho on continuing the swap. Had Edie's friends been uncharacteristically well-behaved? Wasn't Seb annoying her just a little bit by now? Surely the girls' inability to filter any of their thoughts or feelings before wailing them was wearing a little thin? Edie had been sure that it would be the other way around, that Alice would be down on her knees, fervently begging with clenched hands for her ordered life back.

Her phone vibrated next to her. Filled with hope that it was Alice doing a three-point turn and deciding that they could actually go back to normality today after all, with neither of them victors or losers, Edie was flooded with disappointment to read that it was a message from someone called James.

> *Really looking forward to seeing you this weekend*

Who the heck was James? Why would someone called James be messaging Alice? Why would he be looking forward to seeing her? This was very odd. Why had Alice never mentioned a James? Was she having an affair? No, Edie gave herself a mental slap in the face, this was not odd. Why couldn't two people message each other apropos of absolutely nothing? Why did she fall into society's trap of believing this evil myth that human beings are so tightly coiled at any one time, that messaging anyone of the gender they are attracted to would inevitably mean dark and sexy and sinister things. No. So her sister had a secret male friend, who was looking forward to seeing her tomorrow. Hoo-bloody-ray.

Except *she* was her sister. So, she was now going to have to reply, as Alice, to this James person. She thought about messaging Alice to see what she would want her to do, but she didn't want to chance it just in case Alice told her unequivocally not to, and she really wanted a little bit of fun in this very grey world that her sister inhabited.

> Hello! I'm looking forward to seeing you too.

Edie re-read her message after she sent it and winced. The punctation was all wrong. Rosie told her recently that there was a punctuation etiquette in texts that she was previously totally unaware of. Apparently ending your message with a full stop was not polite. It signalled to the other person that you were harbouring some pretty epic levels of anger. And exclamation marks just signalled that you were over forty. Did James fall into that age bracket too? If so, hopefully he would be totally on board with the exclamation marks, and totally in the dark about the connotations with full stops, although she noticed that he didn't use one himself, so maybe he was more

Gen Z than Gen X. Did Alice have a toy boy? With one tiny punctuation gaffe she might have just blown the only non-female friendship her sister had ever had.

A swift thumbs up from James on her message allayed her concerns. Phew. But where and when would she meet him? Should she meet him? How could she not? Thank goodness Alice hadn't wanted to swap back today; if they had, then Edie would be none the wiser as to her sister's secret life. But now that they were definitely not swapping back today, Edie had the whole day to fill. Well, no, that wasn't quite correct, she'd set aside half an hour to whizz round the house giving it a little spruce back up to Alice's standards. She noticed when she was running the bath for Emily last night that the family bathroom had four days' worth of three children's toothpaste and spit clinging on to the sides of the sink like molluscs on a rock, and while she didn't mean to look inside the toilet bowl, she did, and that was a priority to sort out too. Somehow the laundry basket was pretty full again, and the dish she'd used for the macaroni last night had been hardening on the side since last night, as no one thought to put it into soak while she was out, so that needed a good scrub. The carpets probably needed a vacuum too. Edie sighed, what she needed was a cleaner. And Alice could definitely afford it. As she had this idea she was certain she could actually hear a team of angels singing Halleluiah, such was the level of happiness and relief it gave Edie, who quickly set about googling local agencies to bring the house back up to par while everyone was out.

Alice

Alice had decided that what this family needed was some organised fun. She preferred just to call it fun, but recognised that others might differ. It was a Thursday which made it trickier, as everyone needed to be home in bed before it was late. She'd managed to coax Rosie upstairs at around ten last night, and after hiding her phone earlier in the evening on top of the fridge, her niece's lights were out by quarter past. That was still far too late by her own standards, but she planned to bring it forward by five minutes every night of her stay until she was happily retreating to her duvet at a decent time. She thought the cinema might be good. She'd asked Iris last night when was the last time they all went to the cinema together, and Iris couldn't remember when that had ever happened. There was a fairly new Pixar movie out, that had good reviews – from both adults and children – so she messaged Seb to see what he thought.

She had assumed he'd jump at the idea, so was a bit upset when he just replied with, *Nah, I don't think so.*

Rather than changing his mind over text she decided to call him.

'Won't it be fun?' she pressed.

'The cinema is really expensive.'

Alice couldn't tell him that she had a member's discount, so instead said that there was a promotion on. 'A family ticket is now only thirty pounds.' But even as she said it, Edie's friend's offer from the night before rang clear in her ears. Thirty pounds was a midweek manicure to her. Thirty pounds to Edie and Seb was a real treat, as proven by Seb's next words.

'Thirty pounds! I don't think we need to spend thirty quid on a weeknight. And then there's popcorn on top. We'll be easily spending forty, or even fifty. We can watch a film at home.'

'It can be my treat?' Alice said gingerly, knowing that these words would poke a big dent in Danny's masculine pride, but being fairly confident that it wouldn't with Seb.

'No, save your money for something important, like the next

electricity bill. But we could deck out the lounge like a cinema, I can make hot dogs and popcorn, we still have some of those red and white striped popcorn boxes from Iris's last birthday party, and we'll all bring our duvets down and snuggle.'

Alice had to admit that actually did sound much better than schlepping over to the industrial park on the edge of town where the cinema was and handing over a wad of cash to sit in a room with other people. But how could she avoid snuggling with Seb? The cold sore plaster had definitely done the trick as far as warding off any true intimacy, but cuddles? She'd have to make sure she was sitting next to one of the girls instead.

Edie

Edie video-called Alice. They hadn't pre-arranged this, but she just needed to see her family, and she also needed Alice to see how clean and tidy she was keeping her house.

'Hi *Alice*,' Alice said loudly into the screen, panning her phone round so Edie could see everyone. Iris was staring at the microwave waiting for the gap between the pops to reach three seconds, Seb was at the grill turning some sausages over, Rosie was pouring out drinks.

'Hey everyone! Come and say hello to your Auntie Alice!' Edie shouted through the screen, feeling her eyes threaten to spill over with the tears that suddenly sprang up out of nowhere on seeing her family, her kids, her partner, her kitchen, her home.

Iris was the first to bound over. 'Hi Auntie Alice,' she waved.

Was it possible that she had grown in four days?

'We're having a cinema night at home. I'm making popcorn.'

'That sounds wonderful.' Edie blinked to stop her eyes watering. 'I wish I was there. Hey Rosie!'

Rosie gave Edie a wave from across the kitchen; she looked

happy enough. Edie tried to will her nearer the camera so she could chat to her properly but knew Rosie would never think of having a long, extended chat with her aunt, so it didn't work and Rosie stayed where she was.

'What's Seb making?'

'Hot dogs.'

'Oh that is really yummy, hi Seb!'

Seb raised his spatula in a jaunty reply and waved it in the air. 'Hey Alice, sorry I'm at a rather crucial part of the grilling process!'

'Oh no worries, I was just calling to say hello to Edie, and to see what time we're meeting at the studio tomorrow?'

'Eight thirty? Like we always do?'

'Oh yes, sure. Okay, that's perfect.'

'Everything okay at yours?' Alice asked pointedly, widening her eyes a little at the screen in secret code.

'Yes, yes, absolutely, everything is great. Teddy and Rufus are at training, and Emily is being dropped back here after ballet.'

'Is Danny at the gym?'

'Yep.'

'Is Dad remembering to do his blood pressure every morning?'

Edie hesitated; in all honesty, she had completely forgotten her dad lived three doors down. She hadn't popped round there once since the swap. She really hoped Alice wasn't responsible for his meals, or this switch could now take a very dark and sinister turn. 'All is good.' She added after a short pause, 'Not as fun as your house though, wow. It looks like you're going to have a great night. Enjoy everyone!'

Her family all raised their arms in a wave back to her, then went straight back to their tasks. The last sound Edie heard before the screen went black was Seb's laugh. God, she missed that laugh.

Less than a minute and a half later, and still wearing her house moccasins without a single thought to the grime and dog urine on the pavement, she hammered on the front door of her dad's maisonette, while offering up all sorts of promises to the universe to be a vastly improved version of herself if Kenneth answered the door, fit and fed.

It took him a while, adding fuel to all of Edie's worst fears, but when he did, Edie immediately saw the reason for the delay as he was in a pair of black satin boxers, and a silk sort of kimono with a red lining, open at the chest showcasing an impressive meadow of curled grey chest hair.

'Dad?'

'Alice!' he said in surprise, pulling both sides of his kimono together. 'I wasn't expecting you!'

'Clearly. Is this just your Thursday outfit, or have I interrupted something special going on?' Edie winked.

He looked quickly behind him, then back to Edie. 'You normally message first.'

'I hadn't seen you in a while, just checking everything's okay. And everything is clearly, okay. So good.' She took a backwards step towards the gate. 'I'll leave you be.' And another one, accompanied by a strange little Japanese bow for some reason. 'As you were.'

It was fine. More than fine. It was really, *really* fine. Mum had been gardening up in heaven for almost four years, there was no earthly reason why he should not be enjoying a little bit of company on a Thursday evening.

'Alice, let me explain.'

Edie held her hand up to stem his embarrassment, realising as she did so, that she needed to act Alice-like. Alice would find this abhorrent. Alice would cry; actually no she wouldn't. She would be tight-lipped, and polite, and courteous, and then cry at home. None of those reactions would make this any easier on her dad, who was looking like he wanted the ground to swallow him up. There was a reason that this situation happened when Edie was Alice. She could change the narrative right now. She could make this okay for him.

'I'm really pleased you're finding a bit of happiness, Dad, after such a shit time. And for the record, you are rocking that kimono.'

Kenneth stared at his daughter for a beat too long. The lines on his forehead furrowed deeper as he said, 'Edie? Why are you dressed like Alice?'

CHAPTER FIFTEEN

Edie

Edie blinked at him. And blinked again. As much as she tried through the unproven power of telekinesis, the last few seconds just would not erase themselves.

She started to back up further towards the front gate. 'You seem busy, I'll pop round again. Obviously I'll call first next time.'

'Edie wait!'

Edie paused, one hand on the gate, already wincing in anticipation of the next thing to come out of his mouth.

'Where's Alice?' he asked.

'I'm Alice,' she croaked.

'No you're not.'

She could keep up the charade, laugh and gaslight him into believing he'd made a mistake, or she could come clean, tell him the truth, and blow their cover. It had to be the latter. 'Okay fine. You got me. She's uh, back at her house, we were just having dinner together, and we wanted to see if we could still trick you, like the old days. But well done.' She wiggled her finger at her dad. 'You're a canny old fox.'

'Go and get her,' he said, obviously eager to see his estranged daughters together.

'Don't you think you should get dressed first?'

'Good point. Give me five minutes, then bring her round.'

'We don't want to spoil your fun though.'

'You're not, Maggie's been here all afternoon, I'm ready for a break.'

'Too much information Dad,' Edie muttered as she walked the thirty yards back to Alice's front door. Once safely inside, she bolted up the stairs, taking them two at a time, pulling off her top as she went, swapping it for a silk blouse with a big bow on it, and exchanging her high-waist jeans for beige cigarette pants. Both outfits were from Alice's wardrobe, but if Alice ever metamorphosed into clothes-form, the second outfit would be her. She then did a little flick of eyeliner, and a slick of barely-there pink lip gloss. For good measure, she also spritzed herself in Alice's Yves Saint Laurent perfume.

Exactly five minutes later, Edie knocked on the door again, this time using a different, much more sedate tap, tap, rather than her previous frantic hammering.

Kenneth opened the door, and Edie beamed at him, channelling every ounce of her sister. 'Hello Dad, Edie said you wanted to see me?'

Kenneth squinted his eyes at her in suspicion. 'Where's Edie now?'

'Seb called, she's just talking to him and she'll be right round.' Her dad's hanging basket caught Edie's eye, and she had an idea of how to be more Alice. 'Oh Dad, your azaleas are looking really sad, they shouldn't really be in direct sunlight. I've got a spare pot, they'd be perfect under your pergola, I'll repot them for you tomorrow.'

Just then a woman-shaped shadow passed behind Kenneth.

Still very much in character, Edie slanted her eyes, 'Dad, have you got company?'

His face flushed pinker. 'Well, I . . . didn't Edie say?'

'She didn't say anything. Who is it?' Edie craned her neck as if to get a better look, 'Is it Auntie Barbara?'

'I thought your sister might have told you?'

'Told me what? Dad, you're really starting to worry me, what is it? Is it a carer?' That was a bit below the belt, but it just slipped out.

'I have a new friend,' Kenneth coughed, 'who is a lady.'

'A girlfriend?' Edie tried to mould her face into a mask of surprise, laced with her sister's trademark almost imperceptible tinge of disappointment. 'So soon?'

'It's been nearly four years Ally,' he said quietly, almost pleadingly.

The use of her dad's pet name for her sister, combined with his childlike earnestness almost made Edie break character completely and wrap him in a big bear hug, but instead, she took a deep breath, tucked her hair behind her ear, the way that Alice often did, and said, 'Well I hate to think of you lonely, so if she makes you happy, then I guess that's all there is to it. Can I meet her?'

'Why don't you run back and get Edie and you can both come in and say hello?'

'Oh no, Edie looked pretty tied up with one of her clients.'

'I thought you said she was talking to Seb?'

'Yes. Yes. Seb was talking her through some work things.' Edie silently groaned, she was so bad at this.

'I see. Well, I think it would be better for Maggie to meet you both at the same time.'

Edie nodded. Phew, she had totally got away with that one. 'That's probably for the best. Right, I better go and start dinner for the troops.'

'Give Alice my love.'

Edie gave him a little wave, 'Will do Dad, cheerio.' She'd only walked two steps to the gate before his words halted her in her tracks and she closed her eyes. *Dammit. Dammit. Dammit.*

She turned around slowly. 'Was it the Seb/work thing? It was, wasn't it? Or was it something else, do I not sound like her? What was it?'

Kenneth smiled. 'It was the being your dad for forty-six years thing.' He motioned back into the house with his thumb. 'Have you got time for a cup of tea in the garden? I've still got a patch of sunshine up by the shed.'

Edie checked her watch; she had a forty-five-minute window before the kids were home, and it was anyone's guess when Danny might walk through the door, he appeared to have his own schedule. She had been so incredibly lonely the last few days, and after seeing her own family all busy and having fun, even just the suggestion of company and the prospect of having a two-way conversation made a lump form in her throat.

After Maggie had quietly excused herself, giving Kenneth's hand a little squeeze as she left, which made Edie feel an emotion she couldn't quite identify, father and daughter sat alongside each other on a wooden bench, their faces upturned to the last of the day's rays. Edie was the first to speak. 'We've got a bet going. To see who lasts the longest in each other's shoes without getting found out. Kind of based on what you suggested the other week on the bench.'

'I suggested it so you could appreciate each other more. Not so one of you could win and forever torment the loser.'

'I'm the only one being tormented,' Edie muttered.

'What do you mean?'

Edie shook her head, trying to dispel the tears that hovered on the brink once again. Why did she always feel like crying at the moment? She never normally cried in her ordinary life.

'I think Alice is having a better time than me. Well, no, I don't think, I know.'

Kenneth took a second to digest what she said, then quietly asked, 'And why is that?'

'I don't know,' Edie said sadly, before countering that with, 'Actually, I do know. Because my family are more fun, and warm, and she's just slotted into my life. Actually, no, she's a being a better version of me. I video-called them just now, and they're all cooking together, before having a giant movie night, and I know that if I was there, I wouldn't be joining in, I'd be on my laptop or my phone trying to work, and then I'd be seething because Seb was making too much noise with them. And I'm over here, grilling Danny's salmon for his lunchbox, without a single grunt of appreciation in return, and her kids have so many activities I barely see them, and I'm lonely. Really lonely. This is the longest I've spoken out loud for in four days. Actually no, I tell a lie, I've had three Zooms with clients each day, where they just unload all their problems onto me, but no one has asked me how I am, or how I'm feeling. I'm just absolutely invisible, and it's really, *really* shit.'

He nodded, not seeming that surprised. But then, maybe he wasn't surprised. He lived three doors down, he saw Alice's family a lot more than she did; maybe this was why he planted the idea of the switch in the first place, so that Edie could see what he already knew. 'That does sound tough.'

'And it's no wonder Alice has thrown herself into making her house perfect, and getting all these followers on Instagram who think she's great, and send her hearts and tell her how amazing she is because she honestly is invisible in her own family. Apart from Emily, who is just delicious. And actually, I think Rufus could be brought back from the brink too, with a little bit of effort, but Danny and Teddy just completely ignore her... me... most of the time... oh I don't know.'

Kenneth stretched out his legs. 'Sounds like you've got a challenge on your hands.'

'*She* has, you mean. I'm literally here on the world's crappiest all-inclusive, soon to go back to my nice, normal life. It's going to be her problem again very soon.'

'How long was the swap for?'

'To be decided. We left it open-ended, but I've already had enough. But I can't afford to lose the bet.'

'What's at stake? Apart from the obvious?'

Edie looked confused. 'Obvious?' Kenneth was quiet. He'd always been quiet. A lifetime spent among three pretty fierce women had made a man who preferred deeds to words even more introspective. Edie studied his face, but it was hard to predict what he was going to say next.

'Dad, say something.'

'Whatever the *prize* is at the end is neither here nor there, is it? Your mum never put a monetary value on the switches that she made you do, that's not the point. I think you've just got to remember why you're doing this. And I'm not talking about a silly bet. Anyone can spend a couple of days walking in someone else's shoes, realise they're not as comfortable as their own and swap back with nothing changed. Or you can slow down a bit, look at what's going on, really try and see things differently, and come out the other side with a new perspective.'

God, he was a wise old owl. 'How do I do that?'

He shrugged, the answer apparently obvious to him. 'Stop looking at Alice's life through your eyes, and see it through hers, and see what you might be able to change, so that when you switch back, the things that made her life hard before, might be a little easier.'

'Short of giving her husband an intensive course in third-wave feminism followed by electric shock treatment just for the hell of it, I'm not sure it can be made better.'

He smiled at the imagery. 'And you don't think anyone's noticed you've switched?'

'No, you're the first. And don't ask me how that's possible, I notice when Seb's cut his toenails – how the two of us can slip so under the radar no one sees that we're completely different people is mad.'

'I'm surprised Seb hasn't clocked it, he's normally quite perceptive.'

Edie shook her head. 'He's been quite preoccupied lately. I don't think the business is going too well, but you know him, he's always so optimistic that things will pick up, he'd never admit to anything being wrong, so he just compensates by being even more annoyingly cheerful. Something no one can accuse Danny of.'

'He's not all bad, you know. He helped me get a pigeon out of the kitchen a while back. He put a towel over it, like this,' he mimed putting something over something else, 'carried it, cool as you like, to the back door, and vroom!' He flung his hands up in the air to mimic setting something free.

Edie stayed quiet. He wasn't all bad, she just had a different list of priorities to her sister, that was all. The irony was, she had been the one to bring Danny into the family. It was the end of season party for the rugby team, and Edie's boyfriend at the time had been the team's physiotherapist and he had brought both sisters along because Edie had insisted on it. All of Alice's attempts at finding a life-partner using her own wiles had failed, some catastrophically so, and Edie reasoned that if her sister couldn't find a mate amid a twenty-five-strong squad of largely single rugby players then she ought to get her nun's habit fitted STAT. Danny and Alice's mutual appreciation of what the other could offer as a life partner was pretty instant: Danny the strong protector provider who would keep her and their future family safe, Alice the pretty homemaker who thought everything he did was spectacular. It was a win-win by anyone's matrix. By the time the party had ended that night, numbers were swapped, along with some saliva from some enthusiastic snogging, and the rest was history.

In the eighteen years they'd been together, Alice had never given a single indication she'd regretted her choice, but then she wouldn't, would she? Despite living in an age where it was almost rarer not to be divorced, Alice had cultivated a lifestyle much more suited to sixty years earlier. That didn't make it wrong, it just made it difficult for Edie to understand, and now, live in for a week.

Kenneth broke Edie's jaunt down memory lane by patting her hand. 'You better get going if you want to beat the kids back.'

Edie kissed his cheek before she rose. 'Thanks for the chat.'

'You're welcome. I'm here any time.'

'You won't say anything, will you?'

Kenneth mimed zipping up his lips. 'Dad's the word. Oh, one more thing, do my azaleas really need repotting?'

'I have absolutely no idea.' Edie shrugged. 'Ask Alice.'

CHAPTER SIXTEEN

The swap: day 5

Edie

For the first time since they both started on the show, Edie arrived at the studio before Alice. While 'enjoyment' might be too strong a description for how she'd begun to feel about her six am start, it was astonishing how much more you could cram into your day if you got up two or three hours earlier, and had a whiteboard organisational chart stuck to your fridge cataloguing a minute-by-minute checklist of your day. Who knew? So not only had all the lunches been made (achieving a personal best this morning at an impressive nine minutes from when her knife first hit the margarine to clicking the plastic lids down on the four lunchboxes), dinner was also marinating in the fridge and the kids were even dropped off at the school gates with a few minutes to spare. She had also spent a good fifteen minutes carefully tweezering a little line in her right eyebrow to replicate Alice's scar. She hadn't thought to do that before now, thinking that no one would be close enough to her face to notice, but for half an hour this morning the make-up artist would be peering into her pores, so that necessitated a little pruning. Kenneth rumbling the switch had made Edie uber anxious about anyone else spotting their deceit, and now that Edie was here in the studio she felt more determined than ever to put on the performance of a lifetime to win the bet.

'Hey, you're already here!'

Before sitting in the make-up chair next to her, Alice gave Edie a kiss on the cheek, which Edie felt was a little odd. As was her use of the word 'hey'. She was wearing Edie's favourite skirt, a long, floaty yellow satin number embroidered with tiny little beads in the centre of the flowers that Edie had bought in Valencia. She only wore it on birthdays and special occasions, as it was dry-clean only and that was an extravagance she couldn't justify. She didn't know why Alice thought it was the obvious choice for a normal Friday. Except this wasn't a normal Friday. Her hands were never this clammy, and her heart only ever went at this speed when aided by too many double espressos.

'Everything okay?' Alice asked, obviously sensing her discomfort.

'Yes, absolutely.' Edie replied, staring straight ahead at a reflection that wasn't her. 'Why wouldn't it be?'

'We can do this . . . Alice.'

'I know. It'll be fine.'

The floor manager appeared at the door, holding the clipboard that Edie assumed he probably slept with, and looked at the twins in the mirror, 'Morning Alice, Edie. All set?'

'Absolutely,' Alice beamed back. Was Edie imagining it, or was she fluttering her eyelashes more than usual?

'It's a great show today,' he said, continuing to look at Edie in the mirror as she was getting her hair backcombed into Alice's signature Stepford style. The attention was a little uncomfortable if Edie was honest.

'Looking forward to it,' Alice said, maintaining her smile until he left. 'You were so rude!' she said, rounding on Edie once the door shut behind him.

'I was not! I didn't even say anything!' Why would Alice care so much how she interacted with the floor manager?

'Exactly! He probably thinks you don't like him now.'

'I neither like nor dislike him; my only dealings with him are him counting us in and then shouting "cut". To be fair, that's not a great foundation for a friendship.'

'He's actually really nice when you get to know him.'

'When have you got to know him?'

Alice shifted uneasily in her chair, very aware suddenly of the presence of Petra, the make-up artist, who had slowed her hand movements down considerably in order to listen in. 'I just mean, it doesn't hurt to be courteous to everyone.'

'I *was* courteous. I gave him a wave when he walked in. What did you want me to do, flash my boobs at him and invite him to have a squeeze?'

Petra gave a little snort, while Alice tutted loudly and muttered something about going to get a cup of tea.

'I thought Edie was the funny one,' Petra said once Alice was out of earshot, 'but that was hilarious.'

Alice

Gareth's eyes were a little bloodshot. There was a photo doing the rounds on the morning's red tops of him falling out of a taxi outside a club last night, with someone who wasn't his wife helping him up from the pavement. He had made no reference to this so far on the show, and everyone around him was also keeping up the charade of having no idea as to how he evidently spent his downtime, but Alice could smell the booze emanating from his every pore from across the sofa and it was making her feel quite nauseous. To be fair, it could have been the smell of stale alcohol or it could be motion sickness from Edie's incessant jigging of her leg next to her. They were both nervous, she knew. Neither of them wanted to lose the bet by humiliating themselves in front of millions of people. She took a deep breath and prepared to put on a show.

'Good morning, and welcome back. Before the break we asked you to call or message in with your questions for our resident agony aunts, Alice and Edie. Ladies, welcome.'

Edie reached for her water glass, and Alice could see her sister's hands trembling. What was up with her?

Edie's lines were next on the autocue, which Alice read with a faultless smile. 'We have a question here from Susie in Stroud, she says, "We're doing a house swap this summer with a family we've never met from Belgium, and I want to make the house as nice and welcoming as possible for them. What suggestions do you have? Alice, I'm guessing you're the lady for this question!"' As she handed the imaginary baton over to Edie, Alice instinctively held her breath. This was crunch time, the moment when their switch could get completely rumbled.

Edie's eyes widened as she realised that she was indeed Alice. 'Well, that is an interesting one. First of all, I would suggest hiding all your alcohol because the first thing I would do having a free run of someone else's house for the summer is drink their best booze.'

Alice nudged Edie in her thigh.

'Not that I actually drink that much. Edie, you're the lush of the family, aren't you?'

Alice laughed an unnaturally shrill giggle. 'Guilty as charged!'

'You could maybe write them a list of places to go nearby,

your favourite restaurants, independent shops, places like that,' Edie tailed off, clearly running out of ideas.

'Also,' Alice said, butting in, 'I would set out some house rules to make sure your house gets returned to you the way you left it – no shoes inside, no pets on the sofas, no smoking inside, no—'

'Fun at all,' Edie interrupted with a shake of her head. 'Jeez Edie, it's a holiday not a boot camp. I'm supposed to be the sensible one, and even I am finding that overkill.'

'You're right.' Alice pulled a funny face as if to say, *what was I thinking?* 'Just one final thing – just check with your home insurance provider that your building and contents aren't affected by this swap, or you could get a nasty shock if you have to claim.'

'You are coming out with some great advice this morning, *Edie*,' Edie said.

'And the next one is from Greta in Harrogate,' Lauren said, looking down at her notes. 'Now this is a tricky one, probably one for you Edie as a relationship therapist.'

Alice could feel Edie squirming at the same time as she did, for different reasons.

'Greta sent us a voice-note saying that her husband has started to go to the gym most evenings, so is spending a lot less time with their family, and is very distant, and actually quite rude when he is at home, and she wants to know if this might be a sign that he is having an affair? Edie, what do you think?'

Alice took an audible deep breath, while Edie held hers.

'Firstly Greta,' Alice said, looking directly at the camera, 'well done for reaching out, and obviously this has got quite bad if you felt you needed advice on it, so thank you for being brave enough to message in. I think the first thing is to find out from your husband why his behaviour is changing – why is he exercising more? Is it a new thing? Is it just a desire to get fitter? Or is it an excuse to be out of the house? If it is just wanting to be on a new, healthier regime, then ask if you can join him to bring you closer together and have a shared hobby; there are some great deals about for couples' membership. If he still remains quite secretive about it all, then you should talk to him about your suspicions.'

Alice could tell that Edie was impressed because out of the corner of her eye she could see her sister nodding along. Reading Edie's self-help books each night before bed was clearly paying off.

Edie

'And finally,' Gareth said after trying, and failing, to stifle a yawn, 'we have a query just in from Colin, who is forty-two from Northern Ireland. He writes, "After being single for most of my adult life, I have just moved out of my mum's house and in with my new girlfriend who I met online dating. Everything is going well, but she is an absolutely awful cook. How can I tell her this without hurting her feelings?"'

Alice jumped in, clearly forgetting who she was meant to be. 'Why don't you buy her some recipe books Colin, nothing fancy, just some easy basic dishes that even a complete novice could do—'

'Or, Colin.' Edie gave her sister a death stare, before looking down the lens of the lit-up camera. 'Why don't *you* learn to cook?'

'There are some great cooking classes you could book her onto as well?' Alice suggested.

'Or take one yourself without telling her and then surprise her with a gourmet meal,' Edie added.

'Do you cook, Gareth?' Lauren asked conversationally.

'Not if I can help it.'

'*My* partner is a great cook, actually,' Alice said, and it took a second or two for Edie to join the dots and realise that she was back in character as Edie and talking about *her* partner.

'I don't know why cooking has been seen as a female pursuit for so long, when everyone needs to eat, it's bizarre,' Edie interjected, confident that this was still vaguely in the arena of being Alice-like, while not being uncomfortably at odds with her own ideology. But why was she feeling so rankled at Alice calling Seb *hers*? Before she could properly engage her brain, she heard her voice saying, '*My* son, Rufus, is a great cook; he made a fantastic macaroni cheese a couple of nights ago, and a moussaka last night, and I'm really proud of him for it.' The second Edie said it, her blood ran cold. She shouldn't have mentioned it on air, he wasn't her son, it wasn't her secret to tell. She'd promised him. How could she have been so thoughtless?

At least he was at school so wouldn't have heard it, and she was pretty certain that Danny didn't tune in to morning television when he was doing his terribly important job that she wouldn't understand. But what if one of Rufus's friends was off school sick and saw this segment? She'd completely broken his trust, all in the name of one-upmanship.

'All this talk about food is making me very hungry.' Lauren smiled straight into camera three. 'Which is very handy as after the break we have Mario cooking up an Italian storm using pigs' cheeks. Yum.'

The floor manager counted to three silently on his fingers then shouted, 'And cut.'

'Since when does Rufus cook?' Alice whispered as they were having their microphones disconnected.

'Since he told me he really likes it.'

'Does Danny know?'

Edie shook her head. 'Rufus didn't want him to know. Why would he care though?'

Alice closed her eyes to steady herself. 'He's got funny ideas about what girls and boys should do. Oh god, he's going to give Rufus such a hard time.'

Edie felt so bad, and seeing how agitated Alice was getting was only adding to her guilt. 'How will he know? He's at work.'

'His mum and dad watch this; they'll be calling Danny right now. We need to do some serious damage limitation.'

Alice's use of the pronoun 'we' wasn't lost on Edie; only a week ago she would have bowled in to make everything right by herself, so surely this was some progress? Edie still didn't quite understand the root of Danny's prejudice though, even after five days living as his wife. It was the twenty-first century after all, and they were talking about a boy enjoying cooking. It was hardly revolutionary; most of the world's top chefs are men. 'Seriously though, what can he possibly be angry about? So what, his son wants to do a food tech GCSE?'

Alice's head snapped towards Edie on hearing this new information. 'He wants to do what?'

Edie forgot that she'd left that part out. 'He told me a couple of nights ago, he's really keen to learn everything, and he's a real natural.'

'And you cooked with him?'

'Yes, it was really fun; we pretended we were doing a cooking show and we had a real laugh.'

Alice's eyes were narrowed in disbelief. 'With Rufus?'

'Yes. With Rufus. Why is this such a big deal, I don't understand?'

'When Teddy was really young I bought him a little toy kitchen to put in the corner of my kitchen because he loved the one at playgroup, and Danny went absolutely ballistic and threw it in next door's skip.'

'And I'm guessing you didn't immediately march over there, take it out, tell him it was staying, and he needed to take his head out of the last century.'

Alice at least had the decency to look sheepish as she slowly shook her head.

Edie put her hands on her hips. 'Well that's what I'll be telling him tonight if he says anything about Rufus.'

The sound engineer walked away, leaving the sisters alone in the shadows at the side of the studio floor.

'Edie please, it's not worth the hassle. Danny's really old-fashioned with things like this, you won't be able to change his mind.'

'But what about Rufus?' Edie pressed, the image of a frightened Rufus desperately untying his apron and hiding it before his dad walked in was breaking her heart. 'He'll think that I, you, don't care about his point of view. He'll feel really let down.'

'Then let Rufus carry on cooking whenever Danny's not there.'

'The world won't stop turning if you stand up to him, you know.'

Alice sighed dejectedly. 'I know that, but it's just so much easier this way. Trust me.'

'Can I please do this my way?' Edie asked, not that she needed her permission, but it was her sister's family she was talking about, and Alice knew them better than anyone. 'I'm willing to risk the fallout. And if we are going to keep up the swap for a bit longer, then it's me that needs to live with him during that time, so it'll be me that bears the brunt of it anyway. By the time we switch back, it will all have blown over.' Edie could tell Alice was considering what she had said.

Alice

Edie wasn't wrong, Alice stood to get all of the gain, for none of the pain. Not that Danny had ever been violent, not to her anyway, but Alice had plastered over enough holes in walls, and bathed enough bruised knuckles to know that Danny's frustration flooded out through his fists. He wouldn't ever hit the kids though, just men his own size who looked at him funny, or walls that sneered mockingly at him, that sort of thing. Keeping his temper calm and even was a permanent fixture on the to-do list she kept in her brain and not on the fridge for all to see.

Should she let Edie play this out her way?

'Fine. But please tread really lightly. Don't mention anything before he does, then when he does, just keep apologising.'

'What have I got to say sorry for?'

'For not telling him.'

'Do you normally tell him everything?'

Of course she did. 'Of course I do.'

'Everything?' Edie raised one eyebrow and, even in the dim lighting behind the big cameras and next to the black painted wall, Alice knew Edie could see her cheeks were turning a deeper hue.

'What do you mean?'

'James messaged yesterday.'

'Oh?' *Keep calm,* Alice told herself, *this means nothing.* She had nothing to hide, but oh god, why was she blushing so much?

'Don't "oh" me, Alice, when were you going to tell me?'

'Tell you what?' *Nothing to hide at all.*

'About you and James.'

'There is no me and James!' Alice hissed, looking over Edie's shoulder to check no one was eavesdropping.

'So why is he messaging you saying that he's looking forward to seeing you today?' An annoying smile was playing on Edie's lips.

'It's a silly little flirtation, doesn't mean a thing.'

'Have you met up before?'

'Not intentionally.'

'What does that mean? You just found yourself checking into the same hotel room by accident that one time?'

'No! Oh my god, Edie, is that what you think of me? No! His daughter is in the same gymnastics class as Emily, and since his divorce, he always has Zara on a Saturday, so we've started having coffee together at a café down the road while they're in there. That is all. Just two people, vaguely related through their children's sports, sharing a coffee.'

'Don't you think I should have known about this? After all, I am going to be you tomorrow, taking Emily to this class. Don't you think I would have found it a bit forward when I bump into him, and he pats the seat next to him, and on the table is a giant cappuccino with two straws?'

'I've arranged for another mum to take Emily tomorrow and pick her up.'

'Why?' Was it just her or did Edie look a bit disappointed?

'I thought it would be easier. Rufus and Teddy also have a football match, so you can go and watch that instead.'

Edie stuck her bottom lip out pouting, and said in a baby voice, 'I'd rather have a date with James.'

'It's not a date!' Alice's exclamation made a few people standing in a cluster at the other side of the studio floor turn round to look, and she hurriedly lowered her voice and repeated, 'It's not a date.'

'Is he nice?'

Alice didn't know why she paused to consider the question because the unequivocal answer was yes, he was very nice. Very nice indeed. 'He's got a great sense of humour.'

'Well, that would be wasted on you. You've never laughed at my jokes in forty-six years.'

'His are funnier.'

Edie put her hand over heart to act wounded. 'Ouch. Look, I get that you don't want me to go, but Saturday mornings are really quiet at mine, the girls and Seb will sleep until lunchtime, why don't you get dressed up as you, meet him, and be back before you're missed?'

'You're making this sound a lot more clandestine than it actually is.'

Edie raised one eyebrow. 'Am I? Have you told Danny how you spend your Saturday mornings?' There was no need for Alice to answer that as they both knew she hadn't.

One of the camera operators turned around and put a finger to her lips as the countdown to going live was starting. The sisters slipped through a side door to the corridor beyond the studio to carry on their conversation.

'Why are you pushing me into this?' Alice whispered.

'I'm not pushing you into this.'

'You are. You're basically facilitating an affair.'

'I thought it was just coffee?' Edie asked innocently.

'It *is* just coffee. But that's how these things start, isn't it?'

'Is it? You tell me?'

'You're a counsellor, you know. If I was a client, and I told you this, your advice would be to think very carefully about striking up a friendship with another man outside of my marriage, and you would advise against it.'

Edie muttered, 'Not if I'd met your husband.'

'What's that supposed to mean?'

Edie held out her hand and counted an adjective off on each finger. 'Danny is rude, boorish, selfish and totally doesn't deserve you. And before you get all defensive and say how he just works really hard, and is tired, and has so much pressure, and yadda yadda yadda, I just want you to think about how much effort you put in for the family and the marriage, and how much he does. I honestly thought that being you for a week or a month or whatever, would let me see what you see in him, that I'd witness the redeeming qualities he keeps under wraps, but honestly Alice, I can't see any at all. And Teddy's learning from him every day what a husband looks like.'

Alice's instinct was to do exactly what Edie predicted, and immediately leap to her husband's defence, listing the many, many, times he had done something sweet or kind or thoughtful. But as she stood there, waiting for the catalogue of good deeds to appear in her brain, she realised that the only ones she could think of were the expensive gifts he bought her, that didn't reflect her or her tastes at all. She felt so guilty for even thinking it, but the watches, the bags, the vouchers, none of them came with much thought, just the quick transaction of a credit card handed over and whatever the salesperson recommended. Even the gestures that seemed thoughtful at the time . . . Like that time she broke her leg skiing and was in a cast for eight weeks, he'd bought a bar stool the perfect height for the worktop and hob so she didn't need to stand when making dinner. Her friends all thought that was really kind when she told them. She guessed that Edie would have a slightly different take on it. And to be honest, she was starting to as well. After all, Seb would have taken over each and every household task without fanfare or agenda, and if he was the benchmark of what a good partner acted like, then of course Danny would come up short, most people would. It wasn't that Danny was awful, it was just that Seb was so attentive and involved it had skewed her sister's viewpoint as to what 'normal' was.

It actually made her feel really sad that Edie wasn't standing opposite her, five days into the switch, telling her how lucky she was, what a great set-up Alice had, how much she was enjoying the swap. No one wanted to be told that their family had flaws, however much you were aware of all of them. And the irony was, going into this, Alice had honestly believed that *she* was going to have the rougher side of the swap.

The door to the studio opened and the floor manager walked through talking to a runner. He stopped when he saw the sisters, and smiled.

'Hey, I thought you'd left?'

'Hi James, we're going now,' Alice said, 'just catching up with each other.'

'James!' Edie shouted, the penny obviously dropping. Alice elbowed her back into character. Edie made a face of apology. 'Sorry, I'm just really pleased to see you.'

'Um, I just wondered if Emily is going to gymnastics tomorrow?' There was an unmistakeable layer of hopefulness in his voice.

He was looking down at his clipboard as he asked this, which was possibly the reason Alice completely forgot she wasn't the one he was addressing this to and replied, 'Yes, but I've asked Freya's mum to take her, I'm busy tomorrow.'

His eyes shot upwards, puzzled at why Edie was apparently answering for her sister.

'Sorry, that was confusing,' Edie jumped in, as Alice. 'I had asked Edie to take Emily tomorrow to gymnastics as I have a gynaecology appointment I can't miss, but then it turned out that she can't do it, so Edie asked Freya's mum to take her.'

'Ah okay,' James said. Alice thought he looked like a kid who'd been promised an ice cream all week that then never materialised come the weekend. 'I hope everything's okay with the appointment,' he added kindly.

'It'll be fine,' Edie replied. 'To be honest, I quite enjoy the lie-down.'

'Right,' Alice said quickly before Edie could say anything else, 'we should probably be off. Lovely to see you James, same time, next week?' She bundled Edie off down the corridor, hissing through her teeth 'Gynaecology? Could you not have chosen a specialty that did not involve my private parts? You could have said manicure for Christ's sake.'

'I panicked, and we were just talking about starting an affair and so vaginas was the first thing I thought of!'

If Edie had been dressed as Edie, Alice might not have found this so amusing, but seeing her sister standing there, her hair still backcombed in Alice's signature style, her cropped khaki slimline cigarette trousers on, even wearing Alice's diamond solitaire engagement ring and heavy diamond watch, she couldn't help but stifle a smile. But what on earth must James think of her after that bizarre exchange?

'I think you should meet him,' Edie said as she opened the door to the car park, and held it for Alice to walk through too.

'Stop it. Just stop it. You are making this into something far bigger than it actually is. If our floor manager was a woman called Brenda you would not be this pushy.'

'If I thought that Brenda could make you happier than Danny could, then yes I would.'

Alice held her hand up like a policeman standing next to broken traffic lights. 'Enough. I am happily married, end of. I don't need you meddling in things that should not be meddled in. Understand? Edie. Do you understand?'

Edie nodded like a scolded child who had no intention of heeding the instruction.

'Now,' Alice said, changing the subject entirely, 'let's talk about this weekend. Obviously we've got Dad's party tomorrow night, the restaurant's booked for seven, we can swap clothes straight away and stay as ourselves the whole evening, then see how we feel about swapping back at the end, or maybe meet somewhere on Sunday and swap back then. But what do you normally do on Saturday mornings? I've looked in your notes, but there's not a lot to go on. What happens?' Alice asked.

Edie shrugged. 'Not much really. Everyone will lie in, I normally take my laptop up to bed so I'll do whatever I'm working on from bed while Seb sleeps, the girls will surface around lunchtime, then they'll lie on the sofas all afternoon. Seb might cook something, we might take Scooby out for a walk together in the park. Then Sunday morning is normally "couple" time if you get my meaning, but pop your cold sore plaster on, and you'll be fine.'

Alice shifted her weight from one foot to the other, uncomfortable even bringing this up, but it was important. 'I think Seb's missing that *side of things*, to be honest.'

'Has he said something?'

'No, I'm just getting the impression that he's waiting for me to make the first move and then he'd be all over me.'

'That's just his natural state of being. We're a very tactile couple. Sexual intimacy is very important in a long-term relationship, isn't it?'

Alice just nodded. An episode of uncomfortable hand-holding on a family holiday in Tuscany aside, she and Danny had never felt the need to be affectionate outside of the bedroom. And these days, not even in it. They were the only couple in the hotel pool on their honeymoon in Mauritius not to have various limbs wrapped around each other as they lay on sun-loungers, or the only bride not to climb on her new husband's back in the pool as they waded through the water. There was one couple in particular, who were obviously on the same package they were, as they checked in and out of the hotel at the same time as them and shared the airport shuttle and plane with them too, and those honeymooners' lips were stuck to the other one's all week, as if an experiment involving superglue had gone tragically wrong. A hand in a partner's back pocket, an arm wrapped around a waist, a head on a shoulder; it all seemed very unnecessary.

'I might pop over to his studio this afternoon, as myself, not you, and surprise him,' Edie said. 'I've done that once, and I was still finding bits of clay in strange places a few days later.'

Alice was trying not to question why, but this thought made her far more envious than the fact that her sister had just spent the last four nights sleeping in a double bed with her husband. It's not that she wanted to sleep with Seb – the thought actually made her feel a bit ill, as did the idea of finding clay in crevices that had no business having clay in – but to have that kind of spontaneous spark still very much alive and burning after weathering so many years together was something pretty extraordinary. She hoped Edie knew how lucky she was.

CHAPTER SEVENTEEN

Edie

Edie had to stop at a charity shop on the way to Seb's studio to buy something that would make her look like herself again, as turning up to his place of work reeking of sexual intent wearing Alice's clothes would be wrong on so many levels.

She could hear the low strains of jazz through the closed door and smiled. Before she even saw him, she could imagine him sitting at his wheel, his hair pulled back with an elastic band, his T-shirt showing his lithe, muscular forearms, his hands moulding the soft, wet clay; she couldn't wait a second longer to see him, so hurriedly took off Alice's wedding ring, put it in her purse, and pushed the door open.

Forty-five minutes later, her make-up long gone from her face, her relationship well and truly reinstated to peak performance levels and with a renewed desire to see everyone as happily coupled up as she was, she texted Alice on her way to the tube.

> *Heads up: Just had a lovely afternoon with Seb 😍 do you want to swap so you can have a date with Danny?*

> *No, you're okay. We don't really do things like that.*

> *What about with our favourite floor manager?*

> *Stop it! Leave it alone!*

> *Okay. Okay. Just joking!*

With Alice's remonstrations still ringing in her ears, and a huge amount of Friday afternoon extra-curricular clubs to drop off and pick up from, Edie planned to put all thoughts of James out of her mind and leave it up to Alice to restart their Saturday coffee meet-ups when they switched back. That was until around eight that evening, when Danny still wasn't back from work, or the gym, or wherever the hell he went when he wasn't at home. It was quite the coincidence, the viewer calling into the show earlier with the exact same predicament as Alice. Her sister's eyes and voice were giving nothing away though when she gave her guidance – was she imparting the advice to the viewer that she should be listening to herself? Edie had only been living in her sister's world for five days, but that was more than enough time for a giant question mark to form over the legitimacy of Danny's nightly gym visits. If Alice wasn't going to heed her own counsel, then maybe Edie should, on her sister's behalf, and tag along one night, see what he got up to, who he met.

After a dinner of risotto, she forced Teddy and Rufus to play Scrabble with her and Emily, using a good old-fashioned threat of not driving them to their match in the morning as leverage. The subterfuge continued throughout the game as Edie spelled out words she hoped would infiltrate their young minds and perhaps help dilute some of the machismo their father had been peddling. Words like: *partners, loving, respect, gentle, kind*, and she was particularly pleased with *Equity*, which actually got her a score of 38 as the Q was on a triple. Rufus had just put down the word *bumhole* which Edie was certain Alice would have disallowed, but the table-shaking laughter from all three kids meant there was no way she could veto it without breaking a few hearts.

The front door shut with an unnecessary force, and the change in the atmosphere was palpable. The laughter immediately stopped and Rufus reached over to the Scrabble board and quickly removed his last word. Emily actually seemed to shrink a little in her seat.

'Where have you put my dinner?' Danny said, after walking over to the oven, opening it, and finding it empty.

'I didn't make you any as you weren't back and you didn't call.'

He threw his car keys and mobile phone on the counter. 'But you always just leave mine ready to have when I get back.'

'Well, I didn't,' Edie replied. 'If you had messaged or let me know that you hadn't eaten I would have been only too happy to leave some for you, but you didn't. Your turn, Teddy.'

'I don't want to play anymore,' Teddy said sullenly, pushing his letter holder away from him. 'I've got homework to do.'

'But there's only a few letters left in the letter bag Teddy, come on, let's finish the game.'

'I told you, I don't want to.' He got up from the table and went upstairs to his room.

'Well, there's no reason why *we* can't finish the game,' Edie said brightly. 'Do you want to put your word back on, Rufus, or are you going to do a new word?'

'New word,' he mumbled, shaking his head so his hair fell into his eyes.

'What did you all have anyway?' Danny asked.

'Risotto.'

'Did it work? You always either overcook the rice so it's all soft and mushy or don't cook it enough so it's still crunchy.'

'Well all's well that ends well then,' Edie said, deliberately keeping her tone light in front of the children.

'What's that supposed to mean?'

'You missed a dinner you don't like. I'd call that a win. Your go, Emily darling.'

'Well, what can I have? I'm starving,' Danny whined from across the kitchen, making no attempt to open a cupboard to look for himself.

'Anything you like. The fridge is full, so's the freezer.'

'I quite fancy Thai green curry.'

Edie wondered why he was announcing this to the room before realising that he wasn't, he was announcing it to her. She was the chef, caught on an illicit break, and was now being sent back to the kitchen as a new order had just been placed by a regular that no one particularly liked, but who tipped reasonably well. Except this kitchen was closed for the night.

Rufus then put the lesser-scoring word 'home' down on the board, and it was the sheer aura of sadness about him while putting down a word that should be so filled with joy and happiness that made Edie determined to right some wrongs. Enough was enough. 'Why don't we call this a draw,' Edie said, 'and you can both have half an hour playing time before bed.'

Rufus didn't even try to argue about having the same bedtime as his younger sister, as they both gratefully scarpered up to their bedrooms. Edie looked across the kitchen at Danny, who was making no inroads on his preparation of his dinner, and was just leaning against the worktop, scrolling on his phone. She searched her memory bank for any tucked away little recollection of him lying on the floor playing with his children on one of their shared Christmas Days, or showing any affection at all to Alice, or helping their mum up the stairs when she'd got ill, the way Seb had done without being asked. What if it was Alice who became ill and he needed to look after her the way her dad had with her mum during her short illness? Would he scrub the carpet if a post-chemo nausea took hold of her suddenly without warning? Could he be relied upon to take over the running of the house and the kids' welfare if Alice ever succumbed to bone-numbing exhaustion? Edie actually couldn't place Danny in any situation, ever, in the eighteen years of knowing him, when he wasn't doing exactly what he wanted.

'Are you happy?' Edie blurted out, still seated at the kitchen table.

'I'm hungry, if that's what you're asking,' he replied, not even looking up at her.

Edie shook her head. 'It's not.'

'Alice, I'm wasting away here, can you put my dinner on?'

'No, you're more than able to stir some chicken around a pan until it's brown and stir in a pot of paste and a tin of coconut milk.'

He put his phone down on the counter. 'Why are you being so difficult? I've had a long day—'

'Doing what?'

'What do you mean doing what? Working, what do you think I do?'

'I have no idea,' she replied evenly, calmly. 'What do you do?' She wasn't being antagonistic, she literally was just trying to have a chat, the same way she and Seb had every day of their sixteen-year-long relationship.

'I don't have the energy to play this game.'

'It's not a game Danny, games are fun. This is not fun. Are you having fun?'

He leaned back against the counter and crossed his arms, and sneeringly said, 'If you're not going to cook for me, maybe I should ask Rufus; apparently he's a whizz in the kitchen.'

This caught Edie by surprise, Alice was right, his parents must have told him. But she still didn't understand why it was such a big deal.

'Why didn't you tell me he likes cooking?' The word *cooking* rolled off his tongue as though it tasted like gone-off milk.

'Why is it important?'

'He's got the makings of an excellent rugby player.'

'Don't rugby players need to eat? You wouldn't be standing there hungry now if you'd learned how to cook when you were his age.' She carried on, 'You don't have any issue with me teaching Emily how to cook. Why should you be annoyed about me helping Rufus pick up some basics?'

Danny's lip twitched. He obviously wasn't so neanderthal to know that there were some things you shouldn't say out loud, despite wholeheartedly believing them to be true.

'Fine. But only cooking. Not baking.'

Now it was Edie's lips' turn to twitch, this time with mirth, not anger. She got up from her chair and slowly started walking towards him. 'Let me get this right, savoury foods are manly, sweet foods are girly.' She jumped up onto a bar stool. 'What about bread? Technically savoury, but it has to be baked.'

'Don't be ridiculous.'

'I'm not, I'm merely ascertaining the boundaries, that's all.

Cheese scones. Again, very much in the savoury camp, but just one ingredient away from being a teatime treat. Pies, what about pies?'

'Alice, you're being childish.'

Childish? *Childish?* God, he was infuriatingly sanctimonious. 'I'm sorry Danny, but I find your views really offensive and I've had enough. You don't get to make the rules and expect me and everyone else to follow them when they are outdated and just plain wrong. Things are changing around here, they are changing for the better, and you need to get on board with the changes, because I am not subjecting those wonderful children upstairs to this archaic sexist behaviour anymore.'

'Or what?' he replied with the petulance of a child called out in the playground for bullying.

'What?'

'That sounded very much like an ultimatum.' He walked slowly towards where she was sitting, straightening his back, pulling himself up to full height as he neared her, a full head and shoulders above her, and she felt herself shrink slightly.

'No, I . . . er . . .'

'I'm just wondering how you're planning on supporting yourself and three kids if we split up?'

Split up? The back of Edie's neck was getting hot, and her mouth felt dry as she swallowed, 'Well, um, firstly,' she said, stalling for her next sentence to line itself up in her brain, 'have you ever heard of alimony, and secondly, I make really good money, so I actually don't need anything from you. So. . .' That wasn't what she meant to say! She'd gone too far. She knew she'd gone too far the second she interrupted him, and yet she couldn't find a way to stop talking once she'd started. She'd never been afraid of Seb, ever. Even in the midst of some of their loudest, most passionate fights, and they had had loads of them over the years, there had never been a single second where she felt uneasy or in any kind of danger. But sitting there, a couple of feet from Danny, whose big hands could send her flying across the room if they wanted to, she felt an unfamiliar grip of fear.

The next minute of silence stretched interminably as they stared at each other, both one movement away from changing everything irrevocably.

'The game's about to start,' he said slowly, calmly, brushing past her on his way into the lounge, his arm ever so slightly clipping her shoulder.

Edie waited until the door to the living room shut behind him to sink into a chair to stop her falling. She breathed out slowly through her mouth and waited for her pulse to start slowing. She should tell Alice what had just happened. This wasn't what was meant to happen this week; they were meant to switch places, wear each other's clothes, have a fun few days with their nieces and nephews, and then swap back and say, 'that was great, now I understand you so much better, sorry you slipped up, thanks for the new job'. They weren't meant to wreak havoc and break up marriages and split up families. She had been so determined to leave Alice with a happier situation than the one she left five days ago, and yet so far all she'd done was make it far, far worse.

Within seconds the sport was blaring from the living room television, punctuated by Danny's shouts of disgust, which were quickly echoed by Teddy's, and then Rufus's a while later, less passionate, but loud enough for his dad to hear and approve of. Emily was upstairs playing, and Edie was once again alone with her thoughts. If she was Alice, would she even recognise that she was standing at a crossroads in her life? One path beckoning her down more of the same: days melting into weeks, weeks into months, months into years, until the kids had all left home, and it was her and Danny left living in a beautiful home, in a marriage as sterile as her surfaces. Or the other path, one with someone who saw how amazing she was. Without a moment's hesitation she knew which one she would take, but sadly, she also knew, that probably wouldn't be the one that Alice would opt for.

She picked up her phone to call Alice, and then stopped. There was *one* way that she could vastly improve her sister's life.

She could cancel Emily's lift to gymnastics with Freya's mum.

CHAPTER EIGHTEEN

The swap: day 6

Alice

Alice had tried so hard to enjoy an enforced Saturday morning lie-in, but her brain was rebelling in a way that she wasn't used to, since it normally did exactly what she told it to. Edie wasn't wrong; her family had an uncanny ability to completely reset their body clocks for the weekend and stay asleep an unnatural amount of time come Saturday. Whereas Alice, after the blip of her first morning, had reverted to her normal waking hours of six. It didn't help that she was constantly replaying yesterday's conversation with Edie in a loop. Danny was all those things Edie said he was, and yet something had always stopped her calling him out on it, and she couldn't put her finger on what it was. She wouldn't say that she was a particularly passive person, just waiting around for things to happen to her; if anything she was proudly proactive, a get-up-and-go, seize-the-day type of woman, and yet, with Danny, she was, what was she . . . ? Grateful. Yes, at the top of his rugby career, having got twenty-four caps for Scotland, stand-in captain of his regional team whenever the real captain was sent off, Mr October in the Rugby Union calendar 2009, he'd picked her out of a room of fawning twenty-something women. Picked her *up* actually, which looking back, should have been a bit of a red flag. They were only a couple of minutes into their conversation, and hadn't progressed much past the 'how many sisters and brothers do you have' part of small talk before out of nowhere he bent down, put his head next to her hip bone and hoisted her over his shoulder and paraded her through the room to drunken cheering from his teammates. No one had picked her up before, and it didn't occur to her to feel demeaned or sexualised; she just thought how extraordinarily strong he must be. Which, she guessed now, was the point of that whole charade. When the conversation was running dry, dip into the most impressive thing in your arsenal. She found out later, during the best man's speech at their wedding actually, that it was a tried and tested method of impressing women. The only problem with that, though, was that marriage sort of depended on good conversation, and not on good firemen's lifts. Not once, since their early courtship, had the need ever arisen for another shoulder lift, so in retrospect, it wasn't a useful talent to bring to the table at all.

No one could accuse Seb of not being a good conversationalist. Alice and he must have spent two hours last night just talking. And not just surface enquiries as to their days (as he'd kept up a steady commentary all day via text, there really was nothing left to say). They were watching a documentary about a remote tribe in Patagonia, and how, even with no access to modern life, or literature, or knowledge of life outside of their small area, they cultivated their own religion and deity. During this programme, Alice had to admit her mind was wandering a little, as it wasn't a programme she would ordinarily been drawn to, and as the rest of her own family usually commandeered the television for sport and Marvel movies, she rarely had the remote control in her own hand. But Seb was entranced by it.

'So, they had no idea that the Bible, or Torah, or Koran existed, and yet still, their desire for a supernatural being to watch over their lives was so strong, isn't that incredible?' he'd said.

Alice had nodded. It was indeed incredible.

'Why do you think that is? Why are humans so desperate to believe in something that can't be proven?'

Alice had shaken her head, pondering the question. 'It's so strange, isn't it?'

Seb had carried on, 'I mean, I get that a faith then allows you the comfort of believing in pre-determination, thereby relieving you of all autonomy over your life, and therefore, all feelings of regret or remorse. Is that what you think it is?'

Alice hadn't had a conversation like that for over twenty-five years. Not since she and Edie shared a room, and each night Edie would insist on ending each day with a philosophical chat about the universe. She wasn't allowed to be non-committal then either, Edie would press her for an answer. 'But Alice,' she would say, 'can we have happiness without sadness? Who decides what is morally right? If everything came from amoebas, how come amoebas still exist?'

Alice lay next to Seb in her sister's bed early that Saturday morning, the shafts of the sun's rays peeping through the gaps in the curtains, casting ribbons of light on the pretty plaster-pink walls. Wide awake, as Seb slept soundlessly beside her, Alice knew with a sudden clarity what a good partnership was. It was finding your person. Edie had, without a shadow of a doubt, found her perfect match. And Alice also recognised, with a very sad clarity, that she perhaps hadn't.

Edie

James's face took on a warm glow when he saw Edie arrive at the leisure centre. When he'd thought that Alice wasn't coming, it seems he'd decided to save the £3.75 on a pot of tea from the café and instead bring his own thermos flask to drink from while sitting in the chlorine-smelling foyer. It was an act of frugality that Alice would heartily approve of.

'Hi James, I had a change of plan,' Edie said brightly, giving Emily a little push towards the queue of young girls waiting to be let in to the sports hall. 'I'll be back in a couple of hours Em, okay? Try not to fall off anything.' Emily skipped off, and Edie turned back to face James and nodded her head at his flask. 'Is there enough in that for two?'

James moved his anorak from the plastic chair next to him so she could sit down. If this was a real date, Edie would be ascertaining fairly quickly what his love language was, how he gave back to his community, what principle he would never compromise on and if he was ever in a talent show, what skill would he showcase? However, she was not Edie today, she was Alice, so she complimented him on his tea-making skills and asked if he'd like a biscuit from a batch she'd made with Rufus last night before Danny came home. James seemed really nervous, which had the opposite effect on Edie, whose calmness was probably due to the fact that this wasn't her date.

After twenty minutes or so of very pleasant conversation, revolving mostly around the fact that, on reflection, he definitely didn't need to bring his anorak today, and yes, real butter really was superior to margarine in shortbread, and did she know that Americans used oil in their baking, oil! Edie suggested they go down to the basement in the leisure centre and play a game of table tennis while they waited for the girls to finish. At least, that's what she thought she said; his look of surprise and excitement as he scrambled hurriedly to his feet, spilling a little bit of his tea, suggested that she may in fact have propositioned him with a quick fumble on the gym mats.

'I haven't played ping pong in years!' he said, thankfully allaying Edie's moment of self-doubt as to what she might have offered. 'We had one in our sixth form common room, and I used to love it.'

It was an inspired suggestion of Edie's as any awkwardness was slowly stripped away as the ball rallied back and forth between them. They laughed every time it ricocheted off a wall or on the bodies of the teenagers playing on the table next to them. James had an endearing habit of congratulating her after every great serve or return, which reminded Edie a little of Seb's eagerness to please – something Danny was certainly in very short supply of.

After their half-hour session ended, they sat on the floor opposite the squash court, their backs against the wall, drinking from cans of coke they'd just bought from the vending machine. James even held his can out for a little 'cheers' before he sipped from it, which Edie thought was a nice touch.

'I'm so glad your appointment got cancelled, I mean, I hope it can be rescheduled. There was a section on women's bodies last year on the show, and it is really important to keep on top of it.'

'On top of women's bodies?' Edie asked innocently, knowing exactly what reaction her question would receive.

'Oh god, no, that's not what I meant, I just meant with ovary stuff, and the cervix and things, oh Christ—' He banged his head a few times in embarrassment against his drawn-up knees.

Edie put her hand on his arm. 'I'm teasing you. I know what you meant. Sorry, I'll leave the jokes to Edie next time.'

'Thank goodness, I almost got myself into a right hole there.'

Edie spluttered into her can before forcing herself to take a sip of her drink to stop herself saying what she really wanted to. She wished Seb was sitting the other side of her to hear this exchange so they could have a right old giggle about it afterwards.

When he spoke again, the subject had thankfully changed. 'Speaking of Edie, is it weird being a twin?' James asked.

They'd been asked variations of this question pretty much every day of their lives, and Edie rolled out the answer she always did, 'I don't know what it's like not being one.'

'But you're so different.'

'Mm-hmm.'

Warming up to the topic, James continued, 'Is it weird though, knowing there's someone that looks just like you wandering around? Do you get mistaken for Edie quite a lot? Do you ever swap places?'

Edie had a mouthful of cola which she tried not to choke on. 'Not really,' she gasped out, 'like you said, we're quite different.'

'I can definitely tell you apart,' James said with misplaced smugness.

'Can you?' Edie tried not to smile at this blatant lie.

'Yes, you're prettier than Edie.' He blushed. 'Sorry, I don't know why I said that. That was really rude. She's really pretty too, I didn't mean that she was ugly or anything, you're both very attractive women, it was meant to be a compliment.'

Edie smiled, and patted his arm again. 'It's okay. And thank you. I'm not quite sure how to respond to that—' *for obvious reasons* '—but thank you for the sentiment.'

'So if you're always here with Emily on Saturday mornings, what are the rest of your family doing?'

'The boys are at rugby training before a match.'

'What about your husband?'

Edie could tell by the forced nonchalant way James asked that question, he'd been wanting to bring Danny up for a while. This definitely did not feel like a purely platonic line of questioning, whatever Alice maintained. 'I don't know what he's doing,' Edie answered honestly. He had left with his gym bag while she was still upstairs haranguing the boys about getting ready for their lift to the rugby ground. Seb rarely left the room without announcing it, but it seemed that at Alice's, Danny had no qualms about leaving the borough without saying goodbye.

James fidgeted a little. 'I hope you don't mind me saying so, but I sensed something different about you yesterday, at the studio.'

'Oh?'

'You seemed nervous, anxious even, and I wondered if everything was okay, at home?'

'It's nothing I can't handle.' If this was what Alice swore blind it was, just a simple case of two parents killing time while their daughters were in the same gym class, then his line of questioning, not to mention his 'you're prettier than your sister' comment, was really inappropriate, so either he was more socially inept than Alice painted him to be, or her sister's previous chats with him had definitely progressed more than, 'yes, you should have left your anorak at home today and you're right, shortbread without butter is like Chas without Dave.'

He put his hands up in submission. 'Okay, I get it. Subject closed. I won't say anything else about it. But there's actually another reason I'm pleased you're here today. I have some news, well, sort of watch-this-space news.'

Now her interest was piqued a bit more. 'What?'

'You saw the photo of Gareth in the papers a couple of days ago?'

Edie nodded, not really sure where this was going.

'Well, the bosses are not happy at all. They've been wanting to move him off the sofa for ages, and they think this might be the time.'

'Really? But he's been there, what? Eight years?'

'Yeah, but a couple of years ago, they had to get lawyers involved to shut something down before the press got hold of it, and he's just becoming a bit of a liability.'

Edie whistled. 'That is big news. Who are they thinking of as a replacement?'

James listed off a few names of presenters who had covered school holidays and illnesses in the past, then he said, 'I actually heard your name being thrown into the mix by one of the producers.'

'Me? Really?' It took a couple of seconds for Edie to realise that he wasn't, actually, referring to her, and was incredibly grateful that she hadn't exclaimed anything particularly Edie-like to incriminate her. Of course they wouldn't want her, she was merely the genetic add-on. Alice had been right about what she'd said when she suggested the bet, after all.

'Think about it Alice, you'd be perfect. Would you want to do it?'

'I have no idea. I've never even thought about it. Who suggested me?'

'Amelia. There was an emergency meeting on Friday after the show about Gareth, where lots of options were discussed.'

'Why would they consider Al— me and not Edie?' She wasn't asking because she wanted a mini appraisal on the spot, she did actually think the question might be one that Alice might have asked, had she been the recipient of this news. Her sister had always internally doubted her own abilities, so she was bound to have immediately assumed that she wouldn't be able to do it.

'I think you're more . . .'

Edie could tell he was searching for the right word. Considering his audience, the more time he took, the better.

He settled on, 'Reliable. But look, I'm just telling you this to keep you in the loop, I'm not part of any of the decision-making process, so don't get your hopes up, I think they were concerned that maybe you wouldn't go for it anyway.'

'Why?'

'Because of Edie.'

'Edie? What would she have to do with it?' It felt very odd to be talking about herself in the third person. It was also horrible to hear that even if she were to win the bet with Alice, and Alice stepped aside for Edie to take the solo spot on the pink sofa, the producers would feel as though they'd been landed with second best.

'Sister loyalty?'

'I think she'd be really happy for me to do it,' Edie surprised herself by saying. She was shocked that she was now advocating for Alice when a week ago she'd have been doing anything she could to win the bet, including sabotaging Alice's chances now. But things had changed. Living as Alice had made her realise just how much this job meant to her – freedom, both physically and financially, from a husband who was stuck in the 1950s.

'I think you'd be great. And I'd get to see you every day, rather than just Fridays.'

Edie felt herself blush, forgetting for a moment that it wasn't her he was saying this to. 'Why do you like me, James?' Edie knew that Alice would never have asked that question, due mainly to the British social mores of never seeking out validation, and also because it was quite forward. Too forward, she realised, as James's cheeks had flushed red again.

'Can I be honest?' he asked.

'Of course.'

'Please don't be annoyed.'
What on earth was he going to say? 'I promise.'
'I can see how hard you work to keep everything together. I've watched you every week for eight months now, carrying your sister through every show, giving measured, thoughtful advice to the viewers, talking to everyone with the same degree of respect and genuine warmth from the director to the sixth former on a week's work experience who you'll never see again, and under all of it, I can see a real sadness, and it takes every ounce of restraint not to wrap you in a big hug every Friday, and tell you that you can relax now. That you're safe, and it's okay to just breathe.'

Edie was stunned. He had got all of that from across the studio floor? From a few Saturday coffees? She hadn't really seen that from a lifetime of living alongside Alice. But why did it have to be her that heard that beautiful speech and not the woman it was meant for? But possibly, Edie thought as she accepted his hand to help her to her feet, maybe the right person did just hear it.

'You're quiet. Have I upset you?'
Edie shook her head. 'Not at all. The opposite. I think you might be the first person who has actually just seen me.'
They walked down the corridor, flanked by windows on both sides, looking into the squash courts on one side, and the gym on the other. A huge, muscular man in an impossibly small pair of blue shorts where his entire genital area was very much on display between the panels of frosted glass, was doing a set of squats in front of a mirrored wall. A woman walked behind the man and he did a little bum wiggle. This wasn't a gym, this was a peep show.

She looked at James out of the side of her eye, and his expression clearly showed that he'd just clocked the same display that she had, and they both laughed awkwardly.

'I feel a little overdressed,' he said.

'Believe me, you are very appropriately dressed for the occasion.'

As they approached the big hall where the gymnastics class was finishing, Edie wondered how Alice usually said goodbye to James on Saturday mornings. Was there a hug involved? Some sort of awkward cheek kiss? Tongues? No, definitely not tongues. While she was pondering this, as Emily and her friends were putting their trainers back on, James squeezed her shoulder and said, 'I've really enjoyed this morning.'

'Me too. Thank you, you know, for saying what you said.'

'Bye Alice.'

'Bye James.'

Alice

Being around Seb so much, seeing the type of husband he was, had derailed her. She was beginning to lose sight of all the good things in her own life and she needed to be back around Danny, her own family, to remind her what was real and what was not. She checked her watch – two-thirty. They were meeting at the restaurant at seven. Just four and a half hours until she was back with her own tribe. But the night was so fraught with potential pitfalls – how could she greet her own children as an auntie and not as a mum? How quickly after getting there would they be able to swap back into themselves? And Edie's message just now was worrying her too. *Heads up – I've had a couple of arguments with Danny, or rather, you have. He's sulking.* How could she be expected to deal with the aftermath of that without knowing what had been said?

'I think that tray is as clean as you're going to get it,' came Seb's voice from behind her.

Alice looked down where she'd been absent-mindedly

scrubbing at the now sparkling shower tray. She knew that this type of coping mechanism was wildly out of character, but in times of stress, cleaning was the only thing that worked lowering her blood pressure.

'Is everything okay?' Seb asked.

'Of course,' she replied, rocking back on her heels. 'What makes you say that?'

'I've just been feeling that you're a bit distant this week. Is anything on your mind?'

'No, not at all.' If this was distant, what on earth did being close look like? The interaction she'd had with Seb this week was more intense and, ironically, more genuine, than any time she'd spent with a man before. He must be referring to the physical side of their relationship, in which case, she had been distant, for very obvious reasons, but he'd spent the afternoon with Edie only yesterday; surely that interlude would keep him going for a while. She and Danny had only seen each other naked twice since Christmas, and that wasn't a record for them either.

'You would tell me, wouldn't you, if anything was bothering you? If *I'd* done something to bother you? Was it the invite to Rob and Lucy's wedding?'

Why would receiving a wedding invitation be cause for concern? Alice gave him a non-committal smile as a way of reply.

'It'll be our turn soon, I promise. A few more orders, and we'll get a ring, set a date.'

Alice had always assumed that it had been Edie's feminism that had prevented her from heading down the marriage path. What did she call it once? A patriarchal prison? Was that just masking the real reason that they just couldn't afford it?

'I promise, nothing's wrong at all. You're practically perfect in every way,' Alice reassured him, not having any clue that she'd just used a phrase Edie often said.

'Close your mouth Michael, you are not a cod fish.'

'What?'

Seb looked at her with narrowed eyes. 'It's the Mary Poppins reference we always say. Now you're meant to say "rather inclined to giggle, doesn't put things away".'

'Sorry, yes, of course, Votes for Women!'

Seb laughed, turned his back and left the bathroom, and Alice gave a sigh of relief. The sooner Edie could swoop back in and relieve her for a few hours, the better.

CHAPTER NINETEEN

Edie

'Why haven't you laid my party clothes out on my bed?' Rufus asked, standing in the doorway of his parents' bedroom.

Edie looked at his reflection in the mirror on the dressing table where she was seated trying to apply her make-up in a way that looked both like Alice, but that could very easily pass as herself in about an hour. 'Um, because you're a thirteen-year-old who is perfectly capable of choosing what he might like to wear for a party.'

'I can choose my outfit myself?'

'Of course.' Edie swiped a brush full of expensive rose-tinted blush across both cheeks. She was going to miss the contents of this make-up bag when they swapped back.

'Even jeans?'

'If that's what you want.'

Rufus whooped with undisguised joy. 'This is the best day ever!'

Less than a minute later, Edie heard Teddy's heavier footsteps bounding up to their bedroom in the loft conversion, taking the stairs two at a time. 'Mum, Rufus said that you said that he can wear jeans?'

Edie held up a drop pearl earring next to her right ear, and a delicate diamond one next to the other. 'I did indeed.'

'Can I wear jeans too?'

'Of course, knock yourself out.'

Teddy hesitated by the door. 'Are you okay?'

'Yes, why? Pearl or diamond?' She swivelled round on the low stool to face him and turned her face one way, and then the other to model the two choices of earring.

'Er . . . I dunno?'

'You must have a preference?'

He looked really confused, almost like she'd asked him to tell her the square root of pi without using a calculator. 'But I'm a boy,' he stuttered.

'Yes you are. With two eyes that work. Pearl or diamond?'

'Um . . . the white ones?'

'Pearl. Brilliant, good call. Thank you lovely. Be ready to go in about half an hour.'

Around twenty minutes later Danny got out of the bath, after listening to the whole of a sports podcast on a radio he'd propped up next to the tub. Edie had heard him top the bath up with hot water at least ten times through the door. His life was truly amazing.

'Where are my chinos?' he asked, towel drying his hair while another towel was wrapped around his waist.

'I don't know, where are your chinos?' Edie replied, spritzing her pulse points with Alice's signature scent before remembering that she didn't want to smell like her sister. She hastily wiped the perfume off again with a babywipe.

'They're not in my wardrobe?'

'When did you put them in there?'

'I didn't. I put them in the laundry basket on Wednesday after work.'

'Well, that's where they'll be then. Mystery solved.'

He whipped his towel off with no warning, and Edie quickly averted her eyes, but a second too late. Gosh, he was very hairy indeed. Everywhere.

'What do you mean that's where they'll be?' he said, stepping into his trunk-style pants.

'I mean, if you haven't washed them yet, that's where they'll be.' Edie stood up, smoothing down the long navy dress she'd chosen to wear, on the premise that it would be much easier to switch than something with complicated buttons.

'So you're on strike now, is that it? The whole family have to walk around in dirty clothes because you're refusing to do your job.'

'My *job?*' Was she hearing this neanderthal right? 'My *job* is not to wash your chinos.' She could have said more, a lot more. But now was not the time. Tonight was about celebrating her dad's milestone birthday all together, showing him that his two daughters could get along just fine. Tonight was about making sure that Alice and her kids had a good time. Edie was very conscious that she hadn't told her sister that Kenneth knew about the switch, or that he was dating again. Either one of these headlines told in isolation would send her sister off spiralling, both news-bites relayed together would make her spleen burst. She'd have to find the right time to break both bits of news.

*

They'd picked a restaurant a couple of miles away that had a private dining room upstairs, and a set menu for parties that didn't make her eyes water too much. They'd have to put their four meals, and half of Kenneth's on the credit card, there wasn't enough in their current account to cover it, but a bit of a marketing push to get a few more clients next month should cover the repayment. As they neared the restaurant, Edie felt her stomach flip over in anticipation. If someone had told her a week ago that she would feel this amount of excitement about the prospect of seeing her own family, she wouldn't have believed them, and yet, as she sat in the back of a minicab sandwiched between her nephews, a matter of minutes away from being herself again, her whole body was flooded with happiness. They were going to be the last to arrive as she'd just received a text from Alice saying 'here!', which would be surprising to everyone, as *Alice* was always early. But in a weird twist of the universe, it turned out that *Edie* was early this time round, which would give everyone a good chuckle.

It was everything Edie could do not to flatten her niece and nephews as she scrambled to get out of the car and run inside, scoop up her family and never let go. Was this how returning astronauts felt after months on an international space station? She took the stairs two at a time, and burst in through the door with an exuberant, 'We're here!'

'*Alice*, hi,' Alice said, coming up first and kissing Edie on both cheeks, 'that was quite the entrance!'

Edie spotted Seb over Alice's shoulder talking to Uncle Keith and Auntie Barbara, 'Seb!' she exclaimed, running up to him, and just in the nick of time swerving the trajectory of her mouth away from his so her kiss landed plumply on his cheek with an audible smooching sound. 'How are you? It's been ages!'

'Alice!' Confusion flashed across his face, as it would. As in-laws, they'd always got on well, but not *this* well.

Edie gave her dad's sister and her husband a hug too. 'Where's the birthday boy, I thought he was coming with you?'

'He's downstairs getting a round in, he took Rosie and Iris with him too. They'll be up soon.'

Edie linked her arm through Seb's, desperate for as much of

her body to be touching his as possible at any one time. Had he got more attractive in the last six days? She was sure that his jawline had never been quite that sharp before? And were his eyes always that brown? She only saw him yesterday, but here, with the candlelight, and wearing her favourite shirt, she felt a definite flutter.

'Auntie Alice!' Iris came bounding through the door, and Edie took a double take. Her hair had been blow-dried into a sleek bob, and she had an Alice band holding it back. What was more, she was wearing the exact same outfit as Alice, a black dress with a little lace trimmed bolero.

'What the f. . .' Edie didn't know what was worse, the fact that Iris was now Alice's other doppelganger, or the outfit Alice had chosen to wear while masquerading as Edie. She would never have chosen that.

'Look, me and Mummy are dressed the same!'

'Yes.' Edie nodded, doing a great job of keeping a lid on all the expletives her mouth was desperate to say. 'Yes you are, Iris. Very Gatsby.'

Alice

Over on the other side of the room Alice had just had a very polite reunion with each of her children. Possibly made even more lukewarm by her gasp of surprise at the boys wearing jeans. As soon as they saw Iris and Rosie, they went off to join their cousins, leaving Alice standing a foot apart from her husband. 'Hi Danny,' Alice said, leaning in to kiss his cheek.

'Edie.'

'Have you had a good week?' Alice asked him politely.

He shrugged. 'I've had better.'

'Well you can relax now, we've got beer or wine, or soft drinks – are you still on your health kick?'

'It's not a health kick, it's a way of life.'

'He's been at the gym every night this week,' Edie said, joining them. 'He was even there this morning. I asked him if I could go with him next time, but he wasn't keen.'

'Oh that sounds fun,' Alice said. 'You should.'

Danny gave a loud sniff. 'She wouldn't know how any of the equipment works.'

Alice smiled. 'Oh Alice is far cleverer than you give her credit for. She'd pick it up in no time.'

Danny didn't reply. 'Is there any sparkling water?'

'It's on the table, help yourself,' Alice said. 'Alice, I just wanted to run through the menu with you.' The sisters went into the corridor, and after making sure they weren't being followed ran downstairs to the disabled toilet to swap identities. They'd only made it halfway down the stairs when Kenneth appeared holding a tray of drinks at the bottom.

'Girls!'

'Dad! Here, let me take that from you.' Edie ran down the final few steps and took the wobbling tray from his hands.

'Thanks Alice love; you *are* Alice I presume?' he said with a wink for some reason.

Alice laughed from further up the stairwell. 'Of course she is Dad, I thought you could always tell us apart, you must be losing your touch.'

'No, no.' Kenneth touched his nose. 'Still got it. Come on then, let's join the party.'

Once upstairs, Kenneth handed Alice a big glass of white wine, Edie's favourite, from the tray Edie had just put down on the table, and then said, 'Alice, I got you an elderflower as I didn't think you'd want a drink. Unless of course I was wrong and you'd like to swap drinks?' Another wink. What was up with his eye? Alice made a mental note to check when his next optician appointment was due.

It wasn't ideal, she really didn't want to drink tonight, but she had no choice but to pick up the large glass and pretend it was just what she wanted. Edie gave him a tight smile as well. 'That's perfect,' she said, but Alice could tell it wasn't perfect; what her sister would think was perfect would be to down in one gulp the massive glass of Sauvignon Alice was currently holding and order another one immediately.

As soon as Kenneth moved away to say hello to his oldest friend Malcolm who had just arrived, Edie hissed to her sister, 'You're going to have to at least take a sip of that or everyone will think I'm pregnant.'

Edie

'Just give it a couple of minutes and we'll try slipping out again,' Alice said out of the corner of her mouth, before twisting her lips into a big smile as their dad's sister approached. 'Hi Auntie Barb.'

'Can I just say, how lovely it is to see you two getting on. It means so much to Ken to have his two girls here actually looking like they like each other for once!'

'We do like each other!' Edie said, realising as she said it that it was much nearer the truth than it would have been a week ago.

Just then, Rosie's Bluetooth speaker sprang into action from the corner of the room, and Edie's heart expanded in her chest as she saw Seb bow down in front of their eldest daughter, obviously asking her for a dance, before pulling her in close and twirling her around. Rosie was pretending to hate it, accompanying every spin with an 'Oh Daaad', but Edie knew that half-hearted lip curl well enough to know the girl doth protest too much. Seb looked across at them, and made a beckoning wave with his arm. 'Edie! Come and join us!'

No sooner had Edie raised her right foot in the air to take a step, she felt Alice's arm shoot out across her like a barrier coming down. 'Not you,' she hissed through her smile as she went to join them, handing Edie her wine first.

'They're a lovely couple, aren't they?' Auntie Barb said as the two of them watched Seb and Rosie drop their hands to let Alice into their circle too.

'Mmm-mmm,' Edie agreed, swallowing down the big lump forming in her throat with a massive mouthful of warm house white.

'So much in common.'

Edie didn't trust her mouth to open with a reply that wasn't a loud wail, so kept her lips tightly screwed together and just nodded.

Somewhere around the third song, the long dining table had been pushed back, and all five cousins were on the makeshift dancefloor along with Seb, Kenneth and Auntie Barbara. Danny, Malcolm and Uncle Keith were sitting at the dining table talking about Danny's greatest tries for Scotland. Danny seemed a thousand times more animated than Edie had seen him all week. Edie hovered, unsure what Alice would be doing in this situation – would she be haranguing the kitchen staff for the delay? Snipping the stems off the fresh flowers in vases on the table to make them last longer? Polishing the cutlery with a special cloth she'd brought from home? Edie suddenly realised that maybe her sister did these things, these unnecessary little jobs because she didn't quite know what else to do? Perhaps spending hours in the kitchen busying herself with food prep wasn't an act of martyrdom or a desperate desire to host, could it be simply that she hadn't grasped how to just, well, *be*. The thought started to take hold and then everything started to make sense. She looked over at her sister, standing swaying ever so slightly in the group of dancers. The younger five were all completely at ease in their bodies, even Teddy, who before tonight Edie would have staked a large wager on him not leaving Danny's shadow, however much he wanted to join in, but there he was, body popping and laughing with Seb. He'd always liked Seb, probably because he was everything his own father wasn't. Auntie Barbara had put her handbag down on the floor and was dancing round it, while Alice, sort of dressed as Edie, still just stood there demurely swaying and smiling. *What is she doing?* No one would believe she was Edie.

Edie meandered up behind her twin, doing some swaying of her own as she did to stay in character, and whispered through her teeth, 'What are you doing?'

Alice shifted her weight from one foot to the other. 'I'm dancing,' she answered through the corner of her mouth.'

'No, you're not,' Edie muttered quietly. 'You're stepping from side to side while pointing at the ceiling. That's not how I dance, that's how *you* dance. Great moves Auntie Barb!' Edie added more loudly.

Alice turned her head to the side so no one else could hear her talking. 'How am I meant to dance then?'

'Just a little less robot, and more bluebell in the wind.'

'Like this?' Alice lifted her arms up and swayed her whole body as though she was on a boat in rough seas.

'Not exactly, no.'

'Or like this?' Alice managed to make her entire body take part in a Mexican wave.

'Are you doing this on purpose because everyone will think you're me?'

'Whatever gave you that idea?' Alice winked at her. She actually winked.

'Go Mummy!' Iris shouted, clapping in time with Alice's dramatic body thrusts.

Edie rolled her eyes. What did she look like?

She looked like she was having the time of her life, is what she looked like.

Alice

If their dad hadn't interrupted them on the stairs, if they had swapped back at the start of the party, then she'd never have felt that incredible freedom that came when you actually don't give a damn what anyone else thought. She'd seen those signs that said *Dance like no one is watching* but until now had no idea what that felt like, or if that was even possible, but it was, and it felt amazing. There was a part of her though that wished that her own kids could have seen *her* do that, not their aunt, who was able to act that way whenever she wanted. She would have loved to have seen her boys' faces watch their mum throw her head back laughing and attempt the running man dance, or to do the tequila shot that Seb just bought her. She knew, with a definite sadness, that as soon as she and Edie managed to slip away and swap their clothes, that without Edie's mask, she'd retreat again into her self-conscious shell, and she really didn't want to.

'There's an issue with the food *Edie*, can you come and help sort it?' Edie said loudly across the dancefloor.

'You're probably the better person for dealing with that Alice, leave Edie be, she's having fun,' Uncle Keith interjected.

'Don't worry Uncle Keith,' Alice said breathlessly, coming off the dancefloor wiping her forehead, 'every party needs a pooper.'

Once safely locked inside the disabled toilet, the sisters stripped off, and held out the clothes they'd been wearing to the other one, Edie grimaced as the ones she was expected to change into were slightly damp with sweat. 'Sorry about that,' Alice said.

Edie pulled her hair up into the messy bun Alice had been sporting, while Alice pulled her hairband out, and smoothed her hair around her shoulders. Edie ran to the mirror and wiped off her sister's expensive Chanel lipstick, replacing it with her own tinted lip balm from the handbag Alice held out to her, while Alice did the same routine in reverse. The pearl earrings were swapped with hoops, a gold chain for gemstone beads, diamond watch for elasticated crystal bracelet, rings swapped over and elegant nude heels exchanged for beaded sandals. Edie doused herself in her Body Shop coconut body mist, and reached into her handbag and handed Alice the expensive bottle of perfume she'd taken from her dressing table an hour ago.

The switch back complete, they stood side by side looking in the mirror. 'How do you feel?' Edie asked. 'Because I feel really weird. My jewellery feels really heavy.' To emphasise this she held one wrist out and let it drop.

Alice pouted. 'I miss your elasticated waistbands. They were a game changer.'

Edie seemed to be studying her in the mirror. 'You seem really different.'

'I feel different. I know we got into this for a bet, but I've honestly had a really great week. Your family are lovely. And I'm not just saying that. You're really lucky. Seb is just the sweetest man.'

Edie nodded. 'He is.'

'I guess I didn't know him very well before now, and honestly, it's so clear how much he adores you, and the girls.'

Edie flapped her hand in the air. 'Stop it, you're going to make me cry.'

'Honestly. You've literally struck gold with him. And how have you found my family?'

Edie paused. Why was she pausing, Alice wondered. She'd literally just said the most wonderful things about Edie's family; where was the outpouring of compliments about hers? If she had to decipher her sister's expression, she would guess that Edie was working out how truthful she could be after Alice said those lovely things. And as Edie started talking in an uncharacteristically measured way, Alice realised she was right. 'Emily and Rufus are just scrummy. I can tell from tonight that Teddy wants to join in with everything and relax, and it's great to see him dancing and enjoying himself, but at home he won't let himself do anything he thinks Danny wouldn't approve of. Which basically rules out everything apart from watching and playing sports.'

Alice knew the answer to her next question before even asking it. 'And how has Danny been today? You said in your message that you've had words.'

Edie hesitated, biting her bottom lip.

'You can tell me the truth. I know how he can be.'

'I've really tried Alice, I know you think that I have probably aggravated him on purpose, but I really don't think I have; even a normal conversation seems to turn into a row. I couldn't even ask him about his day without him snapping at me. I even messaged him at work once and he got really cross about it.'

'Oh no, never interrupt his work.'

'But Seb messages me all day, every day.'

'Oh I know.' Alice smiled. He'd sent her a photo of a cloud shaped like men's genitals this afternoon on his way back from getting the Saturday newspaper.

Edie bit her lip again, she was clearly not saying something else.

'What are you not telling me?' Alice asked.

'Don't get mad.'

'What?'

Edie's words rushed out. 'I met James for a coffee this morning.' She winced.

Alice's face clouded over. 'You did not.'

'I did, and he was really sweet. We played table tennis.'

'You did what?'

'Ping pong.' Edie mimed having a bat in her hand and swinging it with a backhand.

'I know what table tennis is, I just don't know what possessed you to play it with him?'

'I had to break the ice.'

'What was he saying?'

'He was really sweet, he actually told me something really interesting about Gareth—'

Someone hammered on the door. 'Mum! Are you in there? The food's all come out!'

Edie unlocked the door and grabbed her daughter in a big hug, burying her face into her daughter's neck. 'Yuck,' Rosie said, pushing her away, 'personal space, woman, I did not consent for you to grab me like that.'

'Sorry, sorry, you're right. I was just overwhelmed with love for my eldest, the one who made me a mother, the one for whom my life has purpose and fulfilment—'

'You're really weird.'

'Hang on,' Edie said, reaching out to touch Rosie's forehead, 'have you done something to your fringe?'

Rosie dodged her mother's hand. 'Only three days ago. D'uh, I told you on the day. Ruby cut it in physics.'

'Might you have perhaps also done physics in physics?'

'You're so lame.'

'Perhaps,' Edie said, linking her arm through her daughter's as they headed back to the party room while Alice trailed behind, 'but at least I have a perfectly level fringe.'

Alice's heart hurt a little bit seeing the ease at which mother and daughter walked away laughing together. Their heads bent towards each other conspiratorially, the love they had for each other so clear, buried just beneath the surface of gentle teasing and comfortable banter. Yet the frenetic pace of Edie's existence meant she couldn't enjoy it. Spending this week as her sister had taught Alice that all the ingredients were there in Edie's life for her to be really happy, but she knew she wasn't experiencing the honest reality of it. Alice wasn't the one opening the bills every day, she wasn't the one shoehorning clients in to every spare moment to try to keep food in the fridge, a very special roof over their heads. Just earlier that afternoon she'd seen Rosie secretly gluing the sole of her trainer back down rather than ask for a new pair. Alice's own boys demanded a replacement if there was even a scuff on theirs. There must be something she could do to help this family be as happy as they deserved?

Everyone had already sat down at the table, and the space reserved for Alice was next to Danny. She slid in beside him, feeling an increased amount of trepidation as she smoothed the napkin over her lap and, fingers trembling a little, filled up their water glasses. 'So,' Alice started. 'What's on your mind?'

Danny shrugged.

'You seem down.'

'Not really.' He wouldn't look at her, even the top half of his body was facing ever so slightly away from her.

'Are you particularly stressed at the moment?'

'No more than usual.'

'Is anything bothering you?'

'You're asking a lot more questions recently.'

Alice reached across and put her hand on his. 'I'm your wife, I care about you.'

He moved his hand out from under hers and reached over the table to pick up a bread roll from the basket. 'Do you? Because you've become really argumentative this week, and I don't like it.'

How bad had Edie's rows with him gotten? She and Danny had never argued. Literally never argued in eighteen years. She'd said that as a point of pride in the past – 'we've never even had a cross word, can you believe it?' – but now she realised that was just as unhealthy as full blazing screaming matches that made walls shake. And why hadn't they ever argued? Because she made his life so easy, there was absolutely nothing for him to ever be cross about.

'I wonder why we've argued this week?' Alice asked, making it seem like a rhetorical question, while very much digging for intel.

'Because you want me to do more around the house, with the kids. Don't you?'

Alice hesitated; if he'd asked her this a week ago, she'd have flattened down his feathers, said no, of course not, that actually everything was fine, it was her pleasure to look after him, but after almost a week with Seb, she realised how much easier her life would be if the load was shared, even slightly.

'That would be . . . nice.'

'Are you really earning decent money from your Instagram thing?'

Alice didn't know exactly what Edie had said, so tried to make her answer as vague as possible. 'I have got some sponsors, yes.'

'I'm not going to pretend I understand what it is you do, but that's great if it's a success.'

Alice was about to lean in and kiss him, these were the nicest words he'd tossed her way in months, years even, but before she could, he quickly followed that up with, 'Just don't start letting things slip too much at home. I saw it with my mum and dad remember, the worst thing Mum did was to go back to work.' He'd wheeled out this phrase many times over their marriage, and Alice still wasn't sure how Rita's part-time job in the local library was a lesson on how not to parent.

'Hello you two,' Kenneth said, swapping seats with Teddy so he was now sitting the other side of Danny.

'Kenneth, I meant to ask,' Danny said, 'you've been to the Lake District, haven't you? We're thinking of going up there next month for a few days with the kids. I've got a colleague whose brother runs a log cabin business around Windermere.'

'Yes, the girls' mum and I went there before the girls were born, it was really lovely, I'll dig out the album and show you where we went before we go.' His eyes suddenly widened as he seemed to clock Alice's hand resting on Danny's leg.

'Did you drive to the Lakes, Ken, or get the train?' Danny said, stretching out his arm so it ran along the back of Alice's shoulders.

'I . . . er . . . drove,' Kenneth stammered, looking away, his gaze landing fifteen foot away, on Seb, who was just coming back into the room holding hands with Edie. Kenneth took a big gulp of his elderflower cordial, clearly wishing it was something so much stronger. 'You girls will be the death of me,' he muttered under his breath. *Whatever that meant.*

Edie

While dessert was being served, Edie slipped into the chair next to Alice that Auntie Barbara had just vacated. 'I was thinking,' Edie said quietly, desperate to say what was plaguing her, but equally unsure how her suggestion was going to be taken. But being back here for a few hours had made her so sure of what she needed to say to her sister. 'We don't need to swap back tonight, we could just stay in these clothes and you go home with your family and I stay here. The bet was a stupid idea anyway; this was about understanding each other's lives a bit more and I think we've done that. We don't need to keep it going.'

The speed at which Alice said, 'No!' shocked them both, and had Iris and Emily look up from where they were sitting having their faces painted by Rosie and Rufus at the end of the table.

Alice lowered her voice. 'I just don't think it's been long enough, that's all; we've just figured out how everything works, to stop it now would sort of defeat the object, wouldn't it? We're so close to really understanding each other, and why we act the way do and say the things we say, but there's so much more to learn. Six days isn't enough. It would be so easy to slip back into our old ways. You saw me up there dancing before, I never would have done that a week ago. I'm changing Edie, and I think you are too. We need to give this more of a chance.'

'I'm just worried I'm causing too many waves, with Danny,' Edie said, slumping back in her chair. 'Everything that comes out of my mouth annoys him, and I don't want to make things more difficult for you when we do eventually go back to being ourselves.'

Alice turned her body to face Edie so her back was to Danny and he wouldn't be able to hear their conversation, and kept her voice low. 'I talked to him earlier, and he was really sweet actually. I think you just need to back off him a bit, don't be confrontational, he hates that. He's taken on board everything you've said, and I think you'll start to see some changes.'

Edie scoffed. 'Changes like a personality transplant?'

'Edie!'

'Sorry. I know I shouldn't be so rude about him, but honestly Alice, the expectation and the privilege that just oozes off him, just gets me really riled up. You're a saint.'

'Or an enabler. Isn't that what you and Seb think?'

What did Seb say? Honestly give that man a couple of beers and he'd forget any sense. 'Did he say that?'

'More or less. He said that you both think that I created this monster.'

'Well, I wouldn't call him a monster—' It was as if the

universe had decided that actually that was a very fitting moniker for him because he chose exactly that moment to shout across the room, 'Rufus! What the hell have you got on your face?' Everyone swivelled to look at poor Rufus who blushed so deeply red it was almost difficult to make out the pink butterfly on his cheek, but the silver glitter Rosie had painstakingly applied on her cousin was all too clear.

'I think it looks great,' Seb said quickly. 'Rosie, can I have exactly the same?'

Edie's heart swelled, and catching her sister's eye, she knew Alice felt it too, especially when both sisters watched their own dad get up and stand in line behind Seb to have the same. Teddy hung back, observing. Edie willed him to join the queue, to position himself on the right side, but he didn't move, even though she was sure he wanted to. Danny pushed his chair back in a huff and left the room to go down to the bar.

'Are you okay?' Edie whispered to her sister, who was blinking furiously. 'Don't let it bother you.'

'But it does,' Alice whispered back, clearly furious. 'Had Danny been married to someone like you for eighteen years then he probably wouldn't be like this, he would know it's not okay to say these things, but I've never stood up to him.' She reached for Edie's glass and took a big sip of her wine. 'You're right, it *is* my fault.'

Edie's heart was breaking for her; her sister definitely had a part to play in his behaviour but no one was responsible for someone else choosing to be a certain way. Edie reached out and tucked a tendril of Alice's hair back behind her ear. 'It's absolutely not your fault but for the love of god, stop leaving him inspirational notes in his lunchbox.'

'Yes but—'

'Do you run the house so he does not need to lift one finger from the moment he comes in the door.'

'Well . . .'

'Answer the question.'

'He takes the bins out.'

'Why don't you do that? You're so lazy.'

Alice smiled, conceding that she had definitely made life a little too easy for him. 'How can I start moving the goalposts after eighteen years?'

'Eighteen years is nothing when you might be together for forty or fifty. In fact, now is the perfect time to reassess, to say to him, do you know what Danny, this isn't working for me, what I'd like is this, this and this, and see if he can change. And he might have a few things that he'd like you to do or not do, see what's on *his* list.'

Edie could see Alice stiffening.

'He does not have a list.'

'He might do.'

'But what could possibly be on it?'

'You're right. You are practically perfect in every way.'

'Hang on, what did Seb say was the next line . . . Rather inclined to giggle, doesn't put things away.'

'Wow, you're even saying our sayings now! Watch out, or you'll morph into me without even noticing.'

'If you'd asked me a week ago, I'd have thought that would be horrific, but now I'd be really happy to.'

Edie rubbed her arm against her sister's. 'Aw sis, that's the loveliest thing you've ever said to me.'

'Can you do me a favour though: try not to blow my life to pieces. Don't keep meddling in stuff that doesn't need meddling with.'

'James?'

'James, Danny, Teddy, *Rufus*.'

'But that's why I'm saying we shouldn't swap again. We've had a taste of how our other half lives, now we can just get back to normal.'

'But that's the point, we didn't really like our normal before. I was run ragged, and under-appreciated, you were working far too hard, barely making ends meet while not being able to spend time with your family. We'd lost perspective in our own lives. Maybe what we need is at least another week to really appreciate what we miss about our lives, and a bit more space away from them to see how we can make them different when we swap back.'

Edie wasn't convinced. This whole experience had been akin to picking a five-star resort out of a holiday brochure, getting there, and realising that all the crappy bits of the hotel had been boarded up and covered with a beautiful expensive wallpaper. If there were Trustpilot reviews of Alice's life she would never have agreed to this.

Seb bent down in between their chairs and put his hand on Edie's shoulder. The touch of his skin on hers made her shiver with gratitude that she was back in her rightful body. 'Iris is getting very sleepy,' he said. 'I think we should probably take her home, or do you want me to go on ahead with the girls and you follow in a bit?'

'Gosh, it's nearly eleven,' Alice said, looking at her gold watch, 'we should probably all be off, Edie and I just need to go downstairs a sec and sort something out.'

Edie shook her head. 'No we don't.'

The laser-beams that were shooting out of Alice's eyes could have thawed ice. 'I thought you said that you wanted us to run through the bill again?'

'No, it was fine actually.'

'I'd really like to just double check it with the manager?' Alice was trying to say something entirely different with her eyes.

'I can take the receipt down if you like?' Seb asked.

'No, it needs to be me and Edie, come on. It'll take just one minute. Please.'

Edie had no idea why Alice was so against returning to her own life, unless she hated it as much as Edie did. But on the other hand, Alice was clearly getting so much out of not being around Danny day in and day out, and exploring her fun side. Maybe another week would do her the world of good in realising that there was so much more to her than just being someone's wife and mother. And as much as every part of Edie's body and mind was desperate to go home with her own family tonight, and even the thought of not doing that made her feel like crying, if they swapped back now she wouldn't be able to protect Rufus against the mood that Danny was clearly in, or to continue in her quest for the kids to start pulling their own weight a little bit more to make Alice's life easier for when they did switch back to themselves.

'Fine,' Edie sighed, 'come with me then.'

Alice clapped her hands together. 'Brilliant, thank you.'

Alice

Once back in Edie's clothes, and they'd rejoined the party, everything felt off. Alice imagined she felt like an actor might, portraying someone on stage who was still alive and in the audience watching alongside all their family. She found herself second-guessing everything she did. Was that the way Edie put her coat on? She could hear Edie tutting as she almost forgot the little tin foil package of meat scraps Edie had put to one side to take home for Scooby. She clocked Edie's look of intense sadness when Seb put his arm around Alice's shoulder at the door. Alice disentangled herself the minute he'd done it, but even so, she could tell her sister was fighting every urge not to unveil herself as the rightful recipient of Seb's affections.

'Right, you guys should be off too,' Alice heard herself say. 'Have you got PE on Monday, Emily?' she asked, knowing full well that her daughter did have PE on Monday, and also knowing full well that there was a very high chance that her kit was still lying dirty in her bag from last week, but hearing this might prompt Edie into action on getting home. Home. Her home. The home she had spent hours every day making perfect, every inch of it clean and organised and Instagrammed. The home, that, if she was being honest, she hadn't missed all week.

As her family left, she felt a large pang of regret that she wasn't going with them, but if they swapped back now then it would all have been for nothing; Edie would still be run ragged. No. They had to keep this going for a bit longer, so she could make some subtle tweaks that would improve everything. She'd managed to ruffle Rufus's hair, the way an aunty could, but a mum couldn't, and she'd patted Teddy on the shoulder, which was more contact than he'd allowed her in a couple of years. Might she ever achieve the same laid-back bond Edie enjoyed with her kids? She had a lovely hug from Emily, which she tried to drink in and store up, and a perfunctory kiss on the cheek from Danny, who mumbled a 'see you'. A foot away, Edie was making more of the farewells than her character should be doing, squeezing Iris and Rosie tightly and kissing their heads, running a finger down Seb's cheek, actions totally suited to Edie, but very out of place, and somewhat inappropriate for Alice.

How they'd got away with this for six days was absolutely baffling.

CHAPTER TWENTY

The swap: day 7

Alice

While Alice never thought she would attain the obsessiveness of her sister's feelings towards dog ownership, she was certainly starting to see its merits that Sunday morning as she and Seb stretched out on a picnic blanket under a big willow tree in the park watching Scooby lollop single-mindedly after a ball. They'd left the girls at home; at fourteen Rosie was one year younger than Teddy, and yet Alice had never considered leaving the house without her own children. Undoubtedly Rosie was far more independent than Teddy was, but Alice was starting to see that was her fault, she had deliberately held him back from sovereignty over his own life, because if that happened, well, what did that mean for her?

How many fifteen-year-old boys, three months shy of turning sixteen, had never caught a bus by themselves? Never had their own door key? Never so much as popped a couple of slices of bread into the toaster? All this time she thought that she was being a good mother, but there was so much more to perfect parenting than making sure the kids' vitamin intake was spot on, that they wore clean clothes and took the right PE kit on the right day.

Seb sat himself up to throw the ball for Scooby again. 'You're very thoughtful this morning.'

Alice looked up at him. 'Am I? Sorry.'

'You don't need to apologise for being quiet! Anything I can help with?'

'Not really,' she said honestly – he'd done quite enough in scrambling her brain.

'I really enjoyed yesterday evening by the way. And Friday's visit.'

'Oh. Good.' She guessed that he wasn't talking about the party, and with a blush recalled her sister's ever so slightly dishevelled return to the party with Seb after fifteen minutes' absence.

'I would be very much in favour of other unscheduled drop-ins, should the mood take you again.'

Alice could feel a heat spreading all over her neck and face that had nothing to do with it being mid-June. It also had nothing to do with it being her sister's boyfriend saying this, although, that was admittedly a very inconvenient reality, but the very notion that a middle-aged couple, with teenagers of their own, would feel comfortable talking like this, about *sex*, in a park was unfathomable.

'Noted,' she replied, feeling that was enough to give him a smidgen of hope for more adventures of that kind, but allowing herself to retain some dignity and propriety.

'Why weren't you wearing your ring though?'

Alice's brain raced. The reason was very clear. Edie couldn't wear her eternity ring because she hadn't told Alice she was intending on visiting Seb at his studio, so the ring was still a few miles away firmly slotted on Alice's finger. Alice thought quickly, 'I took it off, before coming to the studio. Just in case you made me recreate that scene from *Ghost* where we both sat at the wheel moulding clay together.'

Seb laughed. 'Do you know, that did actually occur to me as a pretty cool thing to do; great minds.'

'Indeed.'

He lay back down on the picnic blanket alongside her and closed his eyes so the sun could bathe his face in its warmth.

And in that moment, where years of deep connection and an undeniable chemistry between Seb and who he thought was Edie fizzed in the air all around them, Alice absolutely understood what it was that made all the couples in that pool in Mauritius want to give each other a piggyback.

Edie

With her head banging out a tribal drumming rhythm courtesy of all the wine she had put away at the party, all Edie wanted to do that Sunday morning was lie in a park with Seb and Scooby and nap the hangover away, like they always did at weekends when the sun came out. Well not always. Often, *too* often lately, she'd made him go alone, while she stayed behind glued to her laptop. She would literally give anything now to rewind back to every Sunday morning, to the many moments Seb had looked at her with hopeful eyes as he suggested a stroll in the park and, instead of saying no, she'd shut her laptop, grab her coat and then his hand and just go. He'd be going alone again today; Alice would definitely think a stroll in the park was far too frivolous when there were chores to be done.

Meanwhile, she had to take Emily to her maths tutor, and drop the boys at their rugby game. Despite Alice claiming yesterday that Danny had listened to her remonstrations and that changes were afoot, when Edie asked him over breakfast to provide the morning's taxi service for the children, he said he'd arranged a personal training session at the gym that he simply couldn't get out of. After two hours of navigating London's traffic, quite probably still over the limit, with two ungrateful teenage boys telling her to speed up, and a little girl moaning about having to do maths on a Sunday – which Edie absolutely agreed with her about, but Alice had prepaid for the lesson – Edie hated herself for agreeing to swap back. This was hell on earth.

When she and Emily got back just before lunchtime, there was a strange car in the driveway with two elderly people sitting in it, seats reclined, fast asleep. Alice's house was big, but it was unlikely that they'd mistaken it for a hotel. Edie went up to the passenger side, where the woman was sitting and gently tapped on the window, trying not to induce a coronary as she did it. She vaguely recognised the couple as they sprang awake and scrambled to find the door handle, but she couldn't place them, like actors who appeared for only a few episodes in a favourite soap opera.

'Granny! Grandpa!' Emily shrilled, thankfully just before Edie could ask them if they were lost and needed help. She'd only met Danny's parents twice, once at Alice's wedding seventeen years before, and then again at her mother's funeral three years ago, and that whole day was a complete blur.

'Alice,' Danny's mother said as she grabbed hold of Edie's arms to heave herself out of the car, needing assistance due to her recent hip replacement. 'How lovely to see you. You've put on a bit of weight.'

Edie smiled, racking her brain to see if there was a whole section of Alice's folder she had omitted to read about the impending visit of her in-laws. She wouldn't have agreed to the swap had she known, would she? Or was she far more manipulative than Edie gave her credit for, and deliberately swerved this? Judging from her mother-in-law's opening gambit, she really wouldn't blame her.

'Where's Danny?' Emily's grandfather said as he shuffled to the front path.

'I would imagine the gym.' He'd drunk his protein shake in complete silence this morning, giving her no indication what his plans for the day were after his PT session, and he definitely had not said anything about this. 'Come in, come in.' Edie ushered everyone inside, noting that just inside the hallway her sort-of mother-in-law took two pairs of slippers out of a Waitrose bag for life, handed one pair to her husband and then slipped the others on her own feet, indicating that maybe this wasn't just a quick hello. Edie deposited Danny's parents on the kitchen stools at the breakfast bar, deftly doing all this without needing to call them by their actual names, as she had no idea what they were. She placed a steaming mug of tea in front of both of them, along with a packet of biscuits. She knew that Alice would have at the very least artfully arranged them onto a plate but, to be honest, that was just one more unnecessary item of crockery that she'd then have to wash up.

'Can I show Granny my certificates?'

Edie smiled at Emily. 'Yes of course, do you know where they are?' The fridge, the normal place for housing family accolades, just showcased its smooth brushed steel, no certificate or novelty magnet in sight. Emily trotted over to the bookcase where three matching lever arch files stood, and took down the one with her name on it. Edie wished some of her sister's organisation could rub off on her at some point. She'd even missed a trip to the Austrian Christmas markets with her friends six months ago because, on the morning of the trip, as the taxi was waiting outside, she couldn't find her passport.

'Oh, I am so glad you're still doing ballet and gymnastics lessons,' Danny's mum said in her Scottish lilt, leafing through the papers. 'My friend Nuala's granddaughter does some horrible martian art.'

'Bad paintings of aliens?' Edie said under her breath, then louder, 'Can you excuse me for a moment, I just need to go and change.'

Closing the bedroom door quietly behind her, she phoned Alice and tapped her toe impatiently until she picked up.

Edie didn't even say hello, just blurted straight out, 'Danny's parents are here.'

'Wait, hang on a second . . .' The next thing Alice said was muffled, so Edie assumed Alice was covering the microphone while talking to Seb. A few seconds passed and Edie could picture Alice walking away so she couldn't be overheard.

'Okay I'm back, what did you say about Danny's parents?'

Edie paced the width of the bedroom. 'They're here! In your house!'

'What?'

'You didn't say this would happen!'

'I didn't know!'

Edie paused by the window, pulling the curtains back and looking up and down the street for any sign of Danny. 'We need to swap back. I can't do this, I literally know nothing about them! They'll be able to tell straightaway!'

'Calm down, we can't swap back, I'm in the park.'

This made Edie stop still. 'In the park? With Seb?'

'Yes, we've brought Scooby to the park.'

'Are you lying on a blanket under the big willow tree on the slope?'

'Yes, how did you know?' She sounded confused.

'Seb and I have done that most sunny Sundays for years.' Edie heard her lie and flinched. Seb had done that for years.

She made a solemn, silent pledge that when they swapped back to themselves, she would go with him every single time he asked.

'It's honestly really lovely here.'

'I know.' Every atom inside Edie's body was yearning to be lying on that blanket in the park next to her husband, her dog panting beside them, spots of sunlight dappling their faces. Instead, she was trapped in a nightmare of her own making.

'And his parents didn't call ahead and say they were coming?'

Edie opened the bedroom window to lean out and get a better view to the end of the road to try to spot Danny approaching, but the street remained rudely empty. 'No!' she said in frustration. 'And I don't even know what their names are!'

'Rod and Rita. Rita had a hip replacement a few months ago. Rod's got a trawler business.'

'What's that?'

'Fish. Fishing. Fisherman.'

Edie slammed the window shut and sat down heavily at her sister's dressing table. 'Stop saying fish. I already feel like I want to vomit. Tell me something else useful.'

'They've been having a problem with their guttering.'

'Jesus woman, I'm going to puke on your carpet. Tell me something interesting.'

'Don't mention politics, religion, women's rights, Scottish independence, anything about your job, money, social media, London, actually nothing about England—'

Edie put her head down on the top of the dressing table and groaned down the phone. 'Seriously, I can't do this.'

'You can. Just don't talk at all. They won't be expecting you to. Just keep feeding them, and occasionally mention the garden. Danny will do the rest.'

'He's not even here.'

'Where is he?'

'Where do you think?'

'Have you called him?'

'Not yet. I was hoping you'd come back and deal with them.' *Why isn't she hailing a cab and immediately coming back here to deal with them? She could be halfway here by now if she'd have left at the start of the call!* 'Alice, this is way more than I agreed to.'

'You'll be fine. Oh, one more thing, don't mention you.'

'Me?' What an odd thing to say, it didn't make any sense.

'*Edie*. Don't mention anything about Edie.'

'Why?'

'They don't really like you.' At least Alice sounded a little apologetic about admitting this. There was no malice or one-upmanship at all in her tone, just embarrassment.

'They've hardly ever met me!'

'Apparently you were too drunk at my wedding and cried too much at Mum's funeral.'

'Wow, these people really are arseholes.' Edie bit her bottom lip, needing to ask the next question, but knowing she was wrong to even be thinking it. 'Are you sure you didn't know they were coming? It was *you* that chose the date of the swap.'

'I'm going to pretend you didn't say that. Go back downstairs. Now remember, make lots of food and talk about the garden. That's all you need to do.'

'So . . .' Edie paused, knowing that this farce was not of her sister's making, but there was no harm in making her pay for it. 'Just to get this right, I lead with a chat about the merits of an open immigration system, moving quickly onto the importance of making abortion legal and accessible to all, before shoehorning something in about how inspirational my sister Edie is to modern women everywhere. Got it.'

'Edie, please . . .' Alice sounded utterly panicked.

Edie stood up decisively. She didn't know whether she would say all that to Rod and Rita, but at least now the option of having fun with them was on the table she didn't feel quite as rattled. 'I'll talk about whatever I want to in my own home, thank you very much. Bye for now!'

Alice

'Edie! Edie!' Alice stared at the phone in her hand. This wasn't happening. She could feasibly leave the park and be back at her own house in forty minutes or so. But how would she explain that to Seb or her in-laws? Just popping over for no reason, and then what would she say or do? Edie was probably joking anyway. She wouldn't deliberately antagonise a pair of pensioners . . . Who was she kidding, of course she would.

She looked over to the willow tree and Seb wasn't there, Scooby was lying there alone. Her eyes scanned the horizon and paused on an ice cream truck, which Seb was just walking away from, a ninety-nine ice cream, complete with chocolate flake, in each hand. Alice pushed down her anxiety. There was nothing she could do; Danny would be back soon, her being there too would just confuse things. She put on a brave smile and gave Seb a grateful wave.

CHAPTER TWENTY-ONE

Edie

Danny ignored her the first four times she called, but Edie just kept pressing redial until he finally picked up, which she knew that he would eventually.

'Where are you?' It was an unnecessary question – he was either at the gym, or he wasn't, in which case he would lie to her and say he was.

'I'm just leaving the gym.'

She took a smidgen more satisfaction than she should have done in passing over the next piece of information. 'Your parents are here.'

'What?'

She thought that would stop him in his tracks. 'Your parents are currently sat in our kitchen.'

'Why?!' She could hear the panic rising in his voice.

'I don't know! But you need to come back.'

'I was just going to grab some lunch first.'

Is this man for real? 'No, *Daniel*.' Edie didn't actually know if his full name was Daniel, but it seemed that if there was ever a time that called for the use of a full name, this was it. 'You're coming back here. They're your parents.'

'I'm sure you can entertain them for an hour until I'm back.'

'If you're not back in under ten minutes, I will tell them we're considering taking up nude yoga.'

'Come on Alice.' He sounded unsure, and rightly so.

Edie opened the bedroom door a tiny bit to check the in-laws were still downstairs being entertained by Emily. 'I'm serious.' Edie whispered through her teeth, closing the door again, 'I'll even get up a video of one of the classes on my phone to show them. Also, you can't see me, but I'm currently rifling through Emily's drawers to find those temporary tattoos Rosie gave her for Christmas to put one on my neck before I go back downstairs.'

'Alice—'

'Or I could show them the photo on my phone of when Edie picked up Emily to take her to the hairdressers with Iris and they ended up dancing on a float at gay pride. I think it's so important for young people to understand the importance of being an ally, don't you?'

'What are you playing at?'

'I can't hear you running yet, Daniel; you better start running.'

*

Seven and a half minutes later, his face flushed scarlet and so out of breath he had to lean against the doorframe before stepping inside, Danny arrived home. Edie had just replenished the teapot for the second time, and even Emily had run out of conversation, so his gasping entrance was welcomed by everybody.

Rita's whole demeanour exploded in reverent joy in exactly the same way Rosie's had when Edie took her to see Harry Styles at Wembley. 'Hello son!'

'You look great, glad to see you're still training hard. Bet I can still beat you in an arm wrestle though!' With a proud grin, Rod held up his sagging arms and made a bicep curl.

'I hope Alice has been keeping you fed and watered,' Danny said, smiling, but Edie detected an edge to his question, hearing it more as a threat than a simple enquiry. His smile wasn't mirrored in his eyes either. He was clearly livid; it just wasn't clear yet who at.

'Watered yes, but she's only given us biscuits,' Rod replied.

'We were hoping for something more substantial, it is lunchtime after all,' Rita chimed in. 'We're normally given a three-course meal before we've even taken our coats off.'

'She is usually very good at things like that,' Rod agreed, while Danny glowered at her incompetence above their heads.

Edie wondered if she had actually been given the superpower of invisibility without her knowing, because she was standing there while this conversation was taking place, and yet it seemed she was absolutely undetectable. It also was only five minutes past midday, which, on a Sunday, still fell firmly into the mid-morning arena, not lunchtime.

'What would everyone like?' she said brightly, taking out a clean bee pinny from the drawer and tying it round her waist, just to give the audience the full experience of what they expected before hitting them with something they weren't. 'I can pop some frozen baguettes in the oven and do a plate of ham and cheese?'

Danny and his parents stared back at her in undisguised revulsion.

'I don't think we got up at three am to drive the length of Britain to have a ham and cheese sandwich!' Rod laughed. 'I think you can do a bit better than that, Alice.'

'Why *did* you drive all the way here then?' Edie asked, trying not to let her bright and breezy disposition falter.

'We have to talk to Danny about some important business. Nothing that concerns you, hen. You've got your hands full with lunch.'

Edie looked at Danny, naively expecting him to step in and help her conjure up this mystical Michelin-starred feast, but instead he just stared at her with wide eyes while nodding his head at the fridge silently telling her to get a move on.

'Do you know what?' she said, after surveying the contents of the shelves and not seeing how any of the ingredients in it matched up to one another without the help of google, or her sister. 'It's a lovely day, why don't we go and buy some picnic things at the deli, and catch the second half of the boys' rugby match? They'd be thrilled to see you there.'

Her suggestion was actually met with a positive response from all three, which surprised her, not because it wasn't a good idea, but because she had been the one to make it.

They arrived at the game a few minutes after the whistle had blown announcing the start of the second half. It was the final of the county under 16s, a fact she hadn't actually known until she got there, but it made her wonder why Danny hadn't been there since kick-off cheering on his sons, like so many of the other parents lining the white lines around the pitch. She could have understood it had it been a chess championship, or something he had no knowledge of, but when your dad was a former professional player for his country, the least you'd expect is an hour and a half of his time when you were playing his sport. Edie knew very little about the rules of rugby, but accurately surmised that neither did her sister, so felt no compulsion to pretend otherwise and add her voice to the loud shouts of Danny and Rod.

'Pass it!'

'Hold onto it!'

'Spread out!'

'Move closer to him, man!'

If their advice was anything to go by, this was a very baffling game. She was standing alongside the two men at the side of the pitch, with Emily and Rita sitting demurely on a blanket a couple of metres behind them, when Rod said, 'I'm starving here Alice.'

She was confused; they'd all just chosen the food they each wanted to eat and it was all in the cool box on the blanket. Had he forgotten doing that?

'Yeah me too,' said Danny, crossing his arms and rocking back on his heels. 'Throw it, for Christ's sake!'

Edie clapped and cheered as Teddy ran a good twenty metres with the ball before being tackled and falling to the ground, letting the other team have the ball.

'Why are you clapping?' Danny said angrily, pointing at the pitch. 'He lost the ball.'

Edie shrugged. 'But he did really well until that point.'

Rod shook his head. 'He shouldn't have let go, the ref was nowhere near, he could have held onto it a bit longer.'

Danny put his hands under each armpit, thumbs pointing upwards and rocked back on his heels. 'Seriously Alice, we're parched here.'

She suddenly realised that the men actually wanted her to go to the cool box two metres away, fetch their food for them, and deliver it back to them, before pattering her little lady feet back to sit with the other people with vaginas on the blanket. Well, she wasn't going to. If they were hungry and thirsty, they knew where the goods were that would relieve them of both afflictions. She could sense Danny's eyes boring into her side, and heard his sporadic coughs designed to spur her into action, but no, she was not doing it. It was a small act of defiance, but a very necessary one.

A good ten minutes passed by before Danny, obviously

gripped with hunger, trotted back to the food and grabbed his and his dad's rolls, giving Edie a disappointed shake of his head as he came back. She flashed him a winning smile. 'Oh those rolls look yummy, good idea, I'm starving,' she said, leaving the sideline to get her own lunch, feeling Danny's laser-like glare burning a hole in her back.

Despite being one of the smaller players on the pitch, Rufus made a couple of great tackles, winning the ball both times, and taking an incredible drop kick at the goal from near the centre line that sailed over the bar, just seconds before the final whistle blew. It wasn't quite enough to top the leaderboard, but it won him man of the match, and amid much back slapping from his teammates, he jogged over to where they all stood, his proud grin stretching from ear to ear.

'That was brilliant darling,' Edie gushed. 'Well done!'

'That was a great kick Roof!' Emily echoed.

Flushed red with exertion and pride, Rufus said excitedly, 'Did you see it Dad? Grandpa?'

Danny nodded. 'Shame you couldn't have kicked like that earlier in the game; you might have actually won then.'

Rod nodded in agreement. 'Second place is first loser.'

Edie couldn't believe this. Every part of her burned with indignation. Were they so blind as to not see that what Rufus needed in that moment was not a reminder of what he hadn't done, but a massive appreciation for what he *had*. If they weren't going to do it, she would. She knew it wouldn't land quite the same, but it was better than nothing. 'The way you lined the ball up from so far away was incredible, sweetheart, what a shot! Ah, here's Teddy, Ted darling, what a great run you had, you were so fast!'

Teddy looked a bit embarrassed, but underneath Edie was sure she also glimpsed some pride at how hard he'd worked out there, but he knew he couldn't show it. These children were crying out for someone to build them up, to teach them that failure was a part of life, that it only served to make the successes taste so much sweeter. Surely Danny was perfectly placed to impart that nugget of wisdom – he couldn't have won every game he ever played.

Where was the fun in these boys' lives? The joy? She'd seen glimpses of laughter and happiness from them this week, but never when Danny was in the house. Alice worked so hard to organise everything, she didn't have time to just stop and see what they really needed. What *she* really needed.

Just as they'd packed up the food and the blanket, one of the player's dads gingerly approached their group and asked Danny for an autograph. Edie could tell the timing of this request delighted him, as he constantly kept glancing up to check Rod was looking as he put his pen to the stranger's paper. Edie glanced over in Rod's direction too, just to see him yawn, and check his watch. A cloud of sadness flashed over Danny's features, yet he was too blinkered to see that he had two sons of his own so desperate for the same approval he was seeking from *his* father. Edie thought. If she could somehow get through to him, assist him in breaking this generational cycle, help him be the father these kids really deserved, then this swap would be really worth it. Maybe all wasn't lost.

'Right,' Danny said, hoisting the heavy cool box effortlessly over his shoulder, 'we'd better get back so you can get dinner on, Alice.'

Or maybe all was lost long ago.

Alice

'I can't believe you got me slippers! They are so comfortable!' Seb wiggled his toes inside his fur-lined moccasins. He honestly could not have been happier than if she had presented him with a new car. 'Were they expensive?'

'Not at all. I got the girls some too.'

'You are so thoughtful.' He reached over and kissed her on the lips before Alice could pull away or turn her head.

'This doesn't mean that I'm turning into my sister,' she said, a little too quickly, 'I'm just taking inspiration from her good bits.'

'I am here for it. Honestly, the house looks amazing, you've done way more than your fair share of the cooking this week. I promise I'll pull my weight a bit more next week, but I love the fact that you've also been really present, you know? Not glued to your laptop, and just enjoying life a bit more.'

She nodded, feeling a little sad that Edie wasn't able to enjoy her family as much as she should because of work and money and house worries. It also made Alice wonder if *she* was really *present* in her own life? So much of her day was spent organising, and planning, and cleaning, and creating content for her followers, creating and curating the perfect life, how often did she just stop and enjoy it? Never. Her entire life was one long mental distraction, with to-do lists piled on top of to-do lists, tickertapes of duties and responsibilities and chores, and things that only she could do. But here, with Seb and the girls doing so many of things that always fell to just her in her own family, she had the time to be, well, *present*. And she hadn't even missed her Instagram that much. For the first few days of the swap she was always on high alert for content: a nice plate of food, a beautiful window display in a high-street florists, a heart on the top of a cappuccino; each of these things had her reaching for the camera on her phone. But as the week wore on, with Seb encouraging inane messaging throughout the day, she ceased to feel the need to upload these things to followers she didn't know, and instead, just opened up a new message to him. Since that first cringeworthy photo of the sparrow on the windowsill, she was looking out for pockets of joy everywhere to share with him. It was incredible that the validation and affection of one person could top the thousands of digital 'likes' that she craved only a week ago.

He went off humming towards the garden doors, and she stopped herself just in time before she shouted after him, 'Those are indoor shoes, Seb!'

Edie

Danny and his dad had been talking in the living room, behind a firmly closed door, for over an hour, as Edie and Rita amiably prepared dinner side by side. Just as Alice had predicted, the conversation rarely strayed from the planting schedule for the coming year, a topic Edie knew next to nothing about, so limited herself to making encouraging comments like, 'oh yes, good point,' and 'that is very true,' when Rita went ahead designing every inch of Alice's herbaceous borders.

'Your left wall is very shady, so hydrangeas would do well there. But not the blue ones, they can look tacky,' Rita said, finely shredding the lettuce for the salad.

Edie nodded dramatically in agreement. 'I do not want to be tacky.'

'Foxglove would also work well.'

'Do you know what? I was thinking about foxglove actually.' *Foxglove's a funny name for a plant, considering foxes don't have hands.*

'Well,' Rita said, pleased, 'I'd make a start with them then, and see how you go.'

'What do you think about azaleas?' Edie asked amiably, as she swilled some cherry tomatoes under the tap. 'Better in pots?'

Danny and Rod came back into the kitchen, looking very pleased with themselves. Rod even had a hand on Danny's shoulder.

Rita stopped chopping the carrots and looked up expectantly. 'All sorted?'

Rod nodded and smiled. 'He said yes.'

Rita shrieked and ran round the breakfast bar to give Danny a hug – she was about half his size, and reached on tiptoes to kiss his cheek. 'Oh I'm so pleased!'

'What's going on?' Edie asked, smiling, wanting to join in whatever was being celebrated. God knows they needed some merriment in this house.

Rod slapped Danny on the back. 'Danny here has agreed to take over the business so I can retire.'

Edie looked from Rod, to Danny, to Rita, who was holding her hands together in glee, hopping from one foot to the other. 'Um, sorry, what?'

'Dad's asked me to run his business!' Danny said gleefully. 'It's doing really well. We've got fifteen trawlers now, supplying crab, lobster and haddock to supermarkets and restaurants all over southern Scotland.' He headed for the fridge to grab the bottle of champagne Edie had been hungrily eyeing all week, but now the thought of toasting this news made her feel sick.

'And mackerel,' Rod interjected proudly.

Edie tilted her head slightly as she digested this news. 'And you can do that from London?'

'Of course not!' Rod exclaimed, looking at Edie like she had swallowed a pill of stupidity. 'You can move into our house in Fife. We've been wanting to downsize for a while, so you take our home and we'll move into the cottage next door.'

'And you've just agreed to this?' Edie asked Danny, aghast. 'Without even asking me?'

He peeled off the bottle's foil wrapper, discarding it on the worktop for his wife to clean up later. 'Well, it's not as though there's anything keeping you here, you can do your Instagram thing from anywhere.'

The cork made a jubilant pop, prompting aahs and oohs from his parents. Edie had to speak louder over their elation to be heard. 'What about *Britain in the Morning*? The kids' schools and friends? My dad? My sister?'

At the mention of the word 'sister', Rita made a 'pffft' sound through her teeth, which made Edie shoot a look loaded with daggers at her.

Edie rounded on Rod, pointing her finger in his face. 'When I asked you earlier why you were here, you said it was to discuss some business thing with Danny that didn't concern me. I think this concerns me rather a lot, don't you?'

Danny poured champagne into three flutes, hesitating over whether to fill up a fourth. 'Alice, I don't think we need to go over this now—'

Edie knew that her voice was bordering on hysterical, but the thought of her twin being pulled away to a town ten hours away was making her heart burn with fear. 'Really, Danny? Because I think that now is the perfect time to talk about this, because you cannot make decisions that impact the whole family without even discussing it. We will not, ever, be moving to Fife. End of.'

He slammed the bottle down, the remaining champagne fizzing over the top onto the counter. 'That's not your call to make!'

Edie could feel her blood coursing faster through her veins. 'Like it's not *your* call to say that we will.'

'It's not really your decision though, is it?' Rod said, stretching over his wife to pick up a glass for himself.

Edie turned on him. 'And why is that Rod? Because I only have half a vote in this? The 1800s called and want their sexist ideologies back.'

'A wife has to support her husband in his dreams,' Rita parroted primly.

'And you can button it as well, Rita. A wife has to support her husband in his dreams, what about *her* dreams? Give me a fucking break.'

Rod needed to sit down at this, while Rita fetched him a cold glass of water to help with the shock of hearing his daughter-in-law, who'd always been so pleasant and acquiescent, use a word he'd only probably ever heard on the trawlers. Edie imagined that Rita had never heard it said by a real person, outside of a movie, which they probably would have turned off for being so blue.

Edie turned to face Danny head on, trying to recover a sense of decorum and speak as Alice would. 'We will have a sensible conversation about this tonight, whereby we can see if we can reach some sort of compromise where you can flit between here and there, and see if that can work—'

He downed his entire glass in one gulp, then reached for the bottle to fill it up again, turning his back on Edie while he spoke. 'I'm not spending my life travelling. I'm Scottish, I want the kids to feel Scottish, and we're moving to Fife.'

Rod nodded his approval of his son's words as though through the bob of his head he was placing the punctation on the end of Danny's declaration himself. He held out his glass to tap it against Danny's. 'Slàinte Mhath!' the two of them chorused.

Edie didn't think she had ever despised a person more than she did right then.

She picked up her knife to continue making the dinner, but her hand was trembling so much, she could barely keep it in her fingers. She considered, very briefly, murdering all three of them, but thought, on reflection, that her being in prison was probably worse than her sister being in Fife.

CHAPTER TWENTY-TWO

Edie

'You need to tell Alice.'

Edie shook her head, kicking at a tuft of grass in front of her dad's garden bench with her toe. 'I can't, Dad. What if she goes?'

'But that's her choice to make,' he said kindly, clearly knowing that wasn't what she wanted to hear.

Edie blew out slowly. 'I need to make this go away. I need to either change Danny's mind so he turns down the job and stays, or make her life so amazing here that moving to Scotland is the last thing she wants to do.'

He snipped a drooping rose off a thorny branch. 'This is not your life Edie. This is hers. She needs to be part of this decision. It's time to hand her life back to her so that she can deal with this.'

'You don't know what it's like Dad, to be a twin, to have this bond. I know we're different, god are we different, but I can't be hundreds of miles from her, I just can't, my heart would splinter into a million pieces. Plus, like I say, I think I could actually fix this for her. She's never going to stand up to Danny in the way she needs to unless she really feels like her life here is worth fighting him for.'

'This isn't about you Edie. This is Alice's life. And it's up to her to come back and work out a plan with her husband. She might even fancy a change,' he swivelled away from his pruning to face her, waving his secateurs at her, 'have you thought of that?'

'To be what?' she scoffed. 'Rod and Rita's carer as they get older? A fisherman's wife living in a country she doesn't know.'

'It's Scotland, not Sri Lanka.'

Edie shook her head, unwilling to even entertain the idea that Fife could hold any temptation for her sister at all. 'No, there's no way that she'd be happy there. And he'd make her feel that she couldn't say no.'

Kenneth pulled one glove, and then the other off. 'She might surprise you and make her own mind up, do what she wants to.'

'When has she ever done that?' Edie asked, moving up on the bench to make room for him to sit alongside her. 'Because she's spent the first twenty-odd years of her life doing what *I* wanted to do, and now she does what *he* wants.' Edie stopped, stunned at the words that had just tumbled out of her mouth. Oh god, she was doing now exactly what Danny had been doing. Taking Alice's free will away from her. Assuming that her way was the right way.

Kenneth patted his daughter's knee. 'Penny dropped?'

This time when Edie spoke, her conviction was weaker, she could feel a lump forming in her throat. 'No, no it's not the same,' she choked out, 'it's different.'

'How? By not telling her about this, by trying to make this go away before she knows anything about it, I'd say that sounded pretty similar.'

Edie concentrated on a pair of daisies in the grass, the only splash of colour in a sea of green, and she started to cry. 'I can't lose her as well as Mum, I can't. I've only just put my heart back together.'

Kenneth then pulled out the only thing left in his arsenal. 'What would Mum tell you to do?'

Edie sniffed and wiped her nose on Alice's expensive cashmere cardigan, leaving a dark smear on the sleeve. 'To stop playing dress up and start acting like grown-ups.'

A smile played on Kenneth's lips. 'Well then. Where are they all now?'

'Back at mine.' Edie corrected herself. 'I mean Alice's. I said I needed to get some air.'

'Are they staying overnight?'

'No idea. No one tells me anything. Danny hasn't told me to make up the spare room, so hopefully not.'

'Swap back tomorrow and let her sort this out herself. This whole switch thing has done its job, you both know a lot more about each other's challenges than you did before, but this isn't your business to meddle with, she needs to come back into her own life and take control of it.' He knew her well enough to know that the agreeing nod she gave him was not entirely genuine. 'Edie, I mean it darling. This is not about you anymore, this is her life.'

Edie nodded again, this time not listening at all as a plan was vaguely forming.

Alice

Alice side-eyed the woman a foot away, trying not to make it obvious that she was watching her every move. She even picked a scented candle up off the shelf and gave it a cursory sniff to make it look like she too was just an ordinary shopper trying to find a birthday present. The woman turned the vase in her hand over, twisted it round, looking at it from all directions. *Buy it, buy it,* Alice silently willed her. The woman placed it back on the shelf and picked up a hot water bottle shaped like a sloth and took it straight over to the cash desk. Alice resisted the urge to pick up the vase and charge at her, brandishing it in the air shouting, 'Sloths are overrated, they're lazy and move ridiculously slowly, pick this handcrafted piece of pottery that took hours of effort and love to make!' But she didn't. She just moved all the other pieces of ceramics from the other independent artists to the back of the shelf and made Seb's all the more prominent. He had come such a long way since his early prototypes, these designs were really beautiful, each one with the same golden glaze, and thunderbolts of various sizes zig-zagging down its sides. They were really striking.

Earlier, in the park, Alice thought they would just eat their ice creams and head home, but Seb seemed uneasy as he propped himself up on his arm facing her and apologised. He apologised for chasing a dream that every day became more futile, and out of reach. He apologised for giving up a career that while not particularly lucrative, at least came with the promise of a pension and a free car parking space. He apologised for being less than she and the girls deserved. 'I just want you to be proud of me,' he said. 'I'm starting to realise that it was really selfish of me for wanting this. I should never have left a steady job and salary on a whim.'

It wasn't even the right sister he was saying this to, but nonetheless, it absolutely broke her heart. She felt so guilty for hearing about his decision from Edie a year ago, and making a judgement based on the headline of that alone: husband leaves teaching for solo art quest. But lying on that blanket with him, seeing how much he wanted it, believed in it, and yet, not through lack of hard work or faith, wasn't getting it, she realised that perhaps being spontaneous, and free, and hopeful, was something not to be admonished, but admired.

It wasn't that his pottery wasn't pretty, it was; and it wasn't overpriced, or overly fanciful, he had a real eye for shape and colour, and he was really talented, but the sale of a few vases or plates a month would be barely covering the rent of his studio, let alone making a dent in the mortgage repayments or helping towards a weekly shop. No wonder Edie was working so hard to make up the shortfall. She'd found an Excel spreadsheet of all the invoices Edie had sent out this month alone, she was working every hour just to keep the family afloat. Seb needed exposure. He needed a new audience. But first, she needed a new vase and so did all her friends.

*

'You've been ages,' Seb said when she came in, giving her one of his best warm, slow, smiles from the sofa.

She'd left all his pottery in the boot of Edie's car, the haul had come in at nearly nine hundred pounds, a number the lady on the till stated with more than a hint of apology in her voice. It was worth every penny to see Seb's face when the message pinged through on his phone from the owner of the shop, telling him about his mystery benefactor, and putting in a repeat order. His whoops of joy morphed into disbelieving head shaking, before turning into tears of validation, that this pipe dream that earlier that afternoon had seemed selfish and unattainable might now be working out. Alice had only seen Danny cry once, and even then she saw his weeping through the medium of television, not in person. It was his last game with his club, his last final whistle, and the camera panned in with a close-up on his face where immense pride and grief were battling each other. He'd managed to get through the birth of his three children, the death of both his grandparents and his mother-in-law, without a single sniff.

First thing tomorrow, Alice decided that she would package each vase and platter up and send them to other influencers, asking them to post about his designs on their pages. She was also going to drop one of the taller vases into the studio to ask them if they could replace one of the other vases on the shelf behind the sofa with this one instead. A tiny push, and he, and Edie, would be living the life they wanted to.

Edie

Edie walked around the side of the house, and paused just round the corner, out of sight from where Danny was sitting with his parents on the patio. She strained to listen to their conversation.

Rita was saying, 'You wouldn't need to even do any work to the house; we had a new kitchen put in about fifteen years ago, and it's still in pristine condition, and yellow pine is timeless anyway.'

Rod chimed in, 'Whatever you do, don't do anything to the pebbledash on the outside. I know it's apparently all the rage to get rid of it, but it cost us a lot of money in the eighties to put it on and it would break our hearts to see it gone.'

Edie then heard Danny's voice. 'Don't worry, we wouldn't change a thing.'

'I worry, you know, with Alice's social medium thing, that she'd try and paint everything navy and rip out the French windows to put in bi-focals.'

Edie couldn't bear the fact that her sister was being talked about like this, as though nothing she did or said had any value at all. She tried to imagine what Alice would actually do, right now, based on today's events, seeing and hearing what she had. If the switch had never happened, and it was Alice rooted to the same spot next to the wheelie bins and Danny's expensive bicycle, would she feel the same bubbling of blood inside her veins as Edie was, or would she just accept this as her fate, part and parcel of what she'd signed up for? And Edie honestly didn't know the answer. She hoped that Alice would have, at the very least, said that it was a very kind offer, and they'd given them a lot to think about. Knowing her sister, she would have probably sweetened this by offering up a homemade banana loaf at the same time; maybe that was where she was going wrong.

'Are you staying tonight?' Edie asked, walking onto the patio and sitting down on the rattan garden sofa alongside Danny, feeling very much like she'd just gate-crashed a family party she wasn't invited to. 'I totally understand if you want your own space though; there is a lovely Premier Inn that's just opened up off the ring road.'

'Of course they're staying here,' Danny replied, then turning to his dad said, 'give me the car keys and I'll go and get your suitcase and take it up to our room.'

Rita at least had the good manners to look a little uncomfortable at the impromptu imposition, repositioning herself on her garden chair and not meeting Edie's eyes.

'Don't you mean the spare room?' Edie said. She'd slept in there the night before after getting back from the party, so she knew the sheets were clean on yesterday.

'No.' Danny stood up to take the keys from Rod's outstretched hand and put them in his pocket. 'Last time they stayed, Dad had a crick in his neck for days because of the softness of the mattress, and we've got an orthopaedic one, so I already told them that would be better for them.'

Edie looked at Danny. She had no words. Not because she particularly wanted to sleep in the main bedroom, she didn't care where she slept, but this constant belittling of Alice's place in her own home, her own life, was maddening. And not even during the stripping of the bed, and the remaking of it using clean sheets, nor the bundling up of the old linen, and carrying them downstairs to put them in the wash, did any useful, pre-watershed vocabulary come to her. Thankfully Danny was walking his parents around their garden, while Rita talked him through her plans for how to spruce it up ready for house viewings once they put it on the market, saving Edie from pretending to be civil. She shoved the sheets in the washing machine, remembering Danny's dirty gym kit that she'd kicked under the breakfast bar earlier, and she reached for it. As she took out his workout gear she wondered if maybe she should follow the advice Alice gave the viewer on the show who called about her errant gym-loving partner. Perhaps if she did go along with Danny to his 'happy place', she might see a different side to him. Maybe he would be so relaxed and carefree he would redeem himself and they could have a real chat about Fife. She did however hope that this said chat could take place without her having to actually use any of the gym equipment.

CHAPTER TWENTY-THREE

Edie

Later that night, after everyone else had gone to bed, Edie lay horribly close to Danny in the small spare room bed and made a suggestion that was clearly making his head spin.

'You want to come to the gym with me? *My* gym?'

'I didn't know you owned it?'

'Why would you want to do that?' he asked, which really rankled Edie. If Seb had his way, she'd accompany him to the dental hygienist just to spend more time together, and here Danny was, desperate to avoid any time with Alice at all.

'I'd like to get a bit fitter,' Edie said, 'and I feel like we never see each other.'

'Yeah,' Danny said, taking a sip of the herbal sleep tea she had just made for all four adults before they came up to bed, 'but that's one of the reasons I go, just to be out of the house for a bit.'

'You literally leave the house at seven-thirty in the morning, and come back at eight pm; if you were out for any longer you wouldn't be able to put yourself on the census.'

'The gym's my thing Alice. I can find you a nice ladies' gym of your own if you're serious about this. But real fitness takes commitment, and . . .' He shrugged, and gave her a knowing look. 'I don't know if you'd be able to stick at it.'

His insinuation that her sister was unreliable, or inconsistent really prickled at Edie. 'You don't think I'd be able to commit to something? When have I ever proven myself to be flaky or fickle? About anything?'

Danny winced. 'Keep your voice down, you'll disturb Mum and Dad. Please, I just want them to think we're happy.'

This caught Edie by surprise. 'What do you mean?'

'I just want them to think that our marriage is as good as theirs is. That I've got a great family and doing well for myself. And it was all fine until a week or so ago.'

'It was only good,' Edie whispered, 'because I did everything you told me to and waited on you hand and foot. That's not a good marriage; that's good grounds for me demanding a salary to be your housekeeper.'

'But that is part of what a wife is meant to be.'

'My life is so much more than just being your wife and our children's mother, Danny.'

Danny scratched his head while he thought; he couldn't be more like a cartoon bear if he tried.

'As well as looking after you all and making sure you want for nothing, I also maintain nearly a million followers on Instagram, so I spend probably four hours a day creating content.'

There was no mistaking the smirk on Danny's face as she said this, even in the dim light of the bedroom. The childlike vulnerability from a moment before, desperate for his parents' approval was gone, and back in its place was the churlish machismo he wore with pride.

'Why are you smiling?' Edie asked.

'It's not really a job though, is it?'

'I work really hard. From the minute my alarm goes off at six, to when I fall into bed exhausted at the end of the day after cleaning up after all of you.'

'Welcome to married life,' Danny said in a sarcastic tone that only served to amplify Edie's steadily growing rage.

'What's that supposed to mean?' she snapped.

'That's the deal of marriage, isn't it? I go out to work and pay for everything; you look after the home and the family.'

'Have you slept through the last four decades? Times have changed Danny, *I* have changed, and I need a lot more from you than you are currently giving me.'

If the ticking on the alarm clock on the bedside table wasn't so bastardingly loud, Edie was sure she'd have been able to hear Danny's brain whirring. 'I need more help around the house and with the kids, *our* kids. So the days of me doing all the cooking, and cleaning and ferrying the kids about to all their activities and playdates are ending, and you're going to share the load a bit more.'

'You can't just rewrite the rules eighteen years into our relationship,' he stammered, looking more terrified than angry.

'Yes I can, and I am.'

'I know what's going on.' Danny pointed his finger right in her face, a mere inch or so from her nose. 'Your sister's been getting in your ear about all her equal rights rubbish, hasn't she? I couldn't put my finger on what's been buzzing up your bum but now I can. She's been spouting all her feminism nonsense and you've been lapping it up.'

'Yes, that's exactly what it is, except it's not rubbish or nonsense, it's a normal, civilised way of living appropriate to the twenty-first century, and I'm fed up of living like women did before they knew better. So, you can either get on board or ship out to Fife by yourself.' Edie pulled the duvet up closer around her and crossed her arms over it.

'You're serious? You'd prefer me to leave rather than you having to be a wife?'

'A wife isn't someone who does everything you don't want to do. A wife isn't someone who does everything around the house and with the family. A wife is meant to be your co-captain.' Edie thought that if she used a sporting term, he was more likely to get it.

'Teams don't have co-captains,' he replied sulkily, 'no one would know who was in charge.'

'Why does anybody need to be?' Edie was exhausted. Of arguing, of trying to make him understand, of living for a week with someone so unwilling to change, or bend in any way.

'That's ridiculous,' he said, seemingly deliberately misunderstanding the metaphor. 'A captain decides who does the kick-off and penalties, they interact with the referee, you've got to have one.'

Edie closed her eyes to steady herself before replying. She hadn't even managed eight days with this man, how had Alice done eighteen years? 'I wasn't talking about a rugby captain. I was talking about in a family. You don't need one person calling the shots and everyone else doing what they say. This isn't North Korea, it's a family.'

'A family you're trying to split up,' he muttered belligerently.

This was not the plan, Edie told herself. She was not meant to snowball in here and bash Alice's life about like it's a pinata at a child's birthday party. Sit back. Observe. Appreciate. That was all.

'Just have a think about what I've said,' Edie replied, putting her sister's eye mask over her eyes and sticking a pair of foam ear plugs in her ears. 'Good night.'

CHAPTER TWENTY-FOUR

The swap: day 8

Edie

'And that's why I truly believe that Alice is the perfect replacement for Gareth.' Edie beamed at the table of suited producers as she turned her PowerPoint off, ensuring her smile lingered on Shaun the longest. She'd prepared the presentation last night after deciding that sleeping on the sofa in the living room was preferable to spending the night in a small double bed with a disgruntled Danny. She had pulled all her sister's Instagram stats off her social media, pasted some fawning follower comments on the slides, along with a glowing *Good Housekeeping* review of a segment Alice had done alone on how to choose the perfect vacuum cleaner for staircases. It was a pretty compelling case for employment, and it seemed the producers thought so too, as their initial irritated surprise at her interrupting their morning meeting appeared to have morphed into first curiosity, and then interested intrigue. She had originally planned to go to this meeting as Alice, but then decided that doing a presentation about how great you were, and essentially throwing your twin sister under the bus, was not something she felt comfortable doing, even though she *was* that sister under the bus, so she wore the clothes she got at the charity shop the day she surprised Seb at his pottery studio.

'Can I ask how you knew that there might even be an opening, Edie?'

Edie had anticipated this question, and also knew that she couldn't drop James in it, so replied honestly, 'I didn't, not for certain, but *Britain in the Morning* is a show watched predominantly by women. It's watched by women like Alice who want to see themselves represented, and their values honoured. No other show on morning television has two female hosts, and I think we've got a real opportunity for change here. For trailblazing. And I know that Alice would be honoured to be part of this revolution with Lauren.'

There was a murmur of excitement around the table as her words sunk in.

'You've given us a lot to think about, Edie, thank you so much for coming in. I think this goes without saying, but this is a very delicate situation, and we would appreciate your discretion.'

'Diplomacy is my middle name.' It wasn't, it was Elizabeth, but they didn't need to know that.

A few minutes later, after waiting patiently for the lift to stop at the executive floor — after all, hurrying home only meant longer with her in-laws — Edie stepped into the empty elevator. That went well, she thought. If they weren't considering Alice before, she was pretty confident they would be now. And if she was offered a permanent presenting role on morning television, there was no way that being a fisherman's wife in Fife could compete. She'd have to decide to stay here. And what's more,

Alice would be the one making that decision, so while Edie may have helped stack the pros column with a few more items, she wasn't the one making life choices on her sister's behalf like Danny was. It was entirely different.

Alice

At forty-five quid a pop, the pottery was, on reflection, probably a tad too extravagant for a teacher's end-of-term gift, but Alice had a boot-full of Seb's creations and needed to distribute them somehow without him finding out about it. She got the distinct impression that Iris's teacher would have been much happier with Edie's usual offering of a cheap bottle of Cabernet Sauvignon, but at least he gave a good impression of gratitude when Alice handed it over at school drop-off.

On a last-minute whim, she'd grabbed Seb's golden vase with the pink thunderbolt off Edie's mantelpiece at home rather than one of the smaller ones from the shop for her next errand. If she was going to convince the props department to swap this in for the current vase holding the silk peonies on the shelf behind the presenters, it needed to be a real wow piece, and the streak of pink would match the sofa, and its golden glaze would pick up the highlights in Gareth's hair. Alice did the calculations in her head. The show had an average daily audience of three million; if even one percent of those called the show asking where the vase was from, that would rake up nearly half a million pounds in orders, and that would be just the beginning. She'd packaged all the other pottery up before anyone else was awake that morning and dropped them all off at the post office as it opened for a same-day express delivery. All the Instagram influencers would get them later in the day, and soon they'd be plastered all over the internet. Seb's confidence would soar, the bills would be paid, Edie wouldn't have to work so hard, they could employ a cleaner, upgrade their car, take the girls away this summer. It really would be the start of something huge for them. It took every ounce of concentration not to drop it while walking to the television studio from her car, as her mind was still vibrating with everything that had happened in such a short space of time. She and Edie had agreed not to make any changes at all to each other's lives; they were there to observe, appreciate and leave. She didn't know why she was surprised at Edie twirling through her life like a tornado, whipping everything and everyone into a frenzy. Arguing so much with Danny, meeting James for coffee. This was typical Edie, act first, think later. Apologising after the event was preferable to seeking permission before it. This whole switch, this whole experiment, was about understanding each other better, not assuming that you knew the secret to fixing everything. Alice hoiked the heavy vase up to balance it on her hip as she opened the door to the studio, which would have been a lot easier if she was wearing her own leather belt around her waist rather than a flowing maxi dress. She also had another plan up her sleeve. While she was there, she was going to pop up to the executive floor, and try to see Shaun, to put forward a compelling case of why they should hire Edie to be a more regular guest. They had hundreds of viewers phoning or writing in every week with their questions, and they only ever had time to answer three or four on air. Having Edie on the sofa more would not only give the viewers more access to a free counsellor, it would give Edie and Seb's finances a much needed boost too. Edie needed the job – and the money – so much more than she did. Alice would need to make sure Edie was offered the job ahead of her, fair and square. The switch had gone on for too long now for her to even consider deliberately throwing it so that Edie won the bet and therefore the role on the sofa. Their families would be devastated at being duped, and no bet was worth winning for that.

The lift was taking ages to arrive. She jabbed at the button again to take her up to Shaun's office. She could see that it just stopped at the executive floor. Tapping her foot on the floor she glanced at Edie's watch on her wrist, quarter to ten. Just fifteen minutes until the show went live, which would explain why the corridors were so quiet as everyone would be on the studio floor by then.

The lift pinged, and as the doors simultaneously opened, a mirror image of each woman greeted them.

Edie's eyes widened in surprise. 'Alice!'

'Edie! What are you doing here? Why are you dressed as me? You? Why are you you?'

Edie appeared to fumble for a response. 'I, um, had an issue with payroll, so just nipped in to check about it in person rather than emailing, and never hearing back, or it not being read by the right person, and so I thought I'd pop in, and just, you know, sort it out. And I had to be me to do it.'

Alice was barely listening, instead formulating her own excuse while her sister rambled on.

'You?'

'I left your jacket here last week, so just nipped in after drop-off to see if they'd found it.'

'And did they?' Edie said, clearly noting her sister's bare arms were neither wearing a jacket nor carrying one.

'I . . . er . . . couldn't find anyone to ask, they were all really busy before the show.' Alice actually couldn't find anyone from the studio management team to seek permission for the prop swap, so had done something she was now furiously second guessing. She'd switched the vases herself, tucking one of Seb's business cards behind it, not visible to the camera, but anyone enquiring about it would be directed to the right place. It looked so much better than the rather dull original, and she couldn't imagine that anyone would mind, but her heart was still pounding with the subterfuge.

'Are you getting in?' Edie asked, holding the door open button for her sister. One of the ladies that manned the front desk ran for the lift too, and did a double take when she saw two Edies.

'We're trying something new,' Edie said in way of explanation.

'Turns out we *are* identical,' Alice gave a forced laugh, 'who knew?'

The lady got out at the ground floor, and gave them both confused nods as she left the lift.

The lift then started moving down to the basement car park.

'It feels like I'm descending into hell,' Edie said with a tired sigh.

Alice's eyes narrowed at her sister. What an odd thing to say. 'What do you mean?'

'I'm half an hour away from sitting at a breakfast table with Rod and Rita.'

Alice nodded sympathetically; it was a fair point. The only good thing about her parents-in-law was that they lived so far away. She knew that Edie was probably waiting for her to offer to swap back, but she just needed a couple more days to wait for her plans to come to fruition, and then she'd be handing Edie's life back in much better shape. And she had zero desire to sit at a breakfast table with Danny's parents. 'Any plans for the day after that?' Alice asked, trying so hard to be normal and upbeat to cover up the deception she'd nearly got busted for.

'I thought I'd take your in-laws to the Vagina Museum, it's got a special exhibition on at the moment, and Rita would love it.'

Alice couldn't tell by her sister's tone if she was joking or not. She must be joking. Did such a thing even exist? 'Stop it.'

'Well,' Edie added cheerfully, 'it was either that, or a poetry slam by Afghan refugees, honestly, the talent those guys have is incredible, so I'm tossing up between the two.' Edie made a weighing gesture with her hands, to really emphasise the dilemma she was facing.

'They can't help being so closed-off to new things.'

'Vaginas aren't new. They've been around for ages. As have refugees. Jesus was one.'

Alice took Edie's car key out of her bag and clicked the button, making the lights on Edie's ten-year-old jeep flash. 'The best way to deal with them is just smile and keep busy. They'll be gone soon.'

'Yes, that's the saving grace, isn't it, that they don't live next door and you'd have to see them every day.' For some reason Edie eyed her sister carefully as she said this.

Alice gave a theatrical shudder. 'Can you imagine?'

Edie

Edie allowed herself to breathe freely. In that one sentence Alice had green-lighted Edie to do whatever it took to keep her here. Which she would. If she wouldn't stay for her sister, or a job, maybe she'd stay for a man. She waited until Alice drove Edie's car out of the car park before making her phone call.

'Tomorrow?' James seemed a little perplexed at her suggestion. 'On a Tuesday? But there's no gymnastics on a Tuesday?'

'We don't always have to meet surrounded by the smell of sweat and chlorine, James.'

'I know that.' He sounded flustered, Edie could imagine him fanning his clipboard in his face to cool down. 'Where um shall I see you?'

Edie hesitated. 'I'm not sure,' she said honestly. She hadn't thought of any of the logistics involved in this, after actually setting up the appointment, date, meeting, whatever this was. If it was her, she would probably organise to meet at a pub, but she didn't think that was very James, and it certainly wasn't very Alice.

James cleared his throat, clearly gearing himself up to make a suggestion 'I do have tickets to . . . actually no, don't worry.'

'What?'

'I've, um, got tickets for Wimbledon, the fourth round of the ladies' singles.'

'Oh, my goodness, well you should go to that instead!'

'No,' James said quickly, 'I mean, I have *two* tickets, a spare one. If you want to go with me?' The hopefulness in his voice made Edie smile; he was a really sweet man. 'I entered the public ballot last year in a bid to impress my now ex-wife. I wasn't going to go, but . . .'

Edie did a swift calculation in her head. She could ask Rufus to put together some supper for them all, and she'd be back before Danny was home from work. And she'd get to spend a few hours sussing out whether James might be the key to her sister's future happiness. In London. She would have to sit through a whole tennis match, which admittedly seemed a rather dull way to spend a day, but she wasn't being propositioned as Edie, she was being asked out as Alice.

'That sounds perfect, I love tennis, such an exciting sport,' she replied. 'What time is kick-off?'

CHAPTER TWENTY-FIVE

Alice

'What's this?' Alice said, almost stumbling over a small suitcase in her sister's hallway as she got in from the studio. Seb hadn't mentioned that he was going away? She knew that he did sometimes have exhibitions around the country, but surely he would have said? A thought started tugging at her – what if he'd discovered that she'd bought all the pottery or found out about the swap and was enraged about being duped and he was going away for the night to cool down?

'Seb?' Alice called up the stairs, running through to the kitchen, calling his name again. 'Seb?'

He walked in through the back door. 'You're back! Surprise!'

'What's going on?'

'The shop transferred the money from the sales over the weekend, and so with my first proper paycheck, I want to treat the love of my life to a night away.' He held up his hand to stem the remonstrations that were about to pour out of Alice's mouth. 'I've got Iris staying with Freya, Rosie staying with Holly, I've just dropped Scooby next door, you were the only missing piece of the puzzle, and now you're here! I've packed your purple dress for tonight, and your green one for tomorrow, your cleanser, your moisturiser, your make-up bag, your swimsuit, that saucy red lacy number should the mood take us, and I hope it will, and the book you're reading on sanatoriums for madwomen in eighteenth-century Paris. We are ready to go.'

'But, but . . .' It was one thing pretending to be her sister in ordinary daily life, with chores and children to keep them occupied, but when it was just her and Seb on a romantic night away? There was no way that this could happen. No excuse Alice was voicing was quelling Seb's enthusiasm, and he was starting to look a little downbeat that she was even trying to get out of it. She had to come up with a plan fast, but until one came to her she had no choice but to plaster on a big smile and say that it sounded absolutely lovely.

Edie

'The community shop is always looking for more volunteers now that Morag's leg has been amputated below the knee, she can't do as many shifts.' Rita paused, to give Morag's amputated leg the moment it deserved. 'And anyway,' she continued, spraying some of Alice's homemade anti-bac spray on the breakfast bar and wiping it off with a sponge, 'you'll have your hands full making the mackerel pate for the shops. I try to make a hundred jars a day, and they always sell out, so with us working side by side, we'll be able to almost double that. I say almost, because you'll be much slower than me at first, but in twenty years when you're passing the recipe onto Emily and she's making it alongside you, you'll be just as quick as me.'

'Emily wants to be a dancer in the West End,' Edie said,

draining her coffee cup and immediately sticking it under the coffee machine for a refill. It was too early for alcohol, so a steady stream of caffeine straight into her veins would have to do. Danny had taken the day off work and had taken Rod out, thank goodness, leaving Edie and Rita alone at home. This was Edie's chance to appeal to her, mother to mother, woman to woman.

Rita laughed. 'Didn't we all at that age!'

That got Edie's back up. She had been fond of Emily before, but after a week of being her mother, she was just as protective of her as she would have been of Iris. 'She's a really good dancer.'

'I don't doubt it, but money's where the mackerel is.'

'Ah yes.' Edie turned her back on Rita to swill the sponge out under the tap. 'That well known saying.'

'I'm not going to pretend it's a glamorous life, Alice,' Rita said without a hint of mirth or sarcasm in her tone.

Edie gulped back a snort. 'Believe me Rita, no one would assume it is.'

'You'll spend many a night looking out at the black sea wondering if it's swallowed those you love. And I only had Rod to worry about; in time you'll have three men out there.'

'No I won't. Teddy has an unbelievably quick brain and wants to be an engineer, and Rufus—' Edie stopped herself from saying what she was about to about Rufus, not wanting to stoke any bigoted fire more than was absolutely necessary. 'The boys have dreams of their own that don't involve fish. Like Danny did. You supported his dream of playing rugby.'

'Only on the understanding that he'd come home when the time was right. He's always known that.'

Edie wondered if Alice was actually in on this too. If Danny had laid out their plans before their wedding, unfolding the map of their lives for them both to chart together, following the road with their fingertips back to Fife. If she did know, she'd never said anything about it. After their mum died, and Kenneth had fallen apart, Edie and Alice had sat at the funeral home holding hands, choosing which coffin to have, which hymns to sing, standing either side of their dad at the funeral, not sure who was holding who up, but all pledging to be there for each other. Did Alice make that vow knowing in the near future she'd be almost a day's travel away? She couldn't have done. She wasn't that good a liar, whatever the last week had proven to the contrary.

'Was this the life you wanted, Rita?'

The older woman blanched at the question, evidently never having been canvassed for her opinion about anything. Her features softened as she sat gently down on a bar stool, taking her time to give an honest answer, which Edie really wasn't expecting her to do. 'I don't know really,' she said quietly.

'How old were you when you met Rod?' Edie asked, trying to find the right prompt for Rita to start her story.

'Fifteen.'

'What did you want to be?'

Rita laughed. 'Get away with your fancy nonsense, what did I want to be? Grown up, that's what I wanted to be. A grown woman, with my own house, and my own kids, so I could do a better job than my own parents did.'

Edie didn't say anything else. She didn't need to. Her phone vibrated on the counter next to her. Edie glanced at the screen and saw her own name. She turned the phone on to silent, this conversation was too important to pause.

Rita smoothed down the front of her blouse. 'I've never been hungry a day in my life since marrying Rod. I've never wondered if he was carrying on with other women, I've never wanted for anything, he's never raised his hand to me. We've had an understanding, him and me, and it's worked just fine for nearly fifty years.' She waved her hand Edie's way. 'The trouble with you lot is you think life needs to be exciting all the time, fancy restaurants and posh cars that you plug in next to your hair straighteners or whatever, but real life's not like that. The life you'll have in Fife, now that's real life.'

'It's not my idea of real life, Rita,' Edie said quietly. 'It's not somewhere I think I can be happy.'

'Maybe not for a few years while you settle, but you'll soon see its beauty and forget about everything down here.'

'And everyone?'

'If you're talking about your sister, well she can visit, can't she?'

'We haven't been more than an hour away from each other for our entire lives, give or take a few weeks here or there for holidays.'

'It's not as though you're best friends or anything, is it? I see you two arguing all the time on television. You may look alike, but you're chalk and cheese. Before too long, you won't even miss each other. Out of sight, out of mind, you mark my words.'

Alice

Why wasn't Edie answering her phone? She'd said she was just going home. Alice looked out at the changing scenery as the car wove its way out of London, leaving behind the bumper-to-bumper jams on terrace-lined main roads, onto smaller, quieter roads that didn't need permits to park on. Seb said their destination was a surprise, deftly batting away her constant requests for more information, for a clue. She didn't recognise anything they passed. The further away from the city they drove, the more Alice's anxiety increased. Every mile put more distance between her and Edie, lessening the chance of an easy switch back. She even contemplated coming clean, telling him about the swap, putting an end to this charade. But he was so happy, so proud about the sales, about being able to do this for her. Not her, she told herself firmly, Edie. He was doing this for Edie.

They had been driving for an hour and a half when Seb flicked the indicator on, the car slowed, and they turned left up a tree-lined driveway, a manicured golf course rolling down from the left, and a wild meadow of tall cowslips to the right. 'Recognise it yet?'

She didn't. But Edie would. Alice tried to trawl through her mind's memory box for any conversation she'd had with Edie when she described staying somewhere like this.

The trees gave way round the final bend, allowing Alice to glimpse an ivy-covered manor house, its double front doors propped open invitingly. 'Ah!' she said enthusiastically, still having no clue where they were. 'You brought us here! Oh Seb, you're so thoughtful!'

He pulled into a parking space. 'I thought we'd dump our things in our room, and then head to the spa for a couple of hours, what do you say?'

Alice didn't know what to say to that. What *could* she say? So she made a non-committal murmur while reaching into the back seat for their jackets, while Seb got out and opened the boot for the suitcase. As Alice pulled the coats through to the front seat, something small fell out of one of the pockets onto the floor of the back seat. She felt around for it, and her heart plummeted from her chest to her stomach as her fingers closed around the unmistakable shape of a ring box.

Edie

'You'll have to buy lots of thermals. I wear two pairs under my clothes from November to April.'

Edie was mechanically buttering the bread for the teatime sandwiches Rita and Rod would take with them for their journey home, watching as her knife moved across the slice, spreading the yellowness into each corner, making each one perfect. There was little chance of this situation being so easy to smooth over. Rita had painted the picture of the life Alice would have with such a limited palette of colour it was making Edie's heart hurt. Everyone had always pegged Alice as the less vibrant of the two of them, she had been more guilty than most of doing this over the years, but this life that Danny and his parents had carved out for her was as grey as the mackerel pate her sister would be condemned to making for the rest of her days, and Edie wasn't going to let it happen.

Her phone lit up on the counter again with another call from Alice.

'Someone wants to get hold of you, don't they? That thing hasn't stopped. That's one thing you won't need to worry about up in our village, we don't get any reception at all.'

'I better see if it's important.' Edie picked up her phone, glad to be distracted from talk of Rita's thermal underwear. Her brow furrowed. That was odd. Alice had dropped her a location pin, of the country house hotel she and Seb had gone to for their first weekend away, the first time they'd ever left the girls overnight. They'd had all these grand plans of bonking their way through the weekend, yet had a bottle of wine each at lunch, fell asleep mid-afternoon and woke up the next morning just before checkout. They never even got to visit the spa.

Why would Alice be there? Fear suddenly gripped its icy fingers round her heart as she realised what this pin meant. Seb had taken her there as a surprise. Oh god, he'd be expecting romance, and rudeness, and all the things that *she* should be there for, not her sister. She had to get there before Seb rumbled them which would absolutely break his heart.

'I have to go, I'm so sorry, lovely to see you, safe journey back, good luck with the guttering, say bye to Rod for me. Bye.' Edie grabbed her purse, phone and car keys and ran out of the door, leaving a frantic message for Danny as she got in the car that he needed to pick the kids up and stay at home with them until she got back.

Alice

'How nice is this?' Seb said, his face upturned to the warm sun.

'It is very nice,' Alice agreed. One saving grace was that he couldn't propose in the hot tub; she'd checked and his swimming shorts did not have pockets. And there was another woman in the Jacuzzi with them, so as long as she stayed put, Alice reasoned she'd be safe from any romantic outpouring.

Seb stretched out his arms along the back of the whirlpool, one behind Alice's head. 'On a Monday afternoon as well. How decadent are we?'

'Pretty damn decadent,' she agreed, absent-mindedly. Edie must have seen the message by now, and with any luck was at this moment hurtling her way down the country lanes. 'I'm going to get myself a water,' Alice said, thinking that the perfect foil to be able to check her phone, which was in the pocket of the white hotel dressing gown hanging up on a peg across the pool. 'Relaxing is thirsty work.'

'I'll go,' Seb said, standing up in the water. 'Do you want the water with cucumber floating in it, or the lemon one?'

'Cucumber would be great, thank you.'

'My husband would have told me to get my own water, and to bring him back one too,' said the woman from across the hot tub.

'So would mine,' Alice said without thinking, then blushed furiously as she realised what she'd said, particularly when the woman gave her a dirty look and turned the jets up to their highest strength so nothing more could be said over the bubbles.

Half an hour later, Alice's fingertips were so raisin-like they could easily have been served up in a little red box and no one would have batted an eyelid. She tried not to, but she had kept one eye trained onto the door, anticipating Edie swooshing in to relieve her. Not that she actually wanted relieving. In any other scenario than this, she would be having a really lovely time. Seb was funny, and kind, and attentive, and it was very clear that every woman, and a couple of the men, who had joined them in the hot tub throughout the afternoon had sized him up against their partners and found theirs severely lacking in every department. Alice couldn't help doing that herself. What would Danny be doing and saying if it was him here rather than Seb? She closed her eyes against the bubbles massaging her shoulders and tried to swap him in. He'd complain the water was too hot. He'd make her swap seats because her jet looked more powerful than his. He'd constantly check the time, read his emails from his watch, ask the staff to keep up a steady conveyor belt of protein-rich snacks, comment on the cellulite of the other women, mutter under his breath, 'and what first attracted you to the multi-millionaire octogenarian?' whenever an older man with a younger partner came in. There was a reason that in eighteen years they'd never done anything like this.

Seb nudged her. 'Fancy the sauna now?'

'Um, yes, absolutely.' Alice figured she'd be safe as there was no way Seb could propose in the sauna. He got out first, then reached out a hand to help her out of the tub. It would have been rude to ignore it, so she tentatively held out her own to meet his as she stepped out. She could hardly let hers drop now either, they were on a romantic break, he'd be so confused if she shook her hand free, so they walked to the sauna hand in hand, as Alice silently prayed Edie was on her way to step back into her own life in time for one of the most important moments of it.

Edie

Edie's heartbeat hadn't slowed down yet, from the moment she realised what was happening, to now, ninety minutes into her journey. She couldn't remember stopping at any traffic light, giving way at any roundabout, although she supposed she must have done, but her mind was firmly trained on just getting to the hotel. The worst thing would be for Seb to find out about the switch. He would be so heartbroken to know that he'd been duped, lied to. He was such an honest man, there wasn't an ounce of duplicity about him, and he would never understand this. She and Alice had never actually spoken about whether they would tell their families about the swap afterwards. If it had been what it was supposed to have been, just a little fun to see from the sidelines how the other half of them lived, then maybe they could have done. But not now. Not when she had meddled so much. Not now she was trying to line up a new career, a new boyfriend, a new life for her sister. This had gone so far beyond observing. And Alice had only tidied her house up. She didn't deserve the mess Edie was going to hand back to her along with her wedding ring, she really didn't.

Edie screeched her car into a parking space and ran into the hotel, asking for the room for her sister and Seb. The receptionist looked suitably confused at why the lady she'd checked in a couple of hours before was now trying to get in touch with herself, but tried the room regardless and it rang out.

'The room appears to be empty. Perhaps try the spa?'

Of course. The spa. Seb missed out on it last time, but he would be wanting to get the full experience now. She just hoped that he wasn't trying to give Alice *his* full experience. She raced down the corridor following the smell of eucalyptus as it grew stronger and stronger until she could also hear panpipes. No one was manning the spa reception to stop her, so she slipped through quietly, taking off her shoes to mask her hurrying footsteps. She peered through the window into the pool, scanning the water for two recognisable heads, nothing. The relaxation room was empty save for a couple who weren't related to her, so she muttered a rapid apology for bursting in, and went to find the hot tub – Seb loved them. But that too was full of people that weren't them. Where on earth were they? And what was she going to say to them once she found them?

Alice

A bald man in tiny, very tight trunks kept pouring water on the coals, making the sauna so hot Alice's chest was being scalded from the inside out. She elbowed Seb and motioned towards the door. 'Can we go?' He nodded. They rewarded their perseverance with a quick cold shower before heading to the steam room. The air was so thick they put their arms out in front of them like zombies, before tentatively sitting down on what they hoped was an empty bench.

Alice took advantage of not being visible to lean her head back against the wall and close her eyes to stem the panic rising in her chest. Any minute now Seb would suggest going back upstairs, and everyone knew what happened in hotel rooms on romantic mini breaks. She'd need to keep him in the sauna for as long as possible while she worked out how to break the news to him. She'd have to tell him about the swap and he'd be so mad about being lied to. He was so happy, she couldn't burst his bubble, she just couldn't, but soon she'd have no choice. Thankfully, the heat and steam meant that they were sitting further apart, without the risk of Seb putting an arm around her. As Alice pondered how to explain everything to Seb once they got upstairs, she felt somewhat sad that the swap was coming to an end, and that she'd have to go back to her own family. She missed the children dreadfully, and was desperate to be a different type of mum to them when they were reunited, but her heart had an unmistakable heaviness about seeing Danny again. Being around Seb's easygoing genuine warmth had only served to underscore Danny's indifference. Experiencing the feeling of having someone there to catch you, albeit only for eight days, had shone a light into a gaping void that was there in her own marriage, and she had no idea how to repair it, or if she even wanted to.

Just then, the door to the steam room flung open and a voice unmistakably her sister's, albeit masked in a chirpy Australian accent, punctured the thick mist asking if a Ms Edie Dawson was in there as she had a phone call.

Praise to the Lord.

Edie

Wet swimming costumes were so difficult to put on a dry body. Edie was almost doubled over in the small changing room trying to peel it up her torso, while Alice was putting her own clothes back on in embarrassed silence.

'What were you talking about before I came in?' Edie asked, shimmying her shoulders into the arms of the swimming costume. 'That way I can carry on the conversation like I'm the same person.'

'Nothing really. We were just sat in silence.'

With Seb? Edie found that hard to believe. 'We never sit in silence.'

'To be fair, it's really relaxing in there, and we've spent the whole afternoon here.'

'Well, he's going to get a shock when I bowl in chatting nineteen to the dozen. I feel like a coiled spring. I honestly didn't know how we'd be able to swap without him knowing. I was going through hundreds of different scenarios in my head on the way down here.'

'Is there any news from my house that I should be aware of?' Alice said, tying a knot in her favourite silk neck scarf, suddenly finding it restrictive around her neck.

Edie shook her head. 'Nope, same old, same old. Rod and Rita should be long gone when you get back; Danny's picked the kids up and is sorting dinner out.'

Alice stopped, hairbrush in hand, and looked at her sister in disbelief. 'Danny's sorting dinner out?'

'Well by sorting, I mean he's picking up a takeaway as I said I'd be back early evening. How did you have your hair? Up or down?' Edie had called Danny on the way to the hotel on the car's hands free, ostensibly to check he had remembered to pick the kids up from school, but also to ask him for a truce. 'Can we just have one night,' she'd said, trying to keep the note of desperation out of her voice, 'where we don't mention Fife at all? We don't mention fishing, or your parents, or moving, we just take a break from that, and just enjoy a nice quiet evening?'

To her surprise, he'd agreed without hesitation. There was still the risk that he would bring it up anyway, blindsiding Alice completely, but hopefully one night was a short enough amnesty for it to be okay. Then they could swap back tomorrow, and Edie could put the next part of her plan into action.

CHAPTER TWENTY-SIX

Edie

Edie slid through the mist into the seat in the steam room her sister had vacated five minutes before. 'Sorry about that, it was just Freya's mum checking on Iris's dietary preferences this week.'

'Thank god! I was worried it was something serious! Who calls the hotel to ask something like that?' Edie couldn't see him, but the relief in his voice was unmistakeable.

'And I thought I told her,' he continued, 'only raw food, but cooked chicken. That was a bloody nightmare when Iris made herself a raw chicken sandwich for lunch last week; thank god the school saw before she ate it.'

Edie's brow knotted together; Alice hadn't mentioned that. She supposed there wasn't anything to say, the potential disaster had been averted, but even so, a potential salmonella tragedy should have been logged somewhere in some sort of incident report.

'So . . .' Edie started, not sure how to carry on her sentence without giving away that she wasn't there earlier for the announcement of this plan. 'A spa hotel on a Monday in term-time eh? Look at us!'

'You deserve it, and we need to celebrate, don't we?'

'We certainly do.' Edie was completely clueless what they were celebrating, but any further digging would have to be incredibly delicately done. 'I am so happy.' That was good she thought, it was vague enough to be happiness tossed in any direction.

'Are you?' He put his arm around her and drew her in tighter. 'That means so much to me. I know it was a massive risk, wasn't it, me giving up my salary, but knowing that ten pieces of my pottery now stand on people's bookshelves and mantlepieces is just brilliant. And the shop has ordered replacements, so I'm going to be really busy.'

'They all sold?' *That was incredible!* 'Well done, darling!' It wasn't until Edie had flung her arms around his neck that she remembered that this probably wasn't news to her. He hadn't waited until they were together in a hotel's steam room unable to really see each other to impart this information, and he must be thinking that her reaction was really odd.

He disentangled himself, and even though she couldn't see his face clearly through the mist, she could tell by the tone in his voice that he was confused. 'I told you this last night. When I got the call.'

'I know, I know, but hearing you say it again, when we don't have anything else going on around us, just shines a light on it even more. You really are brilliant, Seb.'

She hoped he didn't hear her voice catch in that last sentence, because she wasn't just talking about his pottery skills, or determined ambition to succeed, it was everything. *He was everything*. It had only been a week walking in her sister's shoes and yet it felt like a lifetime, and she had never been more grateful to slot back into her own skin. The moment she had shared with Alice as she left, when Alice held both Edie's hands in her own, claiming she 'had a feeling' Edie was going to have a memorable night, Edie had never felt more grateful to be herself.

Alice

They all looked the same, well almost. Emily's hair had clearly not been blow dried after it had been washed the night before, although a quick sniff of it confirmed to Alice that thankfully it had indeed been washed. Rufus must have missed his barber's appointment which was clearly marked on the calendar for yesterday lunchtime, but with the arrival of their grandparents that was an understandable oversight. Teddy looked exactly the same, but there was something about him that was different, as he ambled back and forth to the various cupboards and drawers getting the plates, cutlery and condiments out to lay the table. It took Alice a moment or two to work it out. Watching Rosie and Iris help around the kitchen this last week had made kids helping out a normality, but she realised with a jolt that she'd never actually seen her own kids doing it. The kitchen floor needed a scrub, there had been some definite outdoor-shoe action on it, and she noted that neither of the boys were wearing their slippers, they were barefoot, but it was nowhere near as bad as she had been expecting. The bananas were lying on top of the rest of the fruit in the bowl rather than hanging from the banana stand, which no doubt was turning all the satsumas underneath bad, but she supposed that rotten fruit went in the same category as spilt milk in levels of catastrophe. The biggest change was the atmosphere. Music was playing in the kitchen, rather than the normal background noise of silence punctuated with sport commentary blaring from another room. Emily even had a little rhythmic wiggle to her hips as she walked around the table distributing the plates in front of each chair in time with the beat.

'Would everyone like bread and butter with their fish and chips?' Rufus called from the open fridge.

'Two slices please mate,' Teddy said, taking the white paper parcels out of the plastic bag on the end of the table and putting one on each plate.

'One please Roof,' Emily said.

Alice stood leaning against the doorframe, watching her children get dinner ready, for the first time ever easily picturing them as adults in their own homes, and realised that she still had so much to learn. Edie was right, who wants to spend their half term going round museum after museum and having a minute-by-minute pre-planned itinerary of forced fun? She walked up to the smart speaker, and could feel at least two of her children's eyes on her, and knew, sadly, that they fully expected her to turn it down or off. Instead, she moved her finger to the right, raising the volume by four, until the joyous sounds of a nineties pop classic rang out and she spun around, grinning at her children. 'Who wants a kitchen disco?'

*

It had definitely been worth it, Alice thought, looking around the table at her children laughing and chatting with one another, for the shift in perspective, the deeper understanding of not only her sister's life, but also her own. Kenneth was right, it had definitely worked. But it was done. There was no point swapping again. The fiction had started to spill into the reality, blurring the pretend and the actual, and any longer, her sense of clarity may have completely left her.

But she was home now.

She smiled across the table at Danny, who had barely said two words to her since she got in, but then he didn't know that she'd been away for a week. 'How's your fish?' she asked him.

He stared at her, with something resembling if not hatred, certainly something very close to it. 'I didn't think we were allowed to mention that word?'

'What word?' For a moment Alice wondered if being Edie for a week had also given her own language choices a blue tinge and she'd cursed without noticing, but was pretty sure that she'd only just enquired whether his fish was nice.

He shook his head and shovelled another large piece of battered cod into his mouth.

Alice could feel tears pricking at her eyes again and blinked them away. Had he always been this dismissive of her?

She felt a gentle kick on her shin under the table and looked up to find Teddy, who was seated to her left, giving her a small lopsided smile. A smile that apologised for his father. A smile that said that everything was okay. She smiled back at her eldest son gratefully, really wanting that to be true.

CHAPTER TWENTY-SEVEN

The swap: day 9

Edie

They'd ordered room service for dinner in the end last night to save them from the hassle of getting dressed. Crumbs from the bread basket were dotted like rain-spots all over the sheets but neither of them cared. Naked, full and reunited, Edie didn't think she had ever been happier. There was not a single cell in her that wanted to swap back into Alice's body later today, but there were so many loose threads that she'd left fraying, and only she could tidy it all up before handing Alice's life back to her like a neat little parcel beautifully packaged. She prayed that Danny had kept his word and hadn't started a fight about Fife. She felt so bad that she'd sent Alice to the front line blind.

While Seb showered, Edie turned the television on. On the very rare occasions she'd slept in a hotel, devouring morning television while having a coffee in bed was a guilty pleasure. Idly flicking through the channels, she tried to avoid *Britain in the Morning* as it brought bubbling to the surface yesterday's secretive sales pitch to the board. But whether it was the paltry offerings on the other channels, or a perverse urge to imagine the sofa with her sister on it, she found herself flicking back to it. Gareth's eyes looked bloodshot, and his skin had an unnatural waxiness about it, as though Petra had used all the products in her arsenal to inject some colour and life into his complexion. Even the viewers watching the television while also doing the housework or scrolling through their phones at the same time, would surely have noticed him messing up and missing a few of his cues. Lauren was really earning her money this morning at trying to cover up his gaffes: introducing the news ten minutes early, calling the resident chef by the name of his predecessor, taking a noisy slurp of his coffee when he was meant to be reading the autocue, and then holding back a very obvious belch while the camera was still trained on him. Surely his days were numbered?

'That shower's amazing,' Seb said, coming back into the bedroom, a towel around his waist, rubbing his hair with a hand towel. 'I've left it on the right setting for you, you just need to turn the tap all the way to the right. Oh look, it's your sofa,' he said, looking at the television.

'Haha, it's not *my* sofa. I sit on it for fifteen minutes every Friday. But I have heard on the grapevine that there might be a space opening up on the main sofa, apparently the bosses are a bit pissed off with all Gareth's after-work antics. Don't you think Alice would be great—'

Seb's hand towel dropped to the floor. Edie stopped talking and looked at him. All the colour had drained from his face and he was staring at the screen as if hypnotised.

'Seb?'

'That vase.'

Edie swivelled her gaze back to the programme, then back to her husband. 'What?'

'Why is that vase there?'

She moved to the end of the bed to get a closer look, unable to see it clearly without her glasses. 'What's wrong with it?'

'It's the one I gave you for Christmas.'

Edie peered at the screen. 'What? How did it get there? Did you lend it to them? I don't know why I didn't think of suggesting that, that's brilliant, what incredible exposure. I bet they'll have loads of people phoning up asking about it, it's so distinctive. I remember when they got those new sofas, the phonelines were jammed about where they were from.' She looked back at him in excitement and saw the colour draining away from his face. 'Seb?'

'I can't believe you would just give away my gift!'

'I didn't, I promise!' She loved that vase, she would never just give it away like it meant nothing. The only explanation was that Alice did, but why?

His head shook in annoyed disbelief. 'Don't lie to me Edie. How else could it have got on national television?'

She grabbed his hands in earnest. 'I don't know, I promise, but it wasn't me. But why are you so angry?' She pointed back at the screen. 'Something *you* made is on TV, Seb! Focus on that, rather than how it got there. This is amazing.'

He looked so forlorn and pulled his hands free from her grasp. 'We promised that we would always be honest, and now you're lying to my face.'

'Why are you saying this? Aren't you proud?' She jabbed her finger again in the direction of the television. 'Look! This is why you gave up your job; millions of people right now are looking at that vase and thinking how freaking talented the creator of that is. And that's you!'

He sank down on the bed, his head in his hands, probably taking in the enormity of what this meant. Free advertising on primetime television was worth its weight in gold to up-and-coming artists. Edie rubbed his back. 'I am just so proud of you darling, if we weren't already in a posh hotel, I'd whisk you away to one to celebrate.'

'It's not meant to be on TV, it's meant to be just for you. It was a prototype, I'm not good enough yet.'

'But that's great, isn't it? Think of the marketing! Surely the whole point of you starting this business was to make a real go of it? Something you made with your own two hands is now on national television, is it too much too soon? Do you not have the stock to cope with any new orders? I mean, that's a great problem to have, you could hire pottery graduates and start a proper production line, even move to a bigger studio if you get loads of new business. Seb, this could be the start of something remarkable!'

His whole demeanour had stiffened, his body, his voice. 'You shouldn't have gone behind my back. We're a team. If you'd suggested this, I would have said no, that I wanted to get there by myself. Not ride on the back of your success, to use your clout to get me noticed. Do you honestly have that little faith in me achieving it for myself?'

'But I didn't—'

'No, you didn't think, you just swooped in and made a decision that has really hurt me.'

It wasn't her that put the vase on the set, but now it was there, she really didn't understand his stance on it. 'But that's just it,' she countered, 'we *are* a team. And teams work together, and having your art front and centre for thousands of people to admire, regardless of how it got there, surely that's a brilliant thing.'

He exhaled slowly, his shoulders dropping. 'I just really wanted to make you proud by doing this myself. It would be so different if the props department had actually chosen my vase to put it on the set, rather than you giving them yours and probably begging them to put it on there. It doesn't prove anything about how good my art is, just how much influence you have.' He picked up his washbag and put it into his case. 'So much was riding on me making a go of this. You're working every hour, we've taken a mortgage holiday, another credit card. I know that I should be happy that this could mean the start of something big, I just wish you had more faith in me that I'd get there on my own merit. You really should have been honest with me.'

His words stabbed her again, and again. Fiction and reality had been dangerously blurred this last week, and she'd been so caught up in the frantic scrambling not to be caught out, she hadn't really stopped to consider the actual deceit involved. If he was this upset and let down over the vase, how on earth would he feel about having had her sister lie in bed with him each night instead of her? About being duped every moment of the last nine days?

They got dressed in silence, packing their clothes up and gathering their toiletries from the bathroom, politely getting out of each other's way, 'you go', 'no, after you.' Each taking their swimming costumes off the radiator, picking their underwear off the floor, so gaily discarded the night before. Over dinner the night before, somewhere between their second bottle of Rioja and their nightcap, Seb had suggested that before checkout time they should go for a walk to the far end of the hotel's estate, where an old Doric temple was. She remembered pulling a bit of a face, anticipating the hangover and much preferring the idea of a lazy lie-in than a long walk to an ancient ruin, however romantic he said it was meant to be, but he was oddly insistent. This morning, as they gave their key back to the receptionist, he didn't even mention it.

'Can you drive?' Seb threw Edie the car keys over the car roof. She nodded, but her own mind was racing with the spaghetti-junction-like mess she'd created in her sister's life that she needed to sort out, which was far greater than the chaos Alice had created in hers. But after this, there was no way she and Alice could swap back today, she needed to make sure that Seb was okay. Every cell inside Seb's body was genuine and honest and pure, and his expression now wore that of a child finding out their parents had conspired in a lie every Christmas for their entire childhood.

She glanced at the clock on the car's dashboard as they rounded the country lanes faster than the speed limit permitted. She was meant to be meeting James in two hours at Wimbledon, but since she had swapped phones again with Alice, and now had her own one back, she didn't have his number to cancel. And even though a sizeable well of guilt had taken up permanent residence in the pit of her stomach about the swap, if she stood James up, then he could block her attempts at getting Alice the presenting job, she'd move to Fife and that would be it.

'Can you drop me at my studio?' Seb said, breaking the silence as they neared the outskirts of London. 'I just want to be by myself for a bit.'

Edie didn't want him to be alone with his thoughts of her apparent betrayal and lack of faith in him, but equally, him being at the studio at least gave her a few hours' grace to try to resolve the loose ends in Alice's life.

*

James had already left the television studio by the time she'd called to try to cancel, and she couldn't stand him up and leave him loitering around the entrance to the courts, looking hopefully towards the car park for her to show up. She had no choice but to put on the least Edie-looking item of clothing in her wardrobe, carefully pin her hair up into a sleek bun and quickly head for south of the river.

It wasn't being unfaithful if she was pretending to be someone else, she told herself over and over as they approached Centre Court to take their seats. Edie and Seb were happily coupled up. Alice and Danny were not. She was not Edie right now, she was Alice, and therefore, it was perfectly fine that another man, a lovely man, who she did not exchange vows or rings with, had just bought her a punnet of strawberries and a flute of champagne and had told her 'don't move,' while he removed an eyelash from her cheek, held it out on the tip of his finger and told her to make a wish. If anyone deserved this kind of wholesome, wonderful attention it was Alice. It was just a bloody shame that she wasn't there to enjoy it.

Edie's heart plummeted when she realised how ridiculously close their seats were to the court. Slap-bang in the left-hand corner, in a prime spot to be picked up by the cameras every other time a player did a serve, which, it turned out in a tennis match, was quite a lot. That last-minute decision to pick up her massive pair of sunglasses, which were unlike anything she'd ever seen her sister in, but did an excellent job of disguising half her face, was genius. Every time a player threw their ball up into the air just in front of her, the serve about to be broadcast to millions, she also lowered her head, unfortunately looking completely disinterested in the sport she had gone to watch, but also, she hoped, nothing like herself or her sister. She ran through the potential fall-out from this: there was no chance of Seb or her girls seeing her, and she assumed that Danny would be at work, Alice's kids at school and Alice would be far too busy cleaning the week's worth of dust and detritus from every surface of her own home to sit down and watch the tennis in the middle of the day. The only person who might spot her would be her dad, and Kenneth had a long track record of keeping her secrets. She might just get away with this.

'Are you enjoying yourself?' James asked, when the players left the court in between a set to sit at the side and drape their heads in a damp towel. There was a note of uncertainty in his voice, no doubt brought on by her refusal to lift her head high enough to actually follow the game.

'Oh yes, it's really good.' She actually wasn't lying. It had never appealed to her before, but being there, with the atmosphere of the crowds, she could see how it might be enjoyable, to someone who wasn't on the precipice of messing up not only her own life, but also her sister's.

'I'm so glad you came.'

'Me too.'

The two players retook their positions, one bouncing her ball a mere ten feet from where they were sitting. Edie's eyes instinctively went down to her lap, as a hush fell on the crowd. James placed his left hand on his left leg, his little finger an inch or so away from where her own hand rested on her thigh. She watched in slow motion as his finger extended out to graze her own pinkie on her right hand, the slightest, subtlest of touches that shot a bolt through her body. She had intended to tell him that she would be open to getting to know him more, to tell him that her marriage was coming to an end, to line him up ready to present to Alice as yet another reason to stay, but it felt all wrong. Her dad's words echoed in her mind, *'But you're doing it again though, aren't you? Forcing her to do what you want . . . you're taking her free will away from her.'*

She let James's touch rest there for a couple of beats before lifting her hand to tuck her hair behind her ear.

*

'Auntie Edie is on the telly!' Emily called excitedly from under a blanket on the sofa in the living room. 'Come and see it! She's at the tennis!'

Alice got up from the kitchen stool. 'You're meant to be sleeping off your migraine, not watching television.'

'Just wait a minute, she's sat there, in that corner.' Emily threw off her blanket, got up from the sofa and jabbed her finger on the screen, making it rock a bit on its stand.

Alice's eyes were trained so intensely on the exact spot in the stands that Emily had pointed to, it didn't even occur to her to tell her not to touch the screen as it would leave awful fingerprints. She scanned the faces on the screen looking for anything familiar. Emily must have been mistaken, Edie would be basking in the afterglow of her new engagement right now, not at the tennis. 'I don't think it could be her Em, she didn't say anything about going to the tennis.'

'It is.' Emily was insistent. 'She's even wearing those big sunglasses that Daddy said make her look like a bug under a microscope.'

'Who is she with? Seb?' Perhaps it was all part of the proposal, Alice wondered. He was one for grand gestures.

Emily shook her head. 'She's got an old lady on one side, and on the other a man wearing one of those straw hats that we see on English men on holiday who also wear socks with their sandals.'

Mother and daughter stood side by side in the lounge, their eyes lasered onto the screen. Every so often Emily would shout, 'there!' followed by Alice narrowing her eyes more at the television, but unable to see what her daughter did. The man Emily talked about very briefly came into shot and there was something oddly familiar about him, though his face was obscured by the shadow of his hat; she had perhaps seen him somewhere before, but it definitely wasn't Seb.

Alice straightened up and shook her head. 'I think you're wrong darling, it could be just someone that looks like Auntie Edie.'

'It doesn't look like Auntie Edie actually, it looks like you, but you're right here.'

Something buried inside Emily's innocent words prickled at Alice.

It looks like you.

Edie wouldn't pretend to be her again, would she? Not without her knowing? None of this made any sense. Alice took her mobile out of her pocket, tapped out an innocuous message enquiring as to Edie's whereabouts and sent it. The next few seconds seemed to happen in slow motion, as no sooner had the text sent from Alice's phone, the camera zoomed in on the Spanish player about to serve, and clearly in shot, just behind her left shoulder, was James. Alice heard herself gasp as sitting right beside him, fanning herself with her programme, was her mirror image, wearing clothes that she herself would wear, the woman's hair pulled tight into a neat bun, exactly the same as Alice had on her head in her own lounge. Her doppelganger glanced at her phone, tapped a few times on the screen and a second later, a new message vibrated in Alice's hand.

> *Sorry lovely, busy working, will call later. #norestforthewicked*

This wasn't possible. None of this added up. Why would Edie race back from a romantic break where she was getting engaged to go to the tennis with James. *James* of all people, Alice was the one who was friends with him, not Edie. Ever so slowly, the fragments started to piece together in Alice's mind.

Edie wasn't at the tennis with James as herself, she was there as Alice. She had deliberately dressed as her sister, intentionally hoodwinking James into believing he was there with Alice. But why? Alice gave Emily a little smile, made noises about needing a little lie down, and went upstairs to her room.

Nothing was as she'd left it ten days ago. Not her husband, not her children, not her friendship with James, not even the book on her bedside table – she'd found the autobiography of the billionaire's wife in the recycling box.

She lay down on her bed and looked up at the ceiling, very aware that silent contemplation was not something she had ever done before. Nor was lying on her bed in the middle of the afternoon. It wasn't that she didn't want to quieten her mind, just that she honestly didn't know how. This latest betrayal in a long list of Edie's thoughtless duplicities was baffling.

Alice's phone buzzed in her pocket. It was a message from Danny saying that he'd decided to go down to Worthing for the night to see his brother. He'd be back tomorrow. There was nothing but relief coursing through Alice's veins as she lay her head back on the pillow and gave in to the tears that had been threatening to fall all day, feeling more lost than she'd ever felt before in her life.

CHAPTER TWENTY-EIGHT

Alice

The call from the television studio came in just after seven am, while Alice was in the shower. Danny not being at home meant Alice gave herself a lie-in, even though she had resolved never to get up early to make him a protein shake ever again, and as for his packed lunch, well if he desired anything more complicated than ham or cheese, he could make it himself. Slipping on her bathrobe, she called the studio back. Both Lauren and Gareth had called in sick, and the usual replacements, a lovely married couple from Bolton called Hayley and Sam, were currently on a beach in Zanzibar sunning themselves before taking over from Lauren and Gareth for the planned summer break in a couple of weeks' time.

'You want me and Edie to present the whole show?' Alice asked incredulously. 'The whole *two-hour* show?'

'Two and a half, yes,' Shaun said. 'I realise this is a huge ask, but in light of recent conversations with your sister, I thought you might welcome the chance to show me what you've got.'

Recent conversations? 'Um, I, have to take the children to school, but I can be in straight after that.' As she raced around the house waking the kids up, flinging goodness knows what into their lunchboxes, Alice thanked the universe that the summons had happened when she was back in her own body. Last week it had been torture trying to be Edie for their fifteen-minute segment, let alone a whole two-and-a-half-hour live show.

Edie was already in their shared dressing room when Alice burst through the doors; perhaps letting your children arrange their own way to school did have its merits after all. She deliberately hadn't called Edie last night after the tennis, there was no point; she'd have only filled the phone call with bluster and bravado. Quite clearly, she was hatching something, and Alice needed to catch her off guard to try to uncover what it was.

A head popped around the door. 'Seven minutes to live ladies, please make your way to the studio floor.'

'Well?' Alice said as they were bustled down the corridor, a runner wearing headsets stalked both in front and behind them. 'Why were you at the tennis with you know who.'

Edie's expression froze, but she kept her gaze fixed dead ahead. 'Um, what?'

'Don't try to pretend you weren't,' Alice hissed, mindful of being surrounded by studio staff.

'It's a long story.'

Alice scoffed, 'I don't have anywhere to be,' even though they both knew that absolutely was not true.

'You'll laugh when I tell you.'

'I'm sure. Go on.' She smiled at her sister sweetly yet with just the right hint of menace.

'Let's wait until after the programme.'

'No, no, we have seven minutes.'

'Five and a half,' the runner in front of them said, without turning their head.

'Edie?' Alice prompted. 'Start talking.'

Edie's face looked like she was bracing herself for impact. 'He had spare tickets,' she said quickly.

'And that's enough of a reason to go behind my back?'

'Look, you've got it all wrong.' The sisters went through a set of double doors.

Alice held the door open behind her for the junior staffer, before doing a running step to catch up level with her sister again, and whispered, 'From where I'm standing it's a massive betrayal, to Seb, to me—'

'But he was so keen to take you to the tennis.'

'Why would he want to take *me* to the tennis?'

'Because he likes you, dummy. So he asked you, and you said yes.'

'That's funny, because I don't recall having that conversation with him.'

Edie at least had the decency to look a little uncomfortable.

'And if he had asked me,' Alice continued after pausing for a second to let the make-up artist powder her nose, by the side of the studio floor while they were still off air, 'I'd have told him that I was very flattered . . .' Alice waited for the woman to move away before adding in a whisper, 'But I am a married woman.'

'But not a happily married one.'

Alice shot her sister a look that held so many meanings. The one that had bubbled right to the top was a simple one telling Edie to be quiet, but nestling just under that was a look Edie couldn't decipher.

'We can't all be married to a saint,' Alice hissed through her teeth.

Another assistant led them onto the floor and they sat down

on the sofa. Not in their usual places, but centre-stage where the hosts normally were. It felt very different, not just the physical perspective of being on the sofa on the right, but the pressure of leading the whole show suddenly felt enormous. This last week had changed her in so many ways, and everything she knew to be true and real about her life, her feelings, had been flipped on their head. And now she was expected to just quash all that down and act like someone she wasn't again.

James called from the corner of the set, 'Ten seconds to live . . .'

'Look, forget about it for now, it's really important we do this right,' Edie whispered, plastering a wide smile on her face in anticipation of the red light appearing on the camera right in front of them.

'But . . .'

'Sssh.'

Edie

'Hello and welcome to *Britain in the Morning* on this gloriously sunny Wednesday. You may be wondering where Gareth and Lauren are this morning. Well Lauren is feeling very under the weather this morning and as for Gareth, your guess is as good as mine.' That wasn't what it said on the autocue, he too had the flu, but a bit of ad-libbing never hurt anybody, and planting the seed of his unreliability definitely couldn't hurt her plan to get him ousted and Alice given permanent residency on this righthand side sofa – which it had to be said, did seem more comfortable than the other one they usually sat on, even though they looked identical, could that be possible?

'We have a packed show for you this morning, we're going live to the American Film Awards shortly in Hollywood, where our roving reporter George Glynn is waiting to give us a round-up of all of last night's winners.' Alice's voice was flat, and a little too monotonous for the content she was reading.

'That *is* exciting,' Edie said, picking up the baton, and trying to cajole her sister to pick up the pace with her own enthusiasm. 'What a great awards season it has been as well! We also have the most incredible selection of mastectomy swimwear coming up, but first we're going to meet Yuri and his talented Yorkshire terrier Kevin, who has successfully predicted every World Cup and Euros winner for the last twelve years.'

Alice was supposed to say, 'Can he also pick out lottery numbers [laugh]?' but her gaze and her thoughts were placed firmly away from the autocue, and Edie had to quickly cover up her sister's misstep.

The camera blinked off as the tape started running with a short film showing Kevin in all his fortune-telling glory, and Edie rounded on Alice. 'You have to step up a bit more Alice!'

'What do you mean?' Alice looked completely lost, as though she'd just wandered onto the set and had her face brushed with powder with no warning.

'This is a massive chance to show everyone how great you are, I mean, *we* are, come on.'

'Sorry,' Alice said, suddenly looking as though she was going to burst into tears. What was wrong with her? 'I've got a lot going on.'

'We've both got a lot going on, but believe me, you're going to want to snap out of it and be the best version of yourself.'

'What does that even mean?'

'Live in five, four . . .' James then mouthed three, two, one, and the camera flickered into life again.

'So, let's welcome into the studio Yuri and Kevin. Hello both of you, and aren't you the cutest?' Edie bent down to stroke Kevin, who repaid the affectionate greeting by baring his tiny teeth and growling, which made her quickly straighten up. 'Look's like he's not a morning person,' Edie said smiling, nudging her sister, 'which makes two of you eh?'

For the whole six-minute segment Edie did most of the talking, ignoring the colour change of the lines on the autocue, and inserting a few off-script jokes that had the crew sniggering along the edges of the set. Just before the fifteen-minute break at eleven for the national and regional news and weather, Edie became aware of Shaun, the executive producer, standing to the side of the set and, as soon as the cameras stopped rolling, he beckoned her over. 'Me?' Edie mouthed, pointing at her own chest. When he nodded, she quietly walked over to him, leaving Alice sitting on the sofa, flicking over the script for the cooking demonstration after the break.

'Edie, we'd like to see you upstairs after the programme please.'

'Me?'

'Yes, we'd like to have a discussion with you about your future with the network going forward.' Instead of sounding ominous, which those words absolutely could have done, there was a tinge of auspiciousness in his voice, something promising even.

'*Me?*'

'Yes.'

'And Alice?' Edie said hopefully. Surely her sister was the obvious person to be having this conversation with. Edie was just a therapist, a listening ear, Alice was the fixer, the one with hundreds of thousands of Instagram followers.

Shaun shifted from one foot to the other. 'Just you.'

Shit. Shit. Shit. In covering for Alice's lethargy, she'd gone too far and done her sister out of a job, out of a reason to stay in London. She checked her watch as she walked back to the sofa, six minutes until they went live again. There was enough time.

'We have to swap,' Edie said quickly into her sister's ear.

Alice looked up from her notes, hearing the words her sister said but not comprehending their meaning. 'What?'

'I'll explain later, but we have to swap clothes, now.'

Alice's confusion was palpable. 'No, I don't want—'

'Trust. Me. Come now.'

It was testament to quite how unlike herself that Alice was, that she followed her sister into the disabled toilets next to the set, and let Edie peel her clothes off her and swap them with hers, right down to their earrings without saying a word.

Petra, who was waiting for them next to the sofa, looked ever so slightly confused when she seemed to clock the delicate eyeliner on 'Edie' and the bare lips on 'Alice', who she could have sworn had her signature dusky rose on just before the news.

'And welcome back, wasn't that weather report a fantastic bit of good news, apart from those of you in Eastern Scotland,' said Edie as Alice. 'What a bit of bad luck if you live in Fife. But then I guess you're used to those black clouds looming.' It didn't actually say that in the script, but any opportunity to diss Danny's homeland, and she was going to take it. She nudged Alice with her knee to tell her to read the lines allocated to Edie on the autocue, which Alice did with a definite robotic tinge to her voice, not unlike a human version of a satnav.

'Well, we're all looking for lighter dishes to cook for supper, and we've got Will in the kitchen today to talk us through some lovely summery salads.'

'Will, we're coming for you!' Edie said, as the sisters got up from the sofa and walked towards the kitchen set up to the right of the set, which was slightly tricky in Alice's high heels – how on earth did her sister walk in these? Whenever she'd worn them before when she'd pretended to be Alice she'd always been sitting down. 'What deliciousness are you preparing for us today?' she asked, grabbing onto the kitchen island with an audible sigh of relief that she'd made it without collapsing to the floor in a heap of limbs.

'We've got a gorgeous mint, feta and pomegranate salad here, and a watermelon and grilled halloumi one here that I'll be talking you through.'

'Oh, fantastic,' Edie said, making a show of elbowing Alice, hoping the sensation of an elbow in the ribs would liven her sister up.

'I was actually really nervous about doing this show with you this morning Alice,' Will said. 'You're much more of a pro in the kitchen than I am.'

'Oh stop it,' Edie replied playfully, swatting him with her hand.

'I wanted to see what you might pair these salads with actually, get your expert opinion on it.'

Edie felt her heart thud with panic as Will looked at her expectantly. Oh god, giving the wrong answer here would kill all her hard work dead. Whether it was the recent mention of Fife that did it, or the subconscious looming doom of her sister's fate should she fail in her mission to line up an alternative future, the only thing she could think of was mackerel pate, and even she knew that would be a vomit-inducing combination for the salads. 'Um, ooo,' she said, stalling for time, 'let's think, mint, feta and pomegranate did you say?' Edie conjured up an image of her sister's immaculate kitchen, and out of nowhere heard herself say, 'I think a lovely leg of lamb would work brilliantly with it personally.'

'Bang on, Alice, that's what I was thinking too,' he slipped a hand into an oven glove to open the oven door, 'and here's one I made earlier.'

For the rest of the show, Alice managed to read the majority of Edie's lines with a half-baked enthusiasm. Her delivery was even disappointingly lacklustre during the gardening segment on how to keep your fresh herbs alive in window boxes, a topic Alice would normally have wished was allotted more airtime. What was wrong with her? As soon as the final goodbyes had been waved to camera four, Edie slumped with exhaustion at keeping the momentum going for the full one hundred and fifty minutes.

James stepped onto the set, his headphones now slung around his neck, and said with a regretful edge to his voice, 'You're both wanted on the exec floor.'

'I'm sorry,' Alice said as they walked slowly towards the lift, both still dressed as the other. 'I've ruined it for both of us, Shaun's going to fire us, I know he is. I just couldn't concentrate, I'm so sorry.'

'It's okay.' Edie thought she was the one with the problems, but something clearly was greatly troubling Alice. 'Do you want to go for lunch and we can chat?'

Alice hesitated, as Edie knew that she would, a lifetime of never giving her own thoughts a voice rendered it almost impossible to try doing so now.

'Let's see after this,' Alice said with a small grateful smile.

Edie ran through the figures in her head as they sat next to each other in the small waiting area outside the boardroom. Without her salary from the show, and with Seb's small contributions from the pottery, meeting next month's outgoings would be really tight. It was only a matter of time that she accepted the sad reality that they couldn't afford to live in her mum's house for much longer and it would have to be sold. She might be able to delay that for a few months by taking on more clients on a Friday once she wasn't doing the show, and perhaps some evenings too.

'Edie, Alice, come on in.'

Edie prayed that they wouldn't reference the meeting on Monday as they took the seats that were pointed at. Alice was already out of sorts, knowing quite how much Edie had meddled in her life would make it so much worse.

Alice

Alice felt numb. Numb with shame at not being able to switch off her brain enough to put on an act for the viewers. Numb with guilt at not liking her own partner very much anymore, now that she'd seen the type of relationship other people had. Numb with the realisation that she didn't like the life she was living very much. Numb with the fact that she was about to get not only herself, but also her sister who so desperately needed the income, fired from a job that they both actually really liked. She reached out to the water jug and as she poured herself a drink noticed her hands were trembling.

'We're a bit confused,' Shaun started. 'Edie, you stole the show in the first half, and Alice, you did in the second. It's like you were doing a relay and tagged each other in the break. What was going on?'

'Sorry,' Edie jumped in, as Alice, 'I had a horrible migraine at the start, but I took a couple of strong paracetamol in the break and felt so much better after that, but I think I must have given something to Edie, because she then started to feel rubbish.'

Shaun slanted his eyes at her in suspicion. 'You can't catch migraines.'

'No, no,' Edie agreed quickly, 'you're right, mine was a migraine, hers was . . . something else.'

'What this proves, is that when you're both at the top of your game, you're great. But this inconsistency really worries us.'

'It's not Edie's fault,' Alice said wearily, suddenly clocking the executive board's looks of confusion at her apparently speaking about herself in the third person as she was clearly still dressed as her twin. She gave a nervous laugh. 'You can tell I'm not myself, I've forgotten which sister I am.' Thankfully everyone around the table sniggered along with her. 'Look, today was a bit of an off day for me, but honestly, you have to give us another chance. If Gareth and Lauren are still ill tomorrow, let us do the show again, and we'll show you how good we can be.'

'Maybe having both of you on the sofa doesn't work; perhaps we should just try it with one of you,' Shaun said with a sigh.

'Just Alice then!' Edie shrilled, before she obviously remembered who she was dressed as, and realised that nominating oneself for a job, over your own identical twin, was a real arsehole move. 'Sorry,' Edie added, touching her temple for added emphasis, 'my migraine's back and it's making me a bit crazy. Look, give us another go tomorrow. We'll sort out our shi. . . zzle and do a great job, we promise. Won't we *Edie?*'

Alice nodded. 'We will *Alice*.' She looked quizzically at her sister, why would she possibly be putting her forward for the sole job? Surely it was Edie that needed the money, not her?

Judging by the looks of utter confusion on the faces of everyone seated around the large oak table, there wasn't a single person in that boardroom who had any idea what was going on anymore.

CHAPTER TWENTY-NINE

Alice

They walked back down the carpeted corridor towards the lift lobby, and catching their switched reflections in a mirror made Alice sigh. 'We have to stop doing this, it's too confusing, it has the potential to go really horribly wrong. When we swap back into our own clothes now, that's the last time we switch, it has to be. We did what Dad wanted, we saw things from each other's side, we've stopped arguing, we just need to get back to normal.' She looked really sad as she added as a postscript, 'whatever normal is.'

Edie turned her head to the side to study her sister's expression as they walked. 'I'm sorry if you feel that it's made more problems than it's solved.'

'What do you mean?'

'Well, first it was meant to be for the bet, then it was meant to be for us to have a bit of fun as the other one, and you don't look like you've had fun.'

The irony was, Alice had had more fun than she'd ever had before, and yet, that was the biggest problem of them all. She simply didn't want her old life back. Her kids yes, but the rest of it? She couldn't care less if she never posted a story online again, just think of the hours that could be saved per year by not writing notes for a grown man's lunchboxes, or making hummus from scratch, or crushing flower petals for a homemade essential oil that didn't smell anywhere near as good as the ones in Marks & Spencer. Hours that could be spent doing things the kids actually wanted to do, or sitting in a quiet room meditating, or trying to make new friends, because the first thing she was going to do when re-entering her old life was to suggest to Louisa they form a splinter group, one where no judgement was ever passed. She would still like coasters to be used, there was no point defacing nice furniture for the sake of it, but a lot of fun could still be had, even with the diligent use of wood protection. She wasn't sure where Danny fitted in. Not yet.

Hopefully she was handing Edie's life back in slightly better shape: her house was clean, Seb's business was booming and the girls didn't retreat up to their rooms with their dinner plates anymore. There was even a new whiteboard planner on the fridge, where each member of the house had written the evenings they'd be home for dinner together.

'Where shall we change?' Edie asked, looking around for a cupboard or somewhere private.

'The disabled loo on the ground floor is the biggest,' Alice replied.

When the lift doors pinged open on the ground floor, the women were greeted by the sight of Seb pacing up and down the marble floor in the reception.

'Seb?' Edie said, charging forward before Alice pulled her back, silently reminding her sister that she wasn't dressed as herself yet.

'Hey Eeds,' he said, looking directly at Alice. 'Where have you been? The show finished ages ago.'

'Sorry,' Alice said, trying to match her words with mannerisms suited to her sister, but she was tired, so tired. 'We were called into a meeting.'

'Is everything okay?' Edie interjected, looking straight at Seb, her voice clearly showing her concern.

Seb looked at Edie dismissively, all his attention was on who he thought was his girlfriend. 'We need to go, sorry Alice, I just need Edie.'

Edie

Edie stood helplessly in the cavernous lobby of the network's headquarters and watched Alice disappear into Seb's car that was double parked outside the building, and weave its way into the midday London traffic. She had to follow them and swap over; this was not Alice's relationship, not her mess. She should have blurted it out then, screamed at Seb that he was taking the wrong sister home, but then she remembered how hurt he was at his vase mysteriously turning up in the studio. There was no way that he'd be able to understand the switch, he'd feel so let down by her lies. She'd text Alice. They were both done with the switch now and ready to go back to their old lives. Edie had done what she could to help Alice and it seemed Alice had done the same for her. They'd have to switch back for good later.

'Alice,' came the clipped voice of the receptionist from behind her, 'your daughter's school has just called, it's an hour past the pick-up time, and she's waiting for you.'

'I'm sorry?' Edie swivelled round and stared at the young woman who had just passed on the message.

'Apparently it's the last day of term and school finishes at midday today? They tried your mobile but it's turned off?'

'What?'

The receptionist looked confused at which part of the message Alice wasn't understanding. 'Your daughter is waiting for you at her school.'

The whole way to pick Emily up, Edie kept trying Alice's mobile and also Seb's, but both were going straight to voicemail. This was a nightmare.

Alice

Despite her near-constant probes of 'what's wrong?' and 'what's this about?', Seb refused to talk until they were back home. *It's not your home,* Alice had to remind herself. *This is not your partner. This is not your relationship to fix.* She made them both tea, thinking while she stirred the pot that she'd never seen this Seb before. Gone was the easy banter and intellectual chat, his warm inviting gaze had been replaced with downcast eyes and his fingers tap, tap, tapped the table continuously. Alice instinctively reached out to place her own hand over his, and Seb placed his other hand on top again, twisting Edie's ring round and round on Alice's finger.

'I'm so sorry to do this on your big day, I wanted today to be a celebration of you, but . . .' He looked up at her. 'I'm still really hurting by the fact that you stepped in and took control of my business. Seeing that vase on TV yesterday was such an odd feeling. On the one hand I couldn't believe that something I'd made was out there for millions of people to see, but then at the same time, I just felt so small that you'd taken it upon yourself to do it without telling me. It felt like you'd had enough at seeing me flounder, and so you just swooped in to take charge.'

Alice's brain leapt ahead, joining the dots, realising that by taking Edie's vase into the studio, she'd completely undermined how their partnership worked. She also felt her stomach sink as she realised how hurt Seb would be if he ever found out the extent to which he'd been lied to.

Seb started talking again. 'I just feel that you didn't believe I could do it alone, and more than anything I want you to be proud of me. I was also just so hurt that you'd lied to me, Eeds. We're meant to be a team. We're meant to work together on things, not go behind the other's back or lie to each other, even if it was with good intentions.'

Alice grabbed his hand, pumping it up and down as she apologised, over and over again, 'I'm so sorry Seb, I really am just so sorry. Please forgive me, I wasn't thinking and it was a stupid thing to do. I honestly won't make the same mistake again if you can just find it in your heart to forgive me. Please.' The desperate begging in her own voice was unlike anything she'd ever heard come out of Edie's mouth, and Seb seemed to cotton onto that too a split second after she did.

His eyes narrowed, his initial frustration now overtaken by what looked like confusion. He pulled his hand slowly out of Alice's grasp and leant slightly back, inching away from her as though she was something to be feared. 'Edie?' He said her name slowly, but the lilt in his voice suggested that it was a question, rather than a statement.

'Ye-es,' Alice replied, in what she prayed was an Edie-like way.

'Oh my god, you're not Edie.'

She froze. She didn't dare say or do anything.

'Alice?' His voice was now a little louder, more insistent.

Alice sank onto the sofa and buried her face in her hands, knowing that by doing so he had his answer. His suspicions were confirmed.

'Do I want to know what's going on?' he asked, sinking into the armchair opposite. His tired sigh suggested he was bracing himself for what she was about to say.

'Probably not,' she replied honestly, still talking through her hands, unable to raise her face to meet his gaze.

'But you *are* Alice?'

She nodded sadly.

'Why are you in Edie's clothes and wearing her jewellery?' He pointed at her hand. 'Her ring?'

Where could she possibly start? 'Umm . . .'

'I don't get it,' he said earnestly, leaning forward in his chair, desperate to understand. 'Why would you pretend to be each other today?'

There was nothing she could say to make this any more palatable.

He shook his head and huffed out a laugh as the truth started to dawn on him. 'It's not just today, is it?'

She slowly shook her head.

'Since when?' he asked quietly.

She couldn't meet his eyes. 'A week last Monday.'

'Ten days ago! You've been living with me, with the girls, for ten days! How could I not know?' His expression suddenly changed from incredulity to revulsion. 'Oh god, we didn't . . .'

'No! For Christ's sake Seb!'

'Well, I don't know, do I?' He shook his head like he was trying to shake swimming pool water out from his ears. 'Why would you both do this? I don't get it. None of this makes any sense.'

Alice exhaled deeply, knowing that any excuse she gave, even the real one, seemed churlish now. 'It seemed like a good way to know how each other lived. To understand each other a bit better. Mum used to make us do it when we were younger, and it worked.'

'You didn't think that me and Danny had a right to know? And the kids? You didn't think to give us a heads up?' His tone had taken on a wounded edge.

'It was just mean to be a bit of fun,' she said weakly.

'At our expense. God, you must have been laughing at how gullible we all were! Did it amuse you both?'

'No, honestly,' she gushed, 'it wasn't like that. We'd grown apart and didn't know anything about each other anymore, and we thought walking a few days in each other's shoes would be the best way to do that. And if you knew, then you wouldn't be normal, or natural. The experiment wouldn't work.' She knew she'd made a mistake calling it that the minute the word left her mouth.

'*Experiment?*' he spat. 'So we were all just lab rats to the two of you. With no feelings or emotions at all.' He leaned back in his chair, tilting his head to the ceiling, and closed his eyes for a moment to calm himself. 'We slept in the same bed Alice! Edie slept with Danny.'

'Well no, they never *slept* together.' *Stop talking Alice*, she told herself.

'And where's Edie now?'

'I don't know. At mine probably.'

'So,' Seb said, 'just to clarify, in the hotel room, that was Edie.'

Alice nodded glumly, aware that he must have so many questions that he deserved answers to.

'But today, at home, that was you.'

'Yes.'

'But last week . . .' A blush started spreading across his cheeks. 'When she came to the studio by herself and we – that was definitely her?'

'One hundred percent,' Alice replied firmly. 'The idea of being naked around clay is revolting to me. And obviously you, being naked around you as well, is revolting.'

'Thanks. And what about at the party? Was that you or her?'

'It was me at the start—'

'That explains the dancing.'

Alice looked up, hopeful to see the familiar twinkle in his eyes, but there was nothing there but hurt.

'Then we swapped when the food came—'

'Thank fuck for that.'

'Then we swapped back again just before the end.' She paused. 'For the record, I forced her to swap back to being me, she didn't want to.'

He raised one eyebrow. 'Oh?'

'I think absence has made the heart grow fonder. She really loves you, Seb.'

He shook his head, still trying to take everything in. 'This is so messed up.'

Alice gave him a hopeful smile. 'The good thing about messes though, is that they can be cleaned up.'

He gave a snort. 'Now I know you're not Edie.'

'The whole vase thing Seb, that was all me. I thought I was helping. I could see how much you're both struggling, I thought that if you had some exposure, if people knew about your talent and your business took off then that would fix everything. I'm so, so sorry.'

Seb stood up and ran his hands through his hair, obviously unsure of what to do, what to say. He turned his back on her, talking to the wall, 'I can't believe this. I'm speechless that you two thought this was okay.' He swivelled on his heel to face her again. 'That you did this without a second thought for any of the rest of us.'

'Seb, I—'

'No. No, you don't get to just apologise and make it fine. I don't know what your relationship is like with Danny, Alice, but Edie and I don't lie to each other. I trusted her. And she thought this stupid game was more important than being honest with me.'

'Please Seb—' Alice reached her hand out to him.

He shrugged her off. 'No. Leave me alone. I'm going to the studio.'

Edie

'Why are you driving Auntie Edie's car?' Emily said, hopping in the front and waving merrily at her teacher, who gave Edie a death-stare for delaying the start of her own summer holiday by an hour and a half.

Seeing Alice sail off with Seb in his car, then being told about having to pick Alice's kids up, just made Edie act on autopilot and get in her own car and drive, without really thinking through the consequences. 'We swapped,' Edie answered simply, hoping that would shut down any further lines of questioning from her niece.

In the rear-view mirror, Edie could see Emily looking around her and wrinkling her nose. 'Our car is much cleaner.'

'Yes.' What could Seb be talking to Alice about right now? Had Alice been forced to come clean? Tell him about the switch? About her being the one to bring the vase to the set? Knowing her sister the way she did, that wasn't an act of malice or intentional betrayal, it was kindness, an attempt to help. But would Seb see it like that?

Emily interrupted her thoughts. 'Mummy? Iris told me that fast food companies kill thirty million chickens in the UK every year.'

'Mmmm.'

'That's a lot of nuggets.'

'Yes, yes it is,' Edie answered absent-mindedly, trying to

concentrate on the road, while most of her mind was firmly elsewhere.

'Do you know that there are four shapes of chicken nuggets?'

'No I didn't.' The car slowed down at a zebra crossing, and Edie rubbed her temples, trying to soothe the headache that was starting. If Alice just apologised at her misjudgement, and left it at that, then Seb would be fine, and as soon as the kids were dropped safely home they could swap back.

'Do you remember that I had one last year that was in the shape of a dinosaur?'

Edie was saved from commenting by the quick follow-up of another fact from the back seat.

'Did you know that the world record for eating nuggets is nineteen in one minute?'

'No, I did not,' Edie replied wearily. She loved Emily, she did, but oh my goodness she just needed her to stop talking.

'Mummy?'

'Mmmm?'

'You don't know very much about nuggets at all.'

'No.'

They pulled into the driveway to find Rufus and Teddy sitting on the doorstep.

Teddy got to his feet. 'Where have you been?' he said accusingly.

'We've been waiting ages,' Rufus moaned.

'I'm starving!'

'Sorry, sorry, I completely forgot that school ended early today, go in and make yourself some sandwiches.' As Edie said this, shooing the kids inside, she did have a moment of reflection to think that two weeks ago, this suggestion would have been met with stares of horror from all three, followed by a complicated list of lunch items they would like presented to them, but instead, they put away their bags in the hall cupboard, and set up an assembly line along the work surface, Teddy buttering the bread, Emily putting ham and lettuce in each one and Rufus cutting them in half. She might be leaving Alice with a completely messed-up marriage, but she'd like to think the kids were slightly better housetrained. 'I need to go and see Auntie Edie and Uncle Seb quickly,' she said. 'Teddy, Rufus, will you look after your sister while I've gone?'

'But Daddy doesn't let us stay here alone?' Emily said, suddenly looking younger than her ten years.

Edie was in the middle of explaining that Daddy wasn't here, and that by Rufus's age she was babysitting for neighbours, when Teddy held up his mobile. 'Dad needs you to collect him from somewhere, his car has a puncture.'

'What?'

'Look.' Teddy held out his phone for Edie to read the message.

> Your mother isn't answering her phone. My tyre has a puncture, I've been towed to a garage, dropping a pin to it now. Can you tell her to get me asap.

Edie's heart once again twisted at how vile Danny was to Alice, not a please, or a thank you, or a pleasantry of any kind. Just a barked order and an expectation of it being followed. She had half a mind to leave him there, and had it not been for the three kids who were now wrapping the sandwiches they'd just made in cling film for the journey, he absolutely would be festering alone by the A212 for the rest of his miserable life, or at least until he realised that perhaps a minicab might have been a more sensible SOS call.

*

Danny wasn't in the garage when they pulled up outside about forty minutes later, and Edie asked Teddy to message him, while she stepped away from the car to answer a call from Alice, so she wouldn't be overheard.

'Alice,' she said quietly into the phone, 'Hold the fort for a couple more hours. I can't really talk right now, I have the kids with me and—'

Alice's voice was frantic. 'Seb knows about the switch. And he got really mad and upset and he's left.'

Edie's heart plummeted to the floor. 'What? How did he find out? What did he say? Where has he gone?'

Just then Danny came stumbling out of the pub opposite. He seemed shocked to find it was so bright outside, putting his hand up to shield his eyes from the sun. He looked around, confused, for Alice's car, and then spotted Teddy standing up out of Edie's sunroof waving at him from the other side of the road.

'Alice, I have to go, please, just try and find him and check he's okay, I'll be back in London in less than an hour, I'll call you then, please, just try to make things right.' Edie hurriedly ended the call, and got back in the car, telling the kids tersely to put their seatbelts back on as her mind raced in time with her pulse.

Danny came and stood by the driver's door. 'Why are you in Edie's car?' he asked through the open window.

'We swapped.' Never was a truer phrase said, thought Edie.

He motioned with his thumb. 'Get out then.'

'No, I'll drive.'

'No,' he said slowly. 'I'll drive. Get out.'

Edie could feel her heart beating a little stronger in her chest. 'Danny,' she said as levelly as she could, 'get in the car, you've obviously been drinking.'

'You were bloody ages, what else was I meant to do?'

Edie sighed, very aware that the three children in the back had stopped laughing and had fallen silent. 'Danny,' she said quietly, 'you're not even insured on this car. Just get in the passenger seat. Please.' She locked eyes with him, silently pleading with him not to make more of a scene and to just acquiesce so they could get the children home and she could go and find Alice.

He stared back at her. For a second Edie was hopeful he would just give in and walk round to the passenger side, but then he slammed the flat of his hand on the roof of the car, 'You have never driven me in your life, and we're not starting that now.'

This small act of anger served to steady Edie's nerve, and she replied steadily even though inside she was raging, 'I'm not arguing with you Danny, I'm telling you to get in.'

'Mum, please, just let him drive.'

Edie turned round in her seat to look at Rufus, who had tears in his eyes, silently begging her to not argue.

'No.' She shook her head. 'I'm not letting him drive you all when he's clearly over the limit.'

Danny bent down further, so his face was inches from Edie's through the open car window. 'I've had a couple of pints, woman. And look at me, I'm fifteen stone, it barely touches the sides. Now move. I look like a right idiot standing out here.'

'Mum—' Teddy implored.

Edie looked first at Danny, then at the children in the rear-view mirror, beseeching her with their eyes to just give in. She thought of Seb upset and angry god knows where, she thought of her girls, did they know the truth too? She thought then of the years that Alice had spent giving into Danny's demands, and she knew in that moment what she needed to do. 'For the very last time, I am telling you to get in the car and to start behaving like a responsible adult. This is not about men and women, this is not about you and me, this is about the fact that you are being an absolute dickhead right now. You have been drinking and I refuse to let you endanger the lives of not only your children but everyone else unfortunate enough to be on the same roads as you today. Now either get in the fucking car or start walking.'

CHAPTER THIRTY

Edie

Please let Seb be okay. Please let Alice find him. Please let him forgive me and understand why we did it. Edie tried not to squeal as she clipped the car's tyres on the kerb as she took a corner a tad too quickly.

'That will be the kerb,' Danny said from the passenger seat.

She could hear her phone ringing in her bag, she knew it would be Alice, but there was no way she could answer it, they just needed to get home.

'Mind the man with the dog,' Danny said.

'He's on the pavement,' Edie replied through gritted teeth.

'Well so are you almost.'

'Teddy's over my side, Mum, tell him to move his arm!'

Edie swivelled round in her seat. 'Teddy, don't stick your elbow out over Rufus, tuck them in.'

'Ow, he just kicked me,' Emily whined, rubbing her shin.

'Rufus,' Edie pleaded in the rear-view mirror, 'just stay still, stop fidgeting,'

'Did you just fart? That is gross, oh my god Mum, Rufus

just farted, he's killing us, I can't breathe, I'm actually going to die,' Teddy stuck the bottom half of his face inside his T-shirt.

Danny banged his hand on the dashboard in frustration. 'Can you shut the kids up? I'm getting a headache.'

Edie undid her seatbelt to stretch her left hand through the gap between the seats, keeping a grip on the steering wheel with her right, trying to soothe the tension in the back with her hand stroking their legs and her pleading eyes in the rear-view mirror. The car hit a bump in the road. Edie's head grazed the car's ceiling. Too late she saw the bright red brake lights of the car she had been following slam on.

The next few seconds played out as if in slow motion.

A screech of brakes. A scream. Drinks bottles, a jumper, Emily's teddy bear, all suddenly weightless. A crushing thud. Giant white bags filled the car.

Then silence.

Somewhere, amid the shrieking, the crying, and the desperate hiss of a dying engine, came the faint sound of a phone ringing from the back seat, snapping Edie back into the moment. She batted at the air bag in front of her, her head throbbing, trying to twist her body round and hearing her own voice weakly say, 'Kids, Emily, Rufus, Teddy, talk to me, are you okay? Are you hurt?' All three stared back at her, their eyes open and staring, but alive, and seemingly unhurt. Teddy tried to furiously blink back tears, Rufus and Emily weren't even trying to stop theirs. Edie reached into the back seat for Teddy's hand, which he gripped gratefully. 'It's okay sweetheart, we're okay.' With the other hand, she reached around to stroke Emily's then Rufus's knees. 'It's all alright.'

'Mum, you're bleeding.'

Edie wiped her head where it hurt the most with the sleeve of her jumper, and tried not to gasp as she saw the dark streak of blood on her cuff.

She couldn't see what they'd crashed into, and prayed it wasn't a person.

'Dad?' Teddy said, sitting diagonally behind Danny. 'Why isn't Dad talking?'

Edie hadn't even thought of Danny until that moment, and her gaze snatched from the children to him. The car's air bag was obscuring his face. She let go of Teddy's hand to frantically push the airbag away from his face.

Emily's crying from the back seat intensified.

'Danny.' Edie jostled his arm a little. 'Danny.' As much as she despised the man, she urged him to open his eyes with every fibre of her being.

Danny let out a little groan, and Edie felt relief coursing through her veins. 'Can you move?' she asked. 'Is anything hurting?'

'Everything,' he groaned weakly. 'Jesus woman, what did you hit? Are you happy now?'

Edie swivelled around again in her seat. 'Teddy, is that your phone ringing? I need it.'

As Teddy handed it to her, she felt him shaking, and after taking the phone with one hand, she held his hand tightly with the other. 'Mum' was illuminated on Teddy's phone screen, Edie declined the call and rang 999 instead. Then everything went black.

*

They'd hit a post box, one of those ones that someone had taken the time to knit a decorative hat for, which was now lying on the floor, covered in mud and engine oil next to where Edie was sitting on the back steps of the ambulance. 'We're going to have to take you in, you've got a nasty cut on your head that will need stitches, and you'll need to be monitored for concussion.'

'What about me?' Danny said. 'I've broken my leg.'

'No,' the female paramedic said kindly, 'you haven't sir, you've bruised your knee.'

'Danny, you need to stay with the kids,' Edie pleaded, trying to stand up, but woozily sinking back down to seated.

'No, I need an X-ray, it's killing me.'

'Sir please, it's honestly just a bump, a day or two of rest and ice, and you'll be fine.'

Danny rounded on the paramedic. 'Are you a doctor?'

'Well no, but I'm—'

'Well then. Load me on the ambulance too.'

'Take him, not me,' Edie said to the paramedic who was holding a gauze pad tightly to the side of her head. 'I can't leave the children.'

'No, you definitely need to go in. Is there anyone we can call for you?'

*

Kenneth arrived in less than fifteen minutes, his calm demeanour exactly what was needed to blanket the whole scene with a sense of perspective and peace. Edie's last words to her dad before the door of the ambulance was shut with both her and Danny inside were simply, 'Tell Alice to come home'. The three youngsters put this naming slip up down to her injury, Danny was too busy groaning with an over-dramatic agony to even notice, but Kenneth knew exactly what she meant.

Alice

Alice had got the address of Seb's studio from one of his business cards, and ran frantically along the corridor, glancing rapidly at the number of each studio tacked to each door she ran past. Seb's was the second door before the end and she didn't even knock, just flung the door open and called his name. He hurried out from the back store room at the sound of her entrance, but his mouth set into a stony line when he saw her. 'I have nothing more to say to you Alice, or Edie, whoever the hell you are.'

'It's me, Alice, and Seb, you've got to come, Edie and Danny have been in a car accident. I've got a taxi outside waiting, please, we have to go to the hospital. Now.'

For the whole journey Seb stared out of his window, his back turned ever so slightly away from Alice, resolutely silent, but the relentless jigging of his knee giving away his gnawing unease. 'Do they know she's allergic to paracetamol?' he said finally. 'Did someone tell them?'

Alice shrugged. 'I don't know. Dad said that she was talking a bit, so maybe she did.'

He started chewing the skin around his thumb. 'She'll be really ill if they give it to her.'

'I know.'

Seb leaned forward and tapped on the glass between them and the driver. 'Sorry mate, do you know a faster route, it's an emergency.'

They ran into the hospital together, the receptionist pointing them both to A&E. The triage nurse took them through, after looking quizzically at Alice for a beat too long, and pulled back a curtain to a small cubicle where a very pale, washed-out Edie was asleep on the bed, five small stitches running through her eyebrow.

'Hey,' she said weakly, when she saw Alice. Seb was a few feet behind talking through Edie's allergies with the doctor on the desk.

'The lengths you go to to make sure that we look exactly the same,' Alice smiled, pointing at her own eyebrow scar.

'Guilty,' Edie whispered with a faint smile. 'How are your kids?'

'Dad's just ordered them a Domino's, they'll be fine. What did they say about you?'

'That I'm incredibly lucky. They've stitched me up, I have a mild concussion, and a bit of whiplash, but they're happy for me to go home tonight if I have someone to keep an eye on me.'

Seb had come through the curtain to catch the end of Edie's sentence. Both sisters looked at him with expectation. He looked from one to the other. 'Of course you have someone to keep an eye on you. I'm mad as hell about this, but I love you and we'll sort it out.'

Edie lifted up her hand and held it out towards Seb, who kissed it and took it in his. Turning her head towards Alice, she said, 'And what about you sis? Will you be able to sort things out with Danny?'

Alice shook her head sadly. 'I honestly don't know.'

Just then Danny's voice cut through the bustle of the emergency room clear and loud. 'Just stop dicking around and give me a bloody bed for the night!'

CHAPTER THIRTY-ONE

Alice

She'd seen this scene so many times on soap operas: husband or boyfriend in the hospital bed, loving wife or girlfriend sitting on a hard plastic chair next to their bed, holding their hand, stroking it, telling them over and over that it's all going to be okay. Except, this time, it really didn't feel like it was going to be. Healthwise, he was going to be absolutely fine, there was nothing wrong with him; the only reason the hospital had admitted him was because it was a very quiet night and he kept noisily groaning every time someone touched any part of his body and they couldn't face the lawsuit if there was actually something wrong with him, which Alice knew instantly just by looking at him that there wasn't.

'Hi,' Danny said, opening his eyes and seeing her there. There was a faint appreciation in his voice, which she hadn't heard for a long time.

'Hello. Well this is a bit of shock.'

'Water.'

Alice poured him a glass out of the jug on his tray table and held it to his mouth. He took a grateful sip but didn't show his gratitude in any words of thanks. Not that she was expecting him to, but it would have been nice.

He lay his head back against the pillow. 'What, no apology?'

'I'm sorry?'

'Well that's a start.'

'No, I mean sorry for what?'

'For nearly killing me and the kids.'

Alice had totally forgotten that he didn't know about the switch and so was assuming that she was the one driving the car. Edie had filled her in about his drinking and the arguing, and she had been in so many similar situations with him, that she knew this was no black and white case. It crossed Alice's mind that Danny hadn't even asked about her head, either.

'This was not my fault, Danny.'

'Well no, the kids were acting up too.'

'No,' she said with a firmness that surprised both of them. 'No. You don't get to do that, Danny. You don't blame our children for your mistake. You got too drunk to drive so I was forced to. You are equally to blame here.'

'But if they hadn't—'

'No. I'm not having you say that.' Alice lowered her voice as the nurse pulled a curtain round them. Not that a thin piece of fabric would block anything out, but at least they wouldn't need to look at everyone staring. 'They are kids. Lovely kids. Take some responsibility for this.'

Danny studied her, his head tilting slightly to the left as he lay in the bed propped up with hospital pillows. 'Why are you wearing your sister's clothes?'

Alice's face hardened. Now was a fine time for him to start noticing her. 'She lent them to me.'

'She's been getting in your head. The sooner we get you

away from her spouting poison in your ear, and move to Fife, the better.'

'Fife?' What a strange thing to say. Fife would be the last place she'd want to move to. It must be the shock talking.

'Yes Fife. And I don't want to argue about it anymore.'

'Okay then,' she said, folding her arms and sitting back in her chair, humouring him until he started talking sense and they could have a proper conversation.

'Good. Because it was really embarrassing you being so rude to Mum and Dad after they've been so kind giving us the business and the house.'

She'd heard stories about people as they came round after surgeries talking jibberish, after Teddy's tonsillitis he thought he was in Tokyo, but there was something about the way Danny was talking that rang frighteningly true. 'So when is this move happening then?' she said, trying to keep her question light and breezy, while her life was on the cusp of slowly slipping out of her grasp.

Danny smoothed the hospital sheet with his hand, 'I spoke to Mum and Dad just now before you came in, and they thought, with the accident and everything, that it would be good to move it all forward. So they're moving out of theirs next weekend, and we'll move up the following week. It will be easier for you to look after me up there without the distractions of down here. I'll have to be off this leg for weeks.'

The nonchalance with which he listed all this information made Alice grip the side of her chair so hard her knuckles were turning white. How dare he make such massive assumptions about her life. 'What *distractions*?' she managed to stammer.

'Edie, Kenneth, social media, the programme—'

'Oh, you mean insignificant things like my *family*, and my *job*?'

'I'm your family, and you'll be more than busy with the fishing business to worry about being on television or Instagram.'

'And our house?'

'I've got an agent coming round tomorrow to value it.'

'When were you going to tell me this?'

Danny at least had the decency, or the common sense, to look a little sheepish at this, even though his tone when he replied was childishly belligerent. 'It's my name on the deeds. It's been my money that's kept us living there.'

'We had a deal,' Alice said slowly through her teeth, 'that you would pay for the house and I would give up work to stay at home while the children were young. You can't turn around now and throw that in my face.'

'I'm not throwing anything in your face. I'm merely stating a fact that it's my house, and I decide what to do with it.' He yawned, a big yawn that allowed Alice to see two fillings in his molars. 'I'm tired now; you better go home and start packing, you've got loads to do.'

Alice nodded. The mist was clearing from her eyes and she knew with absolute certainty what needed to happen next. 'You're right,' she said, standing up decisively and giving him the last smile he was ever going to get from her. 'There is so much packing to do.'

Edie

Edie was sitting on a bench outside the hospital draped in Seb's coat while Seb had walked around the corner to the main road to try to flag down a taxi. She tried to scramble to her feet when she saw the doors open and Alice emerge, but her heavy head made her sit hastily down again. 'All okay?'

Alice nodded. 'Yes and no. Fancy some company?'

Despite it being almost ten o'clock at night, the streets were still full of people trying to eke out every last bit of daylight. Every bench outside the pub opposite was occupied; couples, friends, all starting to reluctantly admit the day was almost over, and that it was time to head home. A group of men wearing suits, their ties hanging out of their pockets, who had clearly been enjoying some hops in the sunlight, passed them on the pavement and all of them looked twice at the sisters.

'You're twins!' one of them said in wonder.

The two women looked up and nodded. 'Yes.'

'Wow, that's amazing, I thought twins were only children.'

'Well, they are, and then they grow up,' Alice said.

The man shook his head in wonder. 'God, that's brilliant, well done.'

'Thanks, we divided the zygote ourselves.' Edie smiled.

It was clear the drunk man had no idea what she was talking about.

'Are you exactly the same?' asked another one.

'Not exactly,' Alice said.

Edie looped her arm through her sister's. 'But maybe more than we thought. Have a good evening.'

'Seb took it well,' Alice started.

Edie nodded. 'I think he understood our reasons for doing it, even if he was a bit upset about it. He's going to be looking at us really oddly for a while I reckon. Did you tell Danny?'

Alice shook her head. 'It wasn't the time. I'm not sure there will ever be a right time for the two of us to be completely honest with each other.'

Three or four seconds passed where the only sound was the music and laughter emanating from the various wine bars and open windows around them. 'Well, *I* need to be honest about something,' Edie said finally. If not now, when?

'Go on.'

Edie's words rushed out with no spaces in between each one, desperate just to impart all the secrets she'd been holding in. 'Danny's agreed to move to Fife, all of you, moving to Fife, to run the fishing thing, and you're going to make two hundred pots of mackerel pate a day with Rita—'

Alice raised an eyebrow.

'—and I couldn't let that happen because you're too beautiful and smart and brilliant, and too important to me, and so I have done some things that I probably shouldn't have done to try to make compelling reasons for you to stay.' Edie paused, trying to interpret the expression on her sister's face with all the information she'd just hit her with. She was expecting wild and untamed fury, or at the very least panicked agitation, but there seemed to be, what was that? *Amusement?*

'Such as?' Alice asked, her mouth twitching as though she was trying to hold back a smile.

'Huh?' Edie had completely lost her train of thought.

'You were just saying. You've done some *things* that you probably shouldn't have done.' Alice didn't sound surprised. Which made this easier for Edie, but it did make her doubly determined to think before speaking or acting in every scenario she would ever find herself in in the future.

'Well . . . I think I've got you a new job presenting the programme instead of Gareth, and James really likes you and wants to spend more time with you, and so you don't need to go to Scotland, you can stay here, and have a fancy job and a lovely man, and just be happy.'

'Is that all?'

Edie was taken aback. She'd literally just told her that she'd interfered in her marriage, her career, and her love life. 'Isn't that enough?'

'It is an impressive amount of chaos to cram into ten days.'

Was that a compliment? It sounded like a compliment. 'Um, thank you?'

'You didn't need to do any of those things though.'

'Why?' Edie took a deep breath, not wanting to hear Alice's answer to her next question. 'Because you're going to Fife anyway?'

'Because I wouldn't stay here because of a job or a man.'

Edie wiped her eyes on the sleeve of her jacket. 'Well, it was worth a try.'

Alice pulled her arm tighter through Edie's. 'I'd stay here for you though.'

'What?'

'I don't need a fancy job on TV, or a new man, in fact, especially not a new man, but I do need my sister.'

'Me?'

'No need to sound so surprised. You're the only sister I've got. And you're barmy, and infuriating, and I may not understand half the things you say or do, but I need you, Edie.'

Tears coursed down Edie's cheeks, and she made no attempt to wipe them away. 'And I need you too.'

On a bench outside a busy city hospital, late at night, the two sisters wrapped their arms around each other in a tight embrace, sobs racking both their bodies, completely oblivious to the looks from everyone else out enjoying the capital that night.

Alice

The empty house was silent when Alice let herself in after midnight. The children were a few doors down at Kenneth's, already asleep. As if on autopilot, Alice hung her coat up in the downstairs cupboard and sat on the bottom stair to untie her laces and swap her shoes for her moccasins. She paused, one shoe off, one on. An overwhelming urge came over her to wear her trainers across the hall carpet and into the kitchen. She shook the thought away, how silly. She started pulling at the laces on her other foot to loosen them, and then stopped again. *Go on,* she heard Edie's voice say, *walk those germs all over your laminate.* Alice slipped her Converse back on and wandered into the kitchen, feeling every inch the rebel with every footstep. *Put on the radio station that won't make you cleverer but will bring you joy.* Alice turned the dial on the radio until the kitchen filled with the strains of a nineties pop band she and Edie used to love. Her stomach started rumbling, and she couldn't remember the last time she ate. Opening the fridge, she saw shelves of items Edie must have bought, as she would never have bought them herself. *Dip some nachos in the shop-bought guacamole and admit that it's quite nice.* Alice poured herself a bowl of tortilla chips and picked up the little green pot of supermarket guacamole and carried it through to the living room. *Tastes good, doesn't it?* Alice smiled as she ran her finger round the inside of the pot to finish it. *Now go and start packing up everything Danny owns, order a removal van to pick it up and deliver it up to Fife. Chop chop.*

Edie

Edie traced a pattern on Seb's palm with her finger. 'I'm literally never leaving your side again. You're going to have to get a sidecar for your bike, because I'm going everywhere with you.'

Seb pulled Edie closer to him on the sofa. 'Suits me.'

'I really am so sorry, it was never meant to turn out like this; we didn't think through the implications for everyone else, it was really selfish.'

'I'm not going to pretend that I wasn't incredibly hurt by your deceit. But I also know that you wouldn't have done it just for fun, I get that it was a last-ditch attempt at you and Alice making up. And if that was the goal, I'd say that it's turned out rather well. Well, car crash, buggered eyebrow, whiplash and concussion aside.'

'Don't forget Danny's bruised knee. And ego.'

'Do you think she'll really leave him?'

'I don't know. I hope so. I think being here, with you, has made her realise how wonderful a good relationship could be. And I certainly realised that being away from you. I know I don't say it, or show you often enough, but I adore you Seb.'

'I adore you too.'

'Would you like me to start leaving you inspirational notes in your lunchbox?'

'No, not particularly.' He laughed, a twinkle returning to his gaze.

'Thank god for that.' Edie paused, then took a big breath in. 'And I've been thinking,' she said, broaching a topic she hadn't been brave enough to even consider before. 'It's time to put Mum's house up for sale.'

Seb looked at her quizzically. 'But I've already had so many enquiries about my pottery after being on TV, things are looking up. We don't need to do that.'

'We do. I was only holding onto it because I wasn't ready to let her go, but she's not in these bricks.' Seb wiped away a tear from Edie's cheek as her lip wobbled. 'She's in me, and in Alice, and she wouldn't want me and you to be crippling ourselves trying to make these payments, she'd want us to start afresh somewhere, build our own memories, not live with hers. She loved us so much and I think she'd just want us to be happy. All of us. Plus, if we don't have the massive mortgage payments every month, I can cut down on my work hours a bit and actually have some time back in the day to spend with all of you guys.'

'We don't have to decide this now. It's a big decision.'

'I'm not going to change my mind.'

Seb put a finger under her chin and raised it so her mouth met his. 'I love you.'

'I love you too.'

'Since you're in the mood for making big decisions . . . I have something I want to ask you.'

Edie laughed. 'A few hours ago you wanted to murder me.'

'Murder is a bit strong. But yes, life with you is exciting and extraordinary, and I will take the rough with the smooth and everything in between if it means spending the rest of my life with you. I even have a ring.'

'You do not!'

'I do. Wait here.' He leapt up from the sofa and ran into the hallway. Edie heard him rifling through his coat pocket. Had it been in there all the time that she'd been wearing it! 'Now I recognise this is not the smoothest proposal in the world, but hopefully it is the most eagerly awaited, and the most heartfelt.'

Edie giggled, and flexed her left hand in anticipation of what was coming next. He knelt down on the carpet next to the sofa, and prised open the ring box to reveal a beautiful small square emerald. 'Edie Elizabeth Dawson, will you do me the absolute pleasure of becoming my wife?'

'I thought you'd never ask,' Edie smiled, and leaned forward until her lips touched his. 'It was worth waiting sixteen years for that though.'

Giggles came from the stairs. 'What did she say?' came Rosie's excited stage whisper from between the banisters.

'She said yes!' Seb shouted back, laughing. 'Mum and Dad are getting married! Girls, come on down and join the party!'

'But only for a bit, it's really late already,' Edie added, before smiling at her own transformation.

Later that night, when Edie was standing by the back door waiting for Scooby to come back in, admiring her new ring in the moonlight, she turned her face to the sky and looked up at the stars. Out of nowhere, a small white feather meandered down and landed softly at her feet. She looked at it for a moment, then smiled. 'Night Mum, and thank you.'

CHAPTER THIRTY-TWO

Six months later...

Alice & Edie

'And welcome to *Britain in the Morning*, we have a packed pre-Christmas show for you today, full of festive fun and frolics. Gosh that's tricky to say,' laughed Edie.

'I don't know about you, but I am ready to party,' Alice said, straight into camera three. 'We have sequins in every colour in our fashion segment coming up just after eleven, and Will is back in the kitchen with some fabulous meat-free alternatives for the big day.'

'And for those of you who don't like the C-word . . .' Edie paused, not sure where the autocue was going with this sentence seeing as she, once again, hadn't read the script before filming started. 'We're going to talk to our travel guru Nell Graham who's got a great round-up of festive-free breaks to enjoy for any budget.'

'So, stick the kettle on, make yourself a cuppa, sit back and let's spend the next couple of hours together.'

As the jaunty music announced the start of the show, and viewers watched the brand-new montage of Edie and Alice in the opening credits, the lure of being the first network show in the world to be hosted by identical twins far too enticing for the producers to pass up, the sisters smiled at one another.

'Does this feel mad to you?' Alice whispered, keeping one eye on the countdown to when they'd be back on air.

Edie smiled back at her. 'Completely bonkers.'

'There's no one I'd like to do this with more than you.'

'Good. Because you're stuck with me.'

'Is that a promise?'

Edie stuck out her little finger. Alice wrapped her own pinkie around it.

'Ready?'

Edie flashed her sister a grin. 'Ready.'

*

An hour later, during the ten-minute break for the news and weather, the sisters started gathering up their notes on the coffee table in front of them, while their microphones were being fiddled with by the sound technicians. James tentatively approached their sofa. 'Um, Alice, we've just made a couple of changes to your script, here are the new notes, can you quickly just look at them?'

Alice smiled politely at him, taking the papers from his outstretched hand. 'Of course. Thank you James.'

'No regrets?' Edie whispered after he walked away.

'None at all. He's a very nice man, and will make someone very happy.'

'Not you?'

Alice gave her head a small unrepentant shake. 'Not me.'

'Is Danny still okay with you having the kids at Christmas?'

'Yes, he's flying down to collect them on the twenty-ninth so they'll have Hogmanay up there.'

'So we're definitely on for Christmas at mine this year?' Edie asked.

'Absolutely. I'm looking forward to taking it easy this year.'

'Well not that easy,' Edie teased, 'you and Rufus are doing all the cooking.'

Before Alice could make a retort, James started counting down from five.

'Welcome back,' Edie said brightly into the camera. 'We have a couple of really special guests joining us in the studio now, come on in Lilly and Evie.'

From the lefthand side of the set, came two seven-year-old girls holding hands. From the shine on their patent leather Mary Jane shoes, to the butterfly-shaped clips holding back their partings, they were a mirror-image of each other in every way.

'It is a pleasure to meet you both.' Alice smiled at them. 'Now you're here because you have just won Britain's most identical twins award, how exciting!'

The two young girls nodded in perfect synchronisation.

'What do you like best about being a twin?' Edie asked, noting with recognition that the hair slide on one of girls was coming loose, and one of her socks was already rolling down lower than the other one.

'I like having my best friend live in my house.'

'I like never being lonely.'

Edie could feel a lump start to form in her throat and the pressing of her sister's hand into her thigh was a sign she wasn't alone in feeling this.

'And are there any downsides to being a twin?'

'When we have to wear the same thing like this really itchy dress,' the one with the rolled down sock said, pulling at the collar as if to show her discomfort. Out of the corner of Edie's eye, she could see their mother flapping her hands at the girls, in the exact same way their own mother used to when trying to take their annual birthday portrait.

'Sometimes people are surprised when we say that we like different things; like I really like ketchup but Evie doesn't, and she really likes swimming, but I still wear armbands and the water makes my eyes sting even when I'm wearing goggles.'

'And I can do this with my tongue . . .' Evie stuck out her tongue as far as it would go until it touched the tip of her nose. 'But Lilly can't.'

'I've actually never tried,' Lilly admitted. 'It looks silly.'

'Try now,' Edie urged. 'We can all be silly together.'

Lilly sat with her lips resolutely pursed together as she watched one of the older women compete with her sister for the longest tongue.

Evie elbowed her sister. 'Come on Lilly, it's fun.'

Alice recognised the mouth twitch in the younger girl, the bewildered pull from one side of wanting to park her propriety and for just a moment give in to the spontaneity and freedom her sister enjoyed so effortlessly, and the tug from the other of staying true to what actually felt right, and natural. She wanted to scoop her up and tell her that it was okay, there was a place for both types of people in the world: those who felt absolutely fine at sticking their tongues out on national television, and those who didn't. She caught Lilly's eye, and gave a conspiratorial nod towards their sisters and an eye roll at her, and the little girl smiled back, suddenly comfortable again in her own shoes.

'Now I have to ask, from one twin to another,' Edie said, once her tongue was firmly back in her mouth, 'do you ever pretend to be each other?'

'Sometimes,' Lilly said, her two missing front teeth making her lisp a little.

'We could be pretending to be each other right now and you wouldn't know,' her sister added cheekily.

'Very true,' Edie winked at them, 'but then again, so could we . . .'

Acknowledgements

I don't think I will ever stop pinching myself that writing books is my job, and seven books in this feeling of awe and bewilderment hasn't lessened a bit. My heartfelt gratitude to my brilliant agent Hannah Schofield at LBA for being by my side throughout this crazy, wonderful, rollercoaster ride.

Massive thanks to the powerhouse team of inspirational women who make up the publishing team at Avon, led brilliantly by Helen Huthwaite. I am lucky enough to have the best editor in the world, Rachel Hart, whose sprinkles of magic fairy dust have made this book so much better; every interaction with you has been a joy. Big thanks to Jess Zahra, Amy Mae Baxter and Emma Grundy Haigh for their support; Emily Hall and Jessie Whitehead in Marketing; Katie Buckley, Hannah Lismore and Emily Scorer in Sales; Francesca Tuzzeo in Production; Dushi Horti for her fabulous copyediting skills – sorry my comma abuse is so widespread – and a special thanks to designer Sarah Foster for such an eye-catching cover. Huge amounts of gratitude also go to Becky Hunter, publicist extraordinaire. Over the pond in the US, thanks to Emily Gerbner and Sophia Wilhelm in the HarperCollins US team and a special mention to Berni Vann at CAA who has championed my books to anyone who will listen.

I want to do a massive shout out to the independent bookshops who advocate for authors so fiercely. A special mention goes to Yellow Lighted Bookshop in Tetbury, Barn Owl Books in Malmesbury, Tea Leaves and Reads in Weyhill, and so many more who are simply marvellous. I also owe so much to online book clubs like Fiction Café Book Club and Linda's Book Bag for their support over the years, not to mention the fabulous book bloggers on Instagram who have hosted me on blog tours and create such gorgeous content for the book-loving community.

As the eldest of three sisters, it was only a matter of time before I wrote a book about the joys of sisterhood, and whilst I believe I may bear a passing resemblance to Edie, neither of my sisters are anything like Alice – although they both have much tidier houses than me! Hannah and Davinia, thank you for being by my side since you were born, and for being my best friends. To Mum, thank you for always being my first reader, and such a supporter of everything I do. To the Butterfields, Coopers, Denfords, Francis family, Haddon McMillans, Harpers, Harveys, Poulains, and Poultneys thank you for being my family, and to Lisa, Netty, Bev, Hana, Nina, Tabs, Sally, Paul & Alex, and all the WBS community, thank you for being my friends.

The last thanks go to my little tribe, Team P – Ed, Millie, Rafe & Theo, thank you for being so patient while I squirrel myself away in my writing shed in the garden every spare minute to follow my dream. Je t'aime, ti amo.

Nell has always known the date she's going to die.

After a psychic predicted her death date twenty years ago, she has lived life accepting she would never see forty – embracing adventure and travelling the world, choosing fun over commitment and laying down roots.

So, when the fateful day comes, Nell feels ready. She sends five excruciatingly honest confessions to her sister, parents and past loves, knowing she won't be around to face the consequences. Then, with her heart laid bare, all that's left to do is check into a glamorous hotel and wait for the inevitable ...

But when Nell unexpectedly wakes up the next morning broke, single and very much alive, she must figure out exactly how to seize this second chance at life. And then it also hits her:

What on earth happens now that everyone knows how she really feels?

This is the perfect book club read for fans of David Nicholls, Holly Smale and Beth O'Leary, asking what it is that makes for a life well lived.